Earthquake?

The throbbing filled the air now, a deep humming that hurt the ears. The three men looked around, but there was nothing to account for the phenomenon—nothing visible.

Joey Vitale's keen young eyes spotted it first, moving in from the north, over the Hudson River. "Look!" He pointed.

It moved majestically through the air, glimmering silver-blue, a massive round shape thickened in the middle, tapering around its edges. It was so huge as it moved over Yankee Stadium that the sun was totally eclipsed; the brightness of the October day quenched as though it had been snuffed like a candle.

His stomach tightened in disbelief. He experienced a sudden, irrevocable certainty that his life—that every life on earth—had suddenly changed. Nothing would ever be the same again.

EAST COAST CRISIS

Howard Weinstein and A. C. Crispin

PINNACLE BOOKS   NEW YORK

V: EAST COAST CRISIS

Copyright © 1984 by Warner Bros., Inc.

An original Pinnacle Books edition, published for the first time
anywhere.

First printing/September 1984

ISBN: 0-523-42259-8

Can. ISBN: 0-523-43251-8

Printed in the United States of America

PINNACLE BOOKS, INC.
1430 Broadway
New York, New York 10018

9   8   7   6   5   4   3   2   1

To Bob Greenberger—
A good friend and editor—and a
fun guy at conventions!

ACKNOWLEDGMENTS:

The authors gratefully thank the following for technical assistance and factual background material:

- Ms. Bevin Sloan, Research Assistant, Corporate Communications Department, Rockefeller Center Corporation
- The Long Island Railroad
- New York Hospital–Cornell Medical Center

And for assistance in typing and photocopying, many thanks to Ms. Hope Skivington and Ms. Polly MacLeod.

Authors' Notes

Strange how certain books come to be written. Like this one. A. C. Crispin (Ann to her friends) was already working on the nifty novelization of the *V* miniseries (that book came out in April of this year, just before the sequel aired on NBC-TV), which was originally to be *two* separate books. Then the decision-makers decreed, *"Let it be one volume,"* and, lo, it became one mighty big book.

But the decision-makers then found themselves in a quandary. They still had the rights to do a second *V* book, and they wanted Ann to do it. Now, she's a good and rapid writer, but even with her dandy new word processor, human fingers can only fly so fast.

At this point, Ann's good, noble, and exceedingly wise editor, Harriet McDougal, worried aloud that Ann might expire in the face of such an undertaking. Ann agreed that she probably couldn't accomplish this feat alone. (Ann likes to write, but she's not nuts . . .)

So Ann wondered rather timidly if a co-author might not be the answer.

"Sounds good," Harriet said, "but who were you thinking of?"

"How about Howard Weinstein?" Ann suggested.

And that's where I came in.

All Ann and I had to start with was the basic premise—this book would focus on an East Coast resistance group, and its action would parallel the West Coast goings-on in the TV series. So in short order we had to create a new story and all-new characters, and write this original novel at the same time as Ann was distilling ten massive screenplay hours into a novelization that would be both interesting *and* small enough to transport without an eighteen-wheeler. The fact that A. C. Crispin managed to do *that*—on time, yet!—is a testament to her skill and professionalism.

We conjured up the outline over two days in the Maryland

countryside where Ann lives with her family. I then raced home to Long Island to write the first draft, aiming to finish just as Ann completed the novelization. No time for her to decompress—she would immediately launch into our second draft. Then we'd polish it together and it would be done (and done well, we hoped).

Somehow we got it finished in time, keeping in mind many of the opinions expressed about *V* by fans at SF conventions, which we both attend regularly. We tried to retain what we felt was best about the original concept as well as creating touches of our own. We hope you enjoy the result.

Howard Weinstein
April 1984

Now that I've become a full-time writer, the support and encouragement I've received from science fiction and Star Trek fans since *Yesterday's Son* came out in August of 1983 has been terrific. To those of you who've written to express your good wishes, many thanks. I'm trying to answer each letter personally, but it takes a long time, especially when one considers the inescapable fact that to continue being considered a writer, one must *write*—books, stories, articles, etc. So please be patient!

I'd also like to publicly extend a standing invitation to Howard to collaborate with me again on a book, sometime. He's great to work with—easygoing, neat, prompt, has reasonably legible handwriting, and he creates wonderful dialogue. He also has that really rare gift of being able to write with a great sense of humor. (Taking oneself too seriously is one of the major faults of beginning writers, I've found.)

It's truly amazing that, despite the sometimes trying experiences we went through while writing *V: East Coast Crisis*, Howard and I ended up still on speaking terms with our story— not to mention with each other. But we did, and it was even fun, most of the time (except let's please forget March 1984—a lost month. Howie didn't tell you the half of it . . .)

May all your lizards be little ones!

Ann C. Crispin
April 1984

Prologue

Journey's End

Ghostly and gray, the small planet rode the loneliest reaches of its solar system, reflecting only the dimmest glow from its distant sun. Five billion miles away, its captor star burned bright and yellow, bathing its closer planets in warmth—even, in the case of one blue-green sphere, life-giving warmth. But this far out, its immensity diminished by sheer distance, it was just another star in the darkness, barely larger and brighter than others studding the void.

Most of the crew aboard the immense ship took little notice of the gray planet except to verify that the computer-controlled engines compensated automatically for its minor gravitational tug. The ship had crossed nearly nine light-years of featureless space—only the crew members posted at the navigation stations actually saw the icy worldlet, but several of them responded to its image on their screens with relief. It was a psychological boost to witness tangible proof that their mission had advanced so much that they were actually entering the system containing their long-awaited goal.

The ship's command center was a dim, silent place. Most of the functions of the gigantic ship were controlled by computers—personnel had little to do except monitor and verify that the computers were performing their functions correctly.

The ship's second-in-command sat perched on the commander's seat, stiff-backed and haughty. Her blonde hair was pulled into a severe ponytail, a utilitarian style that didn't detract from her obvious beauty. It was a cold, brittle beauty, though—ice-blue eyes, lips drawn into a thin line, her face a sculpture of sharp-edged planes and angles.

She glanced down at the navigational, engineering, life-support, communications, and weapons-control stations arrayed before her like the spokes of a giant half-wheel, then focused on one of her subordinates, sitting at the communication console just to the right of the commander's station. The junior officer absently ran a hand through her reddish-brown hair as she scanned her readout screen.

"Jennifer," the command officer said, her voice reverberating in the near silence.

The officer addressed did not respond. *"Jennifer!"* the blonde officer repeated sharply.

This time the younger female started and turned, her fingers digging into the arms of her seat. "I—I am sorry, Angela," she said, careful with her pronunciation of the superior officer's name. "I still have trouble remembering my assigned name. I'll be more alert next time. What did you wish?"

Angela glared. "I wished nothing, Jennifer. I have been instructed to verify that each officer is fully prepared for his or her role in meeting our hosts-to-be. That preparedness includes a thorough familiarity with assigned names. You've had the same training period to learn yours as the rest of us. Your lapse wouldn't be forgivable in a bottom-ranked technician—it's totally unacceptable in the officer third in command of this ship. I doubt you've risen to that rank by suffering memory lapses."

"I said I was sorry," Jennifer said softly. "It won't happen again, Angela."

Angela narrowed her eyes warningly. "It's true that you're awfully young to be taking on this level of responsibility. In fact, I pointed that out to the Commander when he—"

"To *Roger*," Jennifer interrupted, her voice still quiet, but firm now.

"What?" Angela's attack had been diverted. For a moment she drew a blank.

"To *Roger*," Jennifer repeated. "You said, 'the Commander.' *His* assigned name is Roger—or had *you* forgotten?"

Angela stiffened in her seat, but any rejoinder she might have made was forestalled as boot heels rang on an overhead catwalk and the subject of their discussion appeared. The crew acknowledged his presence, but his wave cut short their formal salutations. He sat down in the seat Angela automatically vacated; his eyes, in his weathered, handsome countenance, focused on Jennifer. "Communications standing by, Jennifer?"

"Yes, *Roger*," she said, her glance never wavering from his green eyes. "I'm keying in now."

Her quick touches displayed the information on the screen above their heads, magnified for easy reading. "It seems as though we're about ready," he commented.

"Not in my opinion, sir," Angela said, determined to make her opinions known.

"What do you mean, Angela?" the Commander asked, his face creasing as he frowned, then smoothing as he lifted his fingers to touch the worry lines consideringly.

"I'm concerned that not all of our crew are properly prepared for our mission, sir," Angela said, her eyes flicking coldly to Jennifer.

Roger looked at his officers. "The test ratings on this ship are comparable with the highest in the Fleet. Do you agree with Angela, Jennifer?"

"Well, no, Roger," the younger officer said, moving up to stand beside him and Angela and lowering her voice so that it would not carry to the rest of the bridge personnel. "That is, not exactly. I do agree that we may not be as fully prepared as we should be. Our strategy is based almost entirely on long-range surveillance and monitoring of informational and entertainment broadcasts. In many ways, this is a world still completely alien to us. And our mission . . . ." She hesitated. "The details of the Great Leader's plan are still not clear to many of the officers, Roger. I perceive this to be a possible weak link in our strategy—that so many of our people don't fully realize our purpose, yet will still be interacting with the native population."

The Commander was a bit surprised to hear such apparent pessimism in Jennifer's precise assessment, but nodded thoughtfully. Angela glared at him before whirling to face Jennifer. "How dare you question the Leader's wisdom? Are you privy to things he doesn't know?"

"No," said Jennifer defensively. "It's just that—"

Angela cut her off with an angry hiss. "It seems to me that

you don't have the faith and courage to devote to this mission, Jennifer! How can you question the goals of a mission designed to insure the very survival of our civilization?"

Roger stopped any retort from the younger officer with an upraised hand. "We're tired. This has been a long voyage—for all of us. I know each of us is concerned about what we're going to encounter here. I appreciate both of your opinions, but my command judgment is that we—and the Fleet as a whole—are prepared to fulfill Our Leader's expectations of us." He gestured at the communications console. "Jennifer, we will need your services in just a few minutes."

As the younger officer nodded and resumed her post, the Commander turned to the navigation station, his eyes fixing on the main viewscreen. "Navigation status?"

"Preprogrammed coordinates have initiated deceleration maneuver number three. Estimated time to Earth orbit—six hours."

Roger nodded, carefully keeping his face from reflecting his perplexity. Mentally, he went through the laborious process of converting the local time—"hours"—to his own people's time units. After a second he nodded slightly. *Soon*, he thought, *soon* . . .

He turned back to the viewscreen to see the featureless face of the gray planet receding. It revealed neither sign nor omen nor comment on the chances for success of the Great Leader's mission. The fleet of starships passed it by, and its monochrome clouds swirled in enigmatic salute.

Chapter 1

Where Were You When the UFOs Landed?

Peter Forsythe crouched low, elbows on knees. Ten feet off third base, he was edging in toward the infield grass. His glove was loose and open, but his spikes dug into the dirt, and the muscles of his legs were coiled tightly in anticipation. His eyes bore in on the bat at home plate, just ninety feet away— not on the batter, but on the *bat*, held high and twitching as if it held a life of its own.

Automatically Pete's eyes rechecked the alignment of the batter's feet. The ball would definitely be headed this way. Eight years as the premier third baseman in the American League made him confident in his ability to judge.

He heard the pitch cut the air, straight and fast. The bat whipped forward, too quickly for the human eye to follow except as a tawny blur. The ball came off it like a shot, the sharp rifle crack sounding a split second later.

Even before the sound reached his ears, Pete's reflexes had taken over, his blue eyes tracking the ball as it angled down toward the grass. His compact, lean-muscled body twisted, his left, gloved hand aiming itself where his brain—without any conscious thought—*knew* the ball would ricochet upward after its impact with the grass.

It wasn't enough! He needed another foot of reach, and Pete's body automatically left the ground, diving smoothly, his legs following his trajectory like the tail of a comet. The ball drilled itself into the deep leather pocket of his glove. He landed on his chest, already scrambling to his knees, his bare right hand clutching the ball and effortlessly snapping a hard throw across the field. With a lazy arc belying the speed and power behind it, the ball thudded into the first baseman's mitt.

Panting, Pete listened automatically for the umpire's bellow of "Out!" But there was no bellow, no cheers from the crowd, no disgruntled opposing player glaring at him as he trudged back to the dugout, eliminated from the inning by yet another Pete Forsythe golden play. Yankee Stadium was empty on this crisp mid-October afternoon—except for Pete, his teammate Joey Vitale at bat, the Yankees' owner, Alexander Garr, playing the first-base side of the infield, and team manager Bobby Neal loading and adjusting the pitching machine as he kept a careful eye on Joey's batting stance. All wore dark-blue team warm-up suits.

"Not bad for an old man," said Garr, his rasping voice carrying all too well across the field. "A few more plays like that during the season and we might've been in the Series now."

The taunt stung. Pete recalled all the grounders that had bounced just beyond his reach, the hanging curve balls he'd inexplicably missed hitting for home runs, all the plays he might have made a season or two ago—and all the nights he'd spent wondering if age was really catching up with him. The season's fourth-place finish hadn't been all his fault, but he was ready to accept his share of the blame, and probably more.

"C'mon, Alex," Joey Vitale called from the batter's box. "Ragging Pete ain't gonna help. And he's *not* old—my dad says thirty-three is barely out of diapers!" The tall, whippet-lean young athlete had celebrated his twenty-fifth birthday only last week.

Garr shook his head, a sour smile making his teeth flash in the brilliant sunshine. He started across the diamond toward Pete, circling around the pitching machine on the mound. "Joey, tell that to the insurance people who cover this Methuselah—he's had so many injuries, they've optioned his legs for the Mayo Clinic."

Forsythe stayed on his knees, enjoying the feeling of the cool grass. Then he looked up at Garr. The owner's perfect posture and cropped gray hair still gave him the air of the

Marine he'd been in Korea. He looked younger than his fifty-five years.

"More sweet talk?" said Pete.

"Maybe you *are* tradable after all," Garr said with a sardonic grin. "Can I convince another club you've got a few more years of those impossible plays in you, Pete?"

Pete gave him a level stare, then laughed. "Have you forgotten my no-trade contract? Besides, I may have the knees of a seventy-year-old arthritic cripple, but there's still nobody who makes that play more than I do. Right, Joey?"

Joey watched an imagined drive drop into the stands, turned, looked blank for a second, then nodded. "Sure, Pete—all the way." His slow, warmhearted grin brightened his rawboned, homely features, making him almost handsome. Pete grinned back—it was tough for people to stay stone-faced when Joey Vitale smiled at them.

Garr smiled too, but with all the charm of a cattle owner surveying his prizes as they boarded the stock car. "Swift, real swift, isn't he, Forsythe? It's a good thing he's as strong as a bull, 'cause he's got about as much gray matter." He shook his head, watching Bobby Neal set the young batter up for another pitch. The ball streaked toward Vitale and the kid sent it screaming over their heads, a line drive headed for the stands like a tiny rocket plane.

"He ain't so dumb," said Bobby Neal affably, patting his ample belly. "He hits pretty good, and you pay him a million dollars a year for it. Pretty *smart* if you ask me."

Pete laughed out loud. Neal's down-home common sense always deflated Garr's sarcasm, and the veteran manager was such a sweet-natured man that Garr never hit back. "*Damned* smart," Pete kidded, following Neal's lead. "A million dollars a year, and the kid didn't even go to Harvard Business School like you did, Alex."

Garr's face softened as he watched Joey hit another pitch deep into left field. "He is a classic, isn't he?" Garr said, too low for Joey to hear—not that Joey listened much to what people said about him. "He might be the most graceful outfielder since Joe DiMaggio, Pete. Much as it pains me, I have you to thank for some of this. You've really settled Joey down. I appreciate the big-brother routine. Of course, now that he's matured, I don't need you anymore," Garr quipped.

"Every pup needs a sheepdog," Neal reminded him.

"Only a sheepdog who stays on the wagon," said Garr—the sarcasm was back, full strength and aimed at Pete.

Forsythe felt his jaw tighten as he tried not to show how much it annoyed him when the owner brought up the drinking incident. Once he'd admitted he had a problem three years back, Pete had fought to solve it. He'd *had* it under control too—until that night in Florida. It had been a bad day, one of the worst he'd ever lived through—one he almost *didn't* live through. He'd let his guard down, had one drink, thinking he could stop after that. But he didn't stop even after he left the bar. Not until he'd downed an entire bottle of vodka.

The memory blurred painfully . . . *the car* . . . *the rain . . . headlights blinding him . . . swerving . . . then real pain, physical pain, and the blacking out.*

Driving while intoxicated. The papers loved reporting on athletes messing up their lives, Pete thought bitterly. He'd never forget the accident, and he righteously felt he'd done his public penance, but it had taken Bobby Neal's intervention to smooth things over with Garr. The owner wouldn't even speak to his star third baseman until Neal insisted on a meeting. In a room far chillier than the coldest air conditioner could make it, Garr had exacted a promise—no more drinking or, no-trade clause or not, he'd get rid of Pete in a hurry.

Pete kept that promise. *Haven't had a drink since then . . . nineteen months dry as a bone. Won't he ever forget?*

Garr cocked his head at him, his eyes knowing. "What's the matter, Pete? Scared I really might trade you? Or make it so rough you'll quit? Afraid that if you didn't have training to keep you straight you'd go to pot—or alcohol?" He chuckled at his own pun. "I thought you had your post-baseball future all sewed up, Doc."

Forsythe shrugged. "If I wasn't sure there was life after baseball, I wouldn't be spending my winters in med school, now would I? Besides, with the cost of medical care, the only way I'll be able to afford to keep my legs in working order is to have a bunch of colleagues giving me professional courtesy."

"I knew there hadta be a good reason for you to be crazy enough to go back to medical school," said Neal with a chuckle. "Hey, I'm gonna be sixty-five soon and I've been seein' docs more than my wife lately. Are you gonna be a doctor before I'm dead?"

Pete laughed. "I'll give it my best shot, Bobby. And you stick around for a while, okay?"

"I'll give it *my* best shot."

"Hey!" Joey's voice rang out. "You guys want beers?"

"Sure, kid," said Garr.

Joey went to the cooler in the dugout and came back with three bottles of Bud—and a Diet 7Up for Pete. The third baseman looked at the beers for a moment, then resolutely twisted the cap off his soda. He glanced up at Joey as the younger player drank—at six-three, Vitale was a good four inches taller than the stocky Forsythe. With their difference in height, Joey's dark hair and Pete's thinning blond curls, they made for an arresting contrast in looks.

Joey cocked his head at a questioning angle. The pose reminded Forsythe of a collie he'd had as a kid. "What is it, Joey?"

"I dunno," Joey said, his dark eyes narrowing as he scanned the scudding clouds over Yankee Stadium's upper deck. "Can't you hear it?"

"Hear what?" asked Garr.

Pete frowned, not sure that his ears picked up any actual noise—but his feet sure as hell sensed a vibration. Reflexively, he dug his spikes into the grass as the ground began to shudder the way it does when a subway rumbles underneath the street gratings. But there *was* no subway under the stadium.

Garr's face paled beneath his tan. "Earthquake?"

The throbbing filled the air now, a deep humming that hurt the ears. They looked around, but there was nothing to account for the phenomenon—nothing visible.

Joey Vitale's keen young eyes spotted it first, moving in from the north, over the Hudson River. "Look!" he pointed.

Pete Forsythe's gaze followed Joey's finger, and his stomach tightened in disbelief, the way it had when Jean told him she wanted the divorce. He experienced a sudden, irrevocable certainty that his life—that every life on earth—had suddenly changed. Nothing would ever be the same again.

It moved majestically through the air, glimmering silver-blue, a massive round shape thickened in the middle, tapering around its edges. It was so huge as it moved over Yankee Stadium that the sun was totally eclipsed, the brightness of the October day quenched as though it had been snuffed like a candle.

Miles across, Pete thought, his numbed mind struggling to take in the scale of the mammoth ship. *The sonofabitch is miles across!*

It descended through the clouds, the sun playing off its upper surfaces while its belly remained dark. The edge of its monstrous shadow slid across the stadium, rippling down the bleachers, gliding across the outfield. Then the men were looking at the ship as it moved away, settling over Manhattan.

Garr found his voice first. "Christ Almighty! What *is* that?"

Mayor Daniel O'Connor was in his glory—surrounded by smiling children, clicking cameras, and the soft whirr of videotape minicams. The whole scene on the steps of the new building at the Bronx Zoo was being captured for the local evening news. As City Council President Alison Stein watched him, she was convinced all over again that O'Connor's broad face could hold a wider smile for a longer time than any other human being she'd ever known.

"Y'know," the Mayor began, "when I was a little Irish-Jewish kid growing up in Hell's Kitchen—that's on the West Side, for those of you too young to—"

A chorus of groans had erupted from the regular reporters, and O'Connor broke off, looking around at the grinning faces surrounding him. This was a ritual of every "fun" public appearance and the razzing always accompanied his favorite off-the-cuff speech. "Oh, no, Mayor!" called one reporter, "*not* the little Irish-Jewish-kid from Hell's Kitchen routine again . . . Change the speech, *change the speech*—"

Other members of the press picked up the refrain, and it became a chant of mock protest. The Mayor, a stout fireplug of a man, roared with laughter until he was breathless. "Okay! *Okay!*" He waved for attention. "I promise, no more Irish-Jewish-little-kid stories! Now quiet down!"

The noise subsided and the mayor tried to look serious, returning to his speechifying cadence. "Y'know, everywhere I go, whatever city, when the mayors complain about having to put up with reporters, I always tell them to thank their lucky stars that they don't have to put up with the New York press corps, the wildest, rowdiest bunch I've ever seen—'' The reporters began a chorus of catcalls and mock hisses, and the Mayor finished hastily, "But the *best* too, and don't anyone forget it!''

Alison Stein marveled at the way O'Connor handled these spontaneous appearances, the impromptu press conferences, the streetwise give and take that exemplified her city and its sometimes rough edges. Personally, she detested unscripted appearances—she was a careful, methodical person who felt hideously naked without something written down to prompt her. Twenty years as a lawyer and politician had given her a veneer of calm deliberation, but to this day her hands still sweated and her knees knocked when she faced the microphones. She always got a kick out of watching (and envying) O'Connor's masterful handling of the press.

He was waving his hands for order again, and the crowd quieted to hear him. "Okay, back to why we're here at the Bronx Zoo, the best zoo in the world. When I was a kid, I used to love hopping on the subway and coming up here—and, y'know, I still do. But today I'm even happier and prouder than I was as a kid, because lately, with the support of many local businesses and corporations plus the generosity of private citizens all over the city, the zoo has been raising money for improvements. The zoo we see today is a growing, changing environment, and for hundreds of miles in any direction it's the premier place to see animals in habitats that come as close to nature as possible—right here in the biggest city in America!''

There was a ripple of applause. O'Connor gestured to the building behind him. "Now, today, we're officially dedicating this new reptile house. This alligator pool behind me, I'm told, duplicates a Southern river ecosystem—a bit of the Everglades right here in the Big Apple. Isn't it great?''

The photographers snapped away and the kids in the crowd squealed in joyous fright as doors opened in the stony walls and several alligators slithered through them into the pool, tails undulating in powerful swishes, their tiny eyes nearly hidden amid their dark greenish-brown scales. They didn't look particularly hungry, but with jaws nearly a foot and a half long, nobody wanted to stick his or her hand in to see if they'd be interested.

"Mr. Mayor," called a reporter, "why don't you climb in there and pose with those alligators? It'd make a great shot!"

The crowd laughed and O'Connor smiled benignly. "You're quite a comedian, Ralston."

"Why not?" the young woman grinned cheekily. "Are you chicken, Mr. Mayor?"

O'Connor pursed his lips. "The 'gators might enjoy me more if I was, but no, the Mayor is not chicken. The Mayor is also not a fool. Besides, I'd be perfectly safe. I have it on good authority that these are Democratic alligators."

A burst of laughter rolled over the uninterested heads of the reptiles. O'Connor waved at them. "Alison Stein made sure they had the right party affiliation before she'd agree to let me come here and introduce 'em to the city. Because, you see, if anything *did* happen to me, she'd end up as mayor, and as we all know, she's a lady who prefers to run things from behind the scenes. Alison . . ." O'Connor looked around. "C'mon up here, Alison."

Trying not to color, she pulled her jacket straight and edged toward the Mayor and the hated microphones, wishing O'Connor had let her just hide in the crowd. She glared at him covertly as she mounted the steps toward him. A woman in her mid-forties, she looked her age. She was a shade on the plump side, with yard-long dark hair (which she kept coiled in a neatly braided bun during the day), fair skin, and determined dark eyes. Divorced for more than a decade, she'd somehow managed to juggle raising three children with a full-time job, law school at night, and working her way up through the male-dominated Democratic hierarchy. This was her second term as City Council president.

O'Connor slung an arm around her shoulders as Alison joined him at the top of the steps. "Alison Stein here," he said, "is largely responsible for this new reptile facility, though she'd be the last one to take credit for her own hard work. But she spent a lot of time lining up some of the larger donations from local businesses. I think all New Yorkers should thank her—*I* want to take this opportunity to publicly express my appreciation." He beckoned to the crowd. "How about it?"

The applause was enthusiastic. Alison blushed to the roots

of her hair, and, irritated, realized the flush would probably show on camera. "And what's more," O'Connor said as the clapping began to die away, "I think if you reporters want to hear *the* most heartfelt praise for Alison's work you're likely to hear, you ought to interview the alligators!"

But the line didn't get the laugh O'Connor had expected—the attention of the crowd was suddenly elsewhere. Alison turned on the steps, her gaze searching. There was a gut-quivering hum coming from—from where? It seemed to emanate from everywhere at once. The reporters murmured, wondering. The bass throbbing intensified. Photographers and cameramen and -women turned, searching, trying to be the first to capture the source of the vibrating sound—trying to latch on to a really *big* story for the evening news.

It was big, all right. Somehow they all saw it at once. The huge vessel drifted overhead as lightly as one of the clouds, impossibly huge, impossibly real. The Mayor looked at it for a long moment, his freckles standing out against his pallor, then turned to Alison. "Shit—talk about being upstaged, Ali," he said soberly, his pale blue eyes shining with fear and excitement. "Think I'll get a laugh if I tell 'em it's all a Republican campaign stunt?"

White House Press Secretary Fred Foster cradled the phone on his shoulder as he hastily scribbled notes on a pad. "No, we have no comment as of yet. The report is still uncomfirmed. No, I won't confirm the name of the city. The reports remain unconfirmed. No, no, as soon as we have a statement to make, you'll have it."

He slammed the phone down with a muttered curse just as his cubicle door burst open. Chief of Staff Leonard Katowski stood in the doorway, his knuckles resting on his hips, wrinkling the pinstripes of his ancient navy-blue suit. "Let's go, F. F.—*now*." He ran an urgent hand through his thick black hair, leaving it standing even more on end. His suit was a touch too short for his long thin limbs—Foster had always fancied in idle moments that Katowski would fit right in as the scarecrow in *The Wizard of Oz*.

Foster nodded, standing, ignoring the phone as it shrilled again. "Another one. Christ, how the hell do they expect me to find out anything if they keep me tied up on the phone?"

Automatically he pulled on his jacket, checked the knot on his tie, and smoothed down his wispy blond hair. Katowski fairly danced in the doorway as Foster came toward him, leaving the phone still jangling insistently.

The portly Foster, at least a head shorter than the Chief of Staff, had to jog to keep up with Katowski's quick tread. "Hold all my calls!" he shouted at his secretary as they passed her door, his and Katowski's feet silent on the thick carpet. "What's new?" Foster asked, guessing the answer.

"We've confirmed the sighting. Fighters are being scrambled. We've got to wake up the President *now.*"

"*We* do?" Foster remembered the time they'd awakened the Chief Executive from his afternoon nap, only to discover the reports of new troop movement in Afghanistan were the result of a translator's error.

"*We* do," Katowski stated. "Or else, Freddy, you're going to be the one fielding press questions on why the President wasn't bright-eyed and bushy-tailed when the UFO's invaded from space."

Foster stopped so short he nearly fell. *"UFO's? Plural?"*

Katowski grabbed his arm and pulled him along. "Plural. National Security Agency says the things are being sighted all over the world. We've had formal confirmations from Great Britain, France, and Japan."

"Who gave the order to scramble the jets?"

"Base commanders. SOP. Reconnaissance and radio contact, if possible, to establish their intentions. Now move it, Freddy—quit asking so many questions! We've gotta get our asses in gear and tell Morrow!"

Foster tried to stop again, but Katowski wouldn't even let him break stride. "I *have* to ask questions," he sputtered. "I'm the goddamned Press Secretary!"

They swung into Katowski's office, one door away from the Oval Office. The Chief of Staff began shoveling papers from his blotter into a file folder, his bony hands moving with the precision of a threshing machine—churning, sorting, and sifting. "I thought you were in a hurry," Foster protested halfheartedly.

"Briefing papers. I'm not getting caught with my pants down, and I won't let Morrow or you face the press without doing my job."

Foster began to laugh. "*Briefing papers?* For something that started three minutes ago? Are you nuts? What are you giving him, a synopsis of *Earth Versus the Flying Saucers?*"

Katowski gave Foster a bland look. "I have briefing papers for any contingency you could possibly dream up, Freddy."

"I could never have thought of *this*."

"*That's* why I'm Chief of Staff, and *you're* the Press Secretary." Katowski looked grim.

There was a knock from the open door. They looked up to see a compactly built man looking in. "Ready to go?" asked Gerald Livingston, the perfectly tailored and barbered National Security Adviser.

"One more report," said Katowski, heading for the file cabinets across the room. "How are things downstairs?"

"We're on top of it," said Livingston, sounding miffed that Katowski could think otherwise.

Foster pursed his lips. He'd never liked or trusted Livingston, a man who had no rough edges, no apparent weak spots. He was entirely too calculated for Foster's tastes. "Isn't State gonna be pissed that NSA was in on this from the instant we woke the President up?" asked the Press Secretary.

Livingston shrugged, smiling faintly. "Who cares? Let State be pissed. That's the price Nick Draper pays for having that fancy, plush office out in Foggy Bottom, while I slave in the White House basement."

Katowski yanked one more folder out of a file cabinet, sending the metal drawer slamming back into place. "Got it. Let's go."

"Who's actually going to do the waking?" asked Livingston.

"Do we look like idiots?" growled Foster. "Morrow's *wife* is going to do it."

They took the elevator upstairs to the First Family's living quarters. Foster thought about his secretary and deputy handling a Christmas tree's worth of press office phone lines lit up by cabinet officials, Pentagon brass, citizens, and foreign allies, all wanting to be able to rest easy, to know that President William Brent Morrow had the situation well in hand. In truth, Morrow was probably one of the few Americans remaining who was still resting easy—but that, obviously, was about to change.

The elevator door opened, and Barbara Morrow, a slim, patrician woman in her late fifties, greeted them with a thin smile. "Gentlemen, does anyone have any idea what's actually going on?"

"Not really," said Katowski. "Not yet. No sightings in this area—but they're confirmed in New York, Dallas, St. Louis, and several cities in Europe."

"However bad this may get," said Foster, resisting the urge to drum his fingers on the door frame, "it'll be worse if it gets out that we didn't wake him right away."

Barbara Morrow nodded and led them into the bedroom, clicking the lamp on to its lowest setting. The aides stood back while she gently touched her husband's shoulder. He was stretched out on the handmade quilt, dressed in jeans and a plaid shirt, a big, handsome man with thick gray hair—what a President *should* look like, Foster had always thought. But he did not like being awakened from the naps his physician had prescribed when the Chief Executive had suffered minor chest pains last year.

Morrow rolled over with a grunt, saw his wife, then his aides. "What's wrong?" he mumbled.

"Are you awake, sir?" asked Foster gingerly, remembering the President's heart. Perhaps they should have brought Dr. Washington along.

"I wake up instantly," Morrow snapped. "It's a skill I learned during World War Two in airfield barracks. Now, you boys know what I said the last time you woke me for a bad reason—so I'm safe in assuming this is a good one, am I not?"

Katowski, Foster, and Livingston swallowed in unison, looked at each other to see who wanted to go first, then back at the President. Morrow gave his wife an exasperated glance. "You interrupted my nap for the Three Stooges?"

Suddenly the White House shuddered down to its two-century-old bones. Morrow was on his feet immediately. "Are we under attack?"

"Not exactly," said Katowski, edging nervously toward the window.

"Not *exactly*?" the President echoed. "We don't have

earthquakes here, and it feels like the plaster's going to come down if those vibrations get any worse!"

"We—we don't know if they're hostile," said Katowski, avoiding the President's question.

"*Who* is 'they'?" the President demanded.

Foster pulled open the heavy drapes, feeling his heart pause, then pound with hammer blows that made him wish they'd brought Dr. Washington along for *him*. Morrow strode to the window, stopped, and stared out. His wife and aides arrayed themselves behind him.

"*That* is 'they,' sir," said Foster.

"We don't know who they are," said Livingston, "but there are apparently a lot of them."

It took the Commander-in-Chief of the most powerful nation on earth many heartbeats to find his voice. "Holy shit. You sure I'm not dreaming?"

"No windows. I never know what time of day it is," grumbled Denise Daltrey, rubbing her eyes as she looked at the digital clock on her office desk. It told her it was 4:06 P.M. in the CBS News Building, a former dairy barn in this less-than-chic neighborhood on Manhattan's West Side. It also told her that she'd definitely never make her tennis lesson that afternoon.

As she reached for the telephone to call the pro and apologize, a didactic little voice began a sermonizing monologue: *You're skipping your tennis lesson today, and yesterday you were too tired to get it up to jog. And because you skipped your exercise, you're now so bleary-eyed that you probably don't recall a damn thing you just skipped your tennis lesson to read. Those nice young kids in research did all that digging for you, and when you get on the air tomorrow and the most intelligent thing you can utter is a burp, they'll think it was their fault you blew it, and one of them will try to pitch him or herself out the nearest upper-story window . . . which may be why they make researchers work in an office that has no windows. You're going to have to take better care of yourself, Denise old gal, if you want to keep your job. Viewers will take a dim view of a morning news anchorwoman who falls asleep in the middle of her own show . . .*

"Idiot!" a voice chided aloud, and Denise barely avoided

jumping as she recognized it as her own. Firmly she gave herself a silent remeinder to get a grip on things—after all, she *loved* her job. After a rocky start, she'd gone on to make the co-anchor spot her own. But now, a year into the mad pace, the hours were starting to take their toll—rising at 1:30 A.M. and getting to work by 3:30; being charming, witty, and incisive for two hours while millions of people watched her over their eggs and juice and the sounds of showers, razors, and hair dryers; then meetings on the following day's lineup, followed by lunch and more meetings; then tennis or a workout (when she could squeeze it in and wasn't too exhausted) and back to the office for more work. Finally, she was home by 5:00 for a nap, up at 7:00 to watch the network's flagship, The Evening News, then to sleep, perchance not to dream—*please!*—of all the things she should have done that day but hadn't.

Denise made her apologetic call, then peered into the mirror hanging at eye level over her IBM Selectric. Bags were starting to take up permanent residence beneath her blue eyes and some mornings, even her heavy sweep of sable hair looked tired.

Frowning, Denise quickly wielded her under-eye coverup stick, then freshened her mascara and shadow. Yeah, okay, so the job was grueling. Nobody had ever said it would be easy— and the fact remained that she had never wanted to do anything else and that she was in a very prestigious position for her age. She was getting a ton of experience and exposure—not bad for a kid who'd worked her way up from doing the weather on a Providence radio station. At thirty-three, Denise was what she'd always wanted to be, and she'd achieved that goal without ever compromising her integrity. She'd made it totally on her abilities, her rapport with people, and to be brutally honest, her looks. Homely people had a real disadvantage when bucking for an anchor slot.

Now, her hand resting on the telephone, she faced a turning point—she could read more background on this story she'd be doing tomorrow, or she could call a friend to wangle a late afternoon match. Kathy was a good player, and while she wouldn't give Denise the workout her pro would, at least it would be *something*. She kicked back in her chair, closed her eyes, and mumbled her decision in a small, guilt-ridden voice: "Tennis." Her hips felt bulgy, and she was convinced that only immediate exercise would prevent her looking like a blimp onscreen tomorrow.

She began to dial. "Hi, Kath—Denise. I missed my pro today and came down with a galloping case of the guilts. Want to play for an hour? I can grab a cab and be there in ten minutes." She listened for a moment. "Aw, c'mon, Kath— pretty please? You can get over to Bloomie's tomorrow. I'll even go with you. I've just *gotta* work the kinks out!"

The intercom speaker on her phone burbled insistently. "Hang on a second, Kath. My secretary's buzzing me." With a sigh she switched on the intercom. "I'm not here, Paula. I'm dead, and I won't revive without some exercise," she said, managing a convincingly pathetic whimper. She listened for a moment, then laughed tiredly. "Right. There's a giant UFO over New York City, so I can't leave to play tennis . . ."

She was still chuckling humorlessly when the door to her office slammed back and a tieless Dan Rather stood there in his shirt-sleeves, his dark eyes excited, though his face bore its usual calm. Denise forgot her fatigue, realizing that what Paula had reported *wasn't* her customary zany notion of humor, but the truth. Rather's terse words only confirmed what she knew. "Staff meeting, Bennie's conference room, right now, Denise. UFO over New York and who knows where else. The President has been alerted."

Then he was gone.

Numbly Denise punched back in on Kathy's line. "Kath? Dan Rather just told me there's a UFO over New York. I don't think I can play tennis after all. Call you later. Bye."

Ignoring the sputtering squawks from the receiver, she hung up. The adrenaline was starting to flow the way it always did when a really *big* story loomed, and the rush banished her fatigue. Denise Daltrey grabbed her notebook and tape recorder as she stood. "Hot damn!" she said aloud. "A friggin' *UFO!*"

Lauren Stewart carefully washed a dish, placing it securely into the rack. She ran a finger over the pretty Bavarian floral pattern, remembering how much her mother had loved these dishes, how proud she'd been when her husband's struggling medical practice had blossomed and they'd finally been able to afford this service for eight. That had been shortly after they'd bought this brownstone in Harlem, and Lauren's mother had been so happy keeping everything shining and perfect. Noelani Stewart had never wanted to work outside her home—she'd been perfectly content serving as her husband's receptionist and secretary, and keeping this house the way she'd trained her daughter and her husband to maintain it.

Gets dishes so clean you can see yourself in them, thought Lauren, rinsing the last plate and holding it up to see if she *could* see her face in it. *Not quite,* she thought, seeing only a blurred light-brown oval. Her mind quickly sketched in what the wet surface didn't reveal: her mother's fine-boned Polynesian features, dark-brown almond-shaped eyes, straight black hair, and coloring that fell somewhere between her mother's rich caramel and her father's milk chocolate. She grinned, seeing a white-sugar blur of teeth. *Are sweets all you can think of?* she wondered, amused at herself. *You've been on this diet twenty-four hours and already you're going into carbohydrate withdrawal.*

She laughed aloud, then heard her father's voice behind her. "What're you laughing at, honey?"

"Myself, Dad. I'm trying to lose five pounds before I start on that overseas goodwill tour with Olav, so I'll have a couple of pounds to play with. You know those diplomatic dinners. And I just realized I'd probably *kill* for a bag of M&M's—peanut or plain, I wouldn't be fussy."

Dr. Stewart chuckled. "Lauren, most women would *kill* to have your figure. I can never understand why the fashions say you have to be ten pounds underweight."

Lauren carefully put the last dish into the drainer and let the water out of the sink, turning to see her father sit down at the table behind her. "I'm hurt, Dad." She made a face at him. "The medical statistics all back me up—it's better to be underweight than overweight!"

Dr. George Stewart looked down at his own stomach through his glasses, then patted its comfortable bulge consolingly. "You're right—and you know I think you're gorgeous, baby. Almost as pretty as your mama, and she was the prettiest woman I ever saw." He grinned a lopsided, slightly sentimental grin.

"Do you remember how Mama worked to take care of this

place?" Lauren asked, sitting down opposite him. "I remember once asking her if we couldn't just skip the cleaning for one week, and she just looked at me and said that *her* house got cleaned every week, and that was that. Like the Ten Commandments or something."

Her father nodded, his long dark fingers fiddling with the stack of papers from his anatomy class at Cornell Medical Center, which he'd been grading earlier. "I remember. She wanted you to have this house someday, you know. She'd be disappointed to know you won't be living here after I'm gone."

Lauren stiffened slightly, afraid they might be edging toward one of their painful "discussions." Hastily, she tried to turn the conversation away from her own future. "Is that why you stayed on here after Mama died?"

"No, no, honey. I stayed here because this neighborhood needs a doctor. Why, who else would answer the phone in the middle of the night to help those folks? All the younger fellows have those answering services."

"Oh, Daddy . . ." Lauren said, half-admiring and half-despairing, as she took his hand in hers. "Those folks would find another doctor somewhere, you know they would! Half the time they wake you up for something on the order of a hangnail, and then you have trouble getting back to sleep. You're not the only physician in Harlem, you know. When are you going to cut back? Between your practice here and the classes at med school—" She shook her head. "When are you going to take some time for *you*?"

"I'm fine, baby!" He grinned at her. "Keeping busy keeps me young. If I didn't have those patients and these students to worry about, I'd sit at home worrying about *you*—and then where would we be?"

"I know that," she admitted quietly, patting his hand. "I'm sorry, Dad. Why do we always have this same argument? I can keep a half-dozen Third World delegates from fighting, but I can't keep from fussing with my own father."

He smiled gently. "Those delegates aren't kin, Lauren. Only folks who love each other can fuss the way we do, baby."

Lauren grinned. "I'm almost thirty-five and still your baby, huh, Dad?"

"Always, sweetheart."

They smiled at each other, enjoying the closeness their weekly visit always brought—and heard the dishes in the drain begin to rattle. Jumping up, Lauren raced over to stand by them protectively, her dark eyes wide. The old house vibrated, then began to shake slightly. The stack of papers slid off the table and across the floor, leaving a white swath on the spotless linoleum.

"What in the hell—" George Stewart hurried over to the window. Down in the street people were hurrying out of their homes and apartments, looking up and gesturing. As Lauren joined him at the window, George Stewart looked up too.

Even as Lauren saw the unbelievable apparition of a massive flying saucer hovering over the city, the phone began to ring. Dr. Stewart snatched it up. "Doc Stewart here." He looked up at his daughter. "Yes, she's here."

He handed the phone to Lauren. "Hello?" she said. "Yes, I can see it. Anything official yet?" She listened for a second, then made a face. "Par for the course. I'll be there as soon as I can. I hope I can get a cab."

She hung up. "Gotta go, Daddy. Whatever that thing is, there are more like it hovering over other cities all over the world. The whole UN is going bananas—everyone accusing everyone of being responsible, even though they know the odds against that thing being from this planet." She broke off, realizing that it was odd to think of Earth as only one of a myriad of other planets . . .

Her father kissed her cheek. "Sounds like a job for Super-Diplomat."

"Yes, but I guess they're stuck with me," she said dryly. "I'll call you as soon as I know anything."

"I suspect I might be busy too. UFO's coming to pay a visit are bound to give some folks upset stomachs—not to mention heart attacks and strokes."

"Good luck, Daddy." She started for the door, then reached back to hold his hand tightly. "Remember how much I love you."

"I love you too, honey." Their fingers slipped apart, and he kissed her again, holding her for a long moment.

Chapter 2

Alarums and Excursions

President Morrow was fortunate that he'd taken his nap, for it was the last sleep he got for nearly twenty-four hours. The Oval Office quickly became a command post while Morrow spoke with seemingly endless succession of military officials, congressional leaders, and executive branch assistants. The White House switchboard nearly shorted out with the volume of calls, and the kitchen staff worked around the clock preparing meals, sandwiches, and what seemed like oceans of coffee.

Intelligence agents and station chiefs had begun reporting in from around the globe within minutes of the first sightings. Central Intelligence, National Security, and Defense intelligence personnel vied with each other to see who could bring in the greatest volume of useful information in the shortest order.

Unfortunately, all of the services soon found themselves in possession of only a few—and identical—verifiable facts: (1) the ships were there, hovering a mile or more above most of the major cities of the Earth, (2) each measured about five *miles* in diameter, and (3) there were at least fifty of them hanging over the world's major cities—Washington, New York, Paris, Athens, Tokyo, Moscow, London, Rome, Leningrad, Cairo, Chicago, San Francisco, Los Angeles, Houston, Pretoria, Buenos Aires, Bonn, Peking, New Delhi, Jerusalem . . .

The huge saucers made no moves or sounds once they'd

23

settled in. Every nation with an air force quickly sent fighter patrols up. Actually, the Israelis had been first, taking matters into their own hands without waiting for the superpowers to push their military bureaucracies into motion. Their F-16's, emblazoned with the Star of David, screamed up from desert bases, flitted around the monstrous ship over Jerusalem, then peeled off to check out its twin hovering over (and dwarfing) the pyramids in Egypt.

"Wing commander to base," radioed the patrol leader. The signal was patched into Prime Minister Avram Herzog's office. The Prime Minister was an urbane man who displayed little emotion in the face of this, or any other crisis. He sat by as Defense Minister Yitzhak Dinitz answered the call.

Dinitz, dressed in civilian khaki, was a barrel-chested man whose no-nonsense bearing was softened by a deceptively quiet voice. "Report, Major. Dinitz speaking. Over."

There was a spatter of static, and then: "We can't get any closer than about a kilometer, sir. The intruders are jamming our electronics and navigation computers. They don't respond to any of our hailing frequencies. Over."

"Have they lost anyone?" the Prime Minister whispered to Dinitz. The Defense Minister relayed the question.

"Us? Of course not," said the pilot, sounding indignant. "Besides, they haven't made any hostile moves. Or any moves at all, for that matter. They're just hovering. Request further orders, sir."

Dinitz glanced at Herzog.

The Prime Minister gazed calmly back. "You're the expert, Yitzhak. Do you have a recommendation?"

"They haven't made any hostile moves, true, but they haven't made any friendly ones either. Not even saying hello. I say we give them one more chance to talk to us, then we fire."

The Prime Minister raised a dark eyebrow, stroking thoughtfully at his short beard. "If we do that, we *could* go down in history as the nation that started the first interplanetary war. But we'd like them to talk to us. How about if we aim a bit wide, just to see what they do?"

Dinitz nodded, and tersely gave the order.

In seconds they'd added one more fact about the UFOs to world knowledge: weapons fired at the huge ships simply went astray, detonating harmlessly, high in the upper atmosphere.

And so the world waited. At four in the morning, President Morrow ordered his staff out of the Oval Office. "Come back when you have something new to report," he said. "But not until then. We can sit here and speculate until the stars—or those damned ships—fall out of the sky, and it won't do any of us a bit of good. Beat it, all of you. Get some rest."

Press Secretary Foster was almost to the door when Morrow's words stopped him. "Not you, Freddy. Stick around, if you don't mind."

As Foster nodded and came back into the room, Morrow leaned back in his chair, his heels propped on the desk, waving a weary hand at the triple-screen TV showing the continuous coverage on all three networks. "Turn 'em off, Freddy."

The Press Secretary did so, then sank into a burgundy leather chair facing his boss. Still leaning back, Morrow stretched until his joints cracked. "Ah, peace and quiet at long last."

"Aren't you worried that you'll miss something, sir?" asked Foster.

"If anything interesting happens, seventeen people will be trying to squeeze through that door at the same instant, all dying to be the first to tell me. Maybe the old custom of killing the messenger wasn't such a bad idea—cuts down on doorway traffic jams." Morrow chuckled at the look on Foster's face. "Laugh, Freddy. That was a joke."

"Too close to home, sir. *I'm* usually a messenger."

"Hmm. I see your point." Morrow slumped back in his chair. "Any changes in the national reaction to those silent critters?" He hooked a thumb toward the ceiling.

"The highways out of the cities are beginning to clear out. Seems like the folks who decided to stay put are still staying put. The ones who ran for it have gotten out of the cities by now."

"Where'd they all head? The country? Mountains?"

"Yeah. I wish I'd bought stock in a camping-goods store or a four-wheel-drive lot. General Loman reported that they were having to put the motor pools under tight security—jeeps were disappearing like crazy."

Morrow made a *tch-tch* noise. "This mess is going to wreak havoc with the GNP indicators for the year."

"I agree, sir."

The two men sat quietly for a long moment. The President swiveled his chair around to peer out the window behind his desk, the one the White house photographer used when he wanted to take a dramatic photo of the Chief Executive working late at night during a worldwide crisis. Sure enough, there was the photographer out on the lawn, shivering as the predawn autumn wind whipped around him.

As the man saw Morrow looking at him, he raised his hand in a quick salute and left.

"I can see the photo caption," Foster observed. "'Wild Bill' Morrow burns midnight oil trying to solve UFO crisis."

Morrow chuckled. "Maybe I oughta put my flannel shirt, jeans, and cowboy boots back on, so folks'll recognize me."

Foster smiled wearily. "When did you ever get that nickname, sir? Hardly anyone ever uses it anymore—maybe they've tamed the West out of you."

Morrow's grin flashed for a second. "Shucks, son, you can take the boy out of Texas, but you can't *ever* take the Texas out of the boy. I got that nickname back in World War Two. When I first ran for state senate back in 1958, the campaign people loved it. Gave me 'color,' they said. But then when I started getting nudges to declare my candidacy for President, they wanted me to downplay my cowboy image—even though that image was really me. I told 'em, hell, no! Americans love cowboys, I said, and this is the way I've always been."

"Still are, sir. You've been the same guy all along."

"I wear more suits than I used to," Morrow admitted. "This job changes you no matter how much you think you can stay the same. You sit up nights worrying about things that other people never even know about."

Foster grimaced. "Well, at least you're not alone sitting up tonight, sir. Half the population of the country is probably suffering from insomnia."

"And while we sweat, those little green creeps up there are probably laughing through their teeth—assuming they're green and have teeth."

Foster was quiet for a while, then asked. "How'd you get the nickname during the war, sir, if you don't mind my asking?"

"You don't know?"

"Well . . . I heard some rumors. Nothing confirmed."

Morrow guffawed. "You heard right, Freddy. I used to fly slaloms between telephone poles. Must have been good practice because I came back in one piece from fifty-three bombing missions. Course I was just a youngster in those days—I'd never have the nerve to do anything so foolish now."

Foster looked at Morrow, seeing a twinkle in the Chief Executive's eye, remembering the time he'd insisted on taking the controls of Air Force One for a half-hour during the end of a transatlantic flight—the air traffic controller had become incoherent when Morrow had identified himself as the approaching pilot and then requested landing coordinates. The President had convinced all of them he might actually attempt a landing before grinning and relinquishing the controls to his pilot. The Press Secretary grinned wryly now, then sobered, thinking of the UFO hovering over the nation's capital like a blue-silver thundercloud. "Do you think the country will get out of this in one piece, sir?" he asked.

Morrow sighed. "I wish I knew, Freddy. I wish I knew."

Activity at the United Nations also continued into the small hours of the night. Lauren Stewart stood beside Secretary General Olav Lindstrom as they met with ambassadorial delegations and counseled patience. At least, Lauren thought, it was comforting to know that even if their advice was ignored, there was little anyone could do. The invulnerability of the alien craft was a more powerful argument than any the Secretary General or his special assistant could muster.

Lindstrom was noted for his patience. Depending on who was talking, it was either his most admirable virtue or his biggest failing. Lauren had taken his special seminar at Harvard, while he was the delegate from Sweden and she was completing her master's in International Relations. By the second week of the course, she'd developed a firm and growing admiration for the white-haired man with the neatly trimmed moustache. As she'd listened to him talk about World War Two, how Sweden had managed to walk the fine line of neutrality, not antagonizing the Russians yet still managing to help the British and Americans when they could, Lauren watched his deep, mournful eyes—sad eyes that had learned to observe while others blustered. Lindstrom spoke often about the tactic of calm observation, of finding and seizing the tiniest common ground on which to build a foundation of peaceful coexistence.

But during this long night of too many questions and too few answers, Lauren watched her idol become progressively quieter. The presence of beings from another part of the universe was something that the aging Lindstrom was having trouble accepting. Eventually, Lauren tactfully took over the meetings, moderating with the skill and presence the old man had first spotted in her at Harvard. The young grad student with the exotic looks had easily been the brightest in all the seminars he'd taught, and he'd been pleased when she accepted his invitation to become part of his staff after he was appointed Secretary General.

The UN gatherings ended before dawn, and at Lauren's insistence, Lindstrom retreated to his office for a nap. Lauren could have sprawled on the couch in her own office, but she knew she'd lie there wide-eyed, stiff and listening. Instead, she bundled up in her coat and went up to the outdoor observation deck. For a long time she stood in the cold, staring up at the wash of spotlights against the belly of the dark alien bulk looming over her city.

Slowly she became aware that the city beneath her feet sounded wrong. Wandering over to the railing, she looked down, expecting—but not finding—the light trails of cars, cabs, trucks, and buses. But only a few tiny gleams threaded their way through the street grid. New York was almost totally silent, as though crouching in fear.

Lauren had always felt the self-confidence of a native New Yorker. She was a product of this odd urban mixture of cosmopolitan slick and rough-and-tumble crude. She felt a fierce pride in knowing her city could take on just about anything nature—or man—could throw at it, and come up swinging.

Until now. Down below, the streetlights began to wink out as the sun tinged the bottoms of the clouds near the bridges between Manhattan and Brooklyn, magically turning their cables into a sparkling filigree. Lauren took a deep breath of the morning air and—she couldn't help it—stuck out her tongue at the alien ship. "Screw you," she whispered. "*Don't* talk—see if we care."

She went back to her office, then gratefully poured herself a cup of coffee and picked up the phone. She dialed her father's number.

"Dad? It's Lauren. I hope I didn't wake you, but I didn't know when I'd get another chance to call."

"No, honey." Her father's voice sounded alert. "I've been up awhile. Slept a little, but not much. My guess is that there are gonna be a *lot* of tired people around the world today. How's it going at the UN?"

Lauren stifled a yawn. "Calm, for the moment. They all tired themselves out making accusations they knew were wrong and pointless, just from force of habit. It could have been worse."

There was a soft knock on Lauren's door. A young Indian poked his turbaned head in. "Sorry to disturb you, Ms. Stewart, but there is a meeting in ten minutes, and Mr. Lindstrom requests your presence."

"Okay, Sanjay. Dad, I've got to go. Hang in there. I'll talk to you later."

Almost two hours later, it happened.

A pulsing tone beamed out from the huge spaceships— steady, unvarying, *global*. The pulsing signals sounded for several minutes.

President Morrow was still at his desk in the Oval Office, but the television sets were back on and the room was crowded with people. His eyes—and all other eyes in the room—were on the multiple-screen TV console, watching as the network commentators tried to make some sense out of what was happening. From outside they could hear the pulsing tones being echoed from the ship overhead.

"Turn Channel Nine up," Morrow said, and a staff member fiddled with the remote. "I've always liked Denise Daltrey. Easy on the vision, and she doesn't mince words."

Denise's crisp, even tones filled the Chief Executive's office. ". . . and this literally unearthly sound continues to pulse from the alien space vessels, as it has for about five minutes now. Our correspondents around the world report that the—the beacon, for want of a better word—began at almost the same second from every ship. This morning we're lucky enough to have Dr. Isaac Asimov here with us in our New York studio. Dr. Asimov is, of course, a world-famous science authority and science fiction writer. He's the author of almost three hundred books on everything from black holes to the Bible—"

"I think we would need a combination of the two to figure out what's been happening to our planet since yesterday afternoon," Asimov said, directing his most charming smile at Denise. "And while I have indeed studied black holes *and* the Bible, I've never claimed to understand them fully—especially at the same time."

She finally allowed herself a return smile.

"Ah!" he said. "You *can* smile! You've been so grim since I came in here. I get upset when women react with grim resignation at my arrival. Resignation I can understand, but *grim* resignation—never!"

Denise's mouth twitched as she looked into the camera. "We asked Doctor Asimov to come in to enlighten us, and he's also entertaining us—a double threat. But speaking of threats, Doctor, do you think we *are* in danger from these vessels hovering over our planet?"

Asimov scratched thoughtfully at one bushy muttonchop sideburn. "Well, Denise, speaking from my perspective as a human, if they were going to do terrible things to us, I think they would have done them already. Why wait? It was apparent after the first ten minutes that there wasn't anything we could do to stop them. But in considering the possible motivations of alien beings, you have to remember that they may not *have* motivations that are comprehensible to us."

He grinned at her. "What reasons can you think of to travel to another planet, Denise?"

Denise looked slightly taken aback. "Trade? Commerce with other planets? Friendliness? War?"

"All good reasons," Asimov said. "All reasons that we humans can relate to. But what about aliens who might have come here on a religious pilgrimage—they have it set down in their version of the Bible that they must visit this dinky little world every ten billion years or the universe goes kaput. So here they are!"

Denise nodded. "I see what you mean. Their reasons might be reasons we can't even *imagine*," she said.

"Right," said Asimov approvingly. "In a case like this, predictions are pretty useless—but fun. Until something else happens, I'll reserve judgment as to their intentions." He grinned and shrugged. "What else can I do?"

Denise cocked her head, touching her hidden earphone. "What was that? Excuse me, Dr. Asimov, but I'm being told that something is—" She broke off, listening; then her calm tones sharpened with excitement. "Yes! It's a *voice*! The first voice we've ever heard from another world. We're patching this vocal signal in so we can all hear it. It's being picked up on the international emergency frequency."

She and Asimov both turned to watch the large monitor behind them. The view of the alien ship hovering over Manhattan was unchanged.

A voice filled the speakers, a male voice, neutrally accented, speaking ordinary English. But there was a strange timbre to it, like the resonance of a multitrack recording. The voice was counting: ". . . fifteen, fourteen, thirteen . . ."

"I wonder if this represents a living being," Asimov murmured, "or an electronic voice . . ."

"Perfect English," Denise said, then, listening to her earphone again, continued, "No, I'm told it's in different languages all over the world."

The control-room technicians were frantically switching feeds so that every three numbers heard by the viewing audience came over in different languages—French, Russian, Hebrew, Spanish, then back to English as the voice reached "one."

There was a brief pause that seemed to last millennia, then: "Citizens of the planet Earth. We bring you greetings . . . and we come in peace. May we respectfully request that the Secretary General of your United Nations come to the top of the United Nations Building in New York at 0100 Greenwich time this evening. Thank you."

The transmission ended and there was silence. Denise Daltrey found her voice. "0100 Greenwich time. That's eight P.M. Eastern time. And of course we'll be there covering this story of . . . well, I was going to say the story of the century, Doctor Asimov, but this is really *the* story of all recorded history."

"You're right," said Asimov, for once completely serious. "How many hours do we have to go?"

Denise glanced at her watch. "Just about thirteen and a half hours."

Asimov settled back in his chair, his grin back. "Want to see how many guesses we can rack up in that time as to why they're here? I'll bet I can think of stranger ones than *you* can."

Denise began to chuckle, shaking her head, and held up a pleading hand. "No contest, Dr. Asimov—you're the expert in this field."

Asimov shrugged. "In this situation, there's no such thing as an expert."

·Chapter 3

The Visitors

Olav Lindstrom splashed water on his face, then patted it dry, leaning close to the mirror in his office bathroom. His weathered skin and hands attested to the rugged outdoor life he'd loved back in Sweden, but his recent life here in the United States had left him little time for outdoor exercise. His only escape these days was cross-country skiing, which he did in Central Park when there was enough snow—but New York winters had been uncooperative for the past couple of years. Lindstrom frowned, noticing the sag developing under his chin and the way the lines etched around his eyes were now creeping across his forehead and down his cheeks.

It wasn't only his appearance that troubled him—Lindstrom could feel his physical endurance flagging noticeably of late. He doubted that he'd be able to break kindling anymore, much less chop up a cord of wood—one of his proudest accomplishments in his native country had been keeping his own fireplace supplied each winter.

He sighed, listening to Bach's delicate latticework of flute and harpsichord drifting from his office stereo and wishing he could sit down for just a moment. But a glance at his watch—it was 7:38 P.M.—assured him that he had to keep moving.

Lindstrom reached for the crisp white shirt hanging on the doorknob. Lauren would be coming up to get him at any moment, and he had to be ready. This would be their final chance to talk before Olav went out to confront the unknown.

33

He smiled a small, wry smile at his melodramatic turn of thought, but it was true—he, of all people on the face of this planet, would go down in history as the first human to talk to extraterrestrial beings.

He slowly buttoned the shirt, smoothing it down, noting with detachment how frail his body felt beneath it. He'd been a big man before his heart attack eight years ago, and had easily filled out his elegant European-cut suits. But he'd lost thirty pounds on his doctor's orders, and then five more—and had gained none of it back. Now, no matter how carefully he had his suits tailored, they seemed to hang on him a bit. Lauren was always trying to fatten him up, but he seemed to have lost the hearty appetite he'd always been kidded about.

Turning his collar up, Lindstrom slid his best striped tie around his neck as he heard a light tap on the office door. "Come in," he called.

"Where are you?" It was Lauren's musical voice, a feature he'd always kidded her about. No matter how grave the crisis at hand, there was a bounce, an energy to Lauren Stewart's voice that was irrepressible. It gave even the most dolorous diplomatic pronouncements an undercurrent of optimism. Lindstrom smiled as he finished knotting his tie.

He slipped on his coat and went out into the office. "How do I look?" he asked, pausing on the threshold.

"You look fine, Olav. Very distinguished." Lauren was sitting on the modern pillow-back sofa, sipping at a mug of coffee. She was still wearing the charcoal-gray suit and light-gray turtleneck sweater she'd worn to work yesterday, but she still managed to look amazingly unrumpled. However, in the years he'd known her, Lindstrom had learned to look beyond the signs a casual observer would notice. Now he studied her face, noting the tight-pulled look of the skin about her mouth and cheekbones.

"How are you, Lauren?" he asked, sitting down beside her, his eyes worried.

"How am *I*?" Lauren laughed incredulously. "Olav, I've always said you're a saint, and now I believe it more than ever. *You* have to walk out there and represent Earth to the Martians—or wherever they're from—and you're worried about how *I* am?"

Lindstrom shrugged. "Worrying about the welfare of one's

friends is a good way to stop worrying about oneself, I've always found. I keep telling myself not to be nervous, that beside some of the human beings I've met—and in my seventy years, I've met with Hitler, Stalin, and Mao—these people can't be such monsters . . ." He mused for a moment. "On the other hand, I've also met Einstein, Pope John, Mother Teresa and Albert Schweitzer."

Lauren took his hands in hers, squeezed them, then, with an exclamation, began to rub them between her own. "Cold as ice! Do you want some coffee?"

"No time," he said. "Besides, it's just my nerves giving me away. Silly, isn't it?"

"Not at all. At least those people you mentioned were human beings. You'd read about them, seen their faces before you had to march out to meet them. If you *weren't* nervous now, I'd take your pulse to see if you were still alive!"

He smiled at her. "Thank you, Lauren, for that little dose of much-needed common sense. Now I guess we'd better head for the roof. I must admit they've chosen a somewhat original place for a diplomatic encounter."

High above the city, Roger stood on the catwalk above the central command of his vessel. Jennifer sat at her console, busily keying in characters in her native language. To a human familiar with ancient Hebrew or Sanskrit the characters might have appeared faintly recognizable, but to anyone else they would have been totally indecipherable. The Commander waited until his third-in-command officer completed a screen full of entries before calling her name.

"Sir?" she looked up, rose, and climbed the catwalk until she faced him. "Yes, Roger?"

"Are you on shift, Jennifer?" Roger asked. "I remember seeing your name on the off-duty roster for this interval."

Jennifer nodded, phrasing her English words carefully. "You're right, Roger. I'm technically off shift. I just wanted to finish up some of my personnel evaluations and recommendations."

"Very commendable," Roger said. "You're not finding your additional duties in that area too taxing?"

"No, sir. I wouldn't have requested them if I wasn't sure they'd fit into my schedule."

"Well, I know Angela is glad to be rid of them. Personnel work is not her favorite occupation," Roger said, with just a hint of irony in his voice.

Jennifer knew better than to betray satisfaction at her superior's dig at his second-in-command. "Where *is* Angela, Roger?" she asked. "Shouldn't she have returned by now?"

Roger glanced at the bank of chronometers at the top of the main viewscreen. They showed the time in all of Earth's time zones, with one instrument displaying the time in their own units of measurement for any crew member who might still be confused by human time determination. "She should have arrived with the Supreme Commander by now," he said. "It's nearly 0100. She's probably taking every last second to make sure the Supreme Commander is comfortable—and to let him know *she's* the one responsible for his comfort."

This time, Jennifer had to look away from Roger in an effort to hide her amusement. The hatch behind them slid open and Angela appeared. "The Supreme Commander—John," she announced.

The bridge crew stood, formally saluting, as John entered, acknowledging their greetings. He was shorter than Roger, with a head of thick gray hair and regular, pleasant features. He raised his voice in the dim silence of the bridge: "Please activate the Fleet communications intercom."

Jennifer hurried to obey. When she nodded to him to continue, he spoke again. "In a few minutes I will formally begin our mission here on Earth. If not for your dedication to Our Great Leader's cause, we could not have reached our goal so successfully—I commend all of you for your efforts. I know you will dedicate yourselves to the completion of our task with the single-minded loyalty that enabled us to conserve our resources and undertake this vital mission. In the name of Our Leader, I urge all of you to rededicate your lives to that cause—the very preservation of our kind."

He paused. "The duties of a Supreme Commander, as I am sure you realize, are complicated and numerous. Therefore I will be dividing my time among all the ships in the Fleet. In my absence I hereby designate Roger, the Commander of this vessel, to be my special diplomatic deputy in charge of dealing with United Nations officials as well as with the United States government. I am sure you will give him your full cooperation."

He glanced over at Roger, who looked confident, pleased, and not the least bit humble. "Thank you, John," he said. "I know that I and all my crew will do everything possible to merit your confidence."

"I'm sure you will," said John. "Now I must excuse myself. I have an important meeting to attend—a *vitally* important meeting."

Roger smiled faintly at the understatement.

"Damn," Denise Daltrey mumbled, not for the first time in the past hour. "Damn, damn, damn—double damn!"

"Don't take it so hard, Denise," Sidney, the makeup man, counseled. "At least you got the studio anchor slot tonight. That's something."

"Yeah," agreed Denise glumly. "I get to sit in the studio and watch Kristine Walsh up there on the roof, where everything's happening. The story of a lifetime, and I'll see it secondhand, along with John Q. Public!" She shuffled her intro copy at the anchor desk while technicians checked lighting and cameras.

"Don't know why you're so pissed," Sidney said, brushing minute amounts of blusher onto the newswoman's cheekbones. "You couldn't *pay* me to get that close to monsters from outer space."

"Pay? I'd have given a year's salary to get that story. It's the chance of a lifetime!"

"You look a little tired—have you gotten any sleep since this all started?" Sidney asked, tactfully attempting to change the subject as he patted her forehead with a puff.

Denise nodded, clasping her hands in an isometric tug of war. "Yeah. I caught a couple of hours this afternoon. Actually, I think *you've* got the toughest job of all of us, Sidney."

He stared at her, comparing her left eye with the right. "Me?" He daubed her left eyelid with shadow.

"Yeah. As we on-air types stay cooped up in this damned studio, withering away from lack of sleep and decent food, *you've* got to make us look trustworthy and alive—nobody trusts a cadaverous-looking zombie."

Sidney chuckled. "Couldn't anybody ever mistake *you* for a zombie, Denise. Eyes are perfect."

She squinted, realizing that now she wouldn't be able to rub them when they itched. "Sidney, you're a miracle worker," she said as he held up a small mirror for her.

He dabbed her forehead one last time and smoothed her bangs. Then, with a thumbs-up signal and a smile, he retreated from the brightly lit set. Denise peered past the pool of light centered on her, locating the balding pate and walrus moustache of her producer, Winston Weinberg. "Hi, Winnie. The rooftop team set?"

"Yeah," Weinberg said.

"Come talk to me and calm me down. How many minutes do we have left?"

"We'll be switching over to you, then intercutting between you and the rooftop crew in about five minutes," he answered in his heavy Brooklyn accent. "You look great, hon. Fix your jacket and sit up straight."

"Yes, mother," said Denise, making sure her suit jacket hung correctly, then straightening up and again resisting the urge to rub her tired eyes. "But it's not as though anybody's going to spare me a glance. Nobody'll even notice that I covered this event too. Kristine Walsh will be the one everyone remembers."

"The goddamn *aliens* will be the ones everybody remembers, honey," Winnie said. "I wanted to tell you I'm sorry you crapped out on the pool assignment. I'd rather see you up there than Walsh."

"That's sweet of you, Winnie," Denise said. "But it's the luck of the draw."

"Luck of the draw, my ass," Weinberg growled. "Somethin' stinks about the whole deal. I'd bet money she kissed up to somebody, pulled some last-minute strings, called in a few outstanding debts or something. She hasn't spent the time on this that you and Dan have."

"And they say *women* are catty," Denise said, feigning distaste. "Maybe she's doing the roof because they wanted somebody bright-eyed and bushy-tailed, not overworked and weary."

"Hmph," said Weinberg. "You ever work with her?"

"I know her, but I never worked with her."

"I have. Acts like she's the queen or somethin'. If she

doesn't get her way, you can hear her from Timbuktu to Kalamazoo."

"Maybe I should take her cue. Maybe I've been too easy-going."

He wagged an admonishing finger at her. "Hey, go ahead—kid around. Put yourself down. But you're damn good, Dee, and I know it 'cause I've worked with the best. You wanna know what the scuttlebutt is about you versus Madam Kristine?" Without waiting for her to reply, he continued, "They say, 'Denise'll do anything to get the *story*—Walsh'll do anything to get the *glory*.' No lie, honey."

She reached across the desk to clasp his fingers with her own. "Thanks. No lie, honey."

"Thirty seconds to air time," boomed the director's voice over the loudspeaker. Hurriedly Denise composed herself, checked her posture, arranged her notes, then, finally, tested the small mike clipped to her jacket. The countdown was on.

When it reached "one," the red light on camera two flashed on, and Denise, watching the monitor, saw her image appear under the superimposed words, *"VISITORS FROM SPACE: A Special Report Live from New York."*

The floor director cued her and she smoothly faced the camera. "Good evening, ladies and gentlemen. It is almost eight P.M. here in New York—almost time for the people of Earth to meet, face to face, the first beings encountered from another planet. As we take the ball back from Dan Rather, reporting to you from the nation's capital, the air here in New York is crackling with anticipation. As you can see in this live shot from the United Nations Building, the huge space vessel is still stationary above Manhattan, where it took up residence yesterday afternoon . . ."

Denise went on, recapping the highlights from the previous day, until she switched over to Kristine Walsh on the roof. Then she watched glumly as the Secretary General, accompanied by a tall, exotically attractive woman, came onto the roof. Lindstrom motioned to the UN guards to lower their weapons—then as eight o'clock arrived, Denise, along with the rest of the studio crew, fixed her eyes on the monitor showing the belly of the huge alien vessel.

"I see something!" Winnie shouted after a second.

A moment later they could all hear Kristine Walsh's cool,

professional tones: "A smaller craft is dropping down out of
the Mother Ship and heading directly for the rooftop of this
building. As it heads toward us, it seems to be almost
completely silent, with no exhaust or rocket engines to indicate
its power source."

The smaller vehicle had a curiously duck-billed snout and
gleamed whitely as it came to rest on the top of the UN
Building. Noting its aerodynamic lines, Denise commented
that it seemed to have been designed to fly, at least partly, in the
atmosphere. Her remark earned her an approving thumbs-up
gesture from Winnie. They all noticed a pattern of dots and
bars painted in red on the nose of the craft, vaguely suggesting
a letter or other symbol.

After a second, a hatch opened in the side of the craft and a
ramp extended onto the rooftop. A voice, amplified yet still
containing that odd reverberation they'd all noticed during the
countdown, spoke: "Herr General Secreterare . . ."

"I think that's Swedish," Denise said to Winston, knowing
she wasn't on the air at the moment. "Get me a translation—
quick!"

After a second, the translation came through, and Denise
relayed it to Kristine Walsh on the roof. "Mr. Secretary
General . . . do not be afraid. Please climb the ramp."

Denise watched closely as Lindstrom, with a barely percep-
tible hesitation, stepped forward. The roof camera, wielded by
free-lance cameraman Mike Donovan, followed the slender,
erect figure as it moved forward up the ramp, vanishing into
the darkened opening of the shuttle.

Denise checked the seconds on the studio clock while
keeping one eye on Donovan's closeup of the hatch—
68 . . . 69 . . . 70 . . . 71 . . . 72 . . . 73 . . .

"There he is!" cried Kristine Walsh, and Denise felt a huge
surge of relief.

Pausing on the bottom of the ramp, Lindstrom spoke,
assuring the assembly that he had indeed met the Visitors (as
Lindstrom termed them) and that they looked very human,
although their voices were unusual. He stressed that they
wished to honor all the United Nations covenants and that their
mission was peaceful. He then announced that he'd asked the
Supreme Commander of the Fleet, who was aboard the shuttle,
to address the people of Earth personally.

Booted feet appeared on the ramp, and in silence, Denise and the studio crew watched a gray-haired man with regular, rounded features appear, smiling genially. "Christ!" Denise exclaimed, for once forgetting to check whether she was on the air—she wasn't. "The guy could pass for one of us!"

The Visitor wore a red uniform resembling a flight-deck coverall, with a chest flap across which extended several black stripes. Denise guessed they denoted rank. As the humans watched, the man took out a pair of dark glasses, slipped them on, then said, "I trust you will forgive me, but our eyes are unaccustomed to this sort of brightness." His English was unaccented. If it weren't for the eerie multitrack resonating quality in the voice, Denise thought, the man could be a native American.

He continued, still with a faint smile, "As the Secretary General told you, we have come in peace to all mankind on Earth. Our planet is the fourth from the star which you call Sirius, some 8.7 light-years from your Earth. This is the first time we have journeyed from our system—you, the first intelligent life we have encountered. We are very pleased to meet you!"

The sigh rippling through the studio was profound with relief. The Supreme Commander continued: "Our names would sound peculiar to you, so we—my fellow Visitors and I—have chosen simple names from Earth. My name is John."

Denise stared, fascinated by the thought of a being from another star who could look so devastatingly familiar. John went on to explain that unmanned Sirian probes had been monitoring Earth's radio and television broadcasts for a number of years, which is how the aliens had learned the local languages. One of the phrases he used was "this small fleet"— prompting Denise to glance over at Winston Weinberg. *"Small fleet?"* she echoed incredulously. "Who the hell does he think he's kidding?"

"Shh," said Winnie. "Let the guy make his pitch."

"On behalf of Our Great Leader—he who governs our planet with benevolence and wisdom—we have come because we need your help." John paused for a second. Denise could appreciate the Visitor's innate dramatic ability—he'd make a terrific editorial spokesperson, she thought irrelevantly.

She heard Winnie snort disbelievingly. "They have the ability to cross *nine* light-years and they want *our* help?"

Almost as if he'd heard the producer's comment, John explained, "Our planet is in serious environmental difficulty— far, far worse than yours. It's reached a stage where we'll be unable to survive without immediate assistance. There are certain chemical compounds that can save our struggling civilization. We need to manufacture them. You can help us. And in return, we'll gladly share with you all the fruits of our knowledge. Now that contact is established, we would like to meet with individual governments so that we may present requests for certain operating plants around the world to be retooled for the manufacture of the compounds."

Denise looked over at Winston, then at the other men and women in the studio, feeling a sudden anxiety. *Lord,* she thought, *these people are so far ahead of us technologically— and yet they're still struggling to survive? What does that bode for us in the coming decades?*

John was still speaking, almost as though addressing her worries. ". . . helping you solve your own environmental, agricultural, and health dilemmas. Then we'll leave you as we came—in peace."

They're talking as though they can cure most of what ails us, Denise mused. *So why can't they help themselves?* The answer was obvious, she realized almost immediately. The more complex and technical the civilization, the more complex the environmental chain holding it all together. She watched as John extended an offer for the Secretary General and five journalists to accompany him on a tour of the Mother Ship, and saw, with no surprise, that Kristine Walsh was among those lucky five.

Must've picked them by lot somehow. Damn, I'd give ten years of my life to be in her shoes . . .

The chosen journalists—Kristine, Sam Egan, Michael Donovan and his soundman, Tony Wah Chong Leonetti, plus an old friend of Denise's, Jeri Taylor—all moved quickly toward the ramp, pausing to shake hands with John on their way up. Denise saw the cue and, feeling as though her voice were coming all the way from Sirius, automatically picked up the narrative.

The hatch on the gleaming white shuttle closed, then, as

soundlessly as it had arrived, the vehicle lifted off. Denise watched as it glided upward into the spotlit sky above Manhattan, toward the glistening, looming bulk of the Mother Ship. A hundred bits of reporter's small talk ran through her mind, but she swallowed them all, letting the picture speak for itself.

Chapter 4

Party Time

Alison Stein sipped cautiously at a glass of white wine as she watched the majordomo, Enrico Caldera, move steadily but unobtrusively to Mayor O'Connor's side. For a portly man in his fifties, Caldera was a tribute to quiet grace and gentility, in huge contrast to O'Connor, who was laughing boisterously at a joke Alexander Garr had just told. The majordomo gained the minuscule space next to O'Connor's right elbow and whispered discreetly, "Mr. Mayor—I think the guests of honor may be arriving."

It was obvious Caldera hoped to avoid a stir, and Alison found it necessary to mask a smile when O'Connor grinned at the man and quipped, "Hey, great! The E.T.'s are here!"

Enrico Caldera rolled his eyes as everyone except he and Alison stampeded for the doors to Gracie Mansion. Alison flashed the little man an understanding look. Somehow O'Connor's flamboyance seemed to diminish Gracie Mansion's fading elegance even more quickly than time and budget deficits.

The crowd milled back from the doors with a swelling murmur of disappointment to let a distinguished-looking older black man and a tall, exotically lovely young woman enter, accompanying UN Secretary General Olav Lindstrom. Alison recognized the man as Dr. George Stewart, and guessed the young woman to be his daughter, Lauren. Alison caught Enrico's eye. "Did you do that deliberately, Enrico?"

Caldera shook his head innocently. "Not me, Mrs. Stein. I saw this big limo pull up and all I could think was, it must be them."

Hearing a soft displacement of air from the direction of the open French side door, Alison turned to see a white shuttle—smaller than the one they'd seen that night two weeks ago, but modeled on identical lines—touch down on the grass. She moved toward the door just as somebody shouted, "Hey, look!"

A tall, ruggedly handsome man with curling brown hair and green eyes moved out of the hatchway, followed by two female Visitors. The first woman was petite and blonde, with coolly pretty features and vivid aquamarine eyes, in contrast to the other, who was taller, heavier-boned, with a rounded face, reddish-auburn hair, freckles, and hazel eyes. The Mayor was waiting for them as they entered, his hand outstretched in greeting. "I'm Mayor Daniel O'Connor. Welcome to Gracie Mansion. We're honored you folks could join us."

The crowd made a half-circle around O'Connor, Alison, and the Visitors as the aliens shook hands with the Mayor and City Council President. Alison was struck by the coolness of their flesh—not a clammy coldness, but more as if their natural body temperature were significantly lower than the human norm. "I see John isn't with you," O'Connor said.

"No, Mr. Mayor," the male Visitor said. "He sends his apologies. As Supreme Commander, he has many, many responsibilities, as I'm sure you can imagine. My name is Roger, and this is my second-in-command, Angela." He indicated the young woman with the blonde ponytail, "and my third-in-command, Jennifer. Jennifer is the Fleet's special adviser on interplanetary cultural matters."

The crowd parted to allow Olav Lindstrom through, with Lauren Stewart at his side. Greetings went around the group. Alison was struck by the contrast between the Visitors in their red coveralls and the other guests glittering in evening dress.

O'Connor gestured grandly at the party room. "Please, come in. Lots of people are dying to meet you, and you must be hungry. Dinner won't be served until eight-thirty, but those tables have enough snacks to keep us going until then. The bar is over there."

"Thank you very much," Roger said politely, "but actually,

we've already eaten prior to coming down. Our scientists haven't yet completed their analysis of your planet's flora and fauna, so they've advised us not to partake until we're told it's safe. Just a precaution, I'm sure."

O'Connor nodded understandingly. "Sure, makes perfect sense. I do the same thing when I'm in Mexico. Stuff you can pick up down there can clean you out but good."

Danny! Alison hoped fervently none of the United Nations representatives from Mexico were in earshot. Blushing for the oblivious O'Connor, she saw Lauren Stewart glance at Olav Lindstrom. Hastily, Alison tried to think of something to say, but the moment was already past.

Three Visitors weren't many to go around, but they circulated gamely among the pockets of guests, splitting up to make sure no one of importance was ignored—not an easy task, since the guest list constituted a virtual who's who of New York.

"They almost act like they're running for office," O'Connor whispered to Alison as they watched the party. "They handle the old glad-handing routine better than *I* do."

Alison gave him a sideways look. "And they're less obvious about it too."

He ignored the dig. "They seem to recognize and know something about everyone they're talking to. I wonder how?"

"Well, they said they had probes monitoring our communications. I guess they did their homework."

"It's more than that, more than just news media information," O'Connor insisted, mopping at his glistening forehead with a billowing square of linen. "They know things they could only have discovered by digging through newspaper files or pumping people for information."

"Pumping people?" She gave him a look. "Why such negative terms? Maybe it's a compliment—they're going to be here, living among us for a while. Maybe they'd just like to know more about what makes us tick."

"But why, Ali, *why*? We've already agreed to help them. Why so much interest in finding out about prominent people? I can only think of one . . ." He trailed off with a frown.

"And what reason is that, O wise and sage politician?"

"My, we have a sarcastic tongue about us tonight, don't we?" O'Connor sniffed. "I'll tell you anyway, 'cause it's something you might need to know someday. When you know enough things about people, you may find out some of their weaknesses, enabling you, in many cases, to *control* them."

Alison finished her wine in a single gulp, then grabbed another glass off a passing tray. "You're paranoid, Danny." She glanced around the room. "And judging by the way most people are reacting to the Visitors, I'd keep my unpopular opinions to myself, if I were you." She moved off to mingle, leaving O'Connor to chew over her warning.

"Look at Alexander the Great," Peter Forsythe whispered to the Yankees' manager, Bobby Neal.

"Why?" said Neal in his lazy Oklahoma drawl. "He's my boss, I'm his employee. That means I have to look at him all season. I need a vacation from him by this time each year." He crunched experimentally on an hors d'oeuvre.

"He's right over there—you can't miss him," Pete insisted, pointing with his chin. "He's the one with the egg-sucking grin pasted all over that iron mask of his."

The older man stood on tiptoe, craning his neck, causing the white shirtfront and jacket of his ancient tux to strain noticeably across his paunch. "I see him," Neal said in an answering undertone. "I think he's trying to pick up that Visitor chick. She's cute, ain't she?"

"He's sucking up to all of 'em," Pete mumbled, his eyes following one of the waiters as he took a loaded tray off the bar. "Sonofabitch can't be decent to the humans who work for him, yet butter wouldn't melt when he talks to a bunch of aliens. Disgusting."

Bobby Neal turned to look at Forsythe questioningly. "You been drinking, Pete?"

"Hell no, Bobby!" Forsythe protested, not meeting his friend's eyes. "Just one little glass of wine, that's it."

"Well, it better stop there," said Neal, not unkindly. "You'd better watch it, especially with Alex here."

Pete nibbled viciously at a knish impaled on a toothpick. His eyes were inexorably drawn back to the bar. *One more glass of wine won't hurt,* he thought. *I'll wait awhile. That'll prove I can control it. Nobody gets into trouble on two glasses of white wine!*

"Damn," Neal said, "he's waving to us."

Forsythe began to turn away, but Neal grabbed his arm. "Pete, the man pays us. You've gotta be civil."

"Hey, Bobby, Pete," Alexander Garr called to them. "C'mon over here!"

Pete's feet remained rooted to the floor, but Neal tightened his grip on the third baseman's arm and towed him along. "Button that lip, Peter," Neal said. "The boss doesn't look like he's in the mood for any of your cynical remarks tonight."

"Right," said Pete. "Tonight is unusual. Ordinarily he's just sucking up to politicians from Earth—this is his first chance to do it to politicians from Sirius. Far be it from *me* to interfere."

Bobby Neal elbowed his third baseman in the ribs with a sudden jab, causing Pete to let out a surprised "Oof!" and shut up. Having diabetes and a bad heart may have slowed the older man down a bit, but he could still take his players firmly in hand when he felt the need.

Garr greeted his employees with a broad smile. "Boys, I'd like you to meet Angela, second-in-command of the New York Mother Ship. Angela, this is Bobby Neal, the best manager in major league baseball, and one of my star players, Pete Forsythe."

Neal extended his hand. "It's a pleasure, ma'am."

Peter nodded politely but remained silent, and Garr flashed him a warning look. Turning quickly, Forsythe snagged a glass of wine from a tray and sipped it slowly, his blue eyes wide and innocent.

"We understand baseball and other sports are very important among your people," Angela said.

"Yes, indeed, ma'am," Neal answered. "Got me outta the oil fields when I was a kid. I didn't get much of an education, but look where I am today. Sports have always been a way for a boy with the right determination and athletic skills to better himself. Builds character and a sense of responsibility in *all* kids, even if they don't get to be professional athletes."

"That's very interesting," Angela said, nodding. "Mr. Garr and I were just talking about that, as a matter of fact—building character in youth. We believe it's very important for you to get to know us better, and we would like our visit to your world to be an educational experience—a character-building experience—for your young people."

"May I make a suggestion, Angela?" asked Garr.

"Of course."

Alex struck an inspirational pose as he paused for a dramatic second, and Bobby Neal nudged Peter. "I think I can get the Mayor and the City Council to agree to open Yankee Stadium, one of the shrines of American sports, to help you in your outreach program to young people—the poor and disadvantaged youngsters as well as boys and girls who have had more opportunities in life. I'd like to offer our ballpark, *and* the services of some of my star players as counselors, to assist the efforts you people are making in establishing these Visitor Friends groups you mentioned."

Angela looked duly impressed and deeply grateful. "Why, Mr. Garr, that's a *wonderful* idea. I saw your stadium from the air. It's big enough to land our squad vehicles there and we can co-sponsor gatherings between our people and your youngsters—"

"What we call an 'open house,' Angela." Garr's enthusiasm was expanding by the second. "It will be perfect. We can also set up evening meetings at armories around the city—mix informal sports with discussions and lectures. What do you think, Bobby?"

"Uh, well . . . I think it sounds just dandy. I think the kids'll jump at the chance, 'specially if they get to go up in one of those squad vehicles."

Angela laughed. "That's part of what I was envisioning."

Garr nodded at Neal and Forsythe, then, putting an arm around her waist, steered Angela off to meet another group. As they moved away, he continued, "We used to have a thing called 'Hands Across the Water,' a sort of exchange of ideas and culture with countries across our oceans. This will be the same, except that it's 'Hands Across the Stars.' It'll be a *fantastic* opportunity to—"

Pete watched them go, then shook his head. "Alexander the Great has made another conquest—this time an interstellar one. My God, that man can get in good with anybody—anybody who can help him grab headlines and show what a terrific guy he is. I think the sucker's got political aspirations, I really do." He took a final gulp of wine, looking disgusted. "Can't you see tomorrow's *Post*—'Yankees Owner Interstellar Philanthropist'?"

"I think you got it backwards, Pete," Bobby Neal said softly, watching the unlikely pair consideringly.

"Huh?"

"That Angela spotted Alex a mile away and knew she could use him for somethin' like this."

"What do you mean, Bobby?"

"The Visitors need folks like Alex—people who can show 'em the way to make friends with us Earth people, to get in good with us, show us what good ole boys they are."

"And you call *me* cynical?" Pete snorted.

"Oh, I didn't say their intentions were bad. I just said I could see through what they're doin'."

"Some of us in the cultural-relations field worried that the human religions would have problems accepting our existence, knowing it would prove you aren't the only intelligent beings in the universe, but most faiths seem to have taken it much better than we anticipated," Jennifer commented. "Of course we're delighted it turned out this way."

"Scripture doesn't prepare us for an occasion like this," said Edward Cardinal Palazzo, the Archbishop of New York. "Unless you want to look at generalizations like the first line of the Bible. 'In the beginning, God created the heaven and the earth . . .' Or later, when it says, 'He made the stars also . . .' If you take it in that context, then you Visitors have as much right to be here as we do." He smiled at the auburn-haired Visitor warmly, fingering the gold crucifix on his neck chain. His black vestments hid his small, wiry frame, but couldn't completely disguise his balanced athletic grace. Eddie Palazzo had been a bantamweight boxer while growing up on the Lower East Side. Now, despite his gray hair, he looked far younger than his fifty-three years.

"How do you perceive the way your people have reacted to our arrival?" she asked.

"Everything from joy to despair. For some it was a terrible shock, for others it seemed the fulfillment of a dream." He smiled, revealing beautiful teeth. "Nothing that faith in God can't handle."

"You put a lot of faith in your god, Cardinal Palazzo."

"That's the name of the game, at least in my business. What about religion on your world, Jennifer? How did it prepare you for coping with the fact that *you* weren't alone in the universe?"

"Science prepared us. The religions that existed on our world have mostly faded into items of historical interest—they have little impact on modern life."

Cardinal Palazzo expressed concern. "Don't you Visitors believe in anything greater than science? Where do you think the elements science has discovered came from?"

"Oh, we believe in a greater force—nature, the shaper of the universe. I must admit," Jennifer said thoughtfully, "that I've made sort of an amateur study of your religions, and I was one of the ones who expected more upheaval and fear upon our arrival—the arrival of alien beings outside creation as you've perceived it for all your recorded history."

"Ah—" The Cardinal smiled. "That was your error, if you don't mind my correcting your view of earthly religion. You and your people are *not* outside our sweep of creation and belief. Remember, God created the heavens, the earth, and the stars, as I told you. That makes *you* part of what He created—granted, from a part of the heavens very far away and outside our admittedly very limited experience. But we, as human beings with our short life spans and finite minds, will never have experienced everything God has created. God and His power are, by definition, infinite. So that's why the Church has no trouble accepting and welcoming you, since you come in peace. To us, you're just newly discovered children of God."

Jennifer smiled wryly. "Kind of like long-lost relatives?"

Palazzo laughed heartily. "Exactly! That's a very good way of putting it! I might even steal that for a sermon."

"'Thou shalt not steal,'" quoted Jennifer.

"Hmm—you *have* studied, haven't you?" He smiled at her warmly. "Very well then, will you loan it to me?"

She returned the smile. "I'd be honored."

"That's Peter Forsythe over there on the other side of the room," George Stewart said to his daughter. "He seems to be drifting over in this direction."

Lauren made a face. "Then I think it's time for me to powder my nose."

"Too late, he's seen us. Come on, Lauren, he's one of my best students. I don't know why you don't like him."

"When I met him at that New Year's Eve party, he was drunk as a skunk and a cynic to beat all. He tried to pick up every girl there, and that was while he was still married."

"Oh, he's pretty much got the drinking under control now that he and Jean have actually split up. The months just before and after their separation were pretty rough on Pete, but he's a good guy under all that sarcasm—trust me. And as I recall, *you* were the one who turned a cold shoulder at that party."

"I'm always chilly to cynical drunks who make a million dollars a year and have no reason on earth to *be* cynical drunks."

"Shh—"

"Hi, Doc!" Pete gave George a lopsided grin, his blue eyes a little too bright. "Good to see you. And nice to see—" He blinked, embarrassed, obviously drawing a blank over Lauren's name.

"You remember my daughter, Lauren," said Dr. Stewart, smoothly stepping into the breach.

"Of course," Pete said. "Could I forget one of the most attractive women in New York?"

"Apparently," murmured Lauren, *sotto voce*. George shot her a warning glance, but the remark went over Pete's somewhat fuddled head.

"Well, Pete, have you met the Visitors?" asked Dr. Stewart.

"Briefly," Forsythe said, finishing his glass of wine and looking around for a refill. "They're so much like us they're a little hard to swallow, don't you think?"

"What do you mean?" asked Lauren, challenge plain in her voice.

Pete fumblingly tried to explain. "I dunno. They're just so attentive and complimentary to *everyone*, and they smile all the time. Reminds me of some Hollywood producers I met while I was doing some commercials out there. Guys would treat you like you were the most important person in the world to them, hanging on your every word, then as soon as you weren't standing there to hear 'em, the suckers would ream you out but good, still grinning all the while. Lie right to your face and then stick it to you, like half the politicians and damn diplomats in this world."

Lauren stiffened, a dangerous light flickering in her dark

eyes. George hastened to temporize. "Take it easy, Pete. Remember, Lauren works for the UN."

"Oh, right." Pete had the grace to blush. "Sorry, I wasn't talking about the UN. Everyone knows they're trying to help, not mess the world over. Too bad they don't have much clout."

Lauren gave her father an I-told-you-so look, and George made a conciliatory little gesture, accompanied by a shrug.

The silence lengthened toward awkwardness. Pete smiled winningly at Lauren and tried again. "If you don't mind my saying so, that's a very pretty dress you're wearing, Ms. Stewart," Forsythe said, his eyes traveling over the white silk gown that dramatically bared one of Lauren's slender shoulders. "Not every woman could wear a dress like that. It's sort of . . . what's the word? Daring, or something. You wonder what holds it up."

Lauren smiled fractionally, her eyes distant. "Thank you. I think."

George Stewart coughed suddenly, apparently having swallowed the wrong way. Pete helpfully pounded the older man on the back. In a strangled voice, Stewart announced his intention to get a drink of water, and left. When Pete turned around, Lauren was nowhere to be seen.

Alison Stein eased back into the overstuffed chair in Dan O'Connor's study next to the party room and gingerly slipped her high heels off with a sigh. Her nylon-clad toes wiggled gratefully as she propped her feet on a hassock.

"Rough night on the piggies, eh, Ali?" asked the Mayor from behind her. He balanced a cup of coffee on a tray which the City Council President accepted with a look of profound thanks.

"I'm so glad you don't give these shindigs more than a couple of times a year, Danny," she said, busily taking her heavy silver-and-opal bracelet off and detaching her matching earrings. "I hate getting into long dresses and jewelry."

"But you look so great when you get dressed up, Ali," O'Connor said, looking down at her with frank admiration, his blue eyes holding a sudden warmth. "I think I ought to make all City Council meetings formal-dress occasions."

"Over my dead body," Ali said, resting her head against the back of the chair, careless of the heavy mass of her coiffure.

She avoided his gaze, suddenly conscious of a new current between them. O'Connor had been a widower for several years now, and she'd never seen him show even the slightest interest in women. It was doubly disconcerting now to realize his new awareness was aimed at *her*.

The were both quiet for a moment, and when Stein cast a cautious look up at O'Connor, he was staring into the fire. "The party went pretty well," she said. "I'm glad you seem to be in a better mood about our guests of honor. Lost your paranoia about the Visitors trying to usurp your power or something?"

O'Connor gave her an impatient look. "Cut it out, Ali. I'm not paranoid, and it's not *my* power I'm worried about. And if anything, I'm *more* worried." He sat down on the arm of her chair and dropped his voice confidentially. "They were so goddamned charming to everyone here tonight—the more important the person, the more charming they became."

"Would you have been happier if they'd been grotesque, insulting, and hostile? Would that have made them the perfect dinner guests?"

"They were *too* charming, Ali. I've been in the business too long not to recognize a snow job when I see it. They wooed civic leaders, business leaders, communications moguls—even the Cardinal! They didn't miss a trick. I even saw Roger working on Dan Rather and John Chancellor."

"What about Denise Daltrey? Didn't I see her too?"

"Yeah, they didn't miss anyone. They practically charmed the bunions off all of New York's television VIP's."

"Don't tell me you're worried about people like Chancellor, Rather, and Daltrey losing their objectivity over a little dinner chitchat?"

"No, but they may be the *only* ones whose heads weren't turned here tonight."

"Excuse me, Mr. Mayor." Angela's precise reverberating tones came from the doorway behind them. O'Connor jumped, startled, nearly falling off his precarious perch on the chair arm.

Where the hell did she come from? Alison wondered. *Did she overhear Danny's tirade? Oh, shit!*

Both Mayor and City Council President stood and turned as Angela smiled warmly at them. "I'm sorry I startled you.

Roger asked me to extend good nights for all of us. We have to be getting back, but we enjoyed the evening so much."

"Well," said O'Connor, shaking her hand, "we're delighted you could take time to drop by. We didn't realize any of the guests were still here—good heavens," he looked at his watch, "it's nearly three!"

"Yes, it's a late hour for us too. But we so enjoyed meeting everyone. And we're grateful for your cooperation on that Visitor Friends project I've suggested. We're very anxious to get started."

"Alison and I are at your service, Angela. Good night."

"Good night, Mayor O'Connor, Mrs. Stein."

They stood in the doorway, looking out across the party room, watching Angela join Roger and Jennifer at the door. The Visitors nodded a final farewell to the few stragglers still left, and then they were gone.

Alison glared at O'Connor. "Well, Danny, your tongue certainly leads a life of its own, unfettered by your feeble brain. Evil incarnate, that's what she is, obviously!"

O'Connor shrugged, grinning ruefully. "Open mouth, insert foot."

The three Visitors strolled toward their squad vehicle. "I think that went rather well," Roger said. "We made contact with many of the people we'll need to accomplish this mission. I'm glad you made such a good start with the president of CBS."

"And we learned who may *not* be so cooperative," Angela said softly. "I got the distinct impression Peter Forsythe was only here under duress, and Mayor O'Connor, I think, definitely presents a problem. In my opinion we should consider our options regarding the Mayor."

Jennifer stopped to look at her. "Oh come on, Angela. Aren't you talking in terms that are rather . . . extreme?"

The blonde officer's voice was harsh beneath the alien reverberation. "Nothing can be allowed to interfere with the requirements of our mission. If certain individuals constitute obstacles, those obstacles will have to be . . . eliminated."

Chapter 5

Make New Friends, Lose the Old

Joey Vitale turned his sparkling white Corvette onto the Brooklyn block of neat well-tended brownstones where his parents lived. He drove slowly, his window down, talking to the neighborhood kids who ran down the sidewalk to wave to him.

"Hey, Joey! Long time no see!" called a fourteen-year-old girl in a down vest and leg warmers.

"Hey, Gena, you're gettin' prettier every day!"

"Hey, Joey!" a dark-haired boy yelled, jogging beside the car, "you gonna play football with us today?"

"Maybe later, Johnny. First I gotta go watch the Visitors land at the plant with my mom and pop."

He swung into the driveway and parked behind the custom camper van. Antonio Vitale, a tall beefy man with a beard and moustache, leaned out the side door of the house. "Hey, Joey! Hurry up! Mama's making pancakes for you!"

"Great, Pop. I'm starving." Unfolding his lanky frame from the sports car in careful stages, he climbed out, slammed the door, and stood looking at the street with a grin. Joey still sometimes missed living at home, though his luxurious Manhattan apartment had its obvious advantages. He took a long stride toward the house.

"Hi, Joey," said a quiet voice from the house next door.

Vitale turned, peering into the shadows of the porch, then smiled tentatively at the young woman sitting on the top step.

She was small, with taffy-brown hair and pert features, and was wearing a Yankees sweatshirt and much-faded jeans. "Hi, Marianne. Good to see you."

Hesitantly, Joey crossed the narrow strip of lawn as she came down the steps toward him. He stopped about four feet away, wondering if hugging her would be the right thing to do. "Hey, you look really great. How you been?" No hug.

Simultaneously, she said, "I haven't seen you in months. How've you been?"

They broke off, then laughed. "You first," said Joey.

"Well, I've been pretty good. Studying hard. Grad school keeps me pretty busy. Your turn."

"Same here. We didn't make the play-offs," he shrugged. "But maybe next year. I see you still got the sweatshirt I gave you."

"I've still got everything you gave me," she said, instantly looking as though she wished she could have taken the words back. "Uh, that's some nice camper you gave your folks."

"Yeah, well, Pop always wanted one. And with all the money Alex Garr pays me, the least I can do is make sure Mom and Pop have what they want. They're takin' a trip to Italy next summer."

"That's nice. Are you . . . still seeing that girl? Leslie?"

He glanced over at his car, then down at his Adidas. "Nah. All she was really interested in was going to parties and gettin' expensive presents. Too highfalutin for me. *You* know what I like—a thick shake, a coupla burgers . . . and a good martial arts or horror flick—that's me."

"Yeah, I know," she said, not without irony. "You must not have much trouble meeting girls, though."

"Ahhh, they're all baseball Annies, just hangin' around the hotels and bars. I tried it a couple of times. Not my style. I'd rather watch the late movies and go to sleep by myself, or sit around and talk baseball with Pete and Bobby Neal." He met her eyes squarely. "Why'd you want to know?"

"I don't know. 'Cause I still care about you, I guess. You're a nice guy. Too nice, sometimes. People—women—take advantage of you."

"Not lately," he said with a tinge of bitterness. Then, more hesitantly, "I thought about calling."

"Joey . . ." She looked down, wrapping her hands in the gray folds of the sweatshirt.

"Mare . . ." He paused, then plunged ahead. "Couldn't we try it again?"

She looked up at him for a long second, then shook her head hopelessly. "Nothing's changed. There're still all those nights you'd be on the road and I'd still be Joey's little woman, sitting in the stands, cheering you at the home games. I just don't think I could live like that."

"That's not forever, you know," he said more roughly than he'd intended. "I got enough money. I could retire by the time I'm thirty and never have to work again. Pete's helped me invest it, and I'm learning how to manage it right. Then we'd have the rest of our lives together. No road trips, no baseball Annie's tryin' to put the make on me."

"And you'd always feel that if you'd played another five years, you'd be a Hall of Fame candidate. I can't ask you to give up what you love for me. Besides," she sighed, "I'm almost done with my degree. I want to work for a while before I settle down. Date some other guys. Since we were kids, there's only been you in my life."

"Jo-eeey!" Antonio bellowed. Joey stepped back until his father could see him.

"Be there in a minute, Pop."

"Oh! Okay, son, sorry." The elder Vitale disappeared.

"See?" Joey looked back at Marianne. "They're still hoping we'll get back together. They love you, Mare."

"And I love them," she said, trying not to give in. "It's just—I don't know, Joey. You know I'll always care about you, but I just don't—"

He didn't want her to say anything final, so he gently interrupted, giving her that famous smile. "I won't push you. But promise me you'll think it over, huh?"

"Jo-eeeey!" This time it was his mother's singsong from the kitchen window. "The pancakes are getting cold. Bring Marianne in with you—I got plenty."

Joey and Marianne looked at each other. He rolled his eyes. "She could announce at the stadium without the PA system."

They finally managed to smile, sharing the first really comfortable moment since they'd started to chat. "Well, I never could turn down your mom's pancakes." She linked her arm through his and they headed for Joey's house.

"Denise," said the voice in her earphone. "Camera two in five . . . four . . . three . . . two . . . one . . ."

The demanding red light flicked on and Denise smiled into the lens. "Good morning and welcome back to our second hour of the Morning News. Once again I'm going solo because the Visitors continue to be a round-the-clock, round-the-world story, and our staff of correspondents have been shuttling around the globe, giving you the most comprehensive coverage possible.

"Four days ago, history was made in Visitor-Earth relations when work began at assorted chemical plants around the planet, work designed to retool the plants for processing the Visitors' life-saving chemical." She turned toward the monitor behind the anchor desk. "We thought this would be a good time to give you a quick review of the past two and a half unprecedented weeks in our world's history."

On the monitor, images of the giant ships hovering over world capitals unreeled, then the videotape of Mike Donovan's initial tour of the New York Mother Ship appeared. Denise narrated: "The day after the alien saucers arrived, we finally saw the interiors of these massive space vehicles and found them not all that different from our own largest aircraft carriers—at least at first glance." The monitor ran quickly over shots of blue-gray walls, dimly lit hangars filled with gleaming white shuttles and squad vehicles, with red-coveralled Visitors bustling to attend to them.

The screen flickered, then filled with Kristine Walsh's familiar features, and beside her another woman—dark-haired, imperiously beautiful, with a figure that even the red coveralls couldn't conceal. "We met Diana," Denise continued her voice-over, "Supreme Commander John's second-in-command for the enormous Visitor Fleet, who has subsequently resumed command of the Los Angeles ship in her capacity as science officer for the expedition. Incidentally, our scientists are very curious about the huge ships' gravity drive, which we've been told takes up nearly half their interior. The Mother Ships also have enormous refrigerated holds designed for storage of the compound manufactured here on Earth. As nearly as we've been able to guess—and we've been given no specific numbers—the crew of *each* of the fifty or so ships in the Fleet numbers from *three to five thousand* Visitors.''

Denise turned away from the monitor. "Yesterday I went with a camera crew to visit the opening of a chemical plant located right here in Brooklyn, New York—the borough famous for Coney Island, foot-long hotdogs, and, of course, the old Brooklyn Dodgers baseball team. We were given a guided tour of the facility as the work begun earlier in the week progressed. But first here's what it looked like that first day when the Visitors came to Brooklyn . . .''

As Denise continued her voice-over, the tape showed three large Visitor shuttlecraft landing on the football-field-sized parking lot then disgorging wave upon wave of red-coveralled workers and technicians, all under the watchful eyes of mounted police and area residents.

Denise watched herself appear onscreen with Roger while a Visitor shuttle lifted off behind them with nearly soundless efficiency. The plant was visible behind it, its smokestacks looming overhead, lengths of tube and pipe threading in and out, hugging the concrete slab walls.

"Roger," her onscreen image asked, "as Commander and supervisor of the operations that will begin at this plant today, were you surprised by the greeting you received from the people who live here in Brooklyn?" Denise's videotaped image held the cordless mike closer to the Visitor officer to catch his reply.

"Surprised? In what way?"

"Well, elsewhere in this country, your ships have been greeted with marching bands and an almost festive sideshow atmosphere. But here in Brooklyn, while hundreds of residents *did* turn out to watch, they were much more reserved—as if they had yet to pass judgment on whether they approve of the Visitor activities in their area.''

Roger gave his best boyish grin. "I see what you're getting at. No, Denise, that doesn't worry me. I was warned that New Yorkers are tough—and I mean that in the best possible sense. They're honest and protective of their neighbors, so it's natural they'd be concerned about a large force of outside—and I do mean *outside*—" he grinned again, "workers and technicians coming here."

The scene cut to a sidewalk interview with an elderly man wearing a baseball cap and windbreaker. "We never liked having the plant here to begin with," he was saying, "but we learned to live with it. Now these Visitors are doing who-knows-what to it. What if they ruin it for other uses, or pollute the air and ocean? This is *our* beach here, y'know."

Roger's concerned face appeared again. "Rest assured that we won't be doing anything to endanger the community. In fact, our manufacturing process is much safer than the chemical processing you humans were doing here previously. Much of what we're doing at this plant is simply desalinating seawater to use in our cooling and refining process. You see, Denise, when you consider that we're going to be using cryogenic techniques, it's easy to see that—"

Denise smilingly nodded her head as Roger authoritatively—and nearly incomprehensibly—began on the technical problems of using supercooled substances in chemical processing. Finally she held up a forestalling hand. "I'm sure there are many members of our audience who are following you perfectly, Roger, but others of us, myself included, lost you on the first sentence. Perhaps you can illustrate what you're talking about during our tour?"

The camera followed Denise and Roger through the plant while her voice-over continued: "Unfortunately, we didn't discover a great deal about the nature of the Visitor chemical processes during our tour. The consultants we'd brought with us were able to glean only a little more from the highly scientific jargon the Visitor technicians employed."

Her voice hesitated. "But getting answers to our questions at all posed more of a problem than comprehending any answers we received. Many of our questions were deferred with promises to get back to us with information at some later date, and many of us were left to ponder this increasing evidence of the Visitor high technology and scientific superiority."

Then the poised videotaped Denise stood alone, mike in hand, hair windblown, in front of the plant. "There is a definite wariness apparent here in the sea breezes of Brooklyn, as those who live near the chemical plant watch and wait. This is Denise Daltrey, on location, here in Brooklyn." The recorded voice cut with the image and the monitor blanked. Denise turned back to her audience. "We'll be right back after these messages."

The red light blinked off, and the director's voice boomed over the loudspeaker, "Denise, pick up the phone. It's the president."

"Of the United States?" Denise gasped.

"Of the *network*."

She cocked an eyebrow at Winston Weinberg as he leaned against the end of the anchor desk. "You think the shit just hit the fan?" she asked.

"You'll know in a second," he said.

Denise reached for the phone. "Yes, sir?" She listened for a second. "Yes, I'm free after the broadcast. And I think Mr. Weinberg is too." She hesitated. "A meeting? Well, we have a lot of work to do before tomorrow's—" She winced and bit her lip. "Yes, sir. Yes, sir, we'll be there."

She slowly put the receiver back into its cradle.

"Well?" asked Weinberg.

"He wanted to know why we were picking on the Visitors and how we could have aired such a suspicious, unfriendly, potentially divisive report. Where's our sense of priorities? he wants to know." She twiddled her fingers against the stack of notes at her spot on the anchor desk. "He'll have all our heads on silver platters if the News Division doesn't shape up and fly right—starting *now*."

Weinberg smoothed his droopy moustache. "He said all that?"

"He talks quickly when he's pissed off, Winnie." Denise tried to smile but didn't succeed. "Actually, I think 'enraged' is a better word."

The producer shook his head. "That dumb sonofabitch. He's network president because he's an accountant, and he has the balls to tell us how we should cover the news? What does he expect from us? Puff pieces like the ones Kristine Walsh is doing? She's covering this thing like she's their official spokeswoman, not a journalist. *Jesus H. Christ . . .*" Weinberg clenched his hand into a fist, looked at it, then turned away, his shoulders sagging.

"Ten seconds," came the disembodied director's voice.

* * *

Angela paced in front of the conference table where Roger sat, arms folded. Jennifer stood by the portal, watching her expressionlessly, wishing the Commander hadn't requested her presence.

"We simply *can't* allow any more media coverage like that Daltrey woman's broadcast this morning," Angela snarled. "We're having enough trouble with this damned city already."

"I agree," Roger said mildly. "But we've already taken steps. Diana approached Kristine Walsh yesterday, as scheduled. And the CBS network president came through just as we suggested."

Angela whirled to face her commanding officer. "Yes, but we wouldn't have had him to fall back on if *I* hadn't marked him as an ideal conversion subject back at the Mayor's party. Don't forget that, *Roger*."

The Commander stood abruptly, towering over the small blonde. "And my records give you full credit for your contribution," he said tightly. "I'm sure there's no need to remind you that *I'm* the reason you've risen through the ranks as quickly as you have—the reason you were given this assignment as my second over officers with more time in service."

Angela lowered her eyes, realizing she'd gone too far. "I didn't intend to imply that I had forgotten, Roger. It's just that today's broadcast made me furious. I was just—how does the expression go—blowing off steam."

"Very well," Roger said, mollified. He turned to Jennifer, who was trying not to look at Angela, knowing how the latter—her superior officer—would react to Jennifer's witnessing her rebuke. "I called you in, Jennifer, to ask if you've completed your investigation of Denise Daltrey."

"Yes, Commander," Jennifer replied. "I don't think she's a candidate for a spokesperson slot. She's not the same kind of human as Kristine Walsh—I can't uncover any weaknesses significant enough to control her. In fact, I definitely recommend *against* approaching her with an offer similar to the one we made Walsh. My analysis indicates it would be rejected summarily, and it would cause unwelcome suspicion on Daltrey's part."

Roger nodded. "Very well. Let's see if our word with the

network president takes care of the situation before considering any direct action." His green eyes fixed on Angela's. "Satisfactory?"

"Yes, Commander," the blonde officer replied meekly, but Jennifer didn't miss the glance she cast at Roger's back as he turned away. Angela wasn't much of an actress at concealing her true thoughts . . .

Denise sat alone in her office, still smarting from the morning's meeting with the network president. A tuna on rye toast and a diet Pepsi rested in the white deli bag on her desk, but her stomach flipped over at the very notion of food. *The bastard,* she thought. *You'd have thought we'd done an exposé on his favorite auntie's whorehouse. Why the hell did he take it so personally?*

She popped open the can of Pepsi and took a cautious sip. The liquid stayed in her stomach, so she took another sip, opening her desk drawer to get out a napkin. Her fingers encountered an edge of white envelope, and she tugged a note out of the drawer, seeing her name written in her producer's familiar scrawl. "Hate to say it," the note read, "but I was righter than I knew. Walsh was named Visitor Spokesperson today. I must be psychic—now you know why I bet all the time. Should've put money on it *this* time. At least that way I'd have had something to comfort me while I barfed in disgust. Love and kisses, Winnie."

Denise balled the note up savagely, then prompted by an impulse she didn't care to examine too closely, she tore it into indecipherable shreds. *Something's going on here,* she thought, feeling her anger crystallize into resolution. *And whoever's behind it had better look out . . .*

Joey Vitale savored each and every moment he could spend on the grass and dirt of Yankee Stadium. For his father's generation, nothing could replace the old Brooklyn Dodgers, long gone to Los Angeles. But for Joey, born after the Dodgers had packed up and broken the hearts of baseball fans from Flatbush to Canarsie, and after that old bandbox called Ebbets Field had been bulldozed for a housing project, there was only one ballpark in his childhood dreams—the House that Ruth Built, nestled in a still-habitable corner of the South Bronx.

The presence of the stadium and its baseball dynasty stood as a bulwark against the spreading urban decay that had swallowed most of the surrounding area, transforming a once-prosperous middle-class neighborhood into one of the poorest in the country.

That was the sociology of the place as related to Joey by Pete Forsythe when the younger player had first joined the team. Joey had grown up in the city, but when he was a kid, Yankee Stadium had been an isolated golden haven, a stop on the subway, or an exit off the Cross-Bronx Expressway when his pop would swallow his Yankee-hating pride and take his son to the games. The young player had never known what its surrounding neighborhood was like until Pete took him for a drive through streets that could have been transplanted from World War Two Europe—hollow-eyed shells of once-grand apartment houses, rubble-strewn, often-charred lots that resembled Hiroshima ground zero where jobless teenagers hunched against boarded-up storefronts and where faded and near-indecipherable signs above the doors gave mute evidence that commerce had once existed in this desolation.

Pete's accompanying lecture about social responsibility had made its mark—Joey had vowed never to let his own Brooklyn neighborhood suffer a like fate and had eagerly volunteered for every community-service project he could squeeze in, often contributing money as well as his time to programs that benefited greatly from the backing of a major-league star.

Pete Forsythe took part in many of Joey's projects—a sizable chink in his cynicism-plated armor. He covered his own philanthropy by disclaiming, "Y'know, kid, this won't make a damn bit of difference in the long run. In a hundred years who'll know?" Then he'd add, "But we've got to do it anyway—keeps us off the streets, at least."

Pete called *that* existentialism. Joey wasn't sure what the word meant, but wasn't troubled by it. What he understood was that his friend Pete was a nice guy, but didn't want people finding that out.

All of his memories and thoughts about Yankee Stadium and its environs became excess baggage, quickly dismissed, as Joey drove into sight of the graceful white stadium. He parked his car quickly in the guarded, fenced-in lot, leaped out, slammed the door, and began to trot through the runway to the clubhouse. His feet thudded faster and faster until he was fairly flying past the blur of the halls, then the dugout—

He stopped abruptly, his eyes taking in the emerald green of the real grass, the rich brown of the infield dirt. *No artificial turf for this ballplayer!* Joey sniffed luxuriously, glorying in the smell and feel of this, his home territory. It was great to have a reason to be back.

Today was the first meeting of the Visitor Friends group Alexander Garr had arranged with Angela. Joey, Pete, and Bobby Neal were joined by a few other players who lived in the immediate area, under the supervision of "Field Marshal" Garr. The team owner, having committed himself to the enterprise, was determined that everything run smoothly.

About two hundred children and teenagers gathered in the field-level box seats behind first base. Garr was all decked out in a dark-blue Yankees warm-up suit as he addressed them from a mike on the dugout roof. He explained the ground rules—orderly behavior and good manners were essential, and everyone would get to talk to the Visitors and examine the squad vehicles.

"And Angela has promised," Garr concluded, "that if everyone behaves themselves—and I stress that *if*, kids—then we'll split into groups, ride up in the squad vehicles, and get a special tour of the Mother Ship!"

The group let out a chorus of wild cheers until a single, high-pitched voice overtopped them: "Look! Here they come!"

Garr was easily as excited as the youngsters as they watched four squad vehicles swoop toward the stadium and settle effortlessly onto the outfield grass.

It all went surprisingly smoothly. The kids were divided into groups, each one with two players as "platoon leaders." (Garr couldn't resist military terminology.) Each squad vehicle had a dozen or so Visitors aboard, more than enough to answer the barrages of questions, leaving a few free to stand beside the squad vehicles, keeping a watchful eye on the proceedings.

"It's a good thing they don't have hubcaps on those things," Pete whispered to Joey as their group edged around the outside of the Visitor vehicle. "Did you notice that Alex managed to snare some of the really hard-core gang members?"

"So?"

"So I suspect they would just as soon *strip* a squad vehicle as take a ride in it."

"Give 'em a break, Pete. Some events are so exciting they transcend established patterns of behavior."

Pete stepped back, his lips pursed in a soundless whistle. " 'Transcend established patterns of behavior.' What the hell did you do, swallow a dictionary?"

"A book I've been reading," Joey said proudly. *"Thirty Days to a More Powerful Vocabulary."*

"Hmm." Pete regarded his friend thoughtfully. "Marianne been on your mind lately?"

Vitale scuffled his Adidas into the turf. "Wel-l-l . . . I figured maybe I didn't stack up so hot in the brains department next to those guys in grad school, so I thought, uh—"

"Excuse me," interrupted a tentative female voice—a Visitor voice.

Joey turned to see a tall young woman with chestnut hair waving gently down to her shoulders and the most incredibly long-lashed gray-blue eyes he'd ever seen.

"Forget the college girl," Pete whispered to him, then moved away to follow the tour. The Visitor woman was still looking at Joey, making him flush.

"Uh—um, hi," was all he could come up with. He felt like an idiot.

"My name is Lisa," she said.

It dawned on Joey after a second that he was staring. Almost all the Visitors were physically attractive—watching them troop out of the shuttles at the Brooklyn plant had been like watching a coed beauty contest. But Lisa—Joey couldn't stop thinking that she might be *the* most beautiful woman he'd ever seen. He let his eyes trail down, and it immediately occurred to him that this was not a smart way to get his mind off her looks. Her red coverall was fitted snugly enough to make him wonder what she'd look like in a bikini . . . or out of one. Joey swallowed, searching his mind for something to say.

"What's yours?" she prompted.

"Mine?" he asked numbly. Higher thought processes gradually revived in his brain. "Um, my name? It's . . . uh . . . Joey. Joey Vitale."

Her face registered no change except that her smile widened

as she bobbed her head. Joey stared at her. "You don't know who I am?"

She shook her head, a bit embarrassed. "I'm sorry, should I?"

"Well, no, not really, I guess. It's just that your people seemed to know all about us, and the stadium . . ." He shrugged. "But actually I guess it's pretty silly to expect you to know the names of individual baseball players."

"You play . . . baseball?" she pronounced the word carefully. "Is that a musical instrument, a baseball?"

Joey laughed and Lisa's face fell, leaving him feeling like a jerk. "I'm sorry, I didn't mean to laugh at you. No, baseball is a sport. A . . . physical activity. Didn't they tell you what Yankee Stadium is used for?"

"I missed the briefing, I'm afraid. I was doing some special research for Jennifer. I know what sports are, though. Games, right?"

"Yeah. Baseball is the game we play here."

"What else do you do?" asked Lisa.

"What else?" Joey's mind seemed to be embedded in quick-drying cement.

"Yes, for an occupation. Your work."

"Oh, baseball *is* my occupation, my job. I get paid for it."

Lisa looked doubtful. "You get paid to play a game?"

Joey chuckled. "Yeah. Sometimes I have trouble believin' it myself, that they pay me to do what I like doing most of all." He found it singularly refreshing to talk to someone who'd never even *heard* of baseball—someone who had no idea that he had made nearly a million this season. He grinned at her. "Uh, what was it you wanted to ask me?"

"Nothing in particular. I just thought I'd say hello. The whole idea of these gatherings is for your people and mine to get to know each other, and I'm very interested in your culture." She dropped those incredibly long lashes. "You looked like a nice person to talk to."

Joey grinned. "Well, I'm sure glad you did. It's a great idea, your people and mine getting to know each other better." He put his hand on her arm, leading over toward the monuments and plaques in center field, commemorating baseball greats like Babe Ruth, Lou Gehrig, and Mickey Mantle. "C'mon over here, and I'll tell you about baseball."

"I'd like that," she said.

"And I thought New York Hospital–Cornell University Medical Center could never sink lower than having taken in the Shah of Iran," Dr. Mary Chu announced as she marched into George Stewart's office like a tiny, black-haired tornado. She planted herself on the corner of his desk and glared at Stewart, who peered over his reading glasses at her.

"The man was sick," he said mildly. "What are you raging about now, Mary?"

"I just came from that so-called introductory lecture given by these Visitor characters, telling us what these seminars of theirs will be about. Advanced scientific knowledge, high-tech breakthroughs—my *ass!*"

Stewart craned his neck for an obvious peek at her bottom. "Doesn't look high-tech to me."

She shook her head. "Very funny, George. But making me laugh will *not* make me forget how insulted I feel. Those smooth-talking creeps fed us pure, unadulterated *pabulum*. They were vague and evasive—"

"Like my students on their last anatomy exam."

"Still won't work, George. And the *way* they delivered this so-called information! Well, my God almighty, I've seen first-year med students give more comprehensive, better thought-out lectures. Just who the hell do these guys think they're trying to fool?" She flung herself down in the chair beside his desk, her dark eyes glaring stormily into his. The early November cold and anger had brought up the red in her cheeks—she looked more like a student than a full professor. Her white lab coat contrasted with her bright-red sweater, plaid wraparound skirt, and penny loafers.

Stewart folded his hands on the desk, considering her words seriously. "What are you saying, Mary? That they really *don't* intend to share their advanced knowledge with us as they promised?"

"It's not just what I'm *saying*, George," Dr. Chu said. "Check out the facts, my friend. They postponed the damned thing *twice*—then when they finally give it, it's a total waste. Are you going to tell me that's being up front and forthcoming?"

Stewart held up a placating hand. "No, I'm not going to do

any such thing. I've known you too long to argue with you when you're in your dragon lady *persona*."

She broke up completely at his words, laughing so helplessly that for a moment he was afraid she might have succumbed to hysteria. But that *wasn't* Mary Chu's style. "What's so funny?" he asked.

"Speaking of the dragon lady, she's struck again." Mary held her fingers up and wiggled them, showing off her very long, impeccably manicured nails. "If what I did works, you're going to have to eat every sneering remark you've ever made about my fingernails."

"No!" he exclaimed in mock horror. "How could I go on without looking forward to razzing you about being Ms. Fu Manchu?"

"Old, George, very old, your jokes. But as a matter of fact, I *did* use them as scientific research tools today."

"How?"

"When I shook hands with one of those Visitor characters, I—ahem—*accidentally* jabbed him hard enough to scrape some of the skin off his hand, right under the ol' Fu Manchus. I mumbled an abject apology, of course, sorry for being so clumsy, etcetera, but it was the damnedest thing—he didn't seem to even notice!"

"Did you draw blood?"

"I doubt it, but I came close. If I'd done it to *you*, you'd have yelped, or *something*, but he didn't even blink. And another thing—those Visitors are cold-skinned characters. Temperature at least five to ten degrees below ours. Frankly, he didn't feel much warmer than the air temperature aboard that damned ship of theirs."

"What did you do then?"

"Avoided touching anything else with that hand and raced back to my lab. Sure enough, there were scrapings under three nails, and I set up slides."

George snorted. "And to think you really had me convinced you were pissed off, when you're actually so pleased with yourself you're practically humming the Hallelujah Chorus."

"I *was* pissed off," Mary said defensively. "Still am—to think those guys think we're suckers enough to buy the bill of goods they're trying to push on us. 'Share the fruits of all our knowledge,'—*horseshit*!"

"What are you going to do now?"

"Take you back to the lab with me to take the first look-see at those slides. I've got a feeling we may be on the track of something big."

Stewart checked his watch. "Damn! I'd love to, Mary, you've really got my curiosity raging, but I've got to be downstairs in about two minutes. I've got a CAT-scan scheduled for the Johnson boy, and I promised his parents I'd be there. Then I've got a couple of late appointments at my home office."

Mary nodded. "I understand. But I'm going to start without you."

"Let me know what you find," he said. "You can reach me here until about four, then I'll be home. I'll take a look first thing tomorrow."

"*If* I can squeeze you in," she said airily, buffing the infamous nails on her lab jacket. She rose to her feet and struck a pose on her way to the door. "By then, my fame and detective exploits ought to have spread so far you'll have to take a number and get on line to see those slides."

"Did I ever tell you you're probably certifiable?" Stewart said, beginning to laugh.

"Continually. Ta-ta, George—I'm off to make my name in science!"

Stewart chuckled as he straightened his tie and put on his lab coat, watching his friend as she waltzed out the door and threw him a last wave. Her gleaming fingertips were the last things to disappear into the hall.

It was dark out when the last patient left Stewart's home office. He finished up the paperwork, shooed his receptionist on her way home, and locked the downstairs office door. As he started up the inside steps to his living room, he felt bone-weary—something he'd been noticing more and more lately. Maybe Lauren was right. Maybe he should think about cutting down.

Halfway up the staircase, the phone rang. Go up or down to answer it? If he went down, he'd only have to reclimb the lower steps—might as well finish the journey up. He got to the phone on its sixth ring and had to catch his breath to say hello.

"George," said Mary's voice. "It's me. Can you get back over here right away?"

All his strength seemed to drain away at the thought of leaving the light and warmth of home for the streets again. A fatigue headache throbbed inexorably at the back of his head. "Is it the slides?" he asked. "Can't it wait till tomorrow, Mary? I'm beat."

"George." She was deadly serious under the bantering tone. "Are you getting senile on me? If you are, then wait a while, 'cause I *really* need you to see this. Wear two pairs of socks— what I've just looked at is gonna knock one pair right off."

"What the hell did you find?"

"I can't say. I've probably said too much already over the phone. I'm gonna lock the door till you get here," she said darkly, and he could tell she wasn't kidding at all.

"All right," he said. "I'm leaving now. Sit tight."

"Hurry *up*, George. G'bye."

Snatching a couple of Reese's cups out of a candy dish, George Stewart grabbed his coat and headed out to find a cab.

The taxi stopped outside the hospital gates on York Avenue, and Stewart got out. The air seemed colder here along the East River. He didn't know if it was this making him shiver or Mary Chu's chilling words replaying in his head. There'd been a shakiness in her voice. In the twelve years he'd known her, he'd never heard her sound like that before. He walked quickly up the driveway and into the medical center.

The corridors went by in a blur as he munched on his last peanut-butter cup. Halfway down the final hall, he saw light spilling from the open door of Mary Chu's lab, and the candy seemed to stick halfway down. Telling himself she'd heard him coming and opened the door, he called out softly, "Mary? It's George."

He suddenly realized that silence could be an ugly noise.

Quiet-footed, he went to the doorway and paused. His breath came out in a painful whoosh as he took in the scene— lab stools on their sides, a tossed salad of papers and broken test tubes scattered across the floor tiles. Mary's expensive microscope lay on its back on the floor, its black base sticking out like the stiff legs of a dead animal.

Stewart's mind flashed back to the time his Harlem office

had been burglarized. It had been years ago, over a Fourth of July weekend when he and his family had gone to the mountains. After the break-in, the neighborhood had organized an informal watch over his brownstone. They'd wanted Doc Stewart to stay, and had protected him ever since. He was a precious commodity, someone who knew their names and faces, who'd say hello in the street, who'd help in the middle of the night when a worried mother would call.

But no one had protected Mary Chu, and Stewart felt a sudden, intense grief. He looked carefully at the lock on the door, not touching it, but could see no signs of tampering. He reached for her phone to call security, but stopped. If this break-in had anything to do with the Visitor skin samples—and it beggared coincidence to suppose it *didn't*—he ought to search for signs of Mary's notes and slides, for surely the police wouldn't allow him to remove anything once they arrived.

Carefully, using a tongue depressor to lift the papers, he began sifting through the chaos on the floor.

Fifteen minutes of searching convinced him that there was no more sign of Dr. Chu's detective work than there was of Mary herself. His hands shaking, he dialed security.

There was nothing in the morning paper, no report whatsoever about the break-in. At his hospital office, George Stewart dug patiently through his *New York Times*, but the disappearance of one of the city's most prominent physicians and researchers evidently wasn't considered fit news to print. Not even a tiny mention buried on page forty-seven. Nothing, not a damn thing.

He dialed the hospital's security office. "Can I speak with Mr. Kolker, please?" He sipped at his coffee. "Yes, I can hold."

He was halfway through his cup when a distinctly Brooklyn voice graveled in his ear. "Yes, Mr. Kolker, this is Doctor George Stewart. I was the one who reported the disturbance in Doctor Mary Chu's laboratory last evening, as well as the disappearance of Doctor Chu herself. I was wondering what you'd managed to uncover."

"Not much, Doctor Stewart," said the voice in his ear. It

pronounced his name "Stoo-it." "We don't even know if she was here last night."

"Now just a minute," George said. "I know for a fact she was working late. She called me from her lab and asked me to come see her. That was about seven-thirty. I got there about eight, and I found her lab ransacked. I explained all this to the officer who was up there last night. Myers, that was his name."

"Yeah, I got his report here. But the fact is, no one saw her after she said she was goin' out for a sandwich about five-thirty. Maybe you were mistaken—maybe she called you from home."

"I tried her home. All night. She hasn't been there. I went over there after I left Myers, and her mail hadn't been picked up. She didn't go home."

"Well, Doc, I really don't know what to tell you. We're just an internal security staff. All we found was a mess in her lab. Hell, I've seen labs that looked worse when a strong wind blew through 'em."

"Except for the microscope," George said, his voice tight. "Nobody tosses an instrument worth that much on the floor."

"Yeah, I'll grant you it's strange. But I'm no Dick Tracy. We reported the incident to N.Y.P.D. It's in their hands now."

"All right, I'll talk to them." Stewart hung up. The coffee sloshed acidly in his stomach.

A few minutes later he hung up again, stymied. It seemed that a person had to be missing at least twenty-four hours before the police would even take a report—what a mess!

He thought hard for a few moments, then reached for the phone once more, dialing 411. When the information operator's voice rang tinnily in his ear, he poised his pencil. "May I have the number of *The New York Times*, please?"

Chapter 6

Rat Patrol

Pete Forsythe was increasingly sorry he'd succumbed to Alex Garr's arm-twisting and agreed to help run these Visitor Friends gatherings. There were many places he'd prefer being on a Friday night rather than in a drafty, cavernous armory in a Manhattan neighborhood he wouldn't have voluntarily entered at high noon, much less after dark. But here he was, with Joey Vitale and a handful of other "volunteers," playing camp counselor to about seventy-five unruly street kids from the neighborhood. The first part of the evening had been taken up with target practice by young Visitor troopers demonstrating their prowess with the laser rifles and side arms the aliens had recently begun sporting.

Pete didn't like this. Theirs was supposed to be a peaceful mission, wasn't it? He thought back to the Visitors' arrival, now more than a month in the past, and couldn't recall seeing any of the earlier technicians wearing guns. But now it seemed the only Visitors he saw were troopers, and they wore their side arms as authoritatively as any N.Y.P.D. officer.

The noise of the thudding feet around Forsythe echoed down off the rafters and combined with the pounding beat of several competitive and dissonant ghetto blasters—those huge radios the kids used to broadcast music for a city block. Pete rubbed the back of his neck, reflecting that the possession of even one of the things ought to be an offense punishable by slow torture.

The armory was the size of an aircraft hangar—plenty of

space for the echoes to bounce and re-echo. At the far end, ten boys were playing a version of basketball that seemed to involve more outright violence than some gang rumbles. Pete had found it necessary to lay down some ground rules for the preservation of his own sanity, but as long as nobody drew weapons or blood, he merely watched.

He looked around, noticing that Joey, who had been standing on the other side of the court with the female Visitor Lisa, had disappeared. Pete rubbed the back of his neck again, feeling the need for a drink uncoil within him like a serpent. He settled for a couple of aspirin, swallowed dry, and felt a flash of self-righteous congratulation. Strolling around the fringes of the game, he continued to watch the mayhem.

There was a wintery-crisp clarity to the night air, and Lisa pressed close to Joey as they stood on the armory's concrete steps. The moon looked like an oversized, lopsided street lamp, casting shadows of buildings from across the street. Joey put his arm around Lisa. "You cold?" he asked.

"Yes," she replied, though she didn't shiver. "Our systems don't adjust to temperature the way yours do."

"Here, take my coat," he said, putting it around her.

"I'd benefit more from your shared body heat," she said.

If a human girl had said that to Joey, he'd have taken it as a clear indication of her interest in horizontal recreation, but several encounters with Lisa had taught him that she wasn't the sort to use words to titillate. So he contented himself with putting his arm around her and drawing her against his side while pulling the jacket around both their shoulders.

"Does your planet have a moon?" he asked after a moment.

"Two," she nodded. "But they're both much smaller than yours."

"I'm glad you could get away to come down tonight."

"So am I."

They watched the moon for a few moments while Joey wondered what she'd do if he tried to kiss her. Something restrained him, though. He wasn't sure what. "How do you like Earth so far?" he asked.

"It's very nice. You have a varied climate here in this zone. I like that, even though the cold doesn't agree with us much. Each day is a little different."

"Isn't your world like that?"

"No, our world has much greater extremes of heat and cold. That's due to a combination of slight atmospheric differences and our distance from our star, the one you call Sirius. Our temperate zone is smaller than yours, and most of our planet is considerably warmer. A lot like your equatorial climate."

"You sure know a lot about science."

Lisa smiled. "Did I sound like a textbook? I'm sorry."

"No, that's okay," Joey said. "I like smart people. They put interesting ideas in my head, and I enjoy thinking about 'em. What exactly is your job here on Earth?"

"Well, a combination of tasks. I work some of the time as an environmental monitor technician at the Brooklyn plant, and I'm also studying sociological structures—how your society works and how our people are interacting with yours."

"Yeah?" Joey looked down at her, caught by the way her eyes shone in the moonlight. "And how are we doing?"

She gazed back at him calmly, with a slight smile. "You're doing very well."

He leaned over to kiss her, aiming for her lips, but somehow she moved and he actually connected with her right eye. He felt those incredible lashes quiver beneath his mouth, then he drew back and looked at her. "I'm sorry," he said. "I probably shouldn't have done that."

"I didn't mind," Lisa said. "A kiss is a gesture of liking and affection, isn't it?"

"Uh, well, yeah."

"Well, I like you too, Joey." Carefully she stretched upward and kissed the end of his chin.

He smiled at her. It was amazing how good a kiss on the chin could feel . . .

Pete returned from a quick trip to the john only to notice that the ten basketball players had somehow been reduced to six, and that an electric-blue backpack that had been lying on the floor near the bleachers had also disappeared. He swore softly to himself. The missing kids were Rico, Michael, Stroke, and Julio—all members of the same Spanish Harlem gang. Forsythe sprinted over to the door and yanked it open, seeing two figures side by side on the concrete steps.

"Dammit, Joey, get your butt back in here," he snapped.

"Julio and his buddies have disappeared and I've gotta find 'em. You take over nursemaiding the others."

Vitale gave him a shamefaced look as he came back inside with Lisa. Pete regretted his tone, and said more gently, "Hey, buddy, ordinarily I wouldn't care if you two wanted to get some fresh air. We're just shorthanded tonight. Okay?" His blue eyes held his friend's dark ones for a second.

Vitale nodded. "Yeah. I shoulda told you we were goin' outside."

Circling the gym, Pete kept his ears alert for signs of the missing kids, but the cacophony of the radios made it difficult. He checked one hallway after another, listening as the sounds of the gym receded into a discordant undertone. There was nothing but the concrete walls, some of them lined with lockers and storage bins, smelling faintly of old sweat and cigarette smoke. He noticed locked storerooms of supplies ready for the National Guard's next foray. *If those damn kids have broken in and gotten some of those weapons, Alex will have my ass,* he thought grimly.

Finally he heard smothered giggles as he stood in a dark hallway, and his nose caught the singed, sweet herbal tang of pot. He tiptoed toward the noise, his hand trailing along the wall seeking a light switch. A loud belch and more giggles, and then the swish-clink-pop-hiss of a beer can yanked from its plastic six-pack holder and opened. The smell of beer made Pete's mouth tingle as he realized how thirsty he was. His fingers touched the switch and light flooded the darkened hall.

"Party's over," Forsythe said, eyeing the four boys who sat sprawled against the end of the hall. A fifth figure in a red coverall lay facedown on the concrete. "What'd you do to him?"

The kids were sufficiently blitzed to be beyond fear of anything except perhaps uniformed authority figures, and they grinned at Pete as though he'd said something very funny indeed. "He's drunk," snickered Rico, a short, pudgy kid in a denim jacket with the arms cut out. "We gave him about three cans and the sucker keeled over. My nine-year-old sister can hold her beer better'n that!" He balanced a sneakered foot on the Visitor's rump.

"It's nice that he was willing to go to such lengths to establish good relations with you natives," Pete said, shaking his head. He tried to summon pity for the Visitor, but the sight of the alien's laser weapon sticking out from under the unconscious form drowned any sympathy he might have felt.

"Hey, man," said Rico, "what you gonna do?"

"Well, I'm not going to sit down and have a drink with you guys," Pete said, his mouth twisting. "If you clean up the mess quietly and don't give me any more grief, I may not mention to Mr. Garr that you jerks were drinking in here. That's a real no-no with Alex. If I tell him, you fools won't be allowed back anymore."

"Hey, man, watch who you're callin' a fool," Julio said with the boldness of a leader. He wore a black leather jacket studded with silver, a black T-shirt beneath it. His name was embroidered across his back, and the dark eyes above the peach-fuzz moustache were wary, holding more intelligence than the other gang members. As he climbed to his feet, Pete saw a silver crucifix on a chain swing against the smooth skin of his neck. It should have looked incongruous, but somehow did not. "We were just havin' a little fun. You wanna make a big deal out of it?" His hand twitched near his pocket.

Pete shook his head. "Pull a blade on me, Julio, and you'll find I can outrun you all. I may be twice your age, but I'm a professional athlete, and I'm sober. I'll be out there yelling for help before you guys can get to the end of the goddamn hall."

Julio relaxed visibly, tried to laugh. "Hell, man, don't be so paranoid. I ain't got no blade. It's cool, you keeping quiet for us. C'mon, guys." He kicked at the near-comatose youth they called Stroke, probably because he was always combing his blue-black hair.

"Michael, help him up," said Julio.

"Hand over the booze," Pete said.

"Aw, *man!*" protested Rico.

"Do it!" Julio snapped. "The man's doin' us a favor. We gotta be nice to him." Then he smiled smoothly.

Pete removed the stash from the backpack, checked it over, then stuffed it back in. No hard drugs, thank God. "I'm keeping this," he said. "You guys get on back to the gym and split. I'll tell 'em you weren't feeling so good. If I ever catch you with any of this crap again, forget the nice-guy routine. I'll call the cops."

Rico shook his head vigorously, taking Pete's threat seriously. "Hey, no, man! I'm on probation already!"

"For what?" Pete said, sizing the kid up—he couldn't be
much over fourteen.

"Drunk drivin' a stolen car," Rico said, smirking.

The words made Pete's eyes flash. He swung around and
grabbed Rico by the collar, pinning him to the wall. The look
on the ballplayer's face plainly scared the youth.

"Hey, man, what're you, crazy? What's it to you?" he
protested, trying to sound tough.

Following an impulse he knew he'd regret, Pete dropped the
backpack and took his wallet out of his pocket. "So you think
drunk driving's cool, huh? Makes you proud, a big man, Rico?
Wanna see something?"

Rico's eye narrowed in fear and suspicion. "What? A
badge? You ain't no cop."

"No badge, just a picture." He released his grip on Rico's
jacket. The other kids gathered around, obviously curious but
trying not to seem *too* interested. Pete slid a photo out and held
it up. The gang members stared muzzily at a pretty lady in her
early thirties with a striking smile and auburn hair. She had two
tow-headed little girls balanced on her lap.

"Who's the fox?" asked Julio. "Your wife and kids?"

"*Was* my wife," said Pete tightly.

"She died, man?" asked Julio, masked concern visible in
his eyes.

Pete shook his head. "No. She gave me a choice—drinking
or her."

"So you laid off the booze?" said Michael.

Pete smiled faintly, ironically. "Nope. Next thing I knew,
she packed up and left—with my daughters. Amy and Karen.
Moved to Hawaii."

Rico was still angry at being singled out for physical abuse.
"Why you tellin' us all this, man?"

"You'll know why when I'm done. After they left, I kept
drinking, even though that's *why* they left. But I drank by
myself, so nobody knew how bad it was. Until I showed up for
a night game in Baltimore so stewed I couldn't tie my
shoelaces. My manager hustled me into his office, took me out
of the lineup, and poured coffee down my throat. He told me

he'd keep it quiet—keep it away from Garr—but only if I went to A.A."

"What's that?" said Stroke through his personal haze.

"Alcoholics Anonymous, stupid," said Julio. "Did you go?"

Pete nodded. "Yep. I didn't drink again for a long time—till the next spring training. Then my lawyer called to tell me my divorce was final, and about the judge's decision on child custody—my visitation rights were limited. I had two little girls I loved, and he'd only let *me* visit them—*they* couldn't visit me. My wife's lawyer made damn sure the judge knew all about my drinking."

"But you *quit*," Julio flared, sensing the unfairness.

Pete shrugged. "Didn't matter. You know what I did that night?" He didn't wait for an answer. "I became real close friends with a whole bottle of vodka—told it the whole story. I woke up with the rain hitting me in the face through what used to be the windshield of my car while a cop tried to stop the bleeding." He brushed his nose, which still bore a slight bump.

"I'd wrapped my car around a palm tree," he continued after a moment, his voice remote, passionless. "It wouldn't have been so bad that I almost killed myself, but when I lost control of the car I nearly had a head-on with another one—with a whole family: father, mother, and four kids, one only three months old. The last thing I remembered was seeing their car approaching, and the cop had to tell me about six times that I didn't actually hit them. I wanted to borrow his gun and blow my head off."

He shook himself free of the memory with a visible effort. "They fixed up my face and threw me in the slammer. Bobby Neal bailed me out—for the last time, he told me. Garr wanted to release me outright, but Bobby talked him out of it."

"So, do you still drink?" asked Julio.

"Nope," Pete lied, remembering the white wine at Mayor O'Connor's party a few weeks ago. "Not getting killed that night gave me a lot of second chances. But the accident meant it'd be a good long time before the judge would even *think* about easing up on the visiting privileges." Pete's voice was soft now.

"When's the last time you saw your kids?" asked Julio.

"Last Christmas—almost a year ago. Hawaii's not that close."

"Hey," said Rico, "you got a lotta money. You could fly out there."

"Yeah," Pete said, putting the photo back in his wallet. "I tell myself that every morning. And I don't go." He beckoned to the kids and they walked to the end of the hallway, approaching the sounds of the gym. "Okay, guys, hit the road. I'll take care of your buddy back there."

Rico lingered for a moment, his hands shoved deep into his pockets. "Sounds like you better stay away from the stuff *forever*, man."

Pete nodded. "You, too," he said.

"Yeah, well . . ." said Rico, visibly sobered.

"Get out of here."

Rico left to join his friends as the armory began to empty for the night.

Forsythe turned back in the direction of the drunken Visitor, feeling faintly embarrassed about his sermon. The damned kids were probably laughing their asses off at him. He frowned, wondering if the young alien was still unconscious. He might have to get Joey to help him carry the guy.

The Visitor was up on his hands and knees, facing the wall, as Pete rounded the corner. *Probably puking his guts out,* Forsythe thought with a sigh. *And guess who'll have to clean it up?* He stopped short to allow the alien the dignity of vomiting in private. Then he heard the noise. It was a hissing slur like nothing Pete had ever heard before from human or animal.

What the hell? Forsythe peered around the corner to see the Visitor scrabbling on the floor, still on his knees. Even as Pete watched, he saw a large gray-brown rat scuttle out from the corner, racing toward him.

The Visitor moved so fast he was just a blur. One moment he was drunkenly lurching along the floor, the next he was holding the rat, grinning delightedly. As Pete watched in disbelief, the alien lifted the squeaking, struggling creature toward his face. The rat froze, glassy-eyed, stiff with terror, as the Visitor opened his mouth wide—Pete caught a glimpse of something long and thin writhing inside it, along with what seemed to be *two* sets of teeth—then *wider*, his jaw bulging outward as it dislocated.

One-handed, the alien stuffed the rat into that unnaturally open mouth, and swallowed the frantic creature whole! Then his throat bulged grotesquely with the motions of the squirming body as he gulped it down.

Oh, my God. Somehow Pete managed to back away soundlessly. Forsythe knew instinctively that if the Visitor discovered that he'd been observed, he, Pete, would be a dead man. The aliens had obviously gone to great lengths to be convincing as nearly human, and they might do anything to protect their secret.

So that's why they don't eat in public, Pete thought, backing up very quietly, then turning, soft-footed, to move up the dark hallway. *Shades of Dracula! What are they?* His shoulder blades itched as he thought of the laser gun, and he kept glancing back to see if the Visitor had seen him.

He was sweating and shaking when he made it back to the gym, looking for Joey. Every time he swallowed, he felt the entire contents of his stomach (a bag of Doritos and a Diet 7-Up) threatening to explosively part company.

The kids were all gone. Pete staggered to the door, desperately needing a deep swallow of fresh air. He slammed it open and stood there breathing deeply for several seconds before he saw Joey and Lisa staring at him, concerned. Joey had his arm around the Visitor woman.

"Hey, Pete, you okay?"

Forsythe couldn't answer for a long second. He couldn't take his eyes off Lisa, and it took all his willpower not to yank Joey away from her. *Oh, God,* he thought, looking at the lovely young face before him, *do you do that too? Do you?*

He wondered what she'd say if he asked her.

"I'm okay, Joey," he managed after a second. "Got a hell of a headache from that damned music." He passed a hand over his brow, found it cold and sweating. "I'm okay."

"You're as white as a sheet," Joey said, moving over to take his arm. "C'mon, the kids're gone. I'll drive you home."

Pete moved forward with him, felt the wobble in his knees, and didn't argue further. He wanted Joey to be with him, away from *her*. As he moved slowly down the steps, Forsythe knew he had to find out what was going on. But that would have to wait awhile. For now, he'd be content if he could just get home and lock the door. He needed a drink desperately.

Chapter 7

Conversations in the Park

"I don't believe this!" Lauren Stewart exclaimed to herself in her office in the UN building. *The New York Times* was spread out in front of her. Closing the paper with an angry gesture, she picked up her telephone, impatiently pecking out her father's number.

"Hello, Doctor Stewart here," said her father's voice.

"Dad, it's Lauren. Did you see the *Times*?"

He sighed. "You mean the article about Mary's disappearance? That's all they're talking about at the hospital."

"The article says the police are 'virtually certain' Mary *wasn't* a victim of foul play. They imply she left town under her own steam—even that she ran away! How can they *say* that? Her lab was broken into, and she hasn't been seen since. What the hell do they think happened to her—that she ran off to Tahiti with a traveling salesman?"

"Whoa, baby," he said, sounding weary to the bone. "I'm not real happy about any of this either."

She caught the slight hitch in his voice, and her anger changed to concern. "Dad? Do you know something else about this? Are you okay? You sound really beat."

"I . . . don't want to discuss it. At least not on the phone. Are you busy?"

"Well . . ." She looked at the ever-present stack in her In box and shrugged. "It's nearly eleven—I can take an early lunch. Want to meet?"

"Yeah. C'mon out to my office at the Medical Center. It's nice outside."

"Fine. I'll be there as soon as I can."

As Lauren hung up, she wondered why her father wanted to talk outside. Something stirred within her, pushing her steps ever faster through the corridors, down the elevators and escalators, until by the time she reached the street, she was almost running.

When she saw her father waiting outside the hospital for her, she knew for certain that something was wrong. She hurried over to him, seeing the deepened lines around his eyes, the darkness beneath them. Somehow it seemed that his hair had more gray in it than a week ago. "Hi, Dad," she said, and kissed him.

"Hi, sweetheart. Want to walk a little?"

He took her arm, and they walked together to a park bench set amid the manicured landscape of the vest-pocket Rockefeller University campus adjacent to the hospital. They faced the East River, munching on street-vendor hotdogs and sharing a bag of hot chestnuts. Pigeons lurked nearby, hoping for scraps.

"What happened to Mary, Dad? Was she involved in something she shouldn't have been?"

Her father took a bite out of his hotdog. "Depends on your point of view."

"What's *that* supposed to mean?"

"If you mean, was she involved in anything we humans would consider illegal or shady, I very much doubt it. You've known Mary since you were in college. What do *you* think?"

Lauren shrugged, her dark eyes troubled. "You *know* what I think. She's flamboyant, wild, crazy, funny, and brilliant, not necessarily in that order. But she's the salt of the earth. The idea of her being a criminal is crazy. If she weren't missing like this, I'd laugh."

"Then we agree."

"But what were you trying to imply? Is there anyone who might think differently?"

He fixed her with an intent gaze. "I'm afraid so, honey. I want to tell you about it, but I'm also afraid . . ."

"Of what?"

"I know how closely you've been working with them . . ."

"You mean the *Visitors*? You think *they* had something to do with whatever's happened to Mary? Daddy—" She stared at him helplessly, shaking her head.

"I'm also afraid that if I tell you what I know that you'll be in danger."

"Do you think *you're* in danger?" The thought of any harm coming to her father—of his disappearing like Mary—made Lauren clutch his arm tightly. *Daddy,* she thought, searching his face with anxious eyes, *if anything happened to you, I'd—* She couldn't force herself to complete the thought. "Dad, if there's the slightest chance of that, you'd better tell me. *Everything.*"

After gazing at her for a long moment, her father nodded slowly. "All right." In short, terse sentences, he described Mary's response to the Visitor conference, her actions afterward, and his subsequent involvement when she'd told him about the slides.

"So *you* were the person who told the *Times*?," she said.

"The whole story. And you read what they printed. Somebody, for whatever reasons, didn't want the true story getting out. I'm afraid that whoever that is could discover I'm involved. That's why I couldn't talk over the phone."

"I don't know what to think," Lauren said numbly. "This is bizarre."

"And the worst thing is, in the three days since Mary vanished, I've made some anonymous inquiries—using great caution, let me assure you—and I've found out *she's not the only one*. One of my colleagues, who retired to Florida last year and was doing some consulting work for a lab down there, just up and didn't come home one night. There are at least two others with the same story—one in Kansas and the other in Canada. Whatever's happening here in New York isn't confined to this city—it's all over."

"Oh, no," Lauren mumbled, feeling as though she'd fallen down a rabbit hole. In the sharp November sunshine, the park and the city around her shimmered insubstantially, as though what she saw was nothing more than a rippling reflection in the East River—something that could be destroyed by a carelessly tossed pebble.

Her father was watching her closely, chewing on his last bite of hotdog. "You all right?" he asked gently.

"Yes," she said, straightening, thinking back to something she'd read this morning among the contents of her ubiquitous In box. "Dad, I don't know if this could possibly be connected, but the Visitors have requested that Olav and I fly down to Washington, D.C. Roger and Angela want us to accompany them to a meeting they've scheduled with the President."

"What do they want to talk to Morrow about?"

"I don't know. The memo just said 'security concerns.'"

"Any idea what they could be referring to?"

"I called Olav to ask him, and he said they'd mentioned that there might be a potential threat to Earth-Visitor cooperation."

"Threat?" Stewart laughed without amusement. "What kind of threat could there possibly be? The combined military might of the Soviet Union *and* the U.S. couldn't even touch them." He gestured up at the huge ship hanging over their heads. "What could we possibly do to them?"

"That's what I wondered when I read the request."

He pursed his lips. "There's no way of connecting these happenings, except maybe circumstantially. But I don't like it. When are you supposed to go?"

"Their squad vehicle's coming for us at four o'clock this afternoon."

Stewart grimaced, shaking his head. "Wish you could get out of it."

"I can't. Olav needs me. Besides, I may be able to find out more about what's happening from Angela and Roger."

"You'd better be careful. If there *is* something strange going on and they find out you're suspicious, you could be in trouble."

She smiled tightly. "Subtlety is my business, remember? I'll be the soul of diplomatic discretion."

"All right. But call me tonight, just to let me know you're okay. We'd better not discuss this over the phone, though. We'll wait till you get back."

She nodded. "Agreed. But, Dad, that still doesn't change the fact that Mary's gone without a trace. What if something happens to you? Maybe you ought to—" she shrugged, "I don't know, hide out for a while or something. Take a vacation."

George Stewart considered the suggestion, then shook his head. "I've been careful. I don't think anyone knows anything more than just the fact that I found the mess at Mary's lab. I didn't mention the skin samples when I talked to the reporter. There was nothing conclusive to mention, really. And how long would I have to hide? A week? A month? I can't let paranoia drive me away from my practice. My patients need me. I have classes to teach . . ."

He thought for a moment. "No, I'm staying."

"At least promise me you'll be—"

"Careful," he interrupted her, his eyes fixed on something in the distance past her shoulder. "I promise, honey. Looks like we're about to have company."

Lauren turned to see Peter Forsythe jogging toward them, dressed in a sweatsuit and his Yankees cap. "Great," she muttered under her breath. "That's all we need."

"Hello there, Pete," said Stewart as the man trotted up to them. "You remember my daughter, Lauren."

"Sure, Doc." He nodded at her. "How are you, Ms. Stewart?"

"Fine, thank you," she said with a distant smile.

Forsythe hesitated for a long second, uncertainly. Lauren smiled at his discomfiture. The baseball player obviously had something he wanted to speak to her father about, and just as obviously, didn't want to bring it up in front of her. He jiggled up and down on the leaf-strewn ground, clapped his hands, then flapped his arms. "A little nip in the air today," he observed.

Lauren nodded. "Yes, there is. But if you've been jogging, you should be nice and warm by now." She eyed him, smiling sweetly. "Goodness, you must be in excellent shape. All that running and you haven't even worked up a sweat."

He gave her a glance of poorly disguised hostility, "Uh, Doc, I hate to interrupt a family picnic, but there's something really important I have to discuss with you."

Lauren smiled at her father archly. "Don't tell me your prize student is having problems with his anatomy."

Pete glared at her, then began to chuckle cynically. "No, my anatomy's in great shape, Ms. Stewart. I'd be happy to prove it to you—" He paused for a beat, "at racketball, if you play it."

"As a matter of fact, I do," she said, abruptly abandoning the verbal fencing and standing up. "Daddy, I've got to get back. I'll call you later, okay?"

"Sure, honey. Take care."

"Maybe we can get together for a game sometime, Mr. Forsythe," Lauren said. "It would be *lots* of fun, I'm sure."

Bitch, thought Pete, watching Lauren Stewart walk away with long, arrogant strides. In spite of himself, he admired the tall, slender figure in the camel-hair coat, and his eyes dropped to her legs and lingered for a long second. *Too bad her personality isn't as nice as the rest of her . . .*

He turned back to Stewart, shoving his hands into the kangaroo pockets of his sweatshirt. "Did you teach her to be a Yankees hater?"

Stewart was taken aback. "No, Lauren's never paid much attention to professional sports."

"Oh." Pete gave the retreating woman a final glance. "Well, at least I know she detests me for myself, then."

Stewart chuckled. "I'm glad your feelings aren't hurt. Lauren doesn't make friends very easily—especially male ones. I have a feeling she compares them all to Olav Lindstrom, and next to his old-world charm, they all come up lacking."

Pete smiled. "My suspicion is she compares 'em to *you,* Doc, and that's where we come up short."

Stewart made a self-deprecatory gesture. "What did you need to see me about that was so important you had to put on this jogging act?"

"This is gonna be hard for you to believe, Doc, but let me tell you now that every word is true. I was cold sober when it happened." He grimaced. "I got pretty lit later on that night, but I was so shaky I—"

"Peter—" Stewart held up a hand. "Just tell me what's going on, son."

"Okay. Night before last I was playing big brother down at the armory, and four kids disappeared . . ." Pete paced back and forth before the bench, speaking quietly, until he'd finished the story. Then he slumped down beside Stewart, staring out at the river, afraid to look over at his friend and professor—afraid he'd see nothing but disbelief in his dark eyes.

George sat in silence for a minute, then cleared his throat. "A rat," he said. "A *whole* rat?"

"Big one." Pete measured off an eight-inch space between his fingers, then gulped. Relating the incident had made him almost as nauseous as he'd been that night.

"Pete, are you *sure*? You said it was dark. Maybe you thought you saw—"

"No," Forsythe interrupted, leaning forward intently. "I saw it, Doc."

"I believe you."

Pete's voice was rough with emotion. "Thanks. I appreciate it. What kind of creatures do you think they are?"

Stewart shrugged thoughtfully. "I might be inclined to say they're just people with weird eating habits—"

Forsythe gave him a dubious look.

"Except for that part about the jaw detaching and your being able to see the bulge the animal made as it went down the throat. You say the alien didn't chew the food?"

"Not at all."

"Well, forgetting for a moment how disgusting the idea is of gulping live animals, let's look at it anatomically. No creature with mandibular construction like ours can dislocate its jaw with that kind of motion. It's anatomically impossible. So they may *look* like us, but—" His voice trailed off. The implication was clear.

"I forgot to mention one thing," Pete said. "Just as it opened its mouth at the widest, I thought I saw something inside that . . . Well, it was narrow and slithery, not a human tongue. And there seemed to be a second set of teeth *behind* the human ones they let us see."

"That's even stranger." Stewart thought for long moments. "This just doesn't add up at all."

"Well, one thing we know. They're somehow a lot more different than they're letting on. Why?"

"To quote one of the illustrious security employees at the Medical Center, 'I ain't Dick Tracy,'" Stewart said.

"What's that mean?"

"Well, there's a story I'd better tell *you*, Peter."

When Stewart was done recounting the details of Mary Chu's detective work and subsequent disappearance, Pete sat silently in turn.

"Hmm," he said at last. "Obviously she discovered something about their skin that must have been a real giveaway. And somehow they must've known she had 'em pegged. So they grabbed her."

"Looks like."

"Could they have tapped into the phone call? Or followed her?" Pete wondered.

"I don't know. If they can travel through interstellar space, they can probably wiretap."

"We'll have to be careful," Pete said. "No phone calls from now on. And we talk outside, if at all possible." He glanced around nervously.

"Let's not get paranoid, Peter. I think if we take reasonable precautions, we'll be fine."

"I hope you're right, Doc. Couldn't stand to lose the best anatomy prof I ever had."

"Bucking for an A, are you?"

Pete looked at him directly. "Bucking to keep you around."

Stewart snorted derisively. "Me? If some people are being removed because they're somehow imagined to be security risks or threats to the Visitors, why pick on me? *I* haven't attended any of their briefings or lectures. I haven't asked any embarrassing questions. Nothing subversive to nail me on."

"You hit on the key—*imagined* security risk," Pete said. "These people did *something* that someone *thought* made them dangerous. Who the hell knows what that something is?"

"Don't speculate wildly, Peter."

"You knew Mary Chu—"

Stewart winced. "Please don't use the past tense."

"I'd rather not, Doc, but we better be realistic. Until people like Mary start turning up again, we can't assume they're going to. You knew Mary, and she's gone. Whatever the reasons they took her away, they could stretch those reasons to include *you*."

Stewart ran his hands distractedly through his wiry salt-and-pepper hair. "This is so crazy! *They* took her away . . . Who the hell *are* they, for God's sake?"

"I don't know," said Pete. "I ain't Dick Tracy either."

Chapter 8

"I Suggest a New Strategy . . ."

A tenacious sun had warmed Washington to an unseasonable sixty-eight degrees, and President Morrow closed his eyes against the afternoon brightness, turning his face up to the warmth. The breeze gently riffled his hair as he stood on the White House lawn with Secretary of State Nicholas Draper and Secretary of Defense Farley Mason. After a few minutes, all three men were wishing they hadn't worn dark-blue suits.

Morrow shaded his eyes as he scanned the unrelieved blue of the sky—still no sign of the Visitor squad vehicle that must at this moment be speeding toward him, bearing Roger, Angela, Secretary General Olav Lindstrom, and his special assistant, Lauren Stewart, to this meeting. Morrow wondered if John would accompany them—when Roger had requested the meeting, he'd mentioned that he was acting on the Supreme Commander's orders.

The President glanced over at the cabinet members who had also been requested—by name—to attend. He tugged at his shirt collar with one finger, wishing he could loosen his tie. Why these two particular cabinet officers?

He'd known Farley Mason since the war, when they'd served in the Air Corps together. "Moose" Mason and "Wild Bill" Morrow—the President smiled at the memory; they'd made quite a pair—had some wild times together, both in flight and on the ground. He'd always admired Farley for his cool under pressure and his tenacious refusal to take no for an answer—unless it was the answer he wanted to hear. Depending on who you asked, that quality either made Mason one of the most successful businessmen in the world or one of the most impossible hard-asses you'd ever meet. Morrow suspected both views were true. And both qualities were useful in his job.

His business success had made him an able administrator. He'd worked his way up from a junior engineer's drafting table to chairman of the board of United Aerospace International. During his tenure, UAI had grown from a single small California plant making parts for airplane engines to a billion-dollar conglomerate.

Mason also had an extensive background in world and military history—something Morrow found very reassuring. A man who claimed a thorough familiarity with history's mistakes might stand a better chance of not repeating them.

Physically, Farley was heavier today than when he'd had to fold his lanky frame into the cockpit of his B-17. He was bald now, making his hawk nose—broken once in a tavern brawl—even more prominent. Coincidentally, his nose declared his stance on defense policies. His bright blue eyes squinted behind photo-gray glasses.

In contrast, Secretary of State Nicholas Draper was barely as tall as Morrow's shoulder, and was much more of an enigma to the Chief Executive. He'd chosen this dapper Virginian on multiple recommendations, Draper having served in various capacities in two previous administrations. He had friends in both parties and seemed to have managed the near-miraculous feat of making not a single enemy. The expansive, bluff Morrow had been put off at first by the relaxed country-squire attitude and the cultured drawl, but in the three years they'd worked together, the President had learned to appreciate Draper's calm voice. It was often the only one in the crowd.

While other advisers offered passionate policy positions calculated at least partly to protect their own posteriors, Nick Draper never seemed to worry about protecting his image. Maybe that was one of the reasons he didn't have to protect it: *It's easier to tell the truth, Billy,* Morrow remembered his mother saying, *than to keep track of a pack of lies.* At any rate, the President had learned to trust the little man, with his well-cut suits and wavy grayish-blond hair as much as anyone he'd ever known.

Morrow was roused from his musings when a young Marine guard said quietly, "Over there, Mr. President."

He followed the white-gloved hand as it pointed east. In the distance, the Visitor squad ship gleamed white. Its speed was deceptive. One moment it was a distant glimmer; the next, it settled soundlessly onto the manicured White House lawn.

The hatch opened and the Marine band struck up ruffles and flourishes as a pair of guards efficiently rolled out a red carpet. The throng of reporters who stood several yards away behind velvet ropes began a whispered babble of note-taking comparisons to the accompaniment of the clicking and whirring cameras.

Morrow stepped over to the carpet, stretching out his hand to Roger. He'd met John during the first weeks of the Visitor goodwill tours, but this was his first encounter with the New York ship's Commander. "Welcome to the White House, Commander," the President said. He introduced his cabinet officers, then Roger introduced his second-in-command, Angela. Morrow eyed her and Lauren Stewart appreciatively, thinking that they certainly provided a refreshing change from the usual male-dominated political encounters. The party started across the lawn to the White House.

Morrow guided them directly to the Cabinet Room, skimping on the amenities but knowing from experience that the Visitors would politely refuse both food and drink. Besides, he wanted to find out the reason for the meeting——Roger and Angela looked very sober, almost grim.

They took seats around the dark-wood oval table. A secretary sat unobtrusively in the corner, preparing to take notes. "Mr. President," said Roger, "should a minor staff member be present?"

Morrow eyed him, then smiled, but his voice was firm. "With all due respect, Commander, I would have notes taken of any meeting with any highly ranked representative of a foreign power. That's the way we do things here, sir."

Roger nodded. "Of course. Well, gentlemen and Ms. Stewart, we're all busy people, so why not get right to the point?"

"Fine," Morrow said, watching him alertly. "Go right ahead."

The Visitor solemnly folded his hands on the polished wood. "We have grave concerns about the smooth progress of our cooperative chemical processing project."

"What kind of concerns?" asked Nick Draper softly. He took out a pipe, eyed it wistfully, then contented himself with twirling it in his fingers.

"Security concerns. Angela has been monitoring certain of your scientists, based on information provided to us—"

"Monitoring?" asked Morrow sharply. "What do you mean, monitoring? We have laws against illegal surveillance in this country, Commander, and as long as you people are our guests, you will observe those laws."

"We didn't mean to imply surveillance," Angela said quickly. "We're still not as precise with your language as we'd like to be, Mr. President. Please allow me to explain. Our information has all come from indirect sources—reported to us by some of your top scientists. They've told us that there is a growing conspiracy among certain of their colleagues to disrupt our operations worldwide."

Morrow narrowed his eyes at Roger, recalling how Lyndon Johnson used to intimidate people with a flinty glare. "This is an incredibly serious charge you're making."

The Commander's green eyes never wavered. "We're fully aware of that, President Morrow. We're not making these charges lightly."

"You're talking about something tantamount to treason," Farley Mason said, beating a virtually soundless drumroll with his fingertips. "If such a conspriacy actually existed, it would be in complete disregard of publicly stated U.S. policy, which is to cooperate with you Visitors."

"Well, in most cases we've been getting complete cooperation," Roger said. "And even now that this has surfaced, we're sure it's just a small number of individuals who are involved."

"We just thought it would be prudent," added Angela before anyone else could speak, "to take care of the situation before it grew to serious proportions and could potentially destroy all the goodwill between our peoples."

"And what, in your opinion, would be necessary to resolve this situation?" asked Morrow, though he had no intention of taking the Visitor leader's word at face value. NSA, CIA—

none of the internal security agencies had reported even a hint of any of this.

"Something very simple," said Roger with a reassuring smile. "Angela, would you describe our plan, please?"

She nodded. "We suggest that scientists and members of their immediate families should register their whereabouts with local government authorities. We would then have their names, addresses, and a few minor demographic details, as well as their chosen scientific fields. If they moved about, they'd simply keep these same authorities informed so they could be located if necessary. Your scientists have advised us that you have the technology to do this—that a similar system exists for military registration of young males. If you would like, we'd be happy to assist your computers by allocating storage space in our own banks."

Morrow leaned forward, trying, not with complete success, to hide the cold fury he felt. "You're talking about police-state tactics. I don't know how you run things on *your* world, but here in America, we don't do things that way."

"Oh, Mr. President," Angela put in helpfully, "we've done some research, with the help of your Library of Congress, and there *is* a precedent for this sort of thing. During your World War Two, the United States government interned Americans of Japanese descent, stripping them of their possessions, and placing them into camps behind barbed-wire fences. That action was much more stringent than the simple precautionary listings we're requesting."

Morrow cast a glance of disbelief at the human occupants of the room. Even his normally imperturbable secretary was staring at the Visitors. He turned back to Roger, who was still smiling. "The internment of the Japanese citizens," Morrow said tightly, "was one of the most shameful episodes in our entire history. Such an event will never be repeated in this country, not while *I'm* President."

Roger's assured smile began to fade. Morrow shook his head at the Visitor. "Frankly, Commander, I can't imagine that there is any organized opposition to your presence, but I *will* have our own intelligence agencies look into this . . . theory of yours. *If* they can corroborate what you're saying, I'll let you know, and we'll discuss potential security measures again. But as for requiring registration of every scientist in America . . ." Morrow trailed off, too angry to continue. The only words that were occurring to him in regard to the Visitors' request were short and to the point—most consisting of a mere four letters. They were definitely unsuitable for use in diplomatic relations.

Roger glanced at Angela. "We regret that you feel this way, Mr. President . . ."

Before the Visitor leader could continue, Olav Lindstrom, who had remained silent until now, cleared his throat for attention. "Mr. President," he said. "May I please speak with you privately for a moment?"

"Of course, Mr. Secretary General," Morrow said, pushing back his leather chair. "In my office, if that's acceptable?" At Lindstrom's nod, he ushered the UN representative ahead of him, turning back at the door to address Mason and Draper. "Gentlemen, I'd appreciate it if you'd spend the time enlightening our honored guests about civil liberties in this nation."

"Well, what did you want to discuss?" Morrow asked impatiently once in the Oval Office. He'd never been terribly fond of Lindstrom, with his pleas for caution and patience in international relations.

"Mr. President, I beg you to consider what they ask. If that is impossible, I ask you to at least *seem* to consider it politely."

Morrow sat down on the corner of his desk, his arms folded. "Lindstrom, have you lost your mind? Did they discuss any of this with you before you came here this afternoon?"

"Angela told me, in a private conference during the flight here this afternoon. It's not just the United States, you know. They believe this conspiracy may be spreading all over the world. It wouldn't be the first time scientists linked up to oppose policies put forth by their governments."

Morrow shook his head in amazement. "Do I have to remind you that citizens of free countries are *allowed* to express their disapproval of government policies without being tossed into concentration camps? Even Russian scientists can oppose their government—if they don't mind rotting in a gulag when they're finished speaking out."

Lindstrom sighed. "Mr. President, no one is talking about sending scientists to prison camps. All the Visitors are asking for is a simple registration process."

"And if we comply with this, curtail legally guaranteed civil liberties on the whim of creatures from another star, what'll we do when they ask for another favor—and continue escalating their demands?"

"But they *aren't* demanding, sir," Lindstrom said, his tones level. "As I see it, that's all to their credit. They are *asking* us to consider their legitimate concerns."

Morrow snorted. "Legitimate? This is the first I've heard of any so-called conspiracy. Have they shown you more concrete proof than they've shown me?"

"No," Lindstrom admitted. "But they've given us no reason to distrust them. They've been honest with us."

"As far as we know," Morrow said flatly. "And that's not too far, my friend."

Lindstrom considered for a moment. "Mr. President, I must remind you that they possess the military strength to take whatever they want from this planet. They could enslave or kill every human on the face of the earth. You Americans have no idea what it's like to deal from a position of weakness—having to step gingerly so as not to offend or provoke a power that could crush you if it chose to. We Swedes have had a little more experience at that than you have."

"Are you calling us arrogant, Mr. Secretary General?"

"Not arrogant—naive. I command no great armies, as you do. I am not a head of state. But my position gives me responsibilities in dealing with the Visitors that supersede even your own. I am responsible for *presenting* a united world front—even if that unity is not a reality. I represent the entire planet when I speak with Roger or John. It is my job to meld the differing opinions of world leaders into some kind of coherent policy, and then to negotiate our policy with these Visitors."

Lindstrom ran a hand through his thick white hair. "It is not easy or simple, my task. I have tried to minimize the conflicts as completely as possible. To do that, I recommend that the world cooperate with the Visitors."

"Cooperate with them—or appease them?" asked Morrow pointedly.

Lindstrom ignored the question and its implication. "I agree that we should not go along with these security proposals simply on the Visitors' request. We must have additional proof that such a conspiracy does, in fact, exist. But I ask you, Mr.

President—for the good of the entire world, not just your country—to keep an open mind. *If* they are telling the truth, this registration plan may become a necessary thing."

"All right, Mr. Secretary," Morrow said. "You and I haven't always seen eye to eye. But I trust your integrity enough to withhold final judgment. *If* our own sources come up with proof, I'll consider—*consider*—the registration plan."

"Thank you, Mr. President."

When Morrow and Lindstrom returned to the Cabinet Room and announced the results of their discussion, Angela's face clearly betrayed her dissatisfaction, but Roger was quick to put the best light on matters.

"I only hope you're right, Mr. President," he said, "and this turns out to be undue concern over nothing. That certainly would make our important work proceed much more quickly and easily."

Morrow nodded, spoke a curt farewell, and retreated to the Oval Office. With the meeting over, Secretary General Lindstrom and Lauren Stewart went out to the White House limousine that was standing by, ready to take them to their hotel. The two were staying over to testify before congressional committees the next day. Nick Draper headed for his Foggy Bottom office to direct the intelligence agencies to investigate the Visitor allegations of a scientists' conspiracy. Farley Mason was left to escort the Visitors back across the White House lawn to their squad vehicle.

As they approached the sleek little flyer, Mason expressed interest in its propulsion system. Roger smiled. "I expected that you'd find our vehicle of interest, Secretary Mason. You and President Morrow were both pilots during the war, weren't you?"

"If you don't mind my being direct—" Mason gestured at the white craft, "how the hell does this thing fly without having propellers or a jet or rocket engine? And it barely makes a sound."

"Direct questions are your specialty, aren't they, Mr. Secretary?" Roger asked, smiling casually. "I'll answer yours if you'll answer mine."

" 'Bout what?"

"I must admit that our Moscow ship is having some difficulty dealing with your counterparts in the Soviet Union. I promised the Supreme Commander that I would consult you about them. Apparently you are a man much respected— perhaps even a bit feared—in the Russian hierarchy. It would be of great help if we could get your advice, since you are acknowledged as the foremost expert in peacefully coexisting with a nation that can be—how shall I put it?—a bit exasperating?''

Mason chuckled. "So you want a crash course in dealing with the bear," he said.

Roger blinked. "The bear?"

The Secretary of Defense laughed at the Visitor's expression. "That's our not-so-affectionate nickname for the Soviets. In political cartoons, Russia is often represented as a big bear. Well, Commander, I think we *can* make a trade here. I'll give you a few pointers on dealing with Krasinsky and his crowd if you'll give an old flyboy a ride in this fancy little buggy of yours.''

A Marine guard whispered to the Secretary, but he waved the sergeant away impatiently. "No, I don't need a helicopter escort. Besides, these little buggies can outrun anything we've got short of a rocket, from what I understand. I'll be okay.''

He turned back to Roger. "You've hit me in a weak place, Commander—if I'd been born twenty years later, I'd have tried for the space program, and the hell with business or politics.''

"If that's the case, Mr. Secretary," Angela said, "we have some business to take care of aboard the Washington ship. Would you like a tour after our ride?''

Mason nodded. "Have somebody call my wife and tell her not to wait dinner," he instructed the Marine. Turning to Angela, he nodded. "Let's go.''

Roger gestured toward the open hatch. "Sit up front with me, Mr. Secretary. I'll take the controls.''

Mason climbed into his seat. "I've got to tell you in all honesty, though, I think this whole conspiracy thing is a bunch of malarkey.'' He chuckled as he fastened the safety harness. "The President doesn't like it much when I talk that bluntly, but I believe in just laying things out the way I see 'em.''

"Well," said Roger, easing forward on a lever, "I appreciate that. I want you to feel free to be as honest as possible with us. But while we're aboard the Mother Ship, we'll show you some of our proof.''

Mason laughed. "Okay. The proof of the pudding is always in the eating." He watched the ground fall away with the speed of a jet plane—but with none of the noise and only a fraction of the G-stress. "Who knows? Maybe you'll convince me."

Angela smiled warmly. "I think we may just do that. As a matter of fact, I'm virtually *certain* of it . . ."

Chapter 9

"I Never Knew There'd Be Days Like These . . ."

Peter Forsythe carefully moved a couple of textbooks and placed a cup of coffee onto the end table, then slumped onto his living room couch, thumbing the "on" button of his television's remote control. The screen flickered, then Dan Rather's image appeared. "Okay, lay it on me," Pete muttered, bracing himself for whatever new world crisis or atrocity was making today's headlines.

"Good evening," said the anchorman. "Major new developments today in the continuing story of the Visitors' tenure here on Earth . . ."

Pete sat up so suddenly he had to steady his cup of coffee. He turned the volume up. "In Brussels today, serious accusations were leveled against members of the world's elite scientific community. Nobel Prize winner Doctor Leopold Jankowski of the Brussels Biomedical Institute held a press conference and said he'd been approached to join a conspiracy including many of the world's leading biologists, physicians, and other life-science researchers to undermine Visitor activities here on Earth. Their ultimate goal, according to Jankowski—to seize control of several Visitor Mother Ships."

"Holy shit!" Pete said.

Rather's image was replaced with a videotape of Dr. Jankowski, a stern-looking man in his forties, whose face was strobed by camera flashes as reporters clustered before his podium. "They tried hard to convince me," he said in precise but accented English, "that their goal was to protect the human race. I do believe, however, that their motivation was far more personal . . ."

Rather narrated over footage of Jankowski answering shouted inquiries, reading his prepared statement, then signing it. "Jankowski's sworn statement named twenty-four individuals as being involved in the plot, all prominent scientists from various parts of the world. Many of them have now been detained by local authorities in their home countries. Some of those questioned voluntarily confessed to having been approached by colleagues or to being part of the conspiracy themselves—confirming Jankowski's allegations. The Visitors were unavailable for comment, but their press secretary, Kristine Walsh, did read this statement from the Supreme Commander, John."

A sober-faced Walsh appeared on screen. "The Visitors were shocked to learn of this conspiracy, and fearful of the chaos that could possibly result. Not only would their own plans be threatened, but also all the benefits they intend to share with us."

"Definitely how to win friends and influence people," Pete muttered. "Talk about blackmail . . ."

The entire world scientific community exploded in a barrage of accusations, denials, and counteraccusations. The continuing disappearances of valuable researchers and life-science specialists baffled police departments flooded by so many missing-persons reports they were unable to keep up. Many of the missing were among those implicated by Jankowski or other prominent scientists as part of the alleged conspiracy. Their disappearances often were taken as tacit admissions of guilt.

Denise Daltrey was at her CBS desk when Winston Weinberg dropped by. Her producer's droopy moustache was even more scraggly than usual, as though he'd been gnawing at its edges. "Hi, Dee," he said, his voice booming jovially but with no accompanying smile. Instead, he reached for a yellow legal pad and began to write.

Denise eyed him, then as he gave her a meaningful look, began a lively (and untruthful) account of her latest tennis lesson and the after-practice dinner and evening sports she and her pro had enjoyed. Weinberg scribbled for several minutes, then shoved the pad at Denise. While she read, he regaled her with an endless story about his battles with several credit card companies over his ex-wife's expenditures. Denise already knew that his wife was vacationing in Jamaica at the moment—and that her family was independently wealthy.

The note read:

> *"We've been ordered to play down civil liberties angle on scientists' conspiracy investigations. Congress just proposed registration of all scientists and their families. Info to be entered in Visitor computers. Secretary of Defense Mason says registration is 'essential to internal security and defense welfare.' If damned Congress votes for special act, Morrow'll veto it, of course. I can't believe the support this idiotic notion's gained. Overnight! The stuff is definitely hitting the fan, babe."*

"Well," Weinberg said aloud, standing up and sauntering to the door, "you know what I'm gonna tell MasterCard to do with their twenty percent interest charges?"

Denise shook her head as she hunted for matches and an ashtray. "What, Winnie?"

"I'm gonna do what they tell me and pay it, of course," he sighed. "But I'm gonna hate every minute. I don't know what this world is coming to."

"Yeah," said Denise after he'd left, "I don't know either."

On orders from the White House, the FBI and CIA began investigating the files of scientists accused of belonging to the conspiracy. In many cases, they found evidence of secret meetings, slush funds, arms purchases, and other ominous activities supporting the Visitor claim.

Kristine Walsh made a sorrowful statement to the effect that, as a result of the conspiracy, the Visitor scientific seminars would have to be postponed indefinitely . . .

Peter Forsythe rushed home after a day of clinic rounds and lectures, afraid he'd miss the evening news. His stomach rumbling, he dashed into the living room to turn on the television, his mind churning with more than hunger. *It can't be*, he thought. *I didn't hear right* . . . He'd caught the tail end of a radio report just as he'd left the hospital.

Dan Rather was in midsentence: ". . . with mounting evidence of a scientists' conspiracy and yesterday's discovery of weapons caches for forceful takeovers of Visitor shuttles, Congress has again voted for a special act requiring registration of all scientists and their families, overriding the veto of President Morrow. The President said he would appeal for a special ruling by the Supreme Court. In the meantime, registration procedures will commence the first of next week. We'll have a special report analyzing this new legislation and its effect on the public tonight at eleven-thirty Eastern time. Standing by in Washington, we have UN Secretary General Olav Lindstrom, who presented the Visitor request to world governments. We've asked him to explain more about this unprecedented development, which was set in motion under the auspices of the United Nations."

Rather turned toward a large monitor behind him, where Lindstrom appeared onscreen. The UN official looked weary but calm—almost resigned.

"Is it true that no country has refused to cooperate?"

"Yes. We've been fortunate that all our member nations, plus several nonmember nations, have seen the pressing need for a united front in this matter of world security."

"Jesus!" Pete shook his head. "What's been going on these last two weeks? Has everyone gone fuckin' *crazy*?" He thought about calling Dr. Stewart, but the screen held him nearly mesmerized with shock.

"Mr. Secretary General, you conferred with the President yesterday and congressional leaders today," Rather said, his dark brows furrowed in a near frown. "This development seems awfully sudden. Was this possibility of registration discussed previously with the Visitors?"

Lindstrom adjusted his small earphone. "Uh, yes, Mr. Rather. Just as a contingency. You see, the Visitors had some prior information pointing to this sort of thing around the world."

"Was the registration plan previously discussed with heads of state to see if they would agree?"

Lindstrom nodded. "Yes, it was. My staff and I held exploratory discussions with the major powers to stress the need for cooperation and a united front so that if the conspiracy proved to be a reality, those involved would know they had no place to hide."

Rather hunched his shoulders and his voice took on a sharper edge. "About the proof allegedly uncovered by security agencies . . . Was anything discovered beyond circumstantial evidence? Actual subversive activities? Or threatening incidents?"

Lindstrom balked for a moment and Rather prodded him. "Generally, and this opinion was echoed by many civil liberties authorities we contacted, truly hard evidence would be needed for such a radical step to be taken—something beyond simple accusations and lists of names. Does such evidence exist?"

"Go get 'im, Dan," Pete growled. "This whole thing is the biggest frame I ever saw!"

"We discovered a weapons cache that had been cited in one of the confiscated files from an implicated scientist," Lindstrom said, a trifle on the defensive.

Rather leaned forward. "Did you yourself see this weapons cache?"

"Well, no . . . It was discovered by Visitor troopers patrolling outside one of their plants." He shook his head. "Mr. Rather, I assure you there is no subterfuge here. Evidence has been gathered all over the world, based on information from scientists who have talked with authorities."

"Have you seen that evidence, sir?"

"Well, no—not yet. I was busy coordinating the registration procedures with many, many governments around the world."

"Then how do you know it exists?"

"It is being gathered and will be presented all at once," said Lindstrom. "There will be no doubt of its authenticity."

"Is it being gathered by our authorities and police agencies or by the Visitors themselves?"

"I believe it is a cooperative effort, just as we and the Visitors have been cooperating on their chemical manufacturing since their arrival. But if your implication is that we are no longer in charge of our own planet, I must deny that vigorously, Mr. Rather," Lindstrom said, clearly growing agitated.

"He'll deny it," Pete snapped at the TV, "even if it's true."

"Certainly I didn't mean to imply that, Mr. Secretary," said Rather, polite but without a conciliatory smile, lips set in a grim line. "We'll leave any interpretation to our viewers. Thank you for joining us, sir—"

Pete was already dialing his phone on the end table. "Come on, Doc, answer it," he grumbled as it rang. Finally, he heard George Stewart's voice.

"Hello?"

"Doc, Pete Forsythe here. Were you watching the news?"

"Yeah."

"Do you believe it? Well, I sure don't," Pete said, without waiting for a reply to his question. "Let's talk about this. The park, same bench, A.S.A.P."

Stewart sounded weary. "All right."

When they met, the two men shook hands, then sat down. Pete made a sudden, explosive gesture.

"It's a giant setup. A spider's web—and *you* could be one of the next flies."

"But why me?" protested Stewart.

"How the hell should I know? Who says there's any pattern to it? It just stands to reason that if other people at the hospital have disappeared, none of you are safe."

"Pete, why are you getting mixed up in this?"

"Because if I'd finished med school the first time around, instead of playing a little kid's game for obscene amounts of money, *I* could be the next person vacuumed off the face of the earth."

"You have something in mind?"

"Yes, I do, Doc. It sounds to me like, if the Visitors are—ahem—*cooperating* with local police, they could be planting incriminating evidence." Pete listened to the long silence from Stewart's end of the dark bench. "You think I'm crazy."

"No, not crazy, Peter. Just imaginative. Look, if they were going to go to that trouble, why have Mary Chu up and disappear? Why not plant something in her files and pull that rabbit out of the hat right away?"

"I don't know. Maybe I'm wrong. But I'd rather be safe than sorry. I think we should search your files to see if they've planted anything incriminating."

"All right, Pete. Let me think it over—sleep on it—and maybe in the morning we'll do that."

"I'd feel better doing it tonight," Pete warned.

"I think it would arouse more suspicion to try anything tonight. First thing tomorrow," Dr. Stewart said firmly.

Pete snorted in frustration. "Okay. Morning. Early. Good night, Doc."

As he left the park, Pete said a silent prayer that Stewart would still be *around* in the morning.

His fatigue had sent George Stewart into a deep doze, but the ringing phone shook him back to alertness. He leaned across the bed and picked up the receiver.

"Hello . . ."

"Hi, Dad. I just wanted to let you know I was home."

Stewart smiled softly. "Hi, baby. Glad to hear your voice."

At the other end, Lauren felt her father's affection radiating through the phone, even more surprising because he sounded sleepy. It made her smile too. "Why? Did you have a tough day?"

Stewart hesitated for a moment. "Uh, no. By the way, did you catch any local news reports tonight?"

"No, I literally just walked in the door, and we were pretty busy in hearings on the Hill all day today. We had a quick dinner after Olav did that interview with Dan Rather, then hopped on a plane, and here I am."

"Lauren, did you have anything to do with this registration thing?"

"What do you mean, did I have anything to do with it?"

"Whose idea was it?"

"It was the Visitors' idea, Daddy. Why—what's wrong?"

"I don't like it, honey. It makes me *very* nervous."

"Dad, I have to trust Olav's judgment that it'll be all right. It's just a precaution. People who haven't done anything wrong don't have anything to worry about. Believe me, Secretary of State Draper and Secretary of Defense Mason weren't overly enthused about the idea. So if they agreed to go along with it, there's nothing to worry about." She hesitated. "I hope. I know there are safeguards built in to prevent abuse. And *we'll* be administering the whole program here on Earth, under UN auspices—not Visitor auspices. *I* bucked for that, and won."

"Well, maybe you're right, honey. Maybe there's nothing to

worry about. I hope so. But you must be tired—I know I am.
I'll talk to you tomorrow."

"G'night, Daddy."

"Night, baby."

Peter Forsythe jumped out the rear door of the northbound
M31 bus as it pulled over to the curb on York Avenue. He
sprinted up the hospital driveway and skidded to a stop on the
wet, frosty grass as he spotted the Visitor squad ship parked in
front. Then he saw Dr. Stewart coming out of the building
toward him.

"There's something in the auditorium I think you should
see," Stewart said grimly as they met. "Hurry up, Pete—it's
starting now."

The large room was set up for a press conference, with about
fifteen print-media reporters and a smattering of radio and
television crews hovering expectantly about. Pete and Dr.
Stewart stood at the back of the room, joining at least thirty
white-coated hospital personnel as a female Visitor stepped up
to the bank of microphones. They recognized her as Angela,
Roger's top aide. She was flanked by several other Visitors and
by uniformed and plainclothes police, as well as some FBI
agents.

"Ladies and gentlemen," she said crisply. "As you know,
recent news stories reported the disappearance of one of your
colleagues, a Doctor Mary Chu, held in high esteem by many
of you. As often happens when you think you know someone
well, it's hard to believe he or she could be involved in
anything sinister."

A low buzz of disbelieving comments filled the room, and
Angela paused. She continued: "We also preferred to believe
that she and other scientists were not involved in any way in
undermining Earth-Visitor cooperation. However, we have
called this press conference this morning to show you evidence
found in Mary Chu's files that she was indeed part of the now-
revealed conspiracy."

Pete glanced around to see audience members shake their
heads, wave their hands in denial, and grumble. He almost
laughed when he heard someone growl, in typically feisty New
York fashion, "So's ya muthuh, lady."

Angela nodded to a technician, who dimmed the lights and

turned on an overhead projector. On the screen, Angela pointed to slides of one document after another implicating Chu in the conspiracy.

"Your own police experts have examined these papers and verified Doctor Chu's handwriting all over them . . ."

"I've seen enough," said Pete under his breath. He headed for the nearest exit, and Stewart followed him out to the corridor.

"Let's go," said Pete.

"Where?"

"Upstairs to your office. We've gotta tear it apart for any garbage they might have hidden."

With a groan, Dr. Stewart surveyed the chaos that had been a neat office before Pete Forsythe started wrecking it. There were file drawers and piles of folders and papers on every raised surface, and most of the floor too.

"That's the last drawer," he said to Pete, who was leafing through every single sheet of paper.

"And things are always in the last place you look."

"Not if you don't find them *any*where," said Stewart, rubbing his eyes.

"And what if you do?"

"You *found* something?"

Pete held a sheaf of papers out to him. "You tell me."

Stewart flipped through them. "What the hell are these? I've never seen these before in my life."

"If you can't sound any more convincing than that, you haven't got a prayer, Doc," said Pete sourly.

"I *swear* it, Peter," Stewart exclaimed before realizing Pete wasn't serious. Or *was* he? Stewart took a deep breath.

"Okay, you were right. But I still don't understand. *Why me?*"

"You tell me, Doc. Suppose they somehow made Mary Chu talk. Did she tell you something she knew that they wouldn't *want* you to know?"

Stewart bit on his clenched fist, trying to think. "No, that couldn't be it."

"*What* couldn't?"

"What she was working on the night I came over here and

she was gone. But she never told me what her findings were. They went when she went."

"Maybe they didn't. Maybe she put something in here, just in case."

"But where? We turned the place upside down."

Pete's eyes closed as he rolled the phrase over and over. "Upside down . . . upside down . . ." He kneeled in front of a filing cabinet whose drawers had been removed. "Ah-ha!" he said, reaching up into the hidden inside top surface of the cabinet. He tugged at something taped to the metal and withdrew his hand, clutching a small manila envelope. Inside, he found some scribbled notes on an old prescription pad—and four glass slides in a protective wrapping.

Stewart's eyes opened wide. "The samples!" he said, voice hushed. "Let me see those . . ."

He took the envelope and contents from Pete, unfolded the top piece of paper, and read Mary Chu's last words: "Skin samples, extra set. Protect with your life. Love, Mary, M.D."

Stewart felt his eyes misting, and he wiped them.

"Well? What do we do with this?" asked Pete quietly. *I wonder if the office is bugged?* he thought. He motioned for silence, then turned the desk radio on, volume loud. "Whisper," he said.

Stewart understood the tactic. "We've got to get this stuff out of the hospital, that's for sure. Can't look at it here. Take it home with you—hide it. Come up to my house with it tomorrow. If I'm not there, if you can't find me, that means something's gone wrong—"

"I'll look for you."

Stewart shook his head emphatically. "*No!* If I'm gone, you take this by yourself to old Dr. Hannah Donnenfeld at Brook Cove Lab, out in Oyster Bay on Long Island. Tell her what we know. She'll know what to do with it. And if I do disappear, I want you to promise me something. I know you and Lauren aren't exactly best of friends, but keep in touch with her. She doesn't think she needs anybody, but *I* need to know there'll be somebody looking out for her if I can't." He grinned. "If you two really got to know each other, you'd be friends, you know."

Pete managed a smile. "I can just see the look on her face

once she gets wind of the fact that *I'm* looking out for her—even on her Dad's orders."

Stewart smiled too, and touched Pete's shoulder. "Thanks."

"But why are you being such a martyr, Doc? You should go into hiding someplace only Lauren and I know about. Go before they *take* you."

Stewart shook his head. "I can't, not today. I've got to check on Brenda Johnson's little boy, Gary. Maybe I will after tomorrow. They probably wouldn't risk anything this soon after making the accusations about Mary. They don't want to arouse suspicion."

"But—"

Stewart smiled faintly. "Pete, I have the feeling they could find me anywhere if they really wanted to, and if I did go someplace, I'd only endanger the people who were keeping me out of sight. The world won't stop. I've got students to teach here and patients to care for up in Harlem this afternoon. Don't worry about me—you just keep this safe." He patted the envelope, Mary Chu's legacy. "I'll see you tomorrow morning, eight o'clock sharp. Can you get up to Harlem that early?"

Pete nodded. "I'll be there—you just make sure *you* are." Impulsively, Pete hugged his teacher, then slid the envelope inside his briefcase and left the office.

Chapter 10

Spiderweb

Denise Daltrey looked tired, even for a person whose eccentric schedule had her up in the middle of the night and asleep when most people were just clearing away the dinner dishes. Behind the cameras and the blazing lights, the makeup man watched her on a monitor, fretting at the dark circles under her eyes and the puffiness below her jaw. And Winston Weinberg, perched on his stool just out of camera range, noticed and was not surprised that the liveliness in her voice was missing as she recapped the headlines during the morning show's final moments.

". . . and in one of the most shocking sidelights to the near hysteria surrounding the purported conspiracy, international police claim to have found evidence of suppressed scientific breakthroughs. Senate Medical Affairs Subcommittee Chairman Raymond Burke told newsmen—"

The technical director in the booth punched up the videotape, and the charmless, jowly face of the U.S. Senator appeared, a bit too close to the unflatteringly angled hand-held camera: "I have evidence that new and revolutionary cancer treatments *do* exist and *have* existed for some time, along with many other breakthroughs which our scientific friends apparently kept quiet about and haven't shared with us."

The monitor cut back to Denise's face, clearly displaying concern. "When asked why doctors would keep such secrets,

Senator Burke insinuated that—and I quote—'There's a lot of money to be made from research grants.'"

Denise leaned forward intently. "*Is* there any truth to such charges? What about the almost overnight groundswell of resentment aimed at scientists all over the world? We'll be examining those questions tomorrow on the Morning News. Until then, this is Denise Daltrey, still going solo. Have a good day," she concluded, without her usual smile.

The theme music came up, the logo and credits flashed on the air monitor screen, and Denise slowly removed the clip-on mike from her blazer lapel. When she knew the camera on the set had been turned off, she slid out of her seat and found Weinberg waiting for her at the rim of the brightly lit stage area.

"You're losing it, honey," he said.

"Losing what, Winnie?"

"Your objectivity. 'Insinuated' is not a neutral word. Be careful."

She shrugged. "I don't care. Nobody seems to be *listening* to anything—especially to objectivity. I see the same news reports and read the same headlines as everybody else, and I can't believe anybody could swallow this stuff. And they're not only swallowing it, they're eating it up with a spoon."

He reached over to rub her neck, and she leaned her head forward to enjoy the massage. "Not everybody is, Denise. There are a lot of good reporters, people who care. They're still trying to ask those questions, the ones you want to ask. They're still hoping someone'll listen."

"Want to bet on that?" asked Denise with a mirthless smile. "We're losing, Winnie. Every day, there's less truth and more propaganda. It's like a nightmare, and I want to wake up already. I'm getting real tired of it."

The phalanx of reporters surged toward the curb as Mayor O'Connor's slightly battered limo swung into the space in front of City Hall. The Mayor had the door open before the car had completely stopped. As he got out, the radio and TV reporters brandished their mikes like pistols while the print people held their minirecorders up over the crush. A few old-fashioned writers wielded notebooks and pens as questions were flung at the Mayor. He slammed the door shut and stood as tall as a short man could, feet planted wide apart, looking for all the world like John Wayne minus the six-gun.

"Do I believe it?" he began. "You mean, do I believe the *horse manure* being shoveled at us about scientists hiding cancer treatments from the world because they want more grants?"

The reporters laughed in spite of the tension and jostling. "Think about it, ladies and gentlemen—this shady cabal of studious men and women, plotting to overpower Visitors—big strong people armed very liberally with laser rifles—then flapping their arms and flying up to those Mother Ships and taking them over," he said, his voice heavy with sarcasm. "Have you ever heard anything more ridiculous in your *life*? Dumbest thing since Richard Nixon said, 'I am not a crook.' No, I do *not* like them being here. I don't like the way they've made themselves at home and redefined our civil liberties. Big favor they're doing us, sharing their so-called superiority with us. Democracy and human rights are what make us superior, and I have a question for the American people." For dramatic effect, he glared directly into a camera balanced on a shoulder, his finger wagging.

"Who are we going to believe—some mysterious beings from another planet, or the doctors and scientists who've served us and saved so many lives by pursuing knowledge all these years? Are we going to let them turn this world into one giant police state, spiriting our best minds away in the dark of night on the most transparent, trumped-up charges?"

With that, the Mayor churned his way through the crowd and strode up the steps into City Hall. Alison Stein was waiting for him but had to quick-march to keep up as he passed her like a freight train.

"Not everyone agrees with your opinion of the Visitors, you know, Danny," she said. "Please watch what you say!"

He whirled on her. "Do you? Whose side are you on, Ali?"

"Our side, Dan. I mean, if there *is* any side. All I'm saying is, maybe you should try not to offend so many people by shooting from the lip."

"Frankly, Ali dear, I don't give a shit who I offend. The Visitors? They can't vote, and if they're still here by next election, I'd just as soon not run. *You* want this stinking job? It'll be all yours."

He turned and headed for his office. Neither he nor Alison saw the male Visitor lurking in a dark corner of the foyer . . .

The cab let Peter off in front of Dr. Stewart's brownstone. The street was clean and quiet, with young stragglers leaving for school and adults heading for work. This was one of the solidly middle-class blocks that had survived the turmoil swallowing many surrounding Harlem streets. As the cab pulled away, Pete skipped up the steps to the door and pressed the buzzer. He frowned as he heard only silence inside, then buzzed again. He tried to peek in the window, but the drapes were drawn. He tried one last buzz, but Pete knew it was futile.

"Dammit," he hissed, shoving his bare hands deep into his coat pockets. He slipped the slim leather briefcase with Mary Chu's findings under his arm. It was freezing and he should have worn gloves. He also *shouldn't* have let Doc Stewart out of his sight. He went down the steps two at a time, almost bumping into a short black woman in a massive down coat.

"Excuse me," he mumbled. Then he brightened. "Do you know Doctor Stewart?"

"Yes, I do," she said. "I've lived next door for years."

"Have you seen him this morning? I was supposed to meet him here."

"As a matter of fact, I did see him, real early. He said he had to go down to the hospital where he teaches. Got a call telling him it was some kind of emergency. One of his patients, I think."

Pete bit his lip, then started backpedaling away from the woman out into the street. "Thanks," he called to her as he turned to frantically hail a taxi.

Pete sped through the lobby of the Medical Center at a dead run, leaping between the elevator doors just as they were closing. Despite the morning cold, he was sweating—he wasn't sure if it was the cold sweat of fear or perspiration from his charge across the hospital grounds. The door opened on Stewart's office floor and Pete catapulted himself out—then halted as he spotted a knot of men in front of Stewart's door. They looked like plainclothes cops, maybe a couple of three-piece-suited federal agents. And then he saw the unmistakable red coveralls of a pair of tall Visitor males.

Pete didn't know whether to continue his charge forward or switch to a hasty retreat. Indecision rooted him to his spot at the elevator until he saw Doc Stewart come out of his office accompanied by a cop and a Visitor. Though he wasn't handcuffed or restrained in any way, it was clear that this exit was not voluntary. *Now* Pete retreated around the corner of the midfloor nurses' station. The group took Stewart to the elevator. The black man's face was expressionless as he glanced in Pete's direction. Forsythe knew Stewart saw him, but the doctor's eyes revealed no hint that this sweaty, comparitively elderly medical student was anyone he knew. Pete stayed back until the elevator doors shut, then darted for the stairs and bolted down.

The elevator had already reached the lobby by the time Pete flung the stairwell door open and dashed outside. Stewart was being helped into a Visitor squad ship parked along the driveway. *Damn! How could I have missed seeing that ship before?*

Feeling totally helpless and very winded, Pete sagged to his knees as he watched the spaceship lift off, hover for a moment, then fly toward the Mother Ship hanging in the distance over Manhattan.

Slack-jawed, Pete felt his chest heaving as he tried to catch his breath. His mind reeled and staggered under the accumulated weight of what he'd witnessed these past few weeks. The only person who knew it all, who'd shared it with him and understood, was now a prisoner on an alien ship—at this moment being swallowed up by the giant vessel overhead. Pete couldn't look up anymore. His head drooped, his chin resting on his chest.

*Dammit! But we **found** the evidence they'd planted!*

Then he began to laugh bitterly. He wondered if the Visitors had even bothered to change the incriminating documents they'd put in place of those Pete and Stewart had removed, or just put copies of the same ones back again. Or did local authorities even require visible proof anymore?

*How do you fight people who can do anything they want, who make up the rules as they go, rules you've got to guess? And they're not even **people**. What in hell are they? What do they want?*

Clutching the slim leather briefcase under his arm, Pete got slowly to his feet. Favoring the pain in his side, he walked out onto York Avenue to look for a cab. He had to get away— before he did something crazy like scream in the middle of the street or shriek defiance at the nearest cop. He wanted to stop, to sit down on the nearest stoop and give way to the tears that were building up in his chest, but there was no time. He had to get the briefcase back home safely.

He didn't remember much about getting home, mostly because he didn't allow himself to think. One thing lodged in his mind, refusing to fade no matter what else he tried to think about—there was a bottle of vodka in the top cabinet. It almost seemed to talk to him, and he wanted to use it to dim the terrible bright edges of his sorrow. *Just one drink*, he told himself. *Just one . . . there's no harm in that . . . just one . . .*

His steps came faster and faster, and his mind flashed between images of George Stewart's face and the slides in his briefcase to the bottle that sat in his cabinet. By the time Pete was in the elevator on his way up to his apartment, he was shaking outwardly as well as inwardly. *What's happening to Doc now? How did they get Mary Chu to talk? Torture? Oh, God . . . why is this happening to us?*

He held on to himself long enough to nod hello to the man across the hall and find his keys. When he reached the inside of the apartment, he took the precaution of locking the slides in his concealed safe, then headed for the kitchen—and with the bottle in his hand, stopped.

Lauren. I promised Doc. She doesn't know . . . maybe she can get him free . . . He is her father, and she's got diplomatic connections with Roger . . .

He put the bottle down and picked up the telephone. Information gave him the number for the UN, and several minutes and operators later he'd located Lauren Stewart's number. The phone rang and was answered. "Lauren Stewart's office."

"Hello. This is Peter Forsythe. I'm a friend of George Stewart's . . . Can I speak with Ms. Stewart, please? Her father asked me to give her an important message."

The secretary sounded a trifle dismayed. "Oh, dear. Ms. Stewart went to Washington and Philadelphia for the day. She should be back in town tomorrow morning sometime. May I tell her you called?"

"Is there any way of reaching her? It's really important."

"I'm sorry, Mr. Forsythe. If she calls to check in, I'll give her your name and message, but I don't expect to hear from her. She's going straight from the congressional briefings to a governors' conference in Philadelphia."

"I see." Grimly, Peter gave the woman his number, then hung up. He picked up the bottle and a glass, and went into the living room. This time, he left the television off.

A bright light was spiking its way into his skull. Pete blinked, then wished he hadn't. He seemed to be in a place he'd never been before, but his entire body hurt so abominably that he didn't care *where* he was. He just wanted to drop back down that deep black well he'd fallen down, and stay there . . .

There was a sound. Regular, rasping, nasal. Somebody was snoring. Pete thought about it for a second, then decided it wasn't him—Jean had told him that was one of his best attributes as a husband—he did *not* snore.

The continuing buzz awakened him further, and he realized he was resting awkwardly on a hard surface. He moved his hand. Slick. Hard. Cold where his flesh hadn't warmed it. He stole a quick look from half-open eyes and saw marble. Marbled tiles in his bathroom.

A groan came up from somewhere deep inside him, and Pete tentatively let his awareness begin to extend outward—the light was from the fluorescent ceiling panels in his bathroom. It hurt to move his tongue. He was wearing damp shorts, sitting in his bathtub, and Joey Vitale was sitting on the bathroom carpet, slumped against the vanity, dozing. The place reeked.

I'm hung over, Pete thought. *I've been hung over before, but never like this* . . . His entire body ached the way it had when he'd been in the wreck that time. Had he wrecked his car? No, it gradually came back. He'd been in the living room, and there was a bottle on the end table, and Doc Stewart was gone . . .

He didn't have the faintest notion of when Joey had gotten there—his friend had a key to the apartment from when he'd watered the plants during one of Pete's longer trips.

"Joey," Pete said, and his tongue felt like a huge, inert

whale beached in his mouth. "Joey," he tried again, producing a sound that was nearly intelligible.

Joey stirred and his eyes opened. "Pete?" He saw his friend looking at him, and woke up immediately. "Pete, you okay? You damn near killed yourself!"

"What?" Pete didn't *think* he'd tried to commit suicide—although if he had the strength now, he thought he might try it. "What'd I do?"

"I came over about ten because you weren't answering the phone, and Alex wants us to meet with the kids tomorrow . . . I mean today. I was gonna leave you a note. I found you in the bathroom, passed out. When I tried to move you, you got real sick. I finally ended up puttin' you in the bathtub so I could rinse you off. Took me awhile to get the place cleaned up, then I sat here to make sure you didn't conk yourself on the head or something—guess I musta dozed off. You really scared me, Pete."

"Oh." Pete could envision what a repulsive object he must've made. If he'd had the energy, he'd have felt humiliated. "Joey," he said. "Thanks. Can you give me some water?"

"Sure," his friend said. "Drink it slow, Pete. You don't wanna puke again."

Forsythe's stomach muscles contracted in agony as he moved to sip the water. For a long while he felt the first tiny sip rebelling against its new home, but it finally reconciled itself to its fate. In slow sips, he drank the entire glass. It must have taken him thirty minutes.

He began to feel human enough to remember Lauren Stewart. She'd never called back. *He'd* have to call *her* again and arrange a meeting. *Oh, God, facing her in this condition?* It didn't bear thinking about. Pete had the uncomfortable certainty that Lauren had never been hung over in her life.

"What time is it?" he asked.

Joey checked his watch. "Seven-thirty."

Lauren probably wouldn't reach her office much before nine if she'd been traveling the previous day. Good. That gave him a couple of hours to try and pull himself together.

With Joey's help, Pete stood up and took a couple of salt tablets, a B-complex vitamin tablet, and a potassium tablet. He drank a small glass of V-8, pulled off his shorts, and turned on the shower.

By the time he was dressed and had nibbled at a piece of dry toast, he felt well enough to walk across his apartment unaided—but not much better than that. Joey looked at him soberly. "Pete, you know I'm not the kinda guy to preach. But you better let that stuff alone completely. If you'd been by yourself all night, you could have choked to death."

Pete nodded. "I know. Thanks, Joey. You're right. Don't let anybody ever tell you you're dumb, buddy. You got more smarts than most of us." He took a deep breath—it hurt—and said slowly, "I guess I had to have something this bad—this, and the car wreck—to convince me. I just can't handle the stuff." He raised his head slowly. "I'm an alcoholic, I guess. I *really am.*"

He'd said it out loud before, but never believed it. Now he felt a great wave of relief as well as panic at the thought of never taking another drink. *One day at a time,* he thought, remembering the advice of the counselor at the A.A. meetings Bobby Neal had insisted he attend. *One day at a time . . .*

Pete spotted Lauren in the stream of people flowing across First Avenue toward midtown. He planted the briefcase firmly under one arm, stepped out of the building shadow where he'd been waiting, and intercepted her at the corner. She eyed him with the barely civil coolness he'd come to expect from her. She seemed to have judged him for all eternity on the strength of past sins, and wouldn't admit any new evidence. But that didn't really matter now. What mattered was George Stewart.

"Mr. Forsythe," she said, greeting him with curt neutrality.

How appropriate for a diplomat, he thought. "Please— Pete," he said, trying to find a smile to melt some of the formality, and failing.

"Look, Mr. Forsythe, I'm very busy. You said you had something important to tell me. Could we get right to it?"

He abandoned his forced friendliness and grabbed her by the arm, a little more roughly than he'd intended. "Let's walk."

"Fine. Talk."

"It's about your father."

She tried to stop, but he pulled her along. "What about him? I just talked to him the night before last. Is something wrong?"

"Only if you consider his being dragged off by the police and taken away in a Visitor squad ship something wrong."

This time, Lauren halted, facing him squarely. "*What?* They took my father? On what charge?"

"I didn't know they needed one anymore," Pete said bitterly.

"Tell me what happened. All of it."

Pete limited his recounting of events to what he'd seen at the Medical Center yesterday morning, the actual abduction. By the time he was finished, they'd crossed back over to the UN side of First Avenue and found themselves on the promenade overlooking the East River.

"There's more you're not telling me," said Lauren firmly.

"What makes you so sure?"

"The look on your face the day you came to the hospital to talk to my father. You weren't there to discuss a test grade."

Pete looked away from Lauren and watched a tugboat slowly escorting an empty barge upriver. "Assuming I don't tell you any more, what are you going to do about it?"

"Contact Roger and clear up this obvious mistake."

"That's what I figured. How do I know I can trust you with the rest of it?"

Lauren yanked him by the sleeve, turning him so she could see his face. Her dark eyes were filled with anger. "What the hell do you mean by *that*? This is my *father* we're trying to get released from unwarranted custody."

Pete shook his coat free of Lauren's fingers. "No, Ms. Stewart. We're talking about a lot more. We may be talking about your father's *life,* and the lives of God knows how many other innocent people. We *may* be talking about our *freedom*."

"You're making this sound like a Robert Ludlum novel."

"I'm not making it sound like anything it isn't. Now, you promise me—*swear* to me—that anything I say will not go past you—not even to your boss, Lindstrom. And definitely not to any Visitor. Not to a single living soul."

Lauren stared at him for a long moment. She was wearing heels, and their eyes were nearly on a level. Slowly she reached up and removed Pete's sunglasses, her eyes studying him as he blinked in the onslaught of late November sunlight.

"You've been drinking, haven't you," she declared inexorably. "Are you sure you didn't just dream this all up during some episode of the d.t.'s?"

Peter stared at her for a long moment. "You have one of the nastiest natures of anyone I've ever met," he said slowly. "How a guy like your dad managed to have a daughter like you is beyond me. I oughta have my head examined for even dragging myself out to try and help you. Yeah, I was drinking—after I couldn't reach you. I was facing my last memory of your father's eyes when they took him away, so yeah, I got drunk. *So what?* That's my business."

He turned away. "Go to hell."

She caught him after a couple of strides. "Please! I'm sorry . . . *stop!*"

"Why should I?" Pete growled, still walking.

"Because I said I was sorry," she said. "I don't say that unless I mean it."

"All right." He slowed down, glanced over at her. "You promise?"

"I promise."

Pete started with the night at the armory, toning down the details a bit in deference to his own stomach. He told her everything else—from Mary Chu's disappearance through the planted evidence in her father's office to Dr. Chu's findings and Stewart's being hustled aboard the shuttle by the Visitor guards.

Lauren listened, wide-eyed and silent.

Pete held up his briefcase. "No one's seen Mary Chu's samples yet. I'm taking them out to a lab, to someone your father knows."

"Who?"

"I'm not going to tell you." She started to protest, but he cut her off. "It's not because I don't trust you. It's safer for everybody this way. If you don't know, you can't tell anyone even under duress."

Lauren made a skeptical face. "Under duress? What are they going to do, kidnap high-ranking diplomats now too? Look at this—I said 'too.' Now you've got *me* believing they intentionally kidnapped my father."

Pete was incredulous. "Hold on—you just listened to everything I said and you *still* think this was an honest mistake by the Visitors? Lady, it's about time you opened your eyes and looked around."

"At the world the way you see it? Paranoid, filled with people eating rats?"

Pete barely contained his anger. "Are you saying I'm lying?"

She softened slightly. "No, I'm just saying it's possible you've misinterpreted what you saw. We're dealing with aliens we don't know much about. Maybe there are reasonable, rational explanations for all this."

"And maybe there aren't. Your *father* believed everything I told you."

"Well, as he's not here to tell me himself, I'll withhold judgment on that. I'll get in touch with the Visitor high command today, and I'm sure this will all be straightened out in no time."

Pete glared at her. "So that's it?"

Lauren shrugged. "What did you expect? I'm not the kind to get hysterical. Except for being a little nauseous for a minute when you gleefully told me about the rat—"

"Gleeful? I didn't tell you *half* of it because I didn't want to make you sick."

"Well, thank you for the information on my father, Pete."

Lauren turned to walk away. Forsythe held her by the shoulder and slipped a business card into her hand. "I don't know why I'm giving you this, but here. Keep it, okay?"

She looked at it. "Your phone number?"

"Look, don't toss it, please. I want you to call me and let me know what you find out about your father."

Lauren considered him for a moment. "Okay. I'll call you."

"Thanks," he said coolly, leaning on the railing. He watched her walk away. He wasn't sure what made him angrier—her stubborn attitude or the fact that he'd lost his temper.

Chapter 11

Revelations

Lauren Stewart was grateful that she'd acquired a fair proficiency in dealing with computers as well as diplomats over the years. The fact that she had to confront Roger about her father was daunting enough. Underneath, she was far more distraught than she'd let on to Peter Forsythe.

But by now, sitting down in front of the newly installed computer terminal in her office and punching in to the corresponding set-up on the New York Mother Ship was pretty much second nature. Leaving word with her secretary that she was not to be disturbed, Lauren keyed in the contact code. After the requisite answers to a series of security-check queries, the green lettering on her monitor screen was replaced by an image from the Mother Ship. It was Jennifer, the quiet younger officer who was third in command behind Roger and Angela.

"Yes, Ms. Stewart," said Jennifer as Lauren's picture appeared on her own screen. "May I be of assistance?"

"Yes. I'd like to speak to Roger."

"I'm sorry, he's in a meeting now. Is it something I could help you with?"

Lauren really wanted to talk directly to the Commander.

"Do you know when he might be available?" she asked, sidestepping the other's question.

"No, I'm sorry, I don't. Is there a message you'd like me to relay to him? I'll see that he gets it as quickly as possible, and

I'm sure he'll respond the first chance he gets." Jennifer was trying very hard to be helpful.

"Well, I guess I'd better leave word then. This is *very* urgent. It seems my father, Doctor George Stewart, was taken away by police and some of your people this morning. He was taken to your ship. I would like him released as soon as possible—some sort of mistake has been made."

Jennifer looked genuinely apologetic. "I'm terribly sorry. I'm sure it *was* a mistake—perhaps they mistook him for someone else."

"I hardly think so," Lauren said stiffly.

"Well, there has been some confusion in these early stages of the registration procedure."

"This was not a registration, Jennifer," said Lauren tightly. "This was an unwarranted arrest."

"In any case, your father will be perfectly comfortable during his detention—" Jennifer saw storm clouds gathering in Lauren's eyes and she spoke rapidly, hoping to head off the imminent thunder. "And we'll have him released as soon as we've had a chance to investigate. I'll take your message to Roger myself and see that he handles it personally."

"Please ask him to contact me as soon as you give him the message. That way, I'll be sure he got it. I'll be at my office until about seven o'clock tonight." She paused for a meaningful beat. "I hope I won't have to wait that long to hear from him."

"I'm sure you won't," said Jennifer reassuringly.

"Thank you," Lauren said. The picture blanked out and the Visitor-installed computer screen asked, with a politeness matching Jennifer's careful phrasing, if any further tasks were required of it. Lauren tapped in "NO," and the machine turned itself off.

"She's getting suspicious," Angela said, her hands clasped on the tabletop in the briefing chamber.

Roger sat back, arms folded across his chest. "Was that your impression, Jennifer? You're the one who talked to Miss Stewart."

Jennifer brushed her auburn hair off one cheek as she sat tensely at the edge of her seat. "Not at this time, no. I'd say she was just angry that something unexplained like this could happen without cause, and concerned for her father's welfare."

"How touching," said Angela sarcastically. "We have cause, all right. This clever Doctor Chu had something very interesting to show him—samples of our skin. If our security team hadn't botched the assignment, we might have gotten Chu, Stewart, *and* all the samples."

"Are we sure we *didn't* get all the samples?" asked Roger.

"Sir," said Angela, her tone bordering on condescension, "Mary Chu was too intelligent to have made only one set of slides. It's likely that she anticipated our interference and hid another set—at *least* one additional set—where her friend, Dr. Stewart, would find them."

"Have you learned anything from him?"

"No, sir, not yet. But we'll increase the serum dosage as needed. We *will* get the information from him."

"Will he be harmed?" Jennifer asked, looking more at Roger than Angela. But Angela answered.

"And what if he is? What difference does it make? Minimal brain damage won't affect the man for *our* purposes."

Jennifer glared at her. "Is that *your* reply, Commander?" she said to Roger again. "Does that mean you have no intention of reuniting Doctor Stewart with Lauren?"

Roger raised his eyebrows noncommittally. "It's not a priority."

"Perhaps it should be," said Jennifer, mustering her confidence and steeling herself agaist a challenge from Angela.

"Oh? And why is that, Jennifer?" Angela asked contemptuously.

"Commander," said Jennifer, pointedly ignoring Angela, "Lauren Stewart is in a position to insure that the registration of scientists goes smoothly. She can also help with other procedures involving the UN and world governments. Olav Lindstrom delegates a great deal of responsibility to her—something Angela may not be aware of."

Roger suppressed a smile. He enjoyed seeing the more timid Jennifer emerge as strong enough to stand up to Angela. "Go on. I'm listening."

"She could *also* make things much more difficult for us. Unless we're ready to dispense with all pretense of cooperation, I'd suggest avoiding that."

"We will be soon," said Angela defensively.

"But we haven't yet," Jennifer parried.

"Well, if Lauren Stewart becomes a problem, she can simply disappear too," Angela concluded.

Jennifer smiled. She'd been counting on Angela's lack of imagination to back her into a corner. Jennifer calmly made her move. "I think she'd be much more useful to us if we cultivated her, kept her in her job at the UN—and then, perhaps, converted her. We'd have a powerful secret weapon."

Roger nodded. "Yes, we would. It's certainly a possibility worth considering. For now, then, I agree. Lauren Stewart must be placated. I'll take care of that myself." He pushed his seat back and stood, signaling that the meeting was over. "Thank you both for your advice."

After leaving the conference room, Jennifer walked purposefully down a curving corridor, then through a hatchway into her cabin. The door slid shut behind her. She sat at her computer console and switched the terminal on.

"Personnel computer—log this under security lock, my voice-print or Commander's."

"Logged," said the computer's metallic synthesized voice.

Jennifer inserted a cassette the size of a matchbook. "Complete inserted personnel transfers," she instructed.

"Completed," said the computer.

Jennifer allowed herself a faint smile, shut off the terminal, and left her cabin.

The chemical plant in Brooklyn, near Joey Vitale's old neighborhood, hummed with activity, as it had since the Visitors completed its retooling. Three shuttle ships, serving as tankers, squatted in the parking lot. Another shuttle was hooked up to a pair of heavy hoses from a pump at a corner of the building. Puffs of condensation from the supercooled chemicals clouded up from the terminal like exhaled breath.

Across the street from the plant, a man stood with fingers hooked through the cyclone fence of a schoolyard basketball court. He was a slim black man, wearing jeans and an army fatigue jacket. He had a can of beer in a paper sack in one hand and in the other, inside his pocket, was a miniature camera. He seemed to be watching the noisy junior high school basketball game in the high-fenced court. But every thirty seconds or so, he'd glance toward the plant, slide the camera out of his pocket, raise it to his eye, and snap off a photo.

After a few minutes of this ritual, he walked to a street corner phone booth near a block of shops and dialed. Meanwhile, the shuttle at the filling hoses was detached, and it gracefully lifted out of the parking lot, then banked up toward the giant Mother Ship a few miles away over Manhattan.

"There she goes," said the man in the phone booth. Then he hung up.

Dr. Hannah Donnenfeld nodded to a mop-haired young man sitting at a CB radio transmitter. Donnenfeld placed a dark-blue baseball cap over her wispy white hair. A smile crinkled her face, fine lines and wrinkles etching deeper around her mouth and eyes. She rubbed her gnarled hands together and chuckled. "Now we get down to it," she said, her voice revealing its New England origins.

The young man pressed the microphone button. "Nancy-Charlie two-five, this is Brook Cove. Mama says follow that spaceship. Good luck. And, Sari, make it casual."

The speaker crackled with static. "Roger, Brook Cove. We copy."

A helicopter marked NC-25 edged into the air from a pad along the Brooklyn waterfront. The pilot and a technician, Sari James, spotted the Visitor shuttle immediately. The chopper swung in the opposite direction and circled lazily for a few minutes until the shuttle vehicle had entered the Mother Ship's docking bay.

The helicopter swung around toward the south tip of Manhattan, the reflective glass faces of the World Trade Center's Twin Towers shimmering in the sunshine.

"How much time we gotta kill?" the grizzled pilot shouted over the engine noise. He scratched his stubbly beard.

The technician adjusted the sunglasses slipping down her nose. Sari, a freckled strawberry-blonde, flashed a gap-toothed smile. "A few minutes. Y'know what I've always wanted to do?"

"What?" he asked.

"Fly between buildings. Give the office workers somethin' to talk about at their coffee breaks."

"*That'll* kill a few minutes."

"As long as it doesn't kill *us*," she laughed.

"Hold on, honey . . . here we go!"

He bore down sideways on the control stick and the chopper nearly keeled over, then cut a ragged zig-zag path between skyscrapers.

After about two minutes of aerobatics, they headed north to face the monster Visitor ship again. Sari aimed a cameralike device at the Mother Ship's belly.

"What is that gizmo?" asked the pilot.

"Spectroscopic recorder camera."

"What the hell is that?"

"Well," she yelled over the *whop-whop-whop* of the engines, "we think they've been dumping stuff out of the Mother Ships after these loaded shuttles go back up. We've seen vapor fumes. We want to know what they're dumping. Ooops, there they go!"

"Y'need to be closer?"

"Close as you can get, then swing by a coupla times."

"Ya got it, honey . . ."

Sari triggered the camera as a gaseous jet vented out of ports next to the docking bay on the big vessel's underside.

Pete pulled his Mercedes two-seater over onto the grassy shoulder of a twisting two-lane road, then smoothed out the scrap of paper with Hannah Donnenfeld's directions scribbled on it. He rarely drove on Long Island, and even more rarely on the north shore, where the sameness and clutter of shopping-mall suburbia gave way to narrow country lanes, rolling fields, and tree-shaded mansions set back from the road.

He'd followed the main street into the town of Oyster Bay, seen the signs pointing to Teddy Roosevelt's Sagamore Hill estate, and gone the opposite way. He'd taken a right, then a left, and now the driveway leading to Brook Cove Lab should be right . . . *there*! Ah-ha, there it was, hidden by bushes and trees. He shifted back into gear, made sure no car was rounding the blind bend to clip his dearest possession's rear fender, and gingerly turned into the driveway, aiming between tumbledown stone walls into an opening almost too narrow for any vehicle larger than a motorcycle. On top of one of the low stone walls was a large country-style mailbox with a neat, hand-lettered sign: "Brook Cove Laboratories."

The car skidded slightly on the gravel road winding through the woods and Pete steered carefully. Then the roadway split to surround a magnificent maple tree, its branches spreading like a leafy umbrella over the broad lawn. Going to the right, Pete finally saw the main house, actually a great old Tudor mansion, and perhaps a dozen other buildings and cottages to one side, all built in the same English style. Pete parked with about ten other cars of various vintages and got out. Behind the main house, he could see Oyster Bay Harbor, with small boats anchored in the cove, and a narrow beach perhaps fifty feet below, down a rock-and-grass bluff.

He squeezed his briefcase tightly to his side and walked up the stone steps of the house. The door opened before he could ring the bell, and he was greeted by an elfin woman in her seventies. He recognized her from news coverage of her winning the Nobel Prize a few years ago, but she was even tinier than she'd looked on television. Still, there was a sturdiness about her, confirmed when she shook Pete's hand with a rock-hard grip.

"Doctor Donnenfeld, it's a pleasure to meet you. I've read a lot about your work."

"Little old to be a student, aren't you?" she said with a pursed smile.

He shrugged. "Can't play baseball forever."

"Not with *your* knees," she said with a knowing shake of the head.

Pete laughed. "You follow the sport?"

"Yes, sir, Mr. Forsythe. I used to get to the Bronx whenever I could to root against you boys. Now it's mostly via TV."

"By the accent, I'd guess you're a Red Sox fan."

"Yes, sir. Born and raised in Boston. Come in, come in. It's chilly out here and I'm not as young and warm-blooded as I used to be."

She stepped aside, Pete entered, and she slammed the door. He had to hurry to keep up with her as she led him into a combination parlor and work space—fireplace and couches on one side, lab benches and equipment on the other.

"Interesting decor," Pete noted.

"Eclectic, you might say," agreed Dr. Donnenfeld. "The

kind of people who hang out here, you never know when someone wants to check on a theory right away. Now, let's see what George Stewart sent you out here with."

Pete had been clutching the Chu samples for so long now—at least it *seemed* like a long time—he gave them up a bit reluctantly. She noticed, then gave him that puckered smile again. "Maybe George and Doctor Chu are okay, wherever they got taken." She picked up a phone and tapped in a two-number extension. "Mitchell, will you come in here, please?"

She hung up and slid out the envelope's contents, sifting through the hand-written notes.

A chubby, thirtyish man in jeans and a plaid flannel shirt padded in, and Pete saw he wore bedroom slippers. He wordlessly watched Mitchell as he took the package from Donnenfeld.

"Check it out for anything and everything. Identify and analyze it from top to bottom," she ordered.

"Quick like a bunny, Hannah," said Mitchell in a high-pitched twang.

Donnenfeld was amused as Pete watched Mitchell leave. "We don't bother with white coats here," she said. "Very informal—I see you noticed the bedroom slippers. Working here is like working in your own home, Mr. Forsythe. Or can I call you Peter? I've rooted against you so many times I feel I know you."

She said it deadpan, but Pete couldn't help chuckling. "You know, that's the best laugh I've had since this Visitor thing started."

She stood and gestured toward the door. "*I* have my shoes on. Would you like a tour while we wait? Maybe you'll like it so much, you'll decide to go into research when you're done with medical school. George Stewart says you've got promise." She grabbed a jacket and Pete followed her out as she chattered on. "Hey, you can be both doctor *and* subject—we can test you to see how you managed to rob so many Red Sox of base hits over the years . . ."

They strolled through the compound, which looked standard enough—a mixture of research facilities and living quarters. Donnenfeld explained that scientists chosen to work here received salaries lower than they might get in private industry or at institutions like med schools or think tanks. But housing was free, or subsidized if no room was available, and they had near-total freedom in their work.

"No guidelines or restrictions at all?" Pete asked.

"No need. They have to tell us what they'll be working on and give a proposed schedule when they apply. *What* they're interested in doing is part of *why* they get chosen. And once they start, they just have to show that they're making progress."

"You mean they've got to come up with results? Isn't that a lot of pressure?"

"Oh, no, no. It's entirely possible their progress could be negative—that they've eliminated some possibilities on the road to whatever the goal is. There's no 'publish or perish' deadline pressure."

"How long have *you* been here, Doctor Donnenfeld?"

She looked up and moved her lips silently while she calculated. "Twenty-five years. Come on, let me show you the real nifty stuff."

She led him into a small building scarcely bigger than a shed. In fact, it was a storage shed of some kind, with crates and shelves of books. Donnenfeld reached behind one of the wall-lining bookcases, clicked a latch, and the shelf swung out. There was a door, and behind it a staircase led underground. She went in, Pete followed, and she swung the bookshelf closed behind them. In contrast to the wood-and-tweed, old-world feel of everything else he'd seen, the walls and ceiling were high tech—pristine white concrete with indirect lighting.

The stairs ended at a heavy metal door. Beyond it, they entered a large lab that looked like a set for a science fiction movie—computer terminals all over the place, the most modern lab equipment, and some gizmos that were completely unfamiliar to Pete, even after several of years in med school. There were only four scientists working down here, two stories belowground, and despite the futuristic setting, they were incongruously dressed in jeans, running shoes, work shirts, and denim vests. Pete decided he would have been disappointed if they'd done otherwise. They were all very friendly and relaxed—far from the stereotypical egghead expected at a high-powered research lab.

"So what do you think of our little plant?" asked Donnenfeld.

"I'm overwhelmed. This setup is quite a surprise after the aboveground quaintness."

"There are three more protected facilities like this one."

"Protected from what?"

"Well, the whole place was built around 1950 by Walter Leiber. He was a superrich old bird who'd made his money in a variety of industries, and during the Cold War, he decided the world was sure to end in a nuclear mushroom cloud so he built all this for two reasons. One, to provide scientists with the best possible place to work toward finding ways of avoiding destruction and saving lives. And, two, so they'd have a safe place to *survive* the holocaust if they couldn't *avoid* it, and continue their work to rebuild what might be left of the world. These underground chambers are very well protected and fully self-contained, with filtered air, sleeping quarters, and food storage."

A phone buzzed and a researcher answered it. "For you, Hannah," she said.

Donnenfeld took the phone. "Yes? Thanks, Mitchell. We'll be right up. Come along, Pete—we've got Dr. Chu's results."

Mitchell sat on the rug in front of the flickering fireplace while Donnenfeld sat on the couch, skimming the lab tests. A few other young to middle-aged researchers leaned over the old woman's shoulders while Pete simply paced.

"Very intriguing," Donnenfeld finally said. "Peter, this so-called skin isn't skin at all, at least not in the true biological sense."

"Meaning?"

"Meaning, it's artificial, a plastic-like substance."

Pete stopped in midstride. He'd thought of a wide range of possibilities, but this wasn't one of them. "Plastic? Like a covering of some kind?"

Donnenfeld nodded vigorously. "Yes, sir. What I'd love to find out is, what's it covering? This shows they're *not* like us, and it fits in with what you observed about the rat ingestion." She turned to the assembled staff. "They gobble live rodents, according to this eyewitness's account," she said casually, indicating Pete.

Mitchell turned around from the warmth of the hearth. "That's disgusting."

"Where's your scientific open-mindedness?" chided Donnenfeld.

"Open, shmopen," Mitchell pronounced. "It's still disgusting."

A balding man with a pencil moustache ducked into the living room, waving a folder. His feet hit the loose rug and he skidded directly into Pete's arms.

"Good hands," Donnenfeld chuckled. "What is it, Klaus?"

"Spectro results!" he barked in a slight German accent.

The group's attention, so recently focused on the revelation of the Visitors' plastic skin, turned at once. Klaus drew himself to his full height of about five-foot-five and cleared his throat ceremoniously.

Mitchell rolled his eyes. "Do you have to make everything into a Nobel acceptance speech, Klaus?"

The German was visibly deflated.

"Tell us, already," Donnenfeld hissed.

"Just as we suspected, this chemical compound the Visitors needed so urgently that they came nine light-years to make—"

"Eight point seven," someone corrected.

Klaus made a sour face. "Whatever. They are taking it up to the Mother Ship—and dumping it right back into the atmosphere."

"But why?" asked Pete.

Donnenfeld shrugged. "Who knows? But it's obvious they're lying to us about a lot of things. What they look like, why they're here. I wouldn't trust 'em on anything. Starting now, I want our staff split into two twelve-hour shifts."

"Working on what?" asked Mitchell.

"Going over these biological and chemical results, thinking about what we know, coming up with theories, or doing whatever you want. The idea is, at any one time I want at least half the staff underground, secured in the main labs—doors locked. We will be working under security condition yellow— all precautions."

There were a few groans from the free-spirited among the group, and the old scientist wagged her finger reprovingly. "We're a prime target. If the Visitors do find us and take us away, at least they won't be able to get us all. Under no circumstances can they know about the underground facilities—we've *got* to survive as an institution to keep learning about them and figuring out what their game is."

She clapped her hands and shooed the researchers out of the room—even swatting Mitchell on the rump as he lingered before the fire. "Out, out! Spread the word. This may not be the holocaust ol' Walter worried about, but it'll do until something better comes along."

When the room had emptied, she clasped Pete's hands in hers. "You've been a big help. You should've become a doctor the first time around. No telling what good you might've done—or how many more games the Red Sox might've won."

"I'd like to *keep* helping, Doctor," Pete said earnestly.

"I know. But we have to be very careful. These Visitors could have the whole world under surveillance, for all we know. I'm not sure which would expose us to the greater risk—phone calls or visits. We may have to arrange meetings in Oyster Bay or along the beach. Well, keep an eye out. If you see anything worth reporting, call me on this line from a pay phone." She handed him a card. "It's scrambled and about as bug-proof as modern technology can be. And if it *is* bugged, we can detect it."

She guided Pete to the front door. "We can't thank you enough—both for the information and helping us feel that we *can* do something to fight back." They shook hands.

"Oh, hell," she said, with her little semi-smile. "Even if you are the enemy, how 'bout an autograph, Pete?"

"Sure." He pulled a pen from his pocket and scratched his name on a slip of paper.

Chapter 12

Power Play

Under the glare of television lights, Secretary of Defense Farley Mason signed the long sheet of paper with a flourish. Reporters filled his large office, surrounding him as he sat at his massive oak tank of a desk.

Lauren Stewart was transfixed as the scene played on her living room television. Behind Mason, a chart was balanced on an easel, and the Secretary picked up a pointer and slapped the oaktag as he lectured.

"This map," said Mason, "shows all the countries where we've had hard-and-fast proof of scientists—top people in many important fields—conspiring against the Visitors. That's why I've signed this petition swearing support for the government *and* the Visitors in this ugly war."

"A war, sir?" called a reporter.

"Yes, ladies and gentlemen. A war perpetrated by the elite, who think they can tell us how to run the world, tell us whether or not we can stretch the hand of friendship out to brothers from another star. A war *against* progress led by self-serving scientists seeking to unsettle everything we're building through peaceful cooperation."

"Why haven't we seen President Morrow in a week?" shouted another reporter.

"He's been buried in work," said Mason. "Conferring with world and Visitor leaders privately to try to fight this rising evil."

* * *

William Brent Morrow watched the monitor screen in his cell. As he saw his friend pick up a pen to sign the document, he buried his head in his hands. "No, Moose, no," he moaned softly. He straightened, trying to hide his reaction, knowing he was probably under constant observation by that ice-palace princess, Angela; but positive knowledge of Farley Mason's conversion was a blow that undermined his control.

How many days had he been here? Morrow tried to remember. He rubbed thoughtfully at the stubble on his face, trying to gauge whether it represented three or four days' growth. After the first two, it was hard to tell. The President remembered vividly the night the shuttle had landed, supposedly bringing John to the White House after Morrow had demanded that the Supreme Commander personally explain the outrageous events taking place all over the world. Instead of John, armed shock troopers had erupted from the vehicle, gunning down the Marine guards and police with ruthless precision.

The only person who'd gotten away had been Barbara. When the First Lady's limo had appeared on Pennsylvania Avenue, returning home from a charity benefit, little Freddy Foster had run to meet the car at the White House gate and screamed at her driver to get away. The shock troopers had responded by firing at the rapidly accelerating Lincoln and Foster, lunging like a madman, had jumped in front of the laser bolts.

Morrow too had fought, but they'd been ready with some kind of injection. The President's last memory as the drug took him was of his Press Secretary's back, blackened and charred, stubs of the man's spine protruding like splintered twigs. *If I ever get out of this, Freddy, the President thought, you'll get every high honor this country has, I swear it. I won't let you be forgotten* . . .

But in all likelihood, he'd never get out, buried as he must be in the innards of the alien ship. Morrow wondered if Barbara had had the sense to go underground. He thought she probably had. His wife had grown up in a Pennsylvania coal town, daughter of the newspaper editor, and was one of the more adaptable people the President had ever met. She'd had to be, married to him.

Morrow swallowed, then, realizing he was slumped against the metal bulkhead, tried to sit up straight. Any moment they'd come for him again and escort him under guard to the laboratory in the bowels of whichever vessel this was. Morrow suspected that he was aboard the New York ship, due to Angela's presence.

Stripped of his watch, most of his clothing, and subjected to conversion sessions at carefully irregular intervals (they wouldn't even allow him the tiny stability of knowing *when* the horrors would begin again), Morrow had lost all sense of time, of location, of continuity. And his sessions in the conversion chamber, that glass-walled atrocity, had called up every horror out of his past life, plunging him into excruciating illusionary torture which slowly undermined even the President's stubborn resistance.

Looking at Farley Mason, he could only feel sympathy for his friend, realizing what monsters out of his consciousness the Visitors must have unleashed upon the man to make him betray his country and his President. As he watched, tears filled Morrow's eyes, and he fiercely ordered himself *not* to blink. If he blinked, they'd run free, course down his face, and that bitch Angela would see them. His only hope lay in outlasting the bastards. Maybe if he could hold out they'd give up and kill him . . .

Pete's phone rang. He rolled off the couch to answer it as he watched the circus continuing from Farley Mason's Defense Department office. "Hello? *Lauren?* You calling from a pay phone? I'm surprised to hear from you. It's been four days."

"No, I'm at home. Are you watching the news?"

"The so-called press conference? Yeah. What's the word on your father?"

"Nothing yet. I think they're giving me the runaround. It's been four days and Roger keeps pleading that the confusion caused by the arrests and questioning of guilty scientists makes it hard to track down those picked up by mistake, like Daddy."

"Bullshit," said Pete succinctly. "You know what I think? I think we need to talk about this."

Lauren listened, but kept an eye on the TV screen as Mason kept pointing at charts, then stopped to sign another petition for the still-camera people. "That's it!" Lauren said triumphantly.

"What's it?" asked Pete, miffed that she seemed not to have heard a word he'd been saying.

"Farley Mason is using his *right* hand, that's what."

"So what? Most people do."

"Not when they're lefties," Lauren said.

"How do you know he's a lefty?"

"I've played tennis with the man, and we're always kidding him about being tough to play doubles with because he's wrong-handed."

"And now he's wrongheaded to boot," said Pete.

"You're right—he is," Lauren said. "That first day when we met in the President's office, Mason thought the whole idea of a conspiracy was a pile of cowchips, to quote his colorful phraseology. And now he's talking about it like he invented it and makes a profit on it. Peter, this is very odd."

"I think it's time to start doing something about all this."

"Like what?" asked Lauren guardedly.

"Beats the hell out of me. How about if we both give it some thought tonight, then meet for lunch tomorrow. I know this little Italian restaurant at Fortieth and Lex. It has some quiet private corners. It's called Bella Capri. How's twelve-thirty?"

"That's fine. See you then, Peter."

Something in her voice reminded him she'd probably spent the last four days sleeplessly worrying about her father. "Hey, Lauren? I'm sure he's okay. We'll see him soon, safe and sound."

"Thanks, Peter," Lauren said. "See you tomorrow." She hung up and took a breath. *Maybe I judged Peter Forsythe too harshly,* she thought. *Wouldn't be the first time . . .*

Denise Daltrey hunched over, replacing her high-heeled boots with comfortable running shoes. She sat up and sighed happily. "The agony of the feet . . ." she murmured, reaching for her parka and thinking how good it felt to get back into jeans and sneakers after an eighteen-hour day.

Her office door flew open, nearly smacking her, and the flushed face of Winston Weinberg panted at her. "We have to stop meeting like this," she smirked.

"No time for jokes, Denise. You have two minutes to get into the studio and on the air." He grabbed her by the arm and dragged her after him, rushing down the hallway.

"Aw, no, Winnie. I did the morning news and the evening news—I wanna go home!"

"We've got a pool feed on the Visitors, from L.A."

"No! No more Visitors!" she wailed. "I'm sick of their handsome and beautiful faces and their even white teeth!"

"Denise, honey, it's big stuff."

They entered the elevator. "What is it?" she asked.

"I don't know. No one here has seen it—it's originating from NBC on the Coast. God, I hate it when we've got to take another network's stuff sight unseen. Anyhow, it's some secretly shot footage from the L.A. Mother Ship."

"Who shot it?"

"Michael Donovan, the guy from the pool that first night on the UN Building."

Denise almost smiled. She'd worked with Mike a few times—had dated him once or twice. Nice guy. Short, but a good build. A little too much the cowboy going for the big dramatic shot, sometimes at the expense of the pictures that really told the whole story. But he never quit trying. Gutsy.

As they burst into the studio, Denise could see frantic action up in the control booth.

The director saw Weinberg and Daltrey enter down on the floor, but he was too busy to care that she was wearing blue jeans. Tight shot, no one would know anyway. He had his headset in one ear and the phone up to the other. Perspiration coursed along his silver moustache. "Yeah, this is CBS. We've got our anchor. We're set, Burt."

He glanced over at the test pattern on the monitor for the pool feeds—a monitor that had been largely ignored since the first few dramatic days. All it transmitted were statements of what amounted to pure propaganda by Kristine Walsh—daily briefings of non-news and self-serving commentaries accompanying footage of Visitor-Earth cooperation and the roundup of more and more scientists.

Denise closed her eyes as the makeup man powder-puffed her face. No time for real makeup work. She clipped her mike on to her blouse just as the director's voice came over the speaker and her earphone.

"Everybody ready—we're playing this one by ear. Take logo

slide. Denise, camera one in five—four—three—two—one—
up on camera one."

The floor director cued her and she gave the camera her best
serious-bulletin expression.

"Good evening. We interrupt this program to bring you a
special report. What you are about to see is being fed to us by
the network pool that has been covering the Visitors since they
arrived last month. Only a handful of network supervisory
personnel and technicians have seen this tape beforehand. No
one at our newsroom has viewed it. But we are told it was shot
by cameraman Mike Donovan aboard the Los Angeles Mother
Ship."

She stopped ad-libbing for a moment and listened intently to
her earphone. "I'm told the special tape is ready. We now
switch to our transmission from Los Angeles."

She turned to watch the air monitor along with her viewers.
She recognized the face of Charlie Birnbaum, a cool professional who was almost bursting with the importance of what he
was about to report: "An astonishing occurrence just took
place aboard—"

Suddenly, Charlie's face disappeared and Denise found
herself staring at a fuzzy, blank screen.

"Denise," said her director frantically, "ad-lib!"

"We seem to have lost our feed from the Coast," Denise
said, turning calmly back to camera one. "As soon as we have
it—"

"*We're* off the air too," boomed the director's voice over the
PA speakers. "Shit . . . what the hell is going on? *All* the
networks are off!"

Denise rolled her eyes—she hated technical screw-ups,
especially when she could have been home now, crawling into
bed, pulling her quilt over her head, and ignoring the world.

"Dammit!" said the director. "How the hell could *all* the
lines be out? Wait—what the hell is *that*?"

Denise frowned in perplexity as the air monitor cleared of
snow and resolved into the insignia of the Visitors, the same
one that was emblazoned on their ships. After a couple of
seconds, the symbol was replaced by the unsmiling face of
Kristine Walsh, her auburn hair pulled back.

"This is Kristine Walsh. The Visitors' Supreme Commander, John, is here to make a statement . . ."

The picture switched to John. The alien Visitor symbol on his podium, the stiffly official backdrop, and his uniform clashed ominously with the avuncular tone in his voice and his calmly reassuring face. But the first sentence after his friendly greeting made Denise gasp in outraged surprise.

"I must thank the leaders of each of your countries, who have graciously turned over all their broadcasting facilities to us to help avoid confusion in this crisis. I am sad to say that there has been a carefully coordinated and quite violent attempt by the conspiracy of scientists to commandeer control of our facilities at many key locations throughout the world."

John continued speaking over scenes of refineries and industrial complexes exploding and burning, of emergency personnel and Visitors fighting the fires and carrying injured humans and aliens to ambulances. "The loss of life has been enormous, both to your people and ours. In addition, thousands have been wounded and we're fearful that there will be more attacks."

John's image came back on the screen. "The outbreak is so widespread and so dangerous that most civilian representatives of your governments have asked us for protection—which, of course, we're more than happy to provide. Your leaders are safe aboard our ships."

John allowed his eyes to drop as he took a slow breath— *good use of timing,* Denise thought, with one part of her mind. *I wonder if Kristine coached him or if he's a natural?*

"I'm also very sorry to report that this man, in whom we placed considerable trust"—a slide of a man appeared— "Michael Donovan of the United States, has proved to be the biggest traitor to our cooperative efforts. Any person who gives information leading to his capture will be handsomely rewarded by the UN General Assembly and the government of the United States."

Donovan? A traitor? Denise pondered that one. By reputation, he wasn't always smart enough to stay out of trouble while chasing a story—he'd nearly been killed half a dozen times according to colleagues who'd almost died with him— but Denise couldn't visualize the man she knew as the kingpin in a worldwide conspiracy. *No way.* Denise's attention snapped back to John as the camera closed on him for a super-sincere finish. *Whoever's doing the camerawork knows his stuff.*

"Your national leaders have suggested that a state of martial law will be most helpful at this time, and we agree. Police at local levels will be working with our Visitor patrols, and we will also ask the help of all our Visitor Friends units everywhere," John continued, his face spreading into a warm smile now. "We believe this crisis will pass relatively quickly. In the meantime, friends, my fellow Visitors and I will do our best to see you through it, and maintain control. There will be more announcements later."

John's image faded, and the red Visitor insignia took his place. And stayed.

"Looks like we're out of business, boys and girls," said the director's voice. He sounded numb. "Those fuckers are taking over."

Denise unclipped her mike, realizing that she was about to get all the sleep she'd ever wanted. As if she *could* sleep . . .

Chapter 13

Strange Days, Indeed

"The thought of having to work with *them* makes me crazy, Pete!" Lauren Stewart jabbed her fork into the plate of lasagne with vicious intensity.

"That's not a Visitor, that's your lunch," Pete said in wry amusement. He was intrigued to see her as something other than the chilly professional diplomat. In fact, the more time he spent with her, the more he began to feel that was a mere facade. The woman behind the almond-shaped eyes, the high cheekbones, the carefully modulated voice was becoming more complex and less forbidding.

"Shh," she reprimanded, "keep your voice down."

"We're safe—Guido's an old friend—from Rome, not Sirius. Besides, we're all alone back here."

Indeed they were, for two reasons—the interior of the restaurant was arranged to provide as many private nooks as possible, and few people seemed anxious to go out for lunch now that martial law had been declared.

Life had suddenly become confusing. The streets of Manhattan were nearly empty, almost like an early Sunday morning. Subways and buses ran the way they always had—sporadically—but people seemed unsure of whether they should venture out, go to work, or stay home. Unlike past national and international crises that had melded individuals into a cohesive population linked by radio or television news—as in those terrible, black-draped days following John Kennedy's assassination—this crisis had split people asunder.

The only news came from the Visitors and it emerged in flickers and shadows. Some viewers believed what they were told, others didn't—but all were afraid, partly because they couldn't get confirmation from other sources and partly because their fears had no focus.

On his way to the Bella Capri, Forsythe had counted more police and Visitors on the street than civilians. And the citizens who did venture out scurried like small animals in a forest, not stopping to talk or window-shop. Leaving the cocoon of the home was a purely functional exercise. Which explained why Guido's Bella Capri was all but empty and why the rotund little owner had greeted them with kisses on both cheeks.

"The martial law thing is what pushed me over the edge—I simply *cannot* believe the President would ever have agreed to that," said Lauren.

"But the situation—if you can believe even a tenth of what we're being told—has gotten a lot worse since you met with him."

"I don't care. Morrow's not the kind of man who would give up sovereignty to a foreign power, and certainly not to these characters."

"You don't sound like a diplomat anymore."

She shrugged. "As of last night, I guess I'm not. With most government leaders incommunicado, who is there to be diplomatic with?"

"The Visitors."

Lauren glared at him. "Please—not while I'm eating."

"They never told you a thing about what happened to your father, did they?" Pete asked quietly.

Lauren caught the change in his voice. "You and Dad were good friends, weren't you?"

Pete frowned. "*Are*, Lauren. I hope to continue the friendship for a good long time."

"Peter," her voice cracked, "we have to face the possibility that he's dead."

"*Possibility*, not *probability*," said Pete forcefully. "No news isn't always bad news. We've just got to *do* something about all this."

"Like what?" she asked, digging at the remains of the lasagne.

"Get rid of them, assert ourselves."

"Isn't it a little late for that? I thought they preempted that course of action last night."

"What are you, a quitter?"

She looked offended. "No, just a realist. In my line of work, it's a valuable attribute."

"Well, as you just said, you're out of that line of work, and realism looks very depressing at this point. So why don't we start looking past the bare facts? We live in a violent yet resourceful world. Look at all the terrorists who defy your rules of realism left and right, taking on the superpowers whenever they feel like it. Those wacko Arab fundamentalists in the Mideast taking *us* on, the Afghans taking on the Russians. They ignore the facts, and they literally get away with murder."

"Mr. Forsythe." Lauren glared at him. "My entire adult life has been spent trying to stop things like that. How do you expect me to start thinking of ways to do it to someone else?"

"Pardon me for being a realist, but you folks haven't done a very good job stopping terrorism—and you haven't called me Mr. Forsythe in a week."

"Not since the last time I thought you were being a jackass."

Pete put his glass down with a thump and the Perrier sloshed out. "Dammit, I am *not* being a jackass! Look around, Lauren! We've got to start dealing with the world the way it is *now*, not the way it was, or the way your grad school international affairs classes said it should be."

"I'm with you," said Guido quietly over Pete's shoulder. "But don' break my glasses, eh?" He slapped Pete softly on the side of his head.

"What do you mean, you're with me?" asked Pete.

"I don' like what's going on, I don' like those Visitor posters all over the place, and I don' like having no business. We gotta do something, and whatever you do, I'm with you." Pete watched the short bald man turn and walk away as quietly as he'd come. Then he turned back to Lauren, who surreptitiously wiped a tear away from one eye.

"What's that for?" he asked gently.

She shrugged and tried to laugh. "Oh, I don't know. Daddy, your friend here, everything. And worrying that you're right. But it's so different from everything I've believed for as long as I can remember." She sipped her wine in silence, then changed the subject. "Do you have any family around here, Pete?"

"Not here. My parents live in Florida. I bought them a condo a couple of years ago. They love playing tennis and golf."

"Wife, kids?"

"Divorced. I've got two little girls, seven and nine. They live in Hawaii with their mother."

"Hawaii! I've always wanted to go there. I've got relatives there I've never even met. My mother was Hawaiian, you know. Dad met her when he was a medic there in the Navy, after Pearl. She came back with him when he came home to go to medical school."

"I know. He told me. I knew you had to get those exotic looks from somewhere."

Her face crumpled. "God, I hope he's okay," she whispered.

"He is. I'm sure of it."

"Hawaii," she said, changing the subject again, "you must not get to see your kids much."

"Well, that was part of the settlement. The judge didn't think the kids would gain much by having a drunken baseball player for a father. So my visitation rights were limited for a few years, until I proved I could be a fine upstanding citizen. *You're* going to blow my chances, though."

Lauren stiffened, her formal mask closing down again. "What do you mean?"

"We're sitting here, plotting the violent overthrow of a military government."

She smiled and relaxed. "How're *you* doing since Daddy's been gone?"

"Pretty well." He eyed her, then grinned cynically. "Oh. You mean with the drinking?" Wordlessly, he indicated the glass of Perrier.

"You miss the kids?"

"Yeah, I do. I write a lot, and my phone bill is not modest. But in a way, it would be a lot more frustrating if they lived around the corner and I wasn't allowed to see them. This way, I can rationalize that it's the distance. They have fun there, though. They get to play with dolphins."

"Huh?"

"My ex-wife works with dolphin research at the university." Pete suddenly went grim. "Oh, shit. I just realized—that makes her a scientist, doesn't it? Oh, God—"

"Don't *you* worry, Pete. We haven't heard of any trouble in Hawaii. And it's so far off the beaten path, maybe the Visitors'll just overlook it. They're probably better off there than here."

"Yeah . . . Well, I guess I'd better take you home."

"You don't have to do that."

"Oh, yes I do. I want to make sure you get where you're going. Can't afford to lose a potential comrade-in-arms."

She managed a little smile. "Thank you, sir."

They found a cab in record time on the lonely street and got in. "Where to?" said the driver.

"Seventy-second and Third," said Lauren.

The driver pulled away and turned north up Third Avenue, then made a left on Forty-second Street.

"Hey, wrong way," Pete called, knocking on the glass divider.

"Something I wanna show you," said the driver. "Have you seen Times Square today?"

"No," said Pete.

"Sit tight," said the cabbie.

With traffic almost nonexistent, he zipped over to Times Square, then pointed up to the famous cigarette ad of a giant man's face blowing smoke rings from a rooftop billboard. The ad had been replaced by a smiling Visitor face, complete with black cap and dark glasses. A cartoon balloon pointed to the mouth with words, "Visitors = Friends."

"Ain't that enough to make you wanna toss your cookies?" the cabbie sneered. Then he gunned the engine and squealed away from the curb, heading north toward Lauren's apartment.

Pete paid the taxi driver and walked Lauren to the outside door of the high-rise building.

"Well, I'd like to say thanks for a wonderful time, *but*—" She shrugged.

"That damned billboard really topped the day, didn't it?"

They stood uncomfortably under the awning, neither sure what to say.

"Look, I'd feel better walking you all the way into your apartment," said Pete.

"I—" Lauren began, then stopped and nodded agreement. "I was going to say you were being silly, but I reconsidered."

They went in and rode the elevator up to the tenth floor. Lauren led him down the hall and unlocked her three locks. Pete stepped in front of her and slowly pushed the door open, motioning for her to wait outside. He danced through the living room on tiptoe, darted into the bathroom and bedroom and opened the closets. Lauren stifled a giggle, until he got back to her at the front door. Then she let it out. Pete looked hurt.

"You think I was kidding about that?" he said, jerking a thumb back into the apartment.

"I think you've seen too many spy thrillers. But I've never seen James Bond move like *that*."

Pete smiled but quickly became serious. "We can't take any chances. We have some important work ahead of us."

"We do?"

"Uh-huh. I assume you noticed that people like Guido and that cab driver aren't any too happy about the Visitors and what they've done. And *they're* not famous ballplayers or high-powered diplomats or scientists like the people I met out at Brook Cove. They're the plain old people who make up most of the world."

"Peter, there's a big difference between not liking something and *doing* something about it. Not everyone has the guts to."

"You do."

"Don't be so sure," Lauren warned. "The idea of even touching a weapon makes me shaky."

"*Somebody's* got to take the first step, get the ball rolling. We can't wait for other people. And when *we* start, lots of people'll follow us. But if we don't start, maybe nobody will."

Lauren eyed him, a mixture of amusement and doubt in her eyes. "So you think I've got the guts."

"You went out to lunch with me—you can do anything."

He then surprised both of them by kissing her, quickly and hard. Gently pushing her back into the apartment, he walked out, closing the door behind him. From the hallway, Lauren heard him yell: "Be careful—I'll be in touch."

Pete quickly walked up the steps to his own apartment, then unlocked the bolts as quietly as possible, taking a look inside before actually entering. He figured it was better to be safe than sorry, though the one he was chiefly worried about was Lauren. How well could she play her role of docile cooperation with the Visitors? He thought about the moment that her mouth had been warm against his own, then grinned wryly. *You've been a monk too long, Forsythe, if one little kiss can stay with you like that* . . .

He thought about George Stewart, missing him, and remembered the older man's comment that if he and Lauren would really talk, they'd find they liked each other. Pete grinned, shaking his head as he went into the kitchen. Pouring himself a Diet 7-Up, he sat down to study, but finally pushed Goodman and Gilman's *The Pharmacological Basis of Therapeutics* aside. What was the use? As of today, classes had been suspended at most of the medical schools around the country. "Just as a precaution," John had said.

If I want to be a doctor, Pete thought, *looks like I'm gonna have to become a revolutionary first.* The picture of himself with a machine gun and beard, smoking a Havana cigar and wearing camouflage fatigues, was ludicrous. He'd never even been in the army—hell, he'd never even fired a gun.

Despite Lauren's doubts, he had the feeling he'd have to learn. He wondered where he could get hold of a weapon. Then he wondered what kind of weapon might be most effective against the Visitors. *Shit,* he thought, *I'm sitting here drinking Diet 7-Up and cold-bloodedly plotting to kill people I've shaken hands with. Am I crazy?*

The phone rang. Pete picked it up and heard Bobby Neal's voice. "Pete? You've gotta help me!"

"Bobby? What's wrong?"

"Trouble. After those bastards declared martial law yesterday, I told Alex to shove his Visitor Friends crap right up his wazoo, folded into razor corners. I told him I was an American and that as long as I was one, I wasn't havin' nothin' t'do with creeps that take over like they've done. Alex said he hoped I knew what I was doing. Now," panic sharpened Neal's voice,

"I went home from grocery shopping today, and there was one of those squad vehicles parked outside my building! I know they were looking for me!"

"Where are you?"

"At the stadium. I need some money and—" There was a long, indrawn breath, ending in a grunt. The receiver clunked against something solid in lessening thumps, as though it were swinging against the concrete wall. The line was still open, and Pete heard heavy footsteps approaching the phone. Then a reverberating voice said, "Hello? Who is this, please?"

Pete slammed the phone down, shaking. *Oh, God. What now?*

There was nothing he *could* do for Bobby, he realized, and the knowledge made the pain in his throat nearly intolerable. Tears blinded him, and he rubbed them away savagely. *A Magnum or a big Colt for a concealed weapon,* he thought, his mouth tightening into a hard line. *Then something powerful, with range, and a scope for night fighting. Maybe an M-16 . . .*

Chapter 14

Exeunt, Pursued by . . . What?

Essentially unemployed since the martial law declaration and Visitor takeover of broadcast facilities, Denise had time to relax and catch up on her sleep. Her reporter's instincts told her to snoop around, talk to people, search for hints to what was really going on. But snooping had gotten several of her colleagues arrested within the first twenty-four hours—obviously a signal to the rest of the press to abstain from their usual habits. And there really weren't many people to talk to—most government leaders were aboard Visitor ships, and those who weren't in so-called protective custody were either inaccessible or simply afraid to talk.

Martial law restrictions were starting to take their toll on daily life—travel other than local required special permission, as did long-distance calls. Food and other staples were subject to shortages, with interstate commerce severely limited. Grocery shelves were bare, and people had picked hardware and sporting goods stores clean of things like flashlights, bottled gas, and camping, fishing, and hunting equipment.

From the sketchy reports that filtered through the net of secrecy and isolation thrown over the country by the Visitors, most industry and business had ground to a halt. Except for food production, the only factory complexes working were the Visitor manufacturing facilities.

People were suddenly tethered to their homes, and they didn't know what to do next. Denise walked along Manhattan streets, peering up at apartment houses like a tourist glimpsing tall buildings for the first time. And in a way, she *was* seeing them for the first time, or at least in a different way than she'd ever seen them before. She could almost feel them pulsing with the simmering fears and uncertainties of the people inside, people who waited for this evolving nightmare to run its course.

Finally, she knew she had to get out of the city, away from the concentrations of Visitor squad vehicles flitting through skies suddenly barren of commercial air traffic. It was an odd feeling for a New Yorker—not having jets rumble overhead every few minutes.

It took a few days to get the travel permit, but the Visitor bureaucracy finally approved her request to drive to a friend's vacation cottage in the mountains north of the city.

As she pulled down her suitcases from closet tops and began to pack, Denise flicked on the television, forgetting that the late afternoon soap opera she used to catch every so often was not on anymore. Instead, there was Kristine Walsh interviewing four UN ambassadors. Since she was already across the apartment, wrestling with clothing that resisted orderly folding, she left the set on—even though Walsh's program was making her grind her teeth.

"How dare that woman call herself a reporter," Denise growled.

Kristine's unctuous shilling had lost all pretense of objectivity. Denise wasn't sure which grated on her more—Walsh's rose-colored leading questions or the ambassadors' seemingly choreographed responses, all of which praised the Visitors for their role in stamping out the subversion threatening to girdle the globe.

At the bottom of the screen, Denise noticed the superimposed line, "*Live from the United Nations.*" She slammed her suitcase shut, looked at her watch, and reached for her coat and car keys. Before she turned the television off, she smiled back at Kristine's serene image. "I believe I'm going to pay you a little visit," she said sweetly.

It was dark by the time Denise found a parking space near the United Nations complex. She had no idea if she could even get in to see Walsh. She made it into the building easily enough, but was stopped by well-armed Visitor security officers. A stocky trooper with jet-black hair asked to see her identification.

"Denise Daltrey," he said, reading the contents of her wallet. "You're a journalist, aren't you?"

"That's right. I'm an old friend of Kristine Walsh. I was watching her interview show, and since I was on my way out of Manhattan for a trip upstate, I thought I'd stop by and compliment her."

The Visitor was clearly suspicious. Denise handed him her long-distance travel permit. "See?"

"All this proves is that you were leaving the city. No one is allowed to see Miss Walsh without her express permission."

"Well, why don't you just tell her I'm here and wanted to say hello? If she's too busy to see me, I'll understand. That's not too much to ask, is it?"

The trooper considered for a moment. "I guess not." He motioned to one of his men and gave instructions to relay the message to Kristine.

A few minutes later, the other security officer returned. "She says she'll see Miss Daltrey."

Denise flashed a smile as she was led to a conference room that had been set up as a TV studio. The ambassadors were gone. Except for a few Visitor technicians shutting down equipment and rolling lights out of the way, Kristine was by herself.

"Well, Denise, this is a surprise," Walsh said with a smile.

"So is all this," Denise said, gesturing around the makeshift studio, including the Visitor workers in her sweep.

Kristine motioned to the swivel chairs arranged for the interview. "So, what brings you here?" she asked as they sat down.

"Just came to say hi," Denise said warily.

"They said you were on your way upstate when you passed by. Where are you headed?"

"Oh, just up to a cottage for a couple of days, a change of scenery."

"I envy you," said Kristine, sounding as if she meant it.

"What I wouldn't give for a couple of days off. They've got me working harder than I ever did at the network." She grinned wearily. "No rest for the wicked."

"You said it," Denise responded, not returning the smile. "I'll agree it must be tiring being the sole performer in a trained-seal act."

Kristine drew herself up straight in the chair, her face tightening.

"What the hell is that supposed to mean?"

"You're not brainless, Kristine. I think you know what it means."

"You're right—it means you're jealous that they picked me for this. They trusted me with a very important job."

"I'm glad *someone* trusts you. No human being is ever going to after all this is over and things get back to normal."

Walsh allowed herself a prickly smile. "Has it occurred to you, Denise, that the Visitors are doing our planet a lot of good? This is the new order of things, you know. And I'm part of that order, an important part. You're out of it, and that bothers you, doesn't it? *I'm* the single most important news personality in the *world*."

Denise shook her head slowly. "You don't get it, do you, Kris? This isn't like new management in the News Division. This is martial law—*war*. You've chosen your side, and it's not the right one. You've sold out your own planet. And I have a feeling the Visitors' long-range plans don't include you."

"That's ridiculous," said Kristine stiffly. "John told me—"

"What he *had* to tell you to get you to flush what little integrity you still had right down the toilet."

With that, Denise stood and strode toward the door.

"They *need* me," Walsh called after her, hysteria creeping into her voice. "I've seen to that—"

On the adjacent control booth monitors, Angela watched as Denise left the studio and the door shut behind her. She saw Kristine tremble with rage, then reached for a headset and spoke into the mike.

"Security—Denise Daltrey has just left the studio," said Angela. "Follow her, and when she's someplace isolated, take her and bring her to me aboard the Mother Ship. This is important—*don't lose her*. But I don't want this to be a public spectacle. Is that clear?''

Denise drove straight up First Avenue, then turned onto Seventy-third Street and decided to cut through Central Park on her way across town to pick up Riverside Drive north and out of Manhattan. *Might as well take the scenic route,* she thought.

The traffic light caught her at Fifth Avenue, and she stopped and wiggled her fingers, looking wistfully at the Metropolitan Museum of Art basking in its floodlights a few blocks north.

She loved to lose herself in its corridors, and wished she had the time to stop there now. The splendor of thousands of years of human creativity would be a wonderful antidote to the high-tech nightmare she'd been living through these past couple of months. But she really wanted to make it to the cabin at a decent hour, leaving enough time to unpack and unwind before hitting the sack.

The light changed. Denise slowly turned left and into Central Park. She didn't know that hundreds of feet above her car, a Visitor squad ship did exactly the same thing, silently pacing its quarry.

The park had always been a marvel to Denise, this pastoral enclave smack in the middle of the ultimate concrete jungle, with skyscrapers soaring like mountain ranges on all sides.

The winding roadway and trees made it hard for the Visitor pilot to keep an eye on the car. He dipped lower, trying to stay behind her and out of view . . .

The blanket-and-newspaper-wrapped bum sipped from the bottle in his paper sack, fingertips protruding from torn gloves. He savored the taste as it burned its way down his gullet and thought how lucky he was to have a nearly full bottle, a windless night in the tranquility of Central Park, and clouds parting to reveal a dusting of stars visible even through the city lights. Despite the booze, his poetic sensibilities remained unfogged.

He tilted the bottle back, eyes watching the twinkling stars—and nearly gagged as he saw something moving above the treetops. He edged out toward the curb, pirouetted to catch another glimpse of the shadowy thing through the bare branches—and didn't notice the approaching headlights until he'd tripped and fallen into the roadway.

Denise slammed on her brakes and skidded to a stop.

"Oh, dear God," she said as she snapped open her seat belt, jammed the shift into park, and dove out of the car to see if she'd hit the fallen body.

The lumpish form under her headlight beams was absolutely still for what seemed like forever. She didn't know if she should touch it.

"Are . . . are you all right? Are you hurt?"

There was no response, and Denise winced, anxiously leaning over the body.

"I am not all right," said a slurred male voice from under the blanket. "I haven't been all right for about ten years."

The blanket stirred and the man rolled over on one elbow, bottle cradled protectively. He squinted up at Denise. "However, you din't do anything to me that I din't already do years back, lady."

He rolled some more beneath the blanket, moving like a stubble-faced amoeba. Slowly he found his feet, stood, swayed a bit, then ambled off toward a park bench. Denise let out the largest, longest sigh of relief in recent memory. *This is one for the record books,* she thought—and went to get back into her Toyota. But a massive form hanging in the sky caught her attention. She saw enough to know it was a Visitor squad ship with its running lights off. What was it doing hovering over Central Park?

She put the car in gear and moved slowly ahead. She speeded up, then slowed, repeating the pattern several times. There was no doubt the ship was tracking her. Her throat tightened—and her foot pressed the gas pedal to the floor. The road was badly lit, not intended for nighttime road racing, and the car's tires squealed in protest.

She swerved around a curve, nearly losing control. The car fishtailed, and she wrestled it out of the turn. She took a moment for a glance up and out the window—the squad ship was still with her. Panicking, she spun the wheel hard over and tromped on the accelerator again—*too hard*—the Toyota plowed up the curb, slewed sideways, and clipped a tree with its front fender. It rocked to a halt and Denise was out the door as soon as she could steady her senses.

She ran along the roadway, then realized she was easy

pickings for the Visitor ship while in relatively open view. She cut into the wooded fringe around the lake. The squad ship stayed with her, veering up and around treetops, then down to keep her in sight. All the times she'd run through the park for exercise, she never thought she'd be running for her life.

A bolt of energy slashed into the ground a few yards in front of her, and she screamed involuntarily, more startled than anything. Another laser blast sliced a tree branch off in her path and she dodged around it. Fear was the last reaction on her list right now—anger and determination elbowed for the top slot.

Who the hell are these . . . these aliens . . . to be shooting at me for driving through the goddamned park? Or even for abusing Kristine Walsh? No way are they going to get me! Oh, shit . . . no more woods!

Denise found herself in an open-field stretch of lawn. The Visitor ship swung past her and dropped down, hovering perhaps ten feet off the ground. The laser blasts continued. They could've burned her to the ground any time. It was plain they weren't trying to hit her, just scare her. *Not bloody likely,* she vowed. As she considered her options, the Visitor ship set down and two black-helmeted shock troopers leaped out, laser rifles in hand.

Denise spied a path that would take her into the woods again and out toward Central Park West. *How fast are these aliens in their coverall uniforms and heavy boots?* she wondered. She was about to find out as she tore off toward her only escape route.

Laser bolts sizzled the grass in front of and behind her. She could feel the heat. *Damn!* They were shooting closer to her, getting desperate perhaps. *They want me pretty badly,* she thought. *Will they kill me before they lose me?*

A jagged rock imbedded in the ground caught her toe and she pitched forward into a bush, landing hard and painfully. She rolled over, grateful her wind hadn't been knocked out, and cast a quick glance back toward her pursuers, thinking that her misstep might have been the break they needed.

Multiple footsteps made a rumbling cadence approaching her. No, they didn't sound like footsteps—*hoofbeats!*

Hoofbeats? What the hell?

Scrambling to her feet, Denise darted into the bushes,

crouching, as a huge dark shape came toward her at a fast canter. Out of the corner of her eye, she saw laser bolts blasting down the trail where she'd been heading—evidently her fall had confused her pursuers for the moment. She watched the dark, four-legged shape as it approached. It was a horse all right, and on its back was a rider. Denise stepped out, startling the animal, which shied and stood sidling, uttering a crescendo of cautious snorts. "C'mon, what're you waitin' for?" a human voice said. "Or do you want those creeps to find you?"

"How do I get up?" Denise said doubtfully. In the dark, the horse towered like the bronze bulk of an equestrian statue.

"That stump. Hurry!"

Scrambling onto the narrow stump, Denise managed to vault up behind the man, ungracefully but successfully, as he heaved with a strong pull. She clutched him around the waist and clamped her legs tightly around the horse's flanks. The animal wheeled, the muscles in its back tensing.

"Just hold on to me!" the man ordered. "But don't dig your heels into him or we'll both be on the ground!"

How the hell does this bozo expect me to stay up here, Denise wondered exasperatedly, *unless I hold on any way I can?* Nevertheless, she relaxed her leg muscles from the knee down, and the horse stopped its fretful movements.

Without warning, a laser bolt sizzled in front of them as the shock troopers burst out of the woods path just ahead. With a loud "Yaah!" the man spurred the horse directly at the troopers, who scattered before the animal's headlong charge. Denise clutched the rider's back harder than she'd ever clutched anything in her life as the horse soared over a low bush, directly at the Visitor in its path. The animal seemed directed by rage, and even as the man tried to rein it away, it struck at the alien with iron-shod forefeet.

The trooper hissed—the sound was horrible, as though a great snake lay in their path. With a fighting squeal, the horse struck again, and the Visitor gave a peculiar ululating cry—no sound like that ever came from a *human* throat. With a boot in the side that even Denise could feel, the rider forced the horse away from the creature on the ground.

What are these Visitors? wondered Denise, struggling to keep her balance on the horse's galloping back, as each stride slammed a very tender area against the narrow, rounded cantle of the English saddle.

The scattered troopers regrouped, firing their weapons, but they were rapidly outdistanced by the horse's speed. Low branches whipped Denise's face as the rider slowed to a trot, turning his mount into a tiny side trail, forcing Denise to lie on the horse as flat as possible, her chin buried against her rescuer's spine.

Finally the horse picked its way out of the overgrown trail and they were able to straighten up in a comparative clearing. Denise looked around, trying to figure out where she was, just in time to hear the horseman murmur, "Mind easing up a bit? You've got a grip like a vise, and now that we've gotten away, it'd be nice to breathe again."

"Sorry," she said guiltily, loosening her arms—but not too much. Even at a walk the powerful creature beneath her seemed to sway like a ship at sea. Denise tried without much success to ease herself backward on the rump, certain that the saddle must've left permanent indentations in her groin. *That'll be fun explaining to the next light of my life*, she thought, realizing only now just how crazy this entire episode had been. Her teeth began to chatter.

"Cold?" asked the man in a concerned tone. "You can put on my coat . . ."

"No," Denise said, "just nerves, I think."

"Don't blame you a bit," said the man cheerfully. "My little heart's going pit-a-pat too. I thought we were both cooked." He rubbed the horse's neck affectionately. "Thanks, Barney."

"Well," said Denise, "thank *you*. It's kind of embarrassing knowing the name of your steed here, and not yours, you know. Besides Sergeant Preston, of course."

The man laughed. "You're not too far wrong. Sergeant Sam Yeager, New York mounted police, would you believe?"

—She removed her clasp from around his waist to shake his wrist awkwardly as he held the reins in front of him. "I feel silly," she said aloud. "Here I am shaking hands with a man I've been embracing passionately since the moment we first met." She giggled, thinking that there was more than a suggestion of hysteria in the sound.

"That's okay," Yeager said. "If I hadn't been so scared, it might have been kinda fun." A grin crept into his voice. "But now you have the advantage of me, madam," he said, mock-formally.

"Oh, sorry. Denise Daltrey."

"The *anchorwoman*?" He turned in the moonlight to give her a quick glance. "Well, whaddaya know! I useta watch you every morning!"

As the horse picked its way along the broader trail, Denise felt confident enough to lean out slightly to look at her rescuer's face in the dim light of a street lamp: hair receding slightly, blunt, rather attractive features, a nose that had been broken more than once.

"You're out of uniform, Sergeant," she said.

"And *you're* not on television anymore," he parried.

"None of us are," she said bitterly, "except Kristine Walsh."

"Why were they chasing you, though? If I'm not mistaken, they wanted to take you alive, but they were gonna fry you if they had to."

"I think you're right," she said. "And I don't have the slightest notion of why they were after me. Except that I told Kristine Walsh just what a low-life Benedict Arnold I think she is. But the last I heard, cussing someone out wasn't a capital offense."

"Nope. Especially not in New York. If I had to shoot every person who got pissed and let somebody know it, the city'd be deserted."

"But turnabout's fair play, Sergeant," Denise said. "Why are *you* roaming the park at night, saving lives? You're not in uniform, ergo you're not on duty."

"That's a reporter for you, always figuring the angles. You're right, I'm not on duty. If I was, I'd be turning you over to the Visitors, not saving you from 'em. That's the way the N.Y.P.D. works now." There was barely controlled anger in his voice.

Denise shifted on Barney's rump. "I take it you disagree with official policy?"

"You got it, Ms. Daltrey. But I can't say it out loud. I saw what happened to the guys who told 'em to stick it at the get-go. Suddenly they weren't around anymore."

"Fired? Suspended?"

"G-O-N-E," he spelled, "as in 'off the face of the earth.' Visitors took 'em. But," his voice hardened, "the guys who got real gung-ho about helping those creeps out got some nice perks—pay hikes, stuff you can't get anymore like fancy liquor and steaks, plus the best duty hours. The message was pretty clear, so I kept my mouth shut. To be fair, some of the guys who are going along do it because the Visitors took members of their families, promising that if they were cooperative, they'd get 'em back. Made me glad I'm single."

"That's—" Denise made a disgusted sound.

"Kidnapping, coercion, and bribery," he finished helpfully. "So by day, I do my job . . . sorta. I'm not *real* efficient about helping those bastards out, trust me. Then, at night, I take Barney out for a little secret patrol, keep an eye on things, see who I can find to help out and recruit."

"Recruit?"

"Yeah. For the group we've organized. Guess you could call it a resistance. We're underground, but we're trying to get rid of those . . . things. I don't care how human they look, they can't be. Didya hear that one Barney nailed?"

She nodded. "It didn't sound like any noise I ever heard a person make. Even Kristine Walsh." She laughed sarcastically.

"So what'll it be, Ms. Daltrey? You can get down now and go your own way, or if you want, you can join up with us . . . your choice."

"No choice," Denise said. "If there are people fighting this takeover, I've got to help."

"Okay then. I'll get us out of here."

Denise looked around. "Where *are* we? Do you think I could go back after my car by now? It's not even a month old—I hate to abandon it."

The beam of an overhead searchlight flickered through the trees, and they heard the faint whispery passage of more than one squad vehicle. "Answer enough?" asked Yeager, jerking a thumb upward.

"Yeah," said Denise. "Well, I guess I'll have to trust you to get me out of this, Sergeant, if you don't mind continuing the knight-errant bit.''

"Nope," said Yeager. "Guess I've always wanted to play Galahad."

They threaded through the woods to a paved path. No Visitors were in sight or earshot. They reached the park's edge, crossed Central Park West, and turned on to a quiet side street where an oversized unmarked horse van was parked. "Swing off," Sam said, holding Denise by the arm.

She did—and felt her knees bow apart as she almost kept on going down onto the street. She straightened her legs, moaning in protest as they shook beneath her.

"You'll be eatin' breakfast off the mantelpiece tomorrow," Sam said, amused. He ran the stirrup irons up on their leathers with quick, proficient motions, then quickly unlatched the rear door of the van, swinging a ramp down. Dropping the reins on Barney's neck, he patted the big bay on the rump. "Hup, boy."

Obediently the horse stepped up inside just as a woman leaned out the driver's window. "*Visitor patrol, Sam!*"

Grabbing Denise by the arm, Yeager thrust her into the stall next to the horse's. "Stay down!" he hissed, jumping in, pulling up the ramp, and slamming the door shut.

Denise crouched on the rubber matting as the truck started forward with a jerk. In the other stall, Barney snorted, spreading his legs to keep his balance as the van rounded a corner. Fighting to keep her own balance, Denise's legs gave out, and she sat down abruptly. "Damn," she whispered, feeling the damp matting beneath her hands. She hated to think about *what* had dampened it.

Finally the swaying, bumpy ride was over, and Denise peered out into dim light. They were in a brick stableyard. A young Hispanic-looking woman swung the door open. "Hi, Denise. Need a hand?"

"I think I can make it," Denise said, crawling out. Yeager backed his horse out and went to unsaddle him.

"I'm Brenda Ortiz," the young woman said, holding out her hand. "I work at the Mayor's office."

Denise wiped her hand carefully on the thigh of her jeans before she shook. "Pleased to meet you. Thanks for the help."

"Ms. Daltrey is joining our little group," Sam called from the depths of the stall as feed rattled into the bin. Barney's contented crunching filled the air. "At least I think she is."

"Oh, I am, I am," said Denise with a wry grin. "This may be in poor taste, but—take me to your leader."

Brenda and Sam groaned loudly. Barney munched.

Chapter 15

No More Mr. Nice Guy

Roger stood in his shadowy quarters, glancing at various rodents skittering nervously within their stacked, wall-unit cages. Ten of the twenty cages were empty now. Roger had been hungry, eating almost compulsively—the only behavioral quirk that betrayed his annoyance when things were not going well.

And they were *not* going well now. Oh, nothing major, to be sure. But minor bunglings had occurred that, when added together, made him question the competence of some of his senior crew members.

Particularly Angela. He'd been angry enough when told that she'd ordered the apprehension of Denise Daltrey without his approval, but then he became furious when she'd lost her prey; she'd tried to do the job with a finesse she simply didn't have. Roger had no patience with such errors of judgment.

He opened a cage and plucked out a trembling gray mouse, holding it up by its tail.

"Insignificant little creature," he murmured as he watched the tiny feet wriggle aimlessly. "Like these humans. The Great Leader should have let us take the most direct action." As if demonstrating, he opened his mouth, popped the mouse in, gulped, and swallowed.

He'd become convinced the Leader and his ministers had devised a plan with the same errors as Angela's pursuit of Daltrey—too much complexity, too much time between initiation and completion, leaving too much to chance, too many openings for serendipitous factors to disrupt smooth execution. It was the typical result of bureaucratic planning, something Roger had learned through direct experience to distrust.

The Great Leader had once been a military genius. Perhaps he'd been away from the field of battle for too long to recall all the lessons written with the blood of his soldiers. But Roger hadn't forgotten. This wasn't the time to speak up, though. That would come later, after he and other front-line field commanders had saved the Leader and the Supreme Commanders from their floundering mistakes. One lesson Roger had etched into his memory: Ambition without timing was mere stupidity.

The moment had come for him to tighten the reins of his command and make some shrewd moves of his own design. He reached for the intercom.

Alison Stein put the finishing touches on her makeup, tightened the bun of hair at the back of her neck, and shrugged at herself in the bathroom mirror. The doorbell rang, and she wondered how someone had gotten past the security locks of her apartment building without buzzing her from the lobby.

She approached the door cautiously. "Who is it?" she called from the foyer.

"Police, Mrs. Stein," said a deep voice.

She moved to the door and looked through the peephole. Two uniformed officers stood outside. "What do you want?"

"We've come to escort you to Gracie Mansion, ma'am."

"Why, officer? I'm supposed to be at City Hall in twenty minutes. The Mayor and I had a meeting to—"

"This is about the Mayor, ma'am. I'm afraid we have some bad news."

Alison cracked the door open, keeping the chain in its slot. "Bad news?" There was a tremor in her voice.

"Yes, ma'am," said a tall black patrolman with a thick moustache.

"Oh, God, no—is he all right?"

"I'm afraid not, ma'am. Mayor O'Connor's dead."

Alison felt as if someone had punched her in the stomach as she slumped against the wall. "What happened?" she managed to whisper.

"Detectives think he killed himself sometime during the night. I'm very sorry—I know you worked closely with him."

"How—how—"

"Do you really want to know?" asked the policeman gently. Ali nodded.

"He shot himself. They found him in his bathroom with the gun, and Ballistics matched the bullet with the weapon. It looks pretty cut-and-dried."

Tears filled her eyes. "No," she insisted softly. "No, he wouldn't have done that. Danny wouldn't have. He—he—" She didn't want to cry in front of these men, but she couldn't help it. *Damn him!* She'd warned him, and now he was gone.

"Mrs. Stein, would you please come with us? The detectives and the Visitors would like to ask you some questions—about the Mayor's state of mind lately, that sort of thing. You were about as close to him as anyone was. It would help us figure out what happened."

"He's dead, that's what's happened," she whispered. Then she unlatched the chain. *Oh, God,* she thought. *I'm Mayor now . . .*

For Julio Cruz, his church, the Madonna del Sol, was literally a sanctuary, a haven from the violence and despair that permeated the alleys, streets, and tenements of Spanish Harlem. He loved to come into the church, kneel before the statue of the Madonna, narrow his large dark eyes, and see only the flickering of the candles through his lids. The colors of the statues and holy paintings were so beautiful—so clean. Compared to the threadbare, disinfected, pest-ridden building he'd known as home up to a year ago, the church was his sole bond to another, better life.

Not that Julio kidded himself about ever becoming a priest, or that he was a particularly good kid; he knew he wasn't. He drank too much. He smoked grass and had experimented with angel dust and coke—when he could get it. Sometimes, Julio admitted to himself that he liked getting high a lot, that he'd probably become an addict if he could afford to buy the stuff. It was almost lucky, he thought sourly sometimes, that he *couldn't.*

But Julio didn't steal, so most of the time he stayed straight. He didn't want to go to prison. Some really rough guys he knew were already there, and Julio had no intention of having certain unpleasant things happen to him if he joined them. Besides, Father Roberto Lopez, his parish priest, had made him promise not to steal.

He loved Father Roberto—since Julio's father, Manuel, had died in a construction accident, the priest had helped the Cruz family in every way he could. When Julio's older sister, Terezia, had gotten herself in trouble two years ago, Father Roberto had arranged for her to have the baby in a church hospital, and for it to be adopted. Then he'd arranged for Terezia to take a work-study program so she could finish high school. Julio's sister had a cashier's job now, working in a store. Her salary helped a lot. A year ago, they'd even been able to move to a much better apartment.

So because of Father Roberto, and the oath Julio had sworn to his father as the older man lay crushed and dying that he'd stay with his family and out of prison, Julio had made it to seventeen without anything more serious than some scary near-brushes with the law. He knew he couldn't leave his mother and Terezia alone with his little sisters, five and nine years old.

Sometimes when he knelt in prayer, Julio asked God why he was so poor, and wondered if this was God's means of keeping him off the hard stuff as Julio figured out a way to make something of himself and support his family. Maybe send his little sisters to college, maybe let his mother quit one of her jobs so she wouldn't have to work at a sewing machine in the garment district from eight in the morning until six, and then wash dishes in a barrio restaurant until ten. Maybe it was God's way of making sure Julio didn't kill himself at an age when a lot of his friends had already died, some from overdoses, some in gang fights, some in stolen-car accidents. Two were killed by cops while running away from holdups. In the barrio, life itself was the leading cause of death. But God had let Julio live, and Julio was grateful.

He didn't care that some of his amigos made fun of him because he went to church every Sunday, even stopped by during the week to say a prayer, to light a candle, to go to confession or talk openly with Father Roberto. Julio was never more proud than when his two little sisters had been baptized. Or when he received First Communion. Or when his mother sang in the choir on Sundays and holidays. The church cast some light into Julio's life, a life otherwise defined by looming shadows, bordered by darkness.

It was a Tuesday morning when three Visitor squad ships landed on the street in front of the church. Julio finished his prayer quickly, lit a candle, and followed Father Roberto out onto the front steps to see what the commotion was. They found the Visitors placing barricades on the sidewalk before the building.

"Here now," called Father Roberto, a chubby man of forty-five with dark, smiling eyes, "what are you doing?"

The Visitor trooper in charge, a swarthy, strapping man with a cruel set to his jaw, glared at Lopez for a long moment, contempt obvious even through the alien's dark glasses. Finally, he came up a couple of steps toward the priest. Julio had never seen Father Roberto show harshness toward any person, and even now, his question, though anxious, had been gentle.

The Visitor pulled a folded paper from his pocket and slapped it into the priest's hand. "Authorization."

"For what?" asked Lopez, scanning the paper.

"To use this building as a Visitor headquarters for the area."

"But this building is already in use," said Lopez mildly, "as a church. I don't know if you have a religion, but it's very important to these people."

"We have authorization," the Visitor repeated in a warning tone. "You're not going to make trouble, are you?"

Julio watched from the church doorway, tensing to move in case Lopez was threatened.

"No, that's not what we're here for," Lopez said, handing the paper back. "But authorization or not, this building is already authorized by *God* as a house of worship."

"You have two hours to vacate the premises," the Visitor said.

Lopez shook his head sadly. "I'm sorry, but we can't do that. People come here to pray at all times. I must be here."

The Visitor cocked his head arrogantly. "You don't seem to understand, priest. As of now, this is no longer a church. This is a Visitor Security headquarters. Now, either you cooperate, or we'll have to use force."

Julio stepped brazenly out next to Lopez. "Hey, man, you

don' talk to him like that. This here is a man of God, and you treat him with respect."

"We'll treat him like anyone else. If he follows instructions, he'll be just fine. If he doesn't, he risks serious consequences. And you stay out of it, boy."

Julio took another step forward, but Lopez grabbed him. The boy was thin, but wiry and strong. Lopez used all his weight to stop him.

"*You* treat me with respect, Julio," said Lopez. "Do as I say and behave yourself. The Lord Jesus would not have you raise a hand in hostility, would he?"

"I don' know," Julio said. "He threw those money changers out of the temple, didn't he?"

Father Roberto gave him a warning look. "Julio . . ."

Julio lowered his head. "I wasn't going to, Father. I was just getting closer so he could hear me better."

"Ah, yes, of course," said Lopez, keeping a grip on Julio's arm. "I think he can hear you from here."

Julio glared at the Visitor. "I come here to pray. This is my church, and you ain't gonna turn it into no security headquarters."

The Visitor ignored Julio, turned away, and motioned five troopers toward the entrance. Julio shook loose and leaped down the steps. With a quick motion, he spun the Visitor leader around. The other troopers halted and raised their laser rifles. But before Julio could strike him, the leader slugged him in the belly with his rifle butt. Julio doubled over and sagged to his knees.

Father Roberto rushed to catch the boy and lowered him gently to the sidewalk. Then he came nose to nose with the Visitor leader, anger sharpening his voice. "There was no call for that. He's just a kid. He wasn't—"

The Visitor had heard enough. With a powerful shove, he pushed Father Roberto out of his path. The priest stumbled and fell heavily onto his back. Julio crawled to him and cradled his head as the Visitors marched into the church.

"I'm okay, Julio. More surprised than hurt. Are *you* all right?"

Julio gasped, trying to get his wind back. "I—I been hurt worse. Father, we can't let those bastards do this."

"They're doing it, my son, despite our efforts to stop them."

Julio started to get up. "Over my dead body."

Father Roberto pulled him back down, shaking his head firmly. "No, Julio. Dead bodies can do very little in service to God. Your life is a *gift* from God—it is not yours to throw away foolishly. We have the might of the Lord on our side."

"They *crapped* on the might of the Lord," Julio cried, pointing savagely to the church.

"No, no, Julio. They trampled on two of God's children. But God's enemies have to do a lot more than that if they hope to defeat Him, wouldn't you say? God needs us—*alive*. That's the only way we'll get our church back."

Julio helped the priest to his feet and they hobbled up the steps to stand in the doorway of what was now Visitor Security headquarters. Inside, one Visitor used holy water to douse all the candles. Another was throwing prayer books into a heap. Julio watched with tears sliding down his cheeks.

Father Roberto closed his eyes: "Our Father who art in heaven . . . hallowed be Thy name . . . Thy kingdom come . . . Thy will be done on earth, as it is in heaven . . ." They both crossed themselves and turned away from the church door.

Julio gritted his teeth in a combination of pain and fury. He would be back. The Visitors would pay for this.

Chapter 16

It Begins When You're Always Afraid . . .

Guido agreed without a moment's hesitation when Peter Forsythe gingerly asked if he and a group of friends could meet in Bella Capri's tiny back dining room. Guido wanted to know if these were all people who shared Pete's concern about the Visitors. If they were, Guido wanted to be part of the group.

"I'll keep you posted," Pete told him, "but we've got to keep up appearances. It's got to look like you're just running the restaurant and we're just there to eat."

"Okay," said Guido. He patted his round belly bulging over his apron, as if to advertise his own food. "You'll get plenty to eat when you come here—with a big discount. But if you don't keep me posted on what goes on, I'll get you." He cuffed Pete affectionately on the shoulder.

Pete and Lauren huddled at a small table in one corner. There were six others there—Sam Yeager, a friend of Pete's; Denise Daltrey, brought by Sam; Brenda Ortiz, the pert young woman from the Mayor's office; a couple of bus drivers laid off when service was curtailed; and Guido, darting in and out with food and drinks when he wasn't lingering to listen to the discussion.

"*You* should be doing this," Pete grumbled to Lauren. "You're the professional." She shook her head and pushed him to the center of the room.

"Uh-uh, you're the captain. Think of us as your new team."

Pete introduced himself, then asked the others to do the

same and tell the group why they were there. Each had a personal twist, but it all boiled down to their common desire to wrest control of their lives back from the Visitors—the *invaders*.

"There are lots more people out there who believe what we do," Pete said. "We all know some of them, even though we may not be aware of how they feel. We've got to recruit more members if this resistance is going to amount to anything. So check out your friends and relatives. *Don't* tip your hand until you're sure of how they feel. We've got to keep this secret until we've got the power to back up our convictions."

"And when will that be?" Sam asked.

Pete shrugged. "Not overnight. Meantime, keep your eyes open—notice any and all Visitor activities and try to figure their strengths and their weaknesses."

"If they have any," said Sal, one of the bus drivers, a tall stoop-shouldered man with a gray-flecked crew cut.

"Oh, they *do*," said Brenda.

"Hey, Pete," Sam piped up, "we could use some of your Yankee scouts to get us some charts on the other team."

Pete chuckled. "Good idea, Sam. Now, we're also going to need weapons." He sensed a noticeable stiffening in some of the group, including Lauren. "We can't forget that this is a war. They've used force on *us*. We can't match them for firepower, but sooner or later, if this movement of ours grows, we *are* going to have to face them armed. So think of ways we might get some of the equipment we'll need—small arms, high-power weapons, and explosives."

Lauren stood up. "But an even more valuable resource is *people*. Next meeting, everyone should try to bring three others. Numbers give us more eyes and ears to observe what's going on, more people who might be in positions to throw monkey wrenches into Visitor operations, or intercept information that could be vital to us—things that could help us reach our goals without resorting to killing or blowing things up."

Pete gave her a veiled look of annoyance. She averted her eyes and sat down again, and he turned back to the group. "I guess that's about it for now. We have to vary our pattern so the next meetings won't be at the same time or on the same day of the week. We'll also need a couple of other places to meet so we don't draw too much suspicion. If anybody can think of places, let us know next time. Oh, one other thing: if you're *ever* followed on your way to a meeting, *don't come*! Better to skip a meeting than reveal this resistance to them."

When the others had gone, Guido brought coffee and pastries back to Lauren and Pete. The little man patted Forsythe on the shoulder. "You done good, Pete," he said, then went back up front.

"You look as if something's wrong," said Lauren. "Is it something that can be cured by heavenly Italian pastry?"

"I'm afraid not. Joey was supposed to be here."

Joey Vitale's Corvette pulled up to the curb across the street from the Visitor chemical plant in Brooklyn. Lisa approached the car and Joey reached over and opened the door for her, then kissed her lightly on the cheek as she got in. (For some reason she never let him kiss her mouth. Joey didn't know why, but being *with* her was what was most important.) "I'm glad you could get off for a little while," he said.

"Where are you taking me?"

He was getting so accustomed to the throaty vibrance of her voice, he could almost forget she was a Visitor. "To Coney Island."

"Could this be construed as sociological research into your species?"

Joey laughed. "Yeah, yeah, sure."

He gunned the engine—something he always did when he was happy—and drove away from the plant.

"I almost couldn't see you today," she said.

"Why not?"

"My research is becoming less and less important."

"How come? They brought you all this way to study us and now they won't let you do it?"

Lisa shrugged. "Angela says it's all the troubles you humans are causing—the scientists' conspiracy and all. But I think it's something else. I get the feeling they lied to me about this mission."

Joey unconsciously slowed down and flashed a worried look at her.

A honking horn from behind made him speed up. "Lied to you?"

"You're the only person I can talk to about this," she said, touching his arm. He let go of the steering wheel with one hand and held hers for a second. "I feel as if I'd get into deep trouble if I talked to any of my superior officers, and you're the only human I trust enough to tell. I *can* trust you, can't I?"

"Of course, Lisa. Now, what makes you think they lied to you?"

"Well, it's nothing specific, Joey. Just . . . just the way I hear them talking about the cultural aspects of our visit here. Or the way they *don't* talk about them anymore. When we first got here, we sociologists were told to be friendly and accessible and learn as much about humans as we could, and to communicate with you a lot. But now we're allowed less and less time to be with humans, and we're told such contact could be dangerous to our mission."

"What is your mission, Lisa—*really*?"

"I don't think I know anymore." She flashed him a look of deep concern. "I'm afraid, Joey. Afraid for us, but more afraid for your people."

Joey could offer her no reassurance beyond the grip of his hand. Since Bobby Neal's disappearance, he, too, had been afraid.

Chapter 17

Step Out of Line and They'll Come and Take You Away . . .

Hannah Donnenfeld had loved the dawn for as long as she could remember. Her mother had told her that was because she was born at dawn. But all Hannah knew was that the freshness of sunrise had no rival in nature for her.

In springtime, she awakened to the rhythm of birth, of buds and fledgling birds. She drew strength from that pent-up energy rousing itself to be loosed upon the warming world.

In summer, she inhaled the sweet early moistness of air laced with perfumes of petals and blossoms as she watched, enraptured, the perpetual work of insects up and about, drinking dew and nectars before humans could come out to disturb them.

In autumn, the laziness of summertime was shocked away by the snap of chilled mornings. The later and later sunrises urged Hannah to frenzied activity to take advantage of the dwindling daylight.

And now, on the threshold of deep winter, the dawn skies glowed with profound hues of red and gold and blue, and rolling clouds of fluffed white mixed with glowering gray. It was enough to make her imagine God was a passionate painter, wielding His dramatic brush in the twilight of the year, trying to fight off the coming freeze in this season of His own creation.

Hannah pulled her furry jacket collar up under her chin and breathed deeply as long strides carried her quickly along the stretch of beach below the bluffs and lawns that were home to the Brook Cove Lab.

"Hey, slow down," Mitchell Loomis cried, gasping several yards behind her.

"Can't you keep up with an old lady?" teased Sari James. Her strawberry-blonde ponytail bounced on her shoulders as she jogged a few tantalizing feet in front of portly Mitchell.

"Can't *you*?" Mitchell sneered at her.

"Yep." With that, Sari leaped ahead to catch Donnenfeld, then slowed down to a matching fast walk.

"Not fair," called Mitchell breathlessly. "Women are better at this sort of thing."

Hannah Donnenfeld tossed a withering glance over her shoulder. "Bullshit, my dear." She turned back to Sari. "I'm so glad I can get some of you young people to join me on my little dawn forays. Best time of day."

"I agree," said Sari. "Of course, I lost three boyfriends because I'd never sleep past seven. They'd roll over, and I'd be out jogging."

Donnenfeld laughed. "You know, I used to jog on this very beach twenty-five years ago. Of course that was before they called it jogging and made it fashionable."

"I've never understood why Mitchell comes with us, Hannah."

The older woman leaned close. "Puppy-dog complex—he's fixated on me as his mother figure, only he doesn't *want* to cut the apron strings."

"I heard that!" howled Mitchell.

When they got to a large rock nestled just below the cliff, Hannah and Sari sat on it. Mitchell stumbled up a few moments later. He folded himself over, head as close to his knees as he could manage. Hannah patted him on the back.

"I warned you that all that extra weight would be the death of you."

"Yes, Mom," Mitchell said sarcastically.

The two women started to laugh.

"Yuk it up, ladies," he grouched. "Nobody appreciates me!" Their laughter suddenly ceased and he looked up.

Sari pointed to the sky out west, over the spit of land that protected the cove. A squadron of small Visitor aircraft was approaching.

"Do you think they're headed here?" asked Mitchell in a whisper.

"What do *you* think?" said Hannah gruffly. "It had to happen sooner or later. Let's go." She trotted back the way they'd come and led them up the steep path to the lab complex. Once or twice Sari had to reach back and haul Mitchell to his feet after he'd slipped. When they neared the top, the incline leveled off and they hunched over, skulking through the scrubby bushes that clung by their roots against the steady breeze coming off the water. They reached a stand of pine trees and hid, peering toward the buildings.

What they saw made them shiver more than the damp morning air—six Visitor ships in the compound, perhaps forty heavily armed and helmeted shock troopers herding sleepy scientists and their families out of the cottages, hands clasped atop their heads. Anyone who straggled was roughly shoved along. Poor little Klaus tripped and was dragged to his feet.

"Bastards," Sari hissed.

"What do we do?" Mitchell said.

"We hide," said Hannah, "then we get the hell away from here in case they come back. And we pray that the downstairs shift doesn't come up to see what's going on. They've *got* to escape. If they do, maybe we can come back soon. But even if they get taken, if we can get away safely, we've still got our most valuable equipment with us."

Mitchell looked perplexed. "Jogging shoes?" he asked cynically.

Hannah tapped his head. "Our brains, Mitchell. We're going to need them."

The two officers commanding the raid leaned over a map spread out on the nose of a squad vehicle. A junior trooper stepped up behind them and stood at attention. The raid leaders turned to him.

"Report," ordered Jennifer, who was in charge.

"We found no one else in any of the buildings. We've taken some of the more advanced equipment and destroyed the rest. This installation will be useless to the humans."

Jennifer smiled coldly. "Very good. See to the loading and we'll get back to the Mother Ship."

"Yes, Jennifer," said the young trooper as he turned smartly and quick-marched back toward antigrav sleds piled high with lab equipment.

The officer with Jennifer, a tall man with a boyish smile and curly blond hair, shook his head in admiration. "You're going to get a commendation for this, Jennifer. Roger will be very pleased. You could be in line to replace Angela, you know."

Jennifer shook her head. "No, Paul. Not a chance."

"Don't be so sure. This is one of the most efficiently executed operations of its kind in weeks. You know how Roger likes simplicity and directness."

"As long as you're simply and directly successful."

"You were," said Paul. "And it's not the first time. There were your personnel transfers, for instance."

Jennifer's face froze and she stiffened. "He knows about those?"

"Yes. And he's very pleased."

"I didn't consult him," Jennifer said.

"But it falls within your assignment to make transfers, and he's checked a sample of the people you've brought aboard our ship—they've got impeccable service records and a better mix of skills than our original crew complement. He knows you bent a few rules—but it's results that count. That means a commendation. I hope some of this glory rubs off on me," said Paul with raised eyebrows.

"Oh, it will. My report on this raid will say you played a key role—couldn't have done it without you."

"We only had to kill two scientists here. That means we got nearly maximum yield on the raid. That's rare—an excellent use of resources."

Jennifer shrugged modestly. "Well, keeping up our food supplies is of immense importance. We still have quite a way to go before filling our ship quota of five thousand live humans in food-pod storage."

Paul nodded. "Five thousand—that's a lot."

"We have a lot of mouths to feed on the return trip, not to mention the hungry ones at home."

"I wonder what they taste like," Paul said, almost to himself. "Their lab animals are certainly palatable."

Jennifer snapped a disapproving look at him. "Food is food, Paul," she said harshly. "We're here to serve the Great Leader, not worry about frivolous concerns."

Paul nodded stiffly. "Yes, Jennifer. I'll see to the final loading."

"Very good," she said, folding the map and returning it to the breast pocket of her coverall.

In the twilight near curfew time, the battered Ford cab rolled around the corner, with Julio riding in the front passenger seat, Rico at the wheel, and an older, bearded gang member, Michael Martinez, in the back. Rico pulled over to the curb down the block and across the street from Julio's beloved Madonna del Sol. It still looked like a church, but it made Julio sick to his stomach to know what was going on inside. He'd heard stories since the Visitors had moved in. They'd broken the statue of the Madonna, burned the prayer books, ripped up the pews— some of which Julio had helped install with his own hands when he was twelve, after a fire had damaged the place. And the Visitors had put in a holding cell, a torture chamber. He knew because one of his friends had been taken there after he'd thrown a rock at a Visitor. The boy had been beaten and poked with an electric prod, then thrown down the front steps onto the sidewalk. Fifteen-year-old Jesus had lived long enough to recount his ordeal, speaking between great wracking sobs of pain and shame at the indignities and degradations he'd endured. His injuries hadn't killed him, though. Jesus was found the next morning hanging from a pipe in the basement of his building.

And Julio had found him.

Now Julio cradled the bottle in his lap, the neck held carefully upright. He stuffed the rag in, making sure it reached down into the gasoline. He looked into the back seat. Mike placed three more Molotov cocktail bottles in a tote bag, then nodded to Julio and got out of the car, closing the door quietly. Julio watched while Mike crossed the street quickly, dodging into a doorway three buildings down from the church. He crouched near an empty storefront gaping vacantly on the street.

At Mike's waved signal from the building's shadows, Julio nudged Rico. The driver rolled ahead a car length or two, pausing again a half-block from the church. Julio got out and knelt behind the cab's rusting front fender, hidden from the three Visitor guards facing in different directions at the top of La Madonna's steps.

Julio thrust an arm up over the car's hood. Mike flicked his lighter and touched it to the first of his gasoline bombs. With a deft pitch, he tossed it into the abandoned store, then ducked back and down a second before the bottle exploded with a muffled *whooosh*. The wooden interior of the store ignited immediately, the flames blasting out of what was left of the front window. Martinez escaped the heat by darting into the alley behind the now-burning building.

The Visitor guards left their perch and ran partway down the street toward the explosion and flames. But not yet far enough for Julio's purposes.

Mike climbed the fire-escape ladder, racing to the roof of the burning building only three stories up. Then he edged to the front of the roof, lit another cocktail, and dropped it into the street. It landed closer to the guards and drew them farther away from the church. Mike scampered over the roof and leaped across a gap to the top of the church itself.

"Now," Julio growled to Rico. Julio skipped around the cab, lighting the bomb as he ran, and heaved it at the church front. It tumbled gracefully, spewing a trail of liquid flame, then crashed through the stained-glass window next to the door. But Julio couldn't stop to watch, for Rico had floored the accelerator and swerved the car up onto the sidewalk. As the car moved, Julio dove into the back seat. The tires screamed and smoked as Rico tore past the church, down the street. The Visitors turned and fired a barrage of laser bolts after the fleeing car.

"Shit!" cried Rico. "We're gon' die, man!"

"We're not!" Julio screamed at him. "Just drive!"

The laser fire kept coming. They took a nonlethal hit on the trunk that made the car shimmy. Rico barely retained control as they neared the end of the block.

"Dammit," Julio spat, "where's that last bottle? C'mon, Mike . . ."

At that moment, a sheet of flame exploded in the middle of the street behind them—*between* the car and the shock troopers.

The shooting stopped. Julio and Rico cheered. "Move, shithead!" Julio yelled, half laughing now.

Rico pounded the gas pedal to the floor, reached the corner, cut the wheel hard, and squealed around the turn just as Mike scrambled like a squirrel down the fire-escape ladder on the block-end building. He slid down the last flight, dropped to the sidewalk, and dove through the rear door Julio held open for him. "We made it! We made it! We made it!" he whooped.

"Not yet—go, Rico!" Julio shouted.

Rico floored the old cab one more time, made a seemingly random series of turns, and found himself staring into the floodlight of a low-flying Visitor squad ship. Rico jammed on the brakes. The car spun 180 degrees, slammed into garbage cans, and rocked to a stop.

"Subway!" Julio yelled, pointing back half a block.

They jumped from the car, zigzagging the distance as the ship fired and glided closer. The laser blasts tore up the sidewalk, sending cement chunks and gravel flying.

Julio's long legs got him to the subway entrance first, and he flew down the steps four at a time; Mike followed and Rico trailed. Julio leaped the turnstile before the token booth attendant could react. Other steps, Visitor boot steps, were not far behind. The lasers shattered the quiet and darkness of the station and tunnel.

Julio ran down the platform and then tumbled off it, down into the track well, landing in brackish muddy water. He knew enough to stay clear of the third rail and he stood in a crouch to see over the platform edge. Mike ran toward him as a Visitor stopped far behind, set his weapon and aimed. The laser blast caught Mike full in the back—he spun and fell, twitching, with a scream that split the night, then was still. *What about Rico? He never could run, not ever,* thought Julio through welling tears. Then he saw another Visitor pull Rico along by his handcuffed arms.

"Where's your third friend?" the Visitor said.

Rico was obviously terrified, but mustered his courage. "No other guy—just two of us."

The shock trooper drew back his laser rifle and slammed it across Rico's face. The indescribable sound sliced through Julio's heart. But Rico didn't even cry out. They wouldn't let him fall. They held him up and hit him again. He had to be unconscious by now.

"This one won't die so easily," said the trooper who'd shot Mike. "We'll take him back and work on him."

Julio watched them drag poor, pudgy Rico toward the stairs

to the street, trembling, then realized suddenly his tremors weren't entirely from fear.

The entire track bed was shaking because a subway train was coming into the station. If those Visitors didn't get out of sight in a hurry, Julio would be crushed. He began to panic.

Damn you, Rico, if you were lighter, they could carry you faster. Get out of here, you bastards!

The shaking increased, coming up through Julio's knees. His teeth began to chatter. He braced his hands on the platform ledge, ready to haul himself up. When he looked down the tunnel, he could see the headlights.

When he was a kid, he and his father would play a game— guess how long it took for the train to get to the station once they saw the headlight in the tunnel. *Funny what you think of when you're about to get killed.*

The Visitors and Rico had finally reached the steps. They stopped to change their grip on the unconscious boy. *Hurry up!* Julio screamed silently.

He looked down the tunnel again. The headlight had grown alarmingly. He could begin to feel the stirring of the air, the breeze the train caused when it neared the station. He tensed his hands on the platform. The shock troopers took Rico's arms again. Up the first step. The second. Julio could see their shoulders. Now only their asses . . . now their knees . . . Close enough!

He turned to see the train entering the station, still speeding. Julio vaulted up with all his strength—and made it, rolling onto the platform just as the graffiti-covered subway train passed him and squealed to a stop. Julio leaned on the gaily painted side of the car, then slowly got up. He took a last glance at Mike's body, an ugly black burn blistering his back. He couldn't take the body—the street patrols would surely spot him.

Julio paused in the open door of the subway, then crossed himself. "Rest in peace, Michael Martinez," he murmured. He wiped his eyes and stepped into the nearly deserted train. The doors shut. The electric motors whirred to life. Julio slumped into a seat as the train slid out of the station. His eyes couldn't leave Mike's body. He turned to watch it as long as it was still in view. Then the tunnel's darkness swallowed him.

Chapter 18

Taking It to the Streets

By the time the third meeting of the rebels convened, in Guido's back room again, the ranks had grown considerably. Pete counted sixteen this time, including Hannah Donnenfeld, Mitchell Loomis, and Sari James from the Brook Cove Lab. They'd made their way into the city after three days on the run, contacted Pete, and offered their help. He took them in and let them stay at his apartment. It was cramped, but it was a good feeling not to be alone as the perils and stakes increased. There might not have been an anti-Visitor conspiracy a few weeks ago, but there certainly was one now!

Pete was pleased to see that Joey had made it this time. However, he was too busy conferring with Lauren and Sam Yeager to notice that his young teammate didn't look pleased to be there.

"I think I've got a way to get weapons," Sam was saying. "That armory where your Visitor Friends group meets, Pete. They don't have tanks stored there, but they do have small arms and explosives."

"How do you know?" Lauren said.

Pete's lips tightened as he sensed the antiviolence bias in Lauren's tone.

"Because I'm in the National Guard reserve and that happens to be my armory." Sam grinned.

"Then you know the layout of the building?" asked Denise.

Sam nodded. "But we would stick out like sore thumbs if

we suddenly all piled into the armory during the kids' activities. We need this to be an inside job."

"Get the gangs involved," suggested Brenda Ortiz.

"Will they cooperate?" Lauren wondered.

"We won't know if we don't ask them," Pete said with a sarcastic edge to his voice.

"Judging from what I hear," said Yeager, "the gangs are already doing stuff on their own. There was that church bombing the other day up in Spanish Harlem."

"What bombing?" said Denise. "You get to see police reports, Sam, but we don't get much news."

"Sorry. It's a church the Visitors took over to use as a security headquarters. A few kids attacked with Molotov cocktails. Pretty nervy—"

"Pretty crazy," said Lauren darkly.

"Maybe, but they did a lot of damage, killed a few Visitors," Yeager said. "Pretty much put the place out of commission as a Visitor installation. They caught 'em by surprise. I think we could learn a thing or two from those kids if we could link up with 'em."

"But *we* have to be in charge," said Pete firmly. "We can't have them going off half-cocked, pulling off all sorts of uncoordinated actions if we're going to aim for any kind of cohesive resistance. Do you know who bombed the church, Sam?"

"I can check around. Got some contacts in that area. Does anybody else?"

Yeager was answered by noncommittal shrugs, and Pete looked directly at Lauren. "You do," Pete said.

"That true?" asked Yeager.

"Her father lives up there, not too far from Spanish Harlem," Pete said quickly.

"I can speak for myself," Lauren snapped.

"Fine," Pete said with a brittle smile. "Be my guest."

"Yes, my dad lived—lives—up there, but *I* don't."

"He's a doctor, right?" asked Sam. "So he must know a lot of people as patients. You could be a good contact, Lauren."

"My *father* would be, but the Visitors have him—have had him for weeks."

"Lauren," Pete said, softer now, "they love your dad up

there. I bet a lot of people would be willing to walk on crushed glass to try to get back at the bastards who kidnapped him."

"I—I don't think I—"

"Look," said Yeager, "this is war right now. We're the underground. Also the underdogs. We gotta use any possible advantages we find. We're gonna have to play on people's feelings and loyalties to get them to help with stuff that's sure to be dangerous. I'll do some legwork and get back to you on who to contact. Lauren, will you do it?"

She felt every eye in the small dining room focusing on her. She nodded. "If I think the people you come up with will deal with me. I'm not Hispanic, don't forget."

"Um, I don't know if this is the time or the place," said Denise, "but how many of you remember the night the Visitors took over the TV and radio networks?"

There was a general murmur among the group.

"Well, I was supposed to go on the air with a special bulletin when that happened."

"What kind of bulletin?" said Brenda.

"It was a videotape shot aboard a Mother Ship by a guy named Mike Donovan—"

"The one who's wanted by the Visitors," Sam added.

Denise nodded. "Yes. I didn't see his tape that night, but I know someone who did. And he told me—well, it's pretty incredible. He said the Visitors aren't like us at all. They are *really* alien."

"But the way they look . . ." someone began.

"A fake. They have a skin covering that makes them look like us, but underneath it, they're sort of . . . reptilian," Denise said.

There was a collective gasp, an undercurrent of disbelief. Pete stood. "I didn't know that's what they looked like, but I *can* tell you it's true that their skin hides their true appearance. Dr. Donnenfeld and her Brook Cove Lab confirmed that with tests on a skin sample. And I know for a fact that they eat live rodents."

"Ugh," said Brenda, covering her mouth in disgust.

"Just keep all this in mind," said Hannah Donnenfeld. "They *aren't* like us. It doesn't matter that we don't know their actual appearance. We *do* know they've lied to us from the start. So if we have to do terrible things to fight them, things we never thought we were capable of, we're not killing human beings."

The meeting broke up, and Joey lingered to talk to Pete alone.

"What's up, buddy?" the older player asked.

"That stuff about them being reptilian, is it really true? Or was that just stuff to psyche people into fighting them?" asked Joey, deeply concerned.

"Why? What's the difference?"

"I need to know, Pete. Just tell me."

"Well, it's like we said, none of us here has seen that videotape firsthand. All we've got is secondhand reporting. But the part about their skin being an artificial covering, and how they eat rodents, I know that's true. I saw that personally one night at the armory. What's wrong, kid? You look worse than when we overslept and missed the team flight to the Coast." He hoped the memory would break Joey's melancholy, but it had no effect.

"It's about Lisa, that Visitor girl I've been seeing."

"I didn't know you were still seeing her."

"I am, Pete. And we really like each other. I might even be in love with her."

Pete let out a low whistle. "Wonderful timing, kid."

Joey clutched Pete's shirt. "Am I falling in love with a . . . monster? A . . . fake that's not a real girl?"

If Joey's face weren't so anguished, Pete might have laughed at the absurdity of the question. But this *was* serious. "I don't know what they are, Joe. Tell me, what do you two do?"

"What's *that* supposed to mean?" said Joey defensively.

Pete rolled his eyes. "I didn't mean, what do you *do*. Just, where do you go together, what do you talk about?"

"I don't know . . . everything, I guess. She won't let me kiss her. We talk a lot, about everything. We've never—" Joey stammered and fell silent, blushing.

"You don't talk to her about this underground, do you?" Pete asked sharply.

"Of course not. I'm not a total asshole, Pete." He thought for a moment. "We went to Coney Island awhile ago. Wait a sec—that day she told me something about how they didn't want her to spend much time studying humans anymore, even though as a sociologist she was brought here for that. She said she was afraid they'd lied to her about their mission here."

"Mmmm. Keep seeing her, Joey. Don't let on you know anything about their being different from us. I mean, don't bring her white mice instead of a box of candy as a gift."

Joey looked hurt.

"Sorry, kid. If she's telling us the truth, and they've lied to their *own* people, it may help us a lot. Lisa may help us—"

"I don't want her getting hurt—"

"No promises, Joey. But if she's right, she may turn out to be on our side. Can you handle all this? If you can't, tell me. Now or anytime. You can bail out, and nobody'll think anything terrible about you."

"That's not true and we both know it," Joey mumbled. "But I don't mind seeing Lisa. It'd be hard *not* seeing her."

"I'm sorry to have to ask you, but I have a feeling we're all going to wind up doing things we'd rather not. But we don't have much choice. Not if we want our planet back." He put an arm around Joey's shoulders and they left the restaurant together.

A day later, Sam Yeager came up with a name for them to check out. He was fairly sure that Julio Cruz was their man, the leader of the Diablos but also a religious boy who had regularly attended the burned-out church before its Visitor occupation.

Meanwhile, Pete confirmed that Julio and other Diablo members had been to the armory sports nights. The night after the meeting, he picked Lauren up and they drove to her father's house and office, which had been closed and locked since his disappearance, so they could check his records for Julio's address. The Visitors had never bothered to search the brownstone, since they'd found or planted what they'd needed at the Medical Center office.

Pete sensed Lauren's hesitation as she pushed her key into the front-door lock. She gave him a half-smile. "I haven't been in here since Daddy—well, since—"

"I know. It's okay," Pete said. "Take your time." He gave her a quick, reassuring hug, then shivered. "But brrr—it's cold out here. Almost Christmas."

She blinked in surprise. "My God, you're right. It's so

strange not having the media telling us how many shopping days are left, I'd forgotten."

Pete's distraction worked and Lauren unconsciously opened the door. They went directly downstairs to the office and found the patient files.

"Here it is," said Lauren as Pete looked over her shoulder. "The whole Cruz family are patients of Daddy's. He delivered Julio, in fact."

"Got the address?"

"Uh-hunh." Lauren reached for a pad and scribbled it, then closed the file drawer.

"Okay, Lauren, let's go find Julio Cruz."

She had a faraway look in her eyes.

"What's wrong?" he asked.

"What you just said about Christmas. It's almost here, but you'd never know it. No trees, no lights, no decorations, no crazy shopping."

"So?"

"I miss it."

Pete shrugged. "I do too."

"Pete, don't you see? We can't let them take everything away from us. We *have* to celebrate the holidays. It may not be a military act, but it'll be an act of humanity and defiance. And we've got to hold on to every shred we can. We have to do it for the people who aren't with us to celebrate."

"It won't be a very merry Christmas."

"It may be the last Christmas humans *get* to celebrate. If we can't beat the Visitors, we may not be here in a year," she said quietly. "Besides, the holidays mean hope."

Pete nodded. "Okay. I'll talk to Guido. Maybe we can have a little party at his place. Just our resistance group. Now, let's go talk to Julio."

They were quiet on the ride over to Julio's street. This part of the city was a jarring mix of vacant, crumbling apartment houses, their fine old facades still holding a hint of past grandeur, and partial blocks of brownstones and larger buildings being reborn with the work and sweat of the people who refused to be chased out by the blight of poverty. The courage it took to hold off the surrounding urban decay was something

Pete admired. He wondered if he could have done as well, faced with like circumstances.

Julio's street was one of the pockets of renewal. They parked near the boy's building and went into the lobby, which was freshly painted, with the old stone floor buffed to a sheen. Even the brass highlights around the old elevator had been polished.

It all looked so good, Pete half expected to see a doorman.

They rode up to the third floor and walked along the brightly lit hallway to the Cruz apartment. Lauren touched the buzzer. They heard the click of the peephole cover and a young man's voice: "Who is it?"

"Lauren Stewart, Doctor Stewart's daughter. May I talk to you for a minute? Are you Julio?"

"Who's that with you?" asked the voice. "Is that you, Forsythe?"

"Yeah," said Pete. "Can we come in?"

After an indecisive moment, they heard the scraping of the lock chain and the unlatching of the bolts. Julio opened the door and let them inside. The apartment was sparsely decorated and not yet completely renovated, but the flooring had been replaced by finished wood slats and the kitchen appliances and light fixtures were new. It was a windowed cheery place, and Julio was home alone. He stood in the center of the living room, his stance defiant.

"Okay, what do you want?"

"Mind if we sit down?" asked Pete, not waiting for an answer, sitting on the well-worn but clean couch in front of the boy. Lauren waited a second, then joined him.

"Julio," said Lauren, "did you know that the Visitors framed my father and took him up to their Mother Ship weeks ago?"

Julio looked genuinely shocked. He stepped back, groped for a threadbare easy chair, and sat in it. "No . . . I know my mom tried to make an appointment for my little sister, but there wasn't no answer. She hadda take her to the clinic, and wait all day long."

Pete smiled inwardly—they'd made the emotional connection Sam Yeager said they'd need.

"Julio," he said, "I'm going to ask you a straight question and I want a straight answer. Did you and your friends bomb the church?"

"So what if we did?" came the sullen reply. "I'm not sayin' we did, but it wasn' no church no more anyway. So, whoever did it, and killed some of those muthafuckers, I'm glad."

"We don't like the Visitors any more than you," said Lauren. "I mean, they've got my father, and I don't know whether he's alive or dead." She noticed Julio's face cloud over.

My friends are dead, I know that, thought Julio. But he pointed at Pete and said, "He works for them."

Pete held up both hands, shaking his head. "Whoa, wait a minute. I *don't* work for the Visitors. I started doing that because the man who pays my salary asked me to, and that was long before anybody knew all this stuff about the Visitors being what they are. And believe me, Julio, I know a lot more about what they are than most people do. You can decide for yourself if you trust us, but we need your help and *we're* going to trust *you* right now."

"Help with what?"

"In getting weapons to fight the Visitors," said Pete.

Julio tried to maintain a poker face, but his eyes sparkled with a sudden lust Pete didn't like much. But what choice did he have but to bring Julio in on the plan?

"What kinda weapons, man?"

"Things stored at the armory—small arms and explosives," said Pete. "But these weapons are for the resistance movement, not for any private vendetta you've got going because they desecrated your church."

Julio flared. "Who're *you* to tell *me* what to do with weapons I'm gonna help you get, man?"

Pete almost blew up at him, but opted for a quiet response. "There's an organized group gathering to fight the Visitors. Getting organized and staying that way is the only chance we've got, the only chance we've *all* got."

"We know for a fact," Lauren said, "that some of the other gangs are going along with the Visitors, getting laser rifles from them, drugs, women, fancy cars, because they're helping the Visitors keep their neighborhoods in line. How long do you think it'll be before those other gangs go after the Diablos? Remember that the Black Fury, the Conquistadors, the Toros— they all were busy fighting with the Diablos, *before* the Visitors came, and if they've got better weapons, they'll put your gang out of commission for good."

"And once they turn those laser rifles on your guys, how long do you think you'll last, Julio?" said Pete, continuing the tactic Lauren started. "The Visitors would like nothing better than to have all you uncooperative sons of bitches wiped out by other humans—saves them the trouble of doing it themselves."

"They can't do that so easy, man," Julio snarled. "I'll turn Diablo turf into hell before I let them kill us and take it away."

"You'll be dead before you can move," said Lauren flatly. "The Visitors don't fool around—and neither will the gangs they're backing. The only way you can help save your turf is to help us fight the Visitors all over the city, not just up here."

"Well," said Julio, sitting back more calmly now, "what do you want?"

"First," said Pete, "your word that you'll help us—and keep this quiet. And that you'll do what you're told."

"Do I got *any* say in all this?"

"Yeah, you'll have a say—but what the group decides, you do—like in the army," said Pete.

Julio smiled faintly, considering. "Okay, you got my word."

"Julio, you're crazy, man," said Benny Hernandez, a towering hulk with a trim beard who looked much older than his seventeen years.

Julio shook his head slowly. "No, I'm not. Like they said, those other gangs in the Visitors' hip pockets, they got heavy firepower, man. We got shit. We can't do all this alone."

Hernandez spat on the sidewalk as they walked on Julio's street. "These resistance guys, they the Man, Julio. What do they care about what goes on in this barrio? They gonna use us and we gonna have nothin' to show for it."

Julio reached out and grabbed the bigger boy's arm, turning him so they were staring into each other's eyes.

"Don' worry, Benny. We'll get somethin' to show for it. I want you to talk to your uncle."

"Jorgé?"

"Yeah, Jorgé. He did time, right? For doin' some FALN bombing, right?"

"Yeah."

"Then he's gonna be our 'technical adviser,' man. He can tell us what kinda stuff we need and how to put it together."

Benny rubbed his hands, his eyes narrowing as he thought it over. "Yeah, Julio, yeah. I think you got something here."

Julio nodded confidently, his dark eyes luminous, lit by thoughts of revenge. "Yeah, I got something. *We* got something—and when we're done, everybody's gonna know the Diablos don' get pushed around, not by no Visitors, not by *nobody*."

Pete drove back downtown to drop Lauren off at her apartment. "You were very good in there," he said.

"I'm a negotiator. I negotiated," she said flatly.

"I didn't know you could be that tough. You came up with just the right angle to get us what we want."

"And what makes you think we're going to get what we want?" Lauren asked, eyebrows raised.

"You don't believe what Julio promised us?"

She laughed shortly. "You mean you *do*?"

"What are you talking about?" Pete asked.

"Oh, I believe he'll help with the armory raid. It obviously appealed to him when you told him the details. It's *why* he'll help that I don't trust. And whether he'll take orders. You don't think it was *patriotism* that got him in our camp, do you?" she asked sarcastically.

"Of course not. And there was very little appeal to that emotion during your sales pitch about the other gangs attacking the Diablos."

"We're going to have to keep a very close eye on Julio and his boys once this gets going—assuming we can actually pull it off."

"And you call *me* a cynic?" asked Pete rhetorically.

"Maybe it's rubbing off on me," she said.

Chapter 19

Dreams of a Revolution

"Jennifer."

The auburn-haired officer turned from her bridge console to face Roger as he entered the control room.

"I'd like everyone's attention, please," said the Commander. Angela was the last to stop work at her own station across the bridge.

"This isn't the proper time for a full-fledged ceremony—that will have to wait until we return home. But I wanted this logged for the record, with senior crew as witness: that Jennifer will receive a Mission Commendation, first class, for her leadership and efficiency in the recent raid on the Brook Cove scientific outpost. Now that we've had the time to thoroughly examine the equipment and records taken in the raid, we know that it could have posed a grave danger had the work there been allowed to continue."

"I was just doing my assigned job, Commander," said Jennifer. She could feel Angela's cold gaze boring into her, even from this distance.

"But there are better and worse ways to do one's assigned job," he continued. "You had the judgment and ability to do it the better way. Now, I believe your shift is ending. Dismissed, Jennifer."

"Thank you for the honor, sir. I hope I'll continue to merit your confidence in me."

"I'm sure you will," he said, nodding as she left the bridge.

* * *

When she reached her quarters, Jennifer breathed a weary sigh. A battlefield commendation for doing something she despised was not her idea of success. And Roger's little act was obviously designed to goad Angela, who had hated her enough already. With this, Jennifer would only have to watch herself even more closely.

It was not beyond Angela to go out of her way to sabotage other assignments Jennifer might be given.

Slowly, she unlocked a small compartment in her cabin wall and took out a hand-sized metal case. Opening the lid, she picked up a triangular crystalline medallion attached to a silvery ribbon. She didn't read the inscription, but its words ran through her mind: "For Uncommon Courage and Unselfish Valor in Peaceful Alien Contact—Kisszizk Mission."

She'd earned it on her first mission out of the training academy—long before the Great Leader had led the coup that brought him to power. Things were different in those days—a time when missions to other worlds were peaceful in intent, designed to open new trade and cultural contacts.

There *must* have been another way to solve the environmental crises that seemed to pile up all at once, she thought sadly. But famine, fuel shortages, and economic collapse have a way of dashing reason on the shoals of hysterical fear. The time had been ripe for radical change, and that's exactly what the Great Leader had brought. Jennifer was sorry his solution had turned out to mean despotism and roaming the stars only to spread death. She squeezed her medal in the palm of her hand. The Kisszizk were extinct now, their planet a collapsed slag of debris. Her medal was now only a quaint relic of a time that seemed not so long ago—and yet also seemed never to have happened at all. She placed it back in its case and returned it to the cabinet.

Alexander Garr's Central Park West apartment fit well with the nickname Peter Forsythe, the team wit, had pinned on him—Alexander the Great. It was an opulent duplex with parquet floors, Persian area rugs, and paintings and statues collected from around the globe. "Products of pillage," Pete had dubbed them, asking Garr if he ever had the urge to trade the objets d'art the way he traded players.

"No," Garr had responded. "The players I *thought* were

treasures when I got them, but they turned out to be bums. The art objects are bought as treasures and *stay* that way."

This Christmas Garr waited until all his dinner guests—Roger and Angela, Cardinal Palazzo, and Mayor Alison Stein—had arrived before giving the grand tour.

Garr had spent plenty in black market transactions to scour up a large turkey and the other ingredients for a first-rate dinner . . .

"Chickens," said Guido with a shrug of resignation. "The best I could find. But don't you worry. Leave the dinner to me and I won't let you down, Pete." He patted Forsythe on the shoulder. "Now you go back with your friends."

Pete did as he was told—the other resistance members were already there, artfully decorating a three-foot-tall live tree in a pot.

"How did this get here?" asked Pete.

"With great difficulty," someone piped up.

"By squad ship," quipped Sam Yeager. "Compliments of the Visitors! They're filling in for Santa, y'see."

Food had already been laid out—Christmas cookies and cakes and chips and dips, and Lauren busied herself filling cups with eggnog. She handed one to Pete, held up her own, and they clinked them together. "Merry Christmas," she said, giving him a peck on the cheek, catching him by surprise.

Innocently, she pointed up at the ceiling. "Mistletoe, Mr. Forsythe."

Pete nodded. "Oh. Why do it halfway?" In a quick move, he put his eggnog down, grabbed Lauren, and bent her over backwards in a dramatic embrace. After a startled second, she returned his kiss. A minute later, Denise Daltrey thoughtfully relieved Lauren of her eggnog—which was tipping dangerously.

Pete and Lauren broke the embrace reluctantly, belatedly remembering they had an audience. When they straightened, the group applauded enthusiastically, and Pete and Lauren took sheepish bows.

"Next show," he said, "in one minute. Soon as I get my breath back."

"Oh, no you don't," Lauren laughed, dancing out of range of the sprig of greenery.

* * *

A hired pianist sat at Garr's baby grand, softly playing Christmas tunes as background music. Garr had wanted to sing carols, but there didn't seem to be a lot of enthusiasm for the idea on the part of either Palazzo or Ali Stein, who seemed immensely uncomfortable just being there with the Visitor leaders.

Palazzo took Garr to the side for a private moment. "Alex, why did you invite me?"

"It *is* Christmas."

"One would be hard-pressed to tell—no trees, no lights anywhere in the city."

"The Visitors won't allow any mass gatherings, and they were afraid decorations might stir people up. Then there's the curfew."

"Well," said Palazzo skeptically, "all this does wonders for *my* holiday spirit." He glanced around at the room—Alison Stein sitting by herself, drink in hand, the two Visitors standing together, the piano player oblivious to everyone.

"Not the best party I've ever thrown, huh? Maybe it'll get better when we eat."

"The Visitors don't eat our food, remember?"

"Do you think people are celebrating behind closed doors?" Garr wondered.

"Oh, I'm sure of it, Alex. Thank God," he said pointedly.

Things did not improve with the serving of the meal. Alison recounted lists of the growing number of violent terrorist incidents, wondering aloud if the city would still be standing in a few months. The Visitors assured her that the terrorists would all be rounded up in a matter of days and the city would be safe.

"Cardinal Palazzo," said Roger, "how do you think the spirit of the citizens is holding up?"

"It would have been better if you'd allowed them to celebrate our holidays openly," Palazzo replied firmly. He noticed Angela slyly observing him and met her gaze without fear. "Freedom of worship is very important to us. It's what we're used to, and not having it is taking its toll."

"There was little choice under martial law," said Angela smoothly. "Perhaps we can make some dispensations next year."

"I thought you said this was only a temporary measure," Palazzo countered.

"Resistance proved more widespread than we believed," Roger said. "But I think we've made enough headway to consider lifting many of the restrictions very soon. Perhaps a later curfew . . ." He thought for a moment. "You know what I think we should do, the five of us? Take a goodwill tour of the city—and soon."

"A fine idea, Roger," Angela seconded. "We could pick you three up and tour the city by squad ship—"

"By air? Count me out," said Alison. "I'm terrified of flying. Makes me sick as a dog. We don't want a puce green mayor parading around to calm the citizenry, now do we?"

"Car would be better anyway," said Garr. "That way, we'd be closer to the people we want to see us, rather than just flying around hopscotching from area to area. It's also more traditional. It would be a fine way to let people see you, talk to you, reassure them that you Visitors are really just like us, and have our best interests at heart."

"Cardinal Palazzo, will you join us?" Angela asked.

"Certainly. I agree—it is a good idea, a constructive way of countering all the negative feelings aroused by *martial law*," he said, his voice pointedly disapproving.

"Ali," said Garr, "how about if we coordinate the whole thing through your office? Can you have someone on your staff set an itinerary, contact neighborhood leaders, have the people out there to greet us"—he leaned over and whispered to her—"and make sure there are no embarrassing demonstrations?"

"I think we can handle that. It'll take about a month to set up. Let's set a date."

"How about Valentine's Day? The spirit of love and all that."

"All right," Alison said.

Guido delivered as promised—delicious chicken, bread stuffing, plum pudding, cranberry sauce, minisalads (fresh vegetables were hard to come by), and plenty of wine. And of course his trademark Italian pastries.

"Hey," said Brenda Ortiz between bites, "you know what we need? A name."

"What do you mean a name?" asked Mitchell.

"What self-respecting terrorist group doesn't have a name?" Brenda went on. "You know, like Black September, the Popular Liberation Front of whatever . . ."

"I think she's right," Denise said. "It'll give us some esprit de corps."

"As long as we don't get signet rings and have a secret handshake," Yeager kidded.

Brenda laughed. "Everybody think about it, okay?"

"What is this—a name-the-baby contest?" grumbled Pete.

"Hey, are we going to have a white Christmas?" asked Hannah Donnenfeld.

"Not according to the weather report," said Lauren.

"But that was a Visitor weather report," said Pete with a grin. "And we don't believe *anything* they tell us, do we?"

When they'd finished eating, the group sat quietly. "You know what's missing?" said Yeager. "Music. We have to sing carols. Anybody got a piano?"

"Would this do?" asked Denise shyly. She took a small electronic keyboard out of her tote bag. It was about the size of a loaf of Italian bread.

"How come you never played on the morning news?" asked Pete with a grin.

"My great dream when I was a kid was to be a concert pianist. Obviously, I never made it."

"Play, maestro," said Lauren.

Denise touched the keys and played the instantly recognizable first four notes of "Silent Night." Slowly and quietly, voices joined in.

When the song was over, Denise grinned at the applause. "You know, there's something I've always wanted to perform, but I never had such wonderful choral accompaniment. You don't even need to know the words, just hum along. It'll sound great."

"What is it?" Brenda asked.

"You'll know it," Denise said excitedly. She began Beethoven's "Ode to Joy." And she was right—they didn't need to know the words. Slowly, they began to hum. At first it was tentative and reedy. But each voice added fullness and gave Denise confidence. She increased the tempo, and the music written nearly two hundred years before took on the same soaring sweep it had when performed in elegant, gilded concert halls by hundred-piece orchestras and two-hundred-voice choirs. The times were complex, but the harmonies they were singing were simple, from the heart.

Guido stood at the doorway listening, smiling, his eyes watery. When the song ended, he spoke up: "Hey, everybody, it's snowing. You got your white Christmas."

They broke into cheers. Denise jumped up and waved for attention. "Hey, that's it!"

"That's what?" someone asked.

"Our name, the name of our little terrorist cadre—White Christmas."

She watched their faces expectantly as they mulled the idea, and heads began to nod as tongues turned the two words over and over.

"I like it," said Lauren. "Symbolic, upbeat—any objections?" There were none. "Welcome to White Christmas, everybody."

Then Denise played the first bars of "White Christmas," and everyone joined in the singing. A year ago, none of them would ever have guessed this would be how they'd spend their next Christmas, but as late as a week ago, they didn't expect to have *any* Christmas. And if this one was bittersweet, that was preferable to none at all.

Chapter 20

The Right to Bear Arms . . .

The armory shook with its usual cacophony of thumping basketballs and sneakers, pounding music from a half-dozen radios and tape players, and exuberant voices at top volume, all swirling together in the drafty, increasingly smoky main area.

With Pete's blessing, Julio had passed the word to the kids there this evening—more noise, booze, and drugs, with no questions asked—as long as it was all shared with and directed at the Visitors. And the youngsters responded with relish, almost as if there was a tacit competition going on—which gang or neighborhood group could get the most Visitors high on liquor or controlled substances in the shortest time, and at the same time make the most noise.

What only a few of Julio's friends knew was the reason for the sanctioned anarchy—to cover activities *not* on the announced program.

"Who's the lock picker?" asked Sam.

A fourteen-year-old girl with olive skin and a knit cap glared at him. "You a cop, man. We got immunity?"

"That's the deal," said Sam, speaking quietly to his light-fingered platoon in a back corridor. "Whatever you do in here tonight is our little secret."

"Then I do the locks," said the girl, buffing her fingernails on her down vest.

That evening Sam led his group into the bowels of the old armory. Padlocks on arms-storage rooms were opened, then a storeroom yielded a cache of hand trucks and dollies. Yeager had these dispatched to different parts of the building—they'd make the later job that much easier. Finally, three normally locked emergency doors leading out of the building onto alleys were carefully opened, their alarms deactivated.

The diversions worked and the interlopers completed their tasks without detection. When they were done, all breached doors and locks restored to apparent integrity, Yeager signaled Pete, who gave the word to Julio in turn. Tonight's job was on.

The armory lights went off, the sounds of the switch being thrown by a young male Visitor echoing in the unaccustomed silence. He turned to see Pete putting his coat on at the open front door.

"A good night tonight," said Pete. "What do you think, Gordon?"

The Visitor shrugged. "Your young people can be excessively noisy." He did not seem pleased.

"Well, look at it this way, Gordo—if they didn't burn off all this energy in here, they'd be using it to burn up Visitor facilities, like that incident at the church a few weeks ago."

"I suppose you're right."

"Just between you and me, I think your people were pretty smart to figure that out and plan these sessions. Well, I'll see that everything's locked up. Good night."

"Good night," said Gordon.

Pete stepped outside, holding the door open for Gordon as the Visitor went out into the cold night air. Pete slammed the door behind him, jiggling it to make sure it was secure, and walked away from the armory, turning to wave back at Gordon walking the other way toward a parked squad ship. Pete kept walking away slowly until the Visitor ship lifted off and glided away. Then he moved quickly around the building to the side alley, where Julio's friends were gathering, one by one.

At two other doors on the back and far side of the armory, other gang members huddled in the dark. Julio led one group, Pete another, and Sam the third. At each door, they checked their watches.

"Eleven o'clock," Pete whispered, then opened the unlocked door.

Simultaneously, Julio and Yeager did the same at their posts, waving their platoons inside the deserted armory. Each group's members ranged from urchins to late teens, but they all moved quickly and quietly, the older kids leading as they had been briefed, heading for predetermined storage rooms and corridors. There they found the hidden dollies and hand trucks and set up "bucket brigades," moving crates of rifles, explosives, and ammunition with assembly-line precision back to the three exits.

Others went into the storage areas and came out with surplus duffel bags filled with items of destruction, cold steel carried out like sacks of toys.

Outside, a sanitation-department truck backed into the alley. Duffels were tossed into its yawning rear opening.

Single youths carried bags to other vehicles parked at arranged spots on the blocks around the armory. Some hailed cabs or caught the last buses before the new midnight curfew forced them off the streets.

Throughout the night, they took roundabout routes to the underground garage where Pete and Julio had agreed to rendezvous. By five A.M., all of Julio's people had been accounted for, and the Diablos' leader took big Benny Hernandez aside. "Did you get our stuff, Benny?"

"We got it, Julio. You were right—this *was* worth it. We got machine guns, rifles, dynamite, bullets. But what're we gon' do with all this?"

"I got some things in mind, Benny. We gonna make some people sorry they came to this planet."

Pete arrived with Lauren, Joey, and Yeager at about six—by then, Julio's gang members had loaded the crates and duffel bags onto three panel trucks left in the garage for transport.

"What are you gonna do with all this ammo?" asked Julio ingenuously.

"We're going to let the Visitors know they can't roll over us," said Yeager.

"Are we gonna be part of what you got in mind?"

"You already were," Pete said. "Getting these weapons."

"Hey, man, we wanna be there when they get *used*!" Julio protested.

"We're not sure when that'll be," Lauren temporized.

"Don' call us, we'll call you," Julio said mockingly.

"That's not it," Pete protested, not terribly convincingly.

"I think it is, man," said Julio, spitting out the words. "I think you're kissing me and the Diablos off."

Sam nodded toward the trucks. Pete looked as if he wanted to say something to prove Julio wrong—but he *wasn't* wrong. Pete knew it, and wasn't the least bit comfortable with that fact. But as Sam climbed into one truck and Joey the second, Lauren pulled him to the third and they got in. Engines started and with sunrise just starting to brighten the sky, the trucks rolled out of the garage and onto the street. They turned in different directions and blended into the light flow of traffic that had become the norm in formerly crowded Manhattan.

Pete waved around at the orderly and sparse tide of vehicles, the abundance of parking spaces. "Mussolini made the trains run on time—the Visitors solved New York's traffic problem."

Lauren didn't even crack a smile and sat in silence for several blocks.

"What's wrong?" asked Pete finally.

"I think you're making a mistake, Pete, keeping the gangs out of the mainstream of our activity."

"That's just it—there *is* no mainstream. We can't have a bunch of loose cannons rolling across our decks."

"But that's exactly what we *do* have, Pete," Lauren insisted. "*We* planted this little bug in their ears, the idea of fighting the Visitors."

"Judging by the church attack, Julio had already thought of that on his own," Pete said.

"But now he knows the white middle-class power structure is doing the same thing. And as usual, the poor black and Hispanic people are being shut out. I don't blame him for being pissed."

"I didn't notice you were white, Ms. Stewart,"

"In my case, having money and a prestigious job makes me just as white as you, with your blond curls. To Julio and people in the ghettoes, I'm one of *you*, not one of *them*."

"So what are you saying, Lauren?"

"That we all might live to regret what you just did to those kids."

Pete slammed his fist on the steering wheel. "Did to *them*?

Like it was *my* idea to get them to help us and then shove them back outside, right? I thought we all agreed. For Chrissakes, I'm a goddamned *baseball* player, Lauren! I'm not Fidel Castro or Che Guevara! I don't know what the hell we're doing. Do *you* know? Then you can make *all* the damned decisions yourself from now on!''

"Pete, I didn't mean—''

He cut her off. "I'm just trying to do what I think'll work. And I *don't* think we can trust Julio to go along with us or take orders from us.''

"Don't you realize he had the same access to weapons as we did?''

"I'm sure he did. So what? So they'll use 'em to attack the Visitors with a hell of a lot more firepower than those Molotov cocktails they used on the church. How can it hurt us to have other people punching the Visitors at the same time as we are?''

"How can you *say* that! We need to coordinate, not fragment!''

They finished the drive in grim silence.

The weapons were stored in small consignments around the city—many eggs in many baskets to protect against losing critical amounts of armaments if the Visitors found any of the hiding places or captured any of the White Christmas group and tortured them into revealing secrets. No single member knew more than three weapons locations.

But they still needed a major plan for using their newly acquired arms. They didn't have to wait long. Brenda Ortiz presented the genesis of an idea at a late January meeting, in the sewing room of a garment district factory dormant since the Visitors shut down all unnecessary industry.

"It's some sort of propaganda tour,'' Brenda explained. "The Mayor, Alexander Garr, Cardinal Palazzo, and our good friends Roger and Angela.''

"When?'' asked Pete.

"In two and a half weeks. I've got their itinerary.'' She took a piece of paper out of her pocket and unfolded it. Lauren brought a city map over and spread it out on the sewing table, pushing aside patterns and swatches of cloth left over from the factory's more active days.

As Brenda described the route, Lauren looked over at Pete, whose blue eyes were unfocused, betraying the fact that he was thinking hard while he listened. He caught her gaze and gave her a slight nod. She returned it with a smile.

"I think I've got something," he said. "Tell me what you think of *kidnapping* good ol' Angela and Roger so we can find out what they're up to and maybe get us some bargaining chips." He found all eyes turned his way. "Ah, I see I have your full attention . . ."

Chapter 21

The Face of the Enemy

It was a busy two and a half weeks for the newly christened White Christmas group, as they organized for the "big one," as they came to term their upcoming attempt to kidnap Roger and Angela. The planning required for such a raid proved phenomenal, especially for people still required to put in time at their regular jobs. Pete and Joey, except for their "baby-sitting" at the armory with the Visitor Friends groups, were the ones with the most free time, and much of the burden of preparation fell on them.

They held twice-weekly nighttime practice sessions on the firing range in the basement of Sam Yeager's precinct house, making use of the fact that Yeager had been given unfavorable night duty by the Visitors. Wearing spare uniforms borrowed from lockers in the police barracks and using forged I.D.'s, the White Christmas members practiced with the weapons they'd stolen.

With Lauren's help and UN connections, they even managed to wangle a travel permit up to the isolated mountain cabin, owned by Denise Daltrey's friend. There, in a deserted quarry, they practiced with Molotov cocktails and grenades. Not surprisingly, Pete Forsythe and Joey Vitale proved to have the best throwing arms.

But oddly enough, with the M-16 and .38 Police Special, Lauren Stewart proved to be one of the best shots. She found target practice stimulating and challenging, but never stopped protesting that, while shooting at targets was all very well, she could never—*never*—turn a weapon on anyone, Visitor or human. Pete reassured her that the raid he'd planned did not include any projected combat scenarios. They would capture the Visitors by trickery, and if everything went as planned, nobody would have to shoot anyone.

"Ah," Lauren said when Pete explained this to her as they stood in the precinct house's firing range. "What you're saying reminds me of negotiations with the Russians. They're also very fond of that word '*if*.'"

Coolly, she pulled her protective ear guards into place, raised the .38, sighted carefully, and put six rounds into the heart area of the human-shaped target.

Pete gulped. "Remind me not to make you mad, Ms. Stewart. If only your dad could see you now."

She gave him a superior smile. "Just a little hand-eye coordination, and calculation of ballistics, Mr. Forsythe. If you need some coaching, I'd be glad to offer my services."

Pete grinned at her. "Only if we switch to rifle practice."

"Why?"

"'Cause then you've gotta put your arms around me. Just like in all those movies where the hero teaches the heroine to shoot."

She tried to glare at him, but after a second's pretense, gave up and laughed.

At noon on the day of the "big one," Sam Yeager drove by Guido's restaurant, where three other White Christmas members were waiting for him—Joey Vitale and the two bus drivers: Sal, the tall gray-haired man, and Manfred, a short, round black man with a fringe of white hair over his ears. Sal and Manfred directed Sam to the West Side yard where Metropolitan Transit authority buses were sent for repairs. They had in hand not only the keys to the front gate, but also the keys to four freshly overhauled buses, courtesy of a friend in Maintenance who wanted to help.

They arrived at the yard at about two in the afternoon, entered, found their buses, and made sure they ran. Then they waited out of sight.

The thin crowd gathered at Rockefeller Center was bundled against the February wind whipping the flags around the ice rink. A pair of figure skaters, a man and a woman, danced gracefully to taped music playing over the loudspeakers as the sun shone brightly on this monument to capitalism in the heart of Manhattan. The dozen or so tan Indiana limestone buildings had been put up during the Great Depression, between 1931 and 1939, constructed with the sweat and skills of seventy-five thousand workers. The last rivet was driven in by John D. Rockefeller, Jr., himself.

As the Mayor's limo parked in front of the RCA Building, across from the skating rink, Alex Garr glanced up at the large inscription etched into the stone facade: *"Wisdom and Knowledge Shall Be the Stability of Thy Times."* He wondered if the somber New Yorkers waiting for this public-relations appearance came expecting wisdom *or* knowledge—these times seemed to have very little in the way of stability.

A flying wedge of New York police—watched carefully by heavily armed Visitor security troops in their familiar red coveralls—escorted Garr, Cardinal Palazzo, Mayor Alison Stein, Angela, and Jennifer to the podium set up down on the rink, under the gaze of the great golden statue of Prometheus. Roger was not with them.

As they took their places on the platform, Garr leaned over to Palazzo. "I've seen bigger crowds at two in the morning," he whispered. "And these're a sullen lot too."

"What did you expect?"

Alison Stein stepped to the microphones. A Visitor camera crew was recording the event for later broadcast by Kristine Walsh.

"Ladies and gentlemen," Stein began, a nervous tremor in her voice. Her mouth was dry—she wished it were Dan O'Connor doing this, not her. But she forced a smile. "I'm glad to see so many of you out here on such a nippy Valentine's Day. But that's the nature of New Yorkers, isn't it—triumphing over adversity?"

At the fringe of the crowd, across the plaza, Brenda Ortiz watched. There was a massive marble plaque spread in front of her. She'd been here dozens of time, but never read it. It was a long quote from old John D. and it started with: *"I believe in the supreme worth of the individual and in his right to life, liberty and the pursuit of happiness . . ."*

Brenda found herself smirking—she never expected to feel a

kinship with a robber-baron capitalist, but there on the marble slab, the long-dead industrialist had laid out exactly what Brenda and her rebel friends were fighting for. She walked to a pay phone and dialed.

"Hi—I just wanted to let you know it looks like our dinner guests will be on time," she said.

The cab pulled over to the curb and Denise Daltrey paid the driver. She got out, clutching a shopping bag under one arm. Her bulky down coat, scarf, and woolen cap disguised her, and she sat down on a small folding chair she had in her bag, positioning herself on the sidewalk beside a subway entrance that had a padlocked gate across its bottom and a Closed for Repair Work sign on the gate. She took her electronic keyboard instrument out of the bag and placed it on her lap, putting the case at her feet with its lid open. Then she began to play. The few people passing by in the late afternoon twilight ignored her. After several minutes, one forlorn quarter rattled into the coffer, resting there in solitary testament to music appreciation. Denise glanced at her watch, smiling wryly—almost four-thirty.

A bus stopped at the corner near her and Peter Forsythe got off, an athletic bag in his hand. When no one was looking, he went quickly down the staircase behind Denise, took out a heavy-duty wire cutter, and clipped the chain that bound the folding gate. He opened it enough to slip inside, then closed it behind him, rehung the chain, and moved into the dark at the bottom of the stairwell, out of sight of anyone looking down from the street.

The subway train slowly, sinuously snaked into the station, metal wheels shrieking as the train slid to a stop. In the motorman's cab, the young black engineer heard his compartment door open. Before he could turn, he felt something small, cold, and hard pressed against his cheek.

"Announce that this train is out of service," said Sari James, her long strawberry-blonde hair hidden under a plaid cap. Her hand held the automatic pistol steady as the frightened engineer reached carefully for the public address mike.

"We're not going to hurt you," said Sari, "but we need this train for about the next hour." She smiled reassuringly as he glanced back at her and saw a stunning, dark-skinned woman behind Sari, along with two husky men in blue uniforms—Lauren and two transit workers who'd joined the resistance.

"May I have your attention please, folks. Due to mechanical difficulties, this train is now out of service. We're sorry for any inconvenience. Everyone off the train."

The subway hadn't been very crowded anyway, and it was clear of passengers in no time at all.

"Fine. Close it up," said Sari softly. "Drive nice and easy."

He gingerly pushed the throttle and the train creaked and rocked out of the station into the dark tunnel ahead.

"Okay," said Sari, "pull into the local platform at the next station."

"But I'm not supposed to make that stop, lady. It's closed for repairs."

Sari tipped her gun at him and smiled. "Think of this train as a private charter, okay?"

One of the husky transit workers, Lenny Honaka, took out a walkie-talkie. "Signal Baker three-oh, divert all other trains after us until next transmission."

The device crackled back: "That's a Roger."

Darkness had settled over most of the wintry sky, and Alison reached to turn on the dome light in the limo's rear compartment.

"I think that went pretty well," said Garr unconvincingly. "What a shame Roger couldn't join us."

"I'm sure he'll be disappointed he didn't, after we report to him," said Jennifer, as the Cadillac approached the intersection.

At the traffic signal a half-block away, unseen hands flipped a series of control-box override switches.

The light turned yellow, then red. The limo stopped behind a city bus belching diesel fumes. Another bus pulled up behind the car. Then a third crawled alongside on the right. The limo driver's eyes darted nervously—he'd begun to suspect a setup, but it was too late to do anything about it as the fourth bus pulled up to their left to completely box the car in.

None of his passengers had noticed. Nor did they see Yeager, Joey, Sal, and Manfred put the buses in "park," jump out, and approach the limo with pistols at the ready, ski masks hiding their faces. Sam signaled the driver to lower his window—the gun pointed at his face through the glass convinced him. "Why didn't they listen to me and get one with bullet-proof glass?" the driver sighed. Then, more loudly, "I think we have company, Mayor."

Yeager looked into the car's rear compartment through the open front window. "Would you all get out of the car please? Quickly and quietly, or you're all dead."

"What the hell is going on here?" demanded Garr. He ducked his head toward the Cardinal. "Sorry, Your Eminence."

"No talking," said Yeager roughly. "Out, *now.*"

The five passengers complied, and the four masked gunmen surrounded them and rushed them between the buses, past Denise sitting watch at the subway entrance, down the steps, and through the unlocked gate. Pete was there with a lantern, his face uncovered.

"Pete! What's the meaning of this?" growled Garr.

"You'll find out soon enough, Alex. Now move along, everybody." Forsythe led them down into the station, which was dimly lit and bore signs of interrupted construction— sawhorses, steel piping for railings, bricks, wheelbarrows, and an assortment of other tools—as if the workmen were only out on a break.

Pete looked at his watch, then glanced down the tunnel. Headlights were coming closer. "Where's Roger?" asked Pete.

"He had pressing business," said Angela smoothly. "Your plan to kidnap both of us didn't quite work, did it?"

"Doesn't matter," Pete said in an untroubled tone. *"You'll* tell us what we need to know."

Angela let out a derisive laugh. "You have a lot to learn about us, don't you?"

Pete smiled back. "Not as much as you *think*, lady. Want me to catch you a mouse? Hungry?"

"Peter," Garr began angrily. "You're insulting our—"

Pete cut him off. "Not now, Alex. Just do what you're told and you won't get hurt."

The Con Ed switching substation fed electricity to most of the midtown Manhattan area—including two Visitor headquarters. Julio remembered a couple of summers ago when a water-main break caused a major fire in the switching station, blacking out the entire garment district and knocking out subway service.

Wearing an ill-fitting chauffeur's uniform, Julio parked the Mercedes in front of the building housing the substation. With its DPL plates, the police wouldn't tow the car away—funny how some things never changed. It had been easy to enter the mansion and steal the car and uniform as soon as darkness fell. Julio guessed the embassy wouldn't miss it for a while . . . long enough for it to serve its purpose. He pocketed the keys, taking care to lock the silver Mercedes—wouldn't want anyone to steal it, he thought wryly. Then he walked away.

The subway stopped at the platform and the resistance members and their prisoners stepped into the head car, where they found Lauren, Sari, and the two transit workers, Lenny Honaka and Saul Rosenberg. Sari continued to aim her gun at the engineer. Lauren and the men joined the group surrounding the VIP captives, who were then separated—Garr, Stein, and Palazzo being taken to one end of the car under guard, and Jennifer and Angela pushed into seats. The Visitors were the objects of immediate interest and scrutiny.

"Sari," said Pete, "take us into the tunnel. Then have him stop." Sari turned to the sweating engineer. "You heard the man."

"B-but I can't just stop in the tunnel."

"Is he kidding?" Pete grinned. "They do it all the damn time! Tell him to make believe it's rush hour and we're all commuters in a hurry. That oughta do it."

Sari stifled a laugh, nodded at the nervous man, and the train edged out of the station. A minute later, when they were well along into the isolated darkness, Sari leaned into the cab. "Okay, stop here."

"But there'll be other trains comin' along—"

"Don't worry—we're having them diverted. We don't want to get killed either, fella."

The subway jittered to a halt.

"All right, Angela," Pete said, "we'd like to know what

you Visitors are *really* doing here on Earth. We know you're dumping that supposedly vital chemical."

Angela smiled arrogantly. "Why should I tell you anything?"

"Because if you don't, we'll kill you."

"Oh, spare me your threats. If you kill us, we'll be replaced by other officers who will do our jobs, and our mission will continue until it's been accomplished. You can't stop it now."

"Stop *what*?" said Garr.

Pete glared angrily at his employer. "It's about time you asked an intelligent question, Alex! Only a few months too late, only after you've spent all your time kissing every Visitor ass within reach and ignored all the disappearances and all the martial law bullshit. Sorry, Your Eminence." He laughed shortly. "Well, this'll be a real learning experience for you, Alex."

Leaning casually on a lamp post a block from the Mercedes, Julio Cruz glanced at his watch. Five forty-eight. The dark street was empty. There were no pedestrians near the car, no traffic. Julio reached into his pocket and pressed the button on the small remote-control transmitter. Then he ran.

Two seconds later, the Mercedes exploded into a fireball, shredding the automobile into hunks of deadly shrapnel. The Con Ed substation building took the full brunt of the blast and the fronts of the bottom five floors collapsed in slow motion, concrete caving in like a house of cards, leaving a twisted skeleton of girders and reinforcing rods. The sidewalk and street itself gave way and a crater swallowed up the twisted carcass that had been the Mercedes. Within five seconds, a billowing cloud of acrid smoke blossomed over the site like a miniature mushroom cloud as the gas tank of the car continued to fuel the blaze. A chorus of burglar alarms, coming awake at the moment electricity was cut off, wailed in the hellish firelight.

Twenty blocks away, underground, the lights went off in the subway car and the humming motors died, leaving the rebels and their captives in near-total darkness. Only a pair of emergency bulbs with the collective power of a sick firefly lit the car. Sam quickly grabbed Pete's lantern and turned it up to full illumination—enough for guns to remain trained on Angela and Jennifer.

"What the hell happened?" Pete demanded.

"We don't know," said Sari from the engineer's cab, "but we've got no power. We're stuck, folks."

"Shit," Pete swore quietly. "If that power's not back on in ten or fifteen minutes, we get out through the tunnel. All except you two," he said to the Visitors.

"What good will it do to leave us here? We'd get out eventually," said Angela.

"Not if you're dead," said Yeager.

"Why can't we take them and question them somewhere else?" Lauren asked.

"Lauren," said Pete, "we can't risk our lives guarding them when we're trying to escape through subway tunnels. If they don't talk fast, we'll kill them here and now."

Lauren turned to Jennifer. "You've been awfully quiet. Do you always let Angela do your talking?"

Jennifer bridled at the question. "I do not. *I'll* tell you what you want to know," she said, taking everyone by surprise.

"Don't you dare, you coward!" Angela snapped. "That's an order!"

Jennifer ignored her. "We've lied to your people from the start—as you obviously suspect. It's the magnitude of the lie you can't possibly comprehend."

Angela dove off her seat and lunged, her speed inhumanly fast, and locked hands around Jennifer's throat. Sam dove into the fray, followed by Pete and one of the big transit workers. Joey and Lauren stood back with guns raised, trying to sort out the wrestling on the dark floor. Manfred, the bus driver, grabbed the lantern before it could be knocked off the bench, holding it high for better illumination. Angela, struggling to get up, opened her mouth with a reptilian hiss and a hideous dark tongue a foot or more long lashed forth. A stream of venomous spittle flew out of her mouth, splattering Pete and Sam Yeager in the face. They screamed, falling back, digging at their eyes.

For the moment, Angela abandoned Jennifer in favor of attacking the humans. She threw herself at Peter, hissing again, with that terrifying blurring speed. Blinded, he staggered helplessly as Sam Yeager lunged at Angela, smashing his pistol butt across her face. The others started to close in, but the blonde Visitor whirled like an animal at bay, spitting venom again. The burning drops kept them from grappling with her—and she was between them and the still-blinded Pete.

"Pete!" yelled Sam, trying to sight his gun for a clear shot in the swaying illumination of the lantern. "Get *down*!"

Jennifer suddenly launched herself into a dive straight at her superior officer, grabbing her around the legs. Both Visitors tumbled to the floor.

"Keep that light up!" Lauren screamed. "Pete!"

"Shoot her!" Jennifer's voice was panicky. "*Now!* I can't hold her!"

Angela struggled to her knees again, her tongue flailing once more. For a second the light caught her full in the face, and Lauren saw a thick flap of skin hanging from the blonde Visitor's face—underneath it was a nightmare of greenish-black and scaled skin, with reddish-yellow, black-slitted eyes. She glimpsed it for only a second, then the shadows closed in again, flickering in an insane, glimmering dance. But Lauren could see enough by the tiny emergency lights to tell that Angela was kicking Jennifer in the chest and stomach, struggling furiously to reach Peter. Jennifer made an inhuman sound of pain, and a second later the lantern's light picked up Angela, crawling free, to drag at Pete's legs as he crouched, moaning.

"She'll kill him!" cried Jennifer, gasping for air.

There was flash, an ear-popping reverberation in the close confines of the car, and the .38 jerked in Lauren's grip, not once, but repeatedly. The force of the shots kicked up and back, trying to twist the gun out of her hands, but she held firm. Two more final shots, for a total of five rounds, wrenched Lauren's wrists and elbows and shoulders. Then, as the smoke coiled sluggishly in the car and the smell of cordite rose to nearly choke them, everything was still except for Peter's continuing moans and a rasping sound coming from Angela's throat as she lay half on her back, crumpled where the .38's slugs had thrown her. Her head was propped against the subway bench, a spreading dark, wet stain on her chest.

Lauren's eyes were wide with shock as she tried to fathom what had happened. It had all been so fast! Sam made his way to her and took the gun out of her hands, nodding toward Pete.

"You'd better help him. I'll keep them covered," he said. Lauren stepped over Jennifer and Angela on the floor and helped Pete back onto the seat.

"Are you all right? Can you see?" she asked.

"Yeah . . . it's blurry, and it hurts like hell, but I think I'll be okay."

Lauren turned to take in the whole incredible scene. Garr, the Cardinal, and Mayor Stein stood open-mouthed, staring transfixed at Angela's shattered body. Blood bubbled out of her wounds as she tried to breathe through a lung punctured by Lauren's bullet. Joey helped Jennifer up and onto a seat. She seemed uninjured as she tried to catch her breath—trying not to look at her horribly wounded comrade. Finally, she stood and leaned over Angela—or the thing now visible behind Angela's ruptured mask.

"Wh-what *is* she?" asked Garr, hushed, uncomprehending.

"That's what we look like," said Jennifer quietly. "We're not really like you. Our human skin is actually a miracle of chemical engineering. It duplicates the look and feel of your skin almost perfectly. But we're not mammals."

She reached down to feel for a pulse in Angela's neck. The wounded Visitor tried to hiss out a last word. They heard a dry, gargling sound, then a last, sibilant gasp and her head slumped onto her chest. Jennifer sat down painfully, then looked up at them. "She's dead. I'll tell you everything you want to know— if you still want me to. I've been trying to locate your group for a long time now."

"Of course," said Lauren, helping Pete to sit up now.

He winced, squinting at the surviving Visitor through his burning eyes. Jennifer carefully picked up a piece of Angela's outer skin and peeled it back, revealing all of her real face . . . leathery and dark green with nostril slits instead of a humanoid nose, and a lipless mouth. The head was crested.

"Reptilian?" Pete finally managed to say. "That's what you're like too?"

"That's what we're *all* like." Only Pete heard Joey Vitale's quiet moan of anguish. Jennifer continued, "That's why we don't eat your food—we eat only live animals, or ones that are freshly killed, not cooked."

"All the people you've taken up to the Mother Ships," Pete

said, a whirl of nearly unbelievable thoughts numbing his voice, "they're still alive, aren't they?"

"Yes. Each Mother Ship can hold about five thousand humans in special life-support pods. Their metabolism is slowed down, a sort of suspended animation, so they don't need food—"

"So they can be used . . . *as* food," Pete whispered. "I'm right, aren't I?"

Jennifer nodded.

"Oh, God," Lauren said, hushed. Pete squeezed her hand.

Jennifer continued slowly. "The one truth John did tell you is that we've had extreme environmental disasters on our planet. Some were of our own doing, some were natural. The result is, we're critically short of water and food. The Great Leader's plan was to take the water from your planet—"

"Of course," said Sari, the scientist in her coming back to the fore. "The chemical manufacturing was just a smoke-screen. All the water supposedly used for that is what you *really* wanted. And I'll bet the people you've taken weren't just going to be consumed—"

"That's right," Jennifer said. "They were also going to be used as breeding stock—to breed more food. Like your domestic farm animals."

"But why take people?" Sari asked. "Why not take lower animals that could be raised for food more efficiently?"

"We will—eventually. But at the moment, the Great Leader also needs creatures who can serve as soldiers. Ever since our present military government overthrew a republic that was much like your own United States government, we've been engaged in an interplanetary war with a power that defeated several of our worlds before, early in the Leader's career. He always blamed the weakness of our civilian leaders for that defeat, the only one we've ever suffered, and he vowed he'd have his vengeance. When the environmental and economic problems became critical, he seized control and launched his war of revenge.

"So the thousands of people you've taken from Earth were also going to be cannon fodder for some insane interplanetary war?" Pete said through a jaw clenched to contain his rage. *"What kind of monsters are you?"*

"There's no way I can explain all this away," Jennifer said.

"*I* knew the true purpose of our mission from the beginning. But I was in the minority—many of my people still don't know." She looked over at Joey. "Lisa doesn't, for example. Some were misled, others lied to, to get them to serve on this mission. Most of our crew members were told we were coming to harvest a lower life form—and once we were here, they simply followed orders."

"That excuse doesn't wash, Jennifer," said Lauren. "You're intelligent beings. How can you all follow orders when you know you're killing other intelligent life, not some lower animals?"

"We're not *all* following orders, Lauren. You've got to believe this. Some of us who knew the real mission have been banding together, planning to stop all this before the Great Leader's surrogates take all your water, hundreds of thousands of your people, and kill the rest or leave them to die on a dried-up desert planet."

"Aren't you a little late?" Yeager snapped.

"No, no, we're not. For one second, look at it from my side. If I and others like me—people secretly part of the Alliance, a holdover from the old government—had protested at the start of the mission, what do you think would have happened to us under this military dictatorship?"

"You'd all have been killed before you ever got to Earth," said Yeager.

"Exactly. So we waited until we could do something about it here. We've contacted other officers who hate what we're being forced to do to your planet, we're moving our people into key positions in the chain of command, we're collecting intelligence, and working on ways to get rid of people like Angela—and ways to link up with groups like yours. Whatever we need to do—whatever *you* need to do—we have to do it together. Or the Great Leader *will* get what he sent us for."

"How do we know you're not telling us a new pack of lies to save your own skin and move up to take Angela's place?" said Pete.

She spread her hands. "You don't, I suppose. And I really don't know any way I can prove it to you. No matter what I do, you might wonder if it's just a clever way to set you up, something we had planned to convince you I'm telling you the truth. If you decide not to believe me, you can kill me right now—and I wouldn't really blame you. Maybe *this* will convince you—*I* led the raid at the Brook Cove Lab facility. I'm very sorry that two of your scientists had to be killed, but I had to make the raid look convincing.''

"Gee, thanks a lot. You're a real humanitarian," Pete spat.

"I don't expect your forgiveness for killing *only* two people," Jennifer said, glancing at Cardinal Palazzo. "But when I scanned the site, I *knew* about the underground facilities at the lab. So I made sure I was the only one who did, and volunteered to lead the mission myself. I made sure none of the security people discovered those hidden labs. The scientists working there are still there—and as long as I'm alive, I'll protect that lab and make sure no other raids hit it without ample warning."

Sari looked at the Visitor questioningly. "Does this mean it's safe to go back there?"

Jennifer nodded. "Our Fifth Column *wants* your scientists to come up with whatever they can to disrupt Visitor activities on Earth, slow us down, make Roger and John and Diana bleed. We'll keep retaliation to a minimum wherever we can."

"I don't get it," said Sari.

"You've *got* to help us buy time," Jennifer said urgently. "We still haven't found a way to stop this whole thing."

"What if we come up with a way of killing you all?" asked Sari. "We won't have any way of distinguishing between heroes and villains. Your Fifth Column members will die too."

"If we work together, maybe we'll know what you'll be doing in time to protect ourselves, while those loyal to the Leader—our enemies—die. But if not—if you don't trust us—or just can't tell us in time, then we'll die too. We knew we'd have to pay a price to stop this madness. But some of us will probably survive to carry on the fight in our own ranks."

"How much will you be willing to help us?" said Sari bluntly.

"As much as we can, as long as it doesn't expose us. You have something in mind?"

Sari nodded. "If we're going to do any effective science, we need to reestablish contact with other researchers around the world. We've got to pool what little resources you've managed to salvage for us . . . *if* that's what you're really doing. We need to make computer hookups, to share data. But we can't do that without secure phone lines that aren't tapped."

"You need the clearance codes," said Jennifer.

"Can you give them to us?" asked Pete.

Jennifer flicked her tongue out as she thought. The sight was unnerving to the humans. "It won't be easy—the codes change constantly. The more contacts we have with you, the more we risk detection by security forces."

"Hey," said Pete, "everything we do is a risk. But this particular risk could pay big dividends. Can you do it?"

Jennifer nodded firmly. "All right, you'll have your codes."

"And you'll have your hide," said Pete. "For the time being, we'll trust you. Now, I think it's time we got out of this subway tunnel."

Jennifer reached up and made a deep gash in her throat with her fingernails. The humans gasped before they realized the damage was cosmetic.

"What's that for?" asked Yeager.

"Angela's dead, and I'm getting away. It's got to look like there was a struggle and I escaped."

One of the transit workers found the auxiliary switch, opened the subway doors, and swung the lantern out to survey the tunnel. Widely spaced emergency bulbs on the tunnel walls strung out in a dim chain around a curve.

"Okay, folks," said the transit worker, "do as I say and stay on the catwalk, and nobody'll get fried if the power comes back on while we're out there. And there're probably rats in the tunnel—don't scream if you see any. It's wet and it's dirty, but the escape ladder ain't too far. Ready to go?"

One by one, the transit workers helped everyone out of the train, and they moved off slowly into the dark, damp tunnel.

Chapter 22

Left-Handed Blessings

Edward Palazzo flashed his "don't talk to me" glare when he returned to the Cardinal's residence behind St. Patrick's Cathedral. His aides noticed that he was hours late and that his face and vestments were soiled and streaked, but their curiosity would have to remain unsatisfied. Cardinal Palazzo had never hidden the fact that he had a hot Italian temper when the mood struck him, and they'd learned not to approach him with anything less than pressing church business when thunderclouds gathered in his eyes.

Finding out why he was dirty was *not* pressing church business, they quickly decided, and they left him to work out his black mood on the exercise equipment he'd had installed in a spare room when he'd taken over the archdiocese.

Dressed in blue Yankees team sweats, Palazzo launched himself into as vigorous a workout as he thought he could stand—stretching, presses, leg lifts, the exercycle—all in the fervent hope that he wouldn't think over and over again about the events he'd witnessed that day.

But those thoughts and revelations kept forcing themselves back into his mind, no matter what he did. The exercise was good for the body, but in this case the spirit was on its own. And it was occupied with churning considerations of good and evil, and the ultimate confrontation. He'd always shied away from apocalyptic theology, but now he couldn't help wondering if the Visitors were some latter-day, biblical-style punishment for man's earthly sins. Was this the modern equivalent of the ten plagues or the Great Flood?

He thought about the things Jennifer told them before she made her assisted escape, about the scores of world leaders—including President Morrow—who had been kidnapped or "invited" aboard Mother Ships under false pretenses—and who had been undergoing months of brainwashing through the diabolical conversion process concocted by Diana, the woman Visitor aboard the L.A. ship who seemed to be evil incarnate. Prayer seemed such a futile response, a flailing gesture inadequate to save those poor souls.

And Diana's conversions spawned another problem, one that would multiply beyond itself: how were unconverted humans to know who had or hadn't been affected by the Visitors' mind-twisting? Was *any* human immune from being a suspected spy? Trust would have to be the one thing to bind people together in this test of faith in God and comrades—and Diana's process was an arrow aimed at the heart of that faith.

After a slow, hot shower to wash away the chill of the subway tunnel, a chill that shivered through both body and soul, Palazzo asked for a cup of hot chocolate to be brought to his study. He sat and drank it while watching the late-night news report. The Visitors broadcast a story from Rome, including tape of the Pope blessing people from his balcony, and later from his throne in the Vatican audience room. Then the Pope spoke in his accented English: "God sends us tests, and how we handle those tests determines whether we are good people or evil. How we behave toward these Visitors from another world is perhaps the greatest test humanity will ever face. Will we greet them with hostility, or with love in our hearts and openness in our minds? I caution all our brothers and sisters to remember that the Visitors are *also* our brothers and sisters, and we must cooperate with them if we are to assure our own salvation."

Palazzo stared at the television, slack-jawed. The Pope's words triggered a lightning bolt that struck his soul with the realization that the Pontiff, a man who combined toughness and compassionate spirituality, who was filled with love for all God's children, this most powerful of religious leaders, was blessing people with his *left hand*. And Palazzo *knew* the Pope was right-handed!

He's been converted, thought Palazzo, his vision blurring. Setting his hot chocolate down on the end table, he knelt in fervent prayer.

"Dear Lord, please forgive me for defying the words of the Holy Father. He is no longer responsible for his own thoughts and deeds. I know You will understand in Your infinite wisdom. I know in my heart that what he has told us to do is wrong for the Church, for humanity, and for the future of life on Earth. You gave us that life, and also gave us the intelligence to exercise free will. I must use that gift of free will now. I pray for Your guidance in the days ahead, for only Your guidance can save us. I place myself in Your hands, Lord. Please help thy servant."

The old piers near Manhattan's southern tip jutted into the Hudson River. Some were still in use, others had surrendered to encroaching rot and declining business. These abandoned warehouses were perfect hideouts for a variety of underground and underworld endeavors. It was in one of these warehouses that White Christmas had located its main headquarters. Lower Manhattan gave them the cover they needed—approaches from different directions through the maze of narrow streets and alleys, many of which dated back to two and three hundred years ago when the remainder of Manhattan Island was still wilderness.

Following the escape from the subway tunnel, the group split up and members made their way back to the warehouse. Deeply shaken, Alison Stein and Cardinal Palazzo, after pledging their support to the group, returned to their residences—they'd be missed otherwise. But Alexander Garr wanted to stay with the rebels.

He wasn't precisely sure why—a mixture of feelings: guilt, curiosity, frustration, the need to express his repentance. After Pete had his eyes carefully rinsed to cleanse them of Angela's venom, Garr sat down with him in what used to be the warehouse management office, a battered room filled with rusting filing cabinets, lopsided desks, and a naughyde couch with stuffing oozing out of rips in its black cushion.

"I'm not surprised to see you in charge," said Garr.

"Well, I'm not really, Alex. It's more a collective thing. Me,

Lauren, Sam Yeager—who's a city cop—and anybody else can chime in with ideas or comments . . . even criticism."

"And they won't get traded?" asked Garr, kidding.

"Nope."

"Are you the only team in the league?"

Pete scratched his head. "We're the sole New York entry. No, I take that back. I think we're the *major* league team, but there's at least one minor league club," he said, thinking of Julio.

"How about elsewhere?"

"I've got to believe we're not the only people in the country, or in the world for that matter, who are doing this sort of thing. But we just don't know—that's one of our problems. That's why Jennifer's offer to help us get in touch with other resistance groups is so important."

"Maybe I could help," said Garr. "I'm still in pretty tight with the Visitors, you know. You might be able to make use of my brown-nosing, Pete."

"I don't know. They might think you helped set up the ambush that killed Angela."

"I don't think so," said Garr. "I hate to admit it, but you don't know just how much of an asshole I actually made of myself playing up to them. I think I'll still have some pull. Maybe I can play double agent."

"What do you mean?"

"Go in and tell them that I've heard something about the New York underground wanting to get in touch with other groups in other cities, that you came to ask for my help, and suggesting to them that they use me as a double agent. Then I can ask them to feed me info on what they know about resistance in other cities. That'll help give you specific targets for contact, and I can warn you if they're going to try any reprisals."

"Would they really believe you'd turn in your own kind, Alex?"

Garr hung his head. "I'm ashamed to admit it, Pete, but I've given them that impression, yes."

"How could you have done it?" Pete asked sadly.

Alex shrugged. "Ambition, fear . . . I don't know myself. I'm used to being on top, Pete, used to running things—or knowing the people who do. I've spent my whole life that way.

You ever wondered why people like me keep trying to accumulate more and more wealth?"

"Yeah, I've wondered."

"Well, I can't speak for everyone, but a lot of people do it because wealth can buy power. Oh, up to a certain point, it's to buy *things*—but there are only so many things you can put on display. After that, you realize wealth gives you authority over other people—it makes people come to you, willing to do almost anything you want them to do. That's scary—it's also addictive. You get used to it, maybe even learn to like it. At the very least, you learn to live with it. And when that power is suddenly threatened, you get frightened. You're faced with the possibility of life without that authority, and you'll do almost anything to keep it."

"Even sell out the rest of humanity?" Forsythe asked.

"I *really* didn't know what they were doing, Pete."

"Oh, come on, Alex. How can I believe that?"

"I saw what I wanted to see. Today, I saw more than I ever *imagined* I'd see, more than I could pretend I *didn't* see."

He paused for a moment, looking straight into Pete's eyes. "Y'know, as a Marine I swore never to let my country down. Well, I was, until today, but no matter what you think of me personally, Pete, I'm no traitor. I want to fight for my country again, and I'll do anything to prove that. How about it?"

He extended his hand to Pete, who took it firmly in his own.

"You're going to have to take orders from me, you know," Peter said. "Are you going to have a problem with that?"

"The irony did occur to me," said Garr dryly.

"You step out of line and you're traded."

"Hey, that's my line," Garr protested with a grin.

"Not anymore—at least not until next baseball season—if there *is* a next baseball season.."

"You're following a fine tradition, Pete."

"Huh? What do you mean?"

"Ever hear of Mo Berg?"

"Sure—he caught for the Red Sox in the thirties, right?"

"Ever hear of the OSS?"

Pete nodded. "The forerunner of the CIA, during World War Two."

"Very good. Well, Mo Berg was sort of a master spy during the war when he became a top aide to the head of the OSS."

"Well, Alex—just because we're ballplayers doesn't mean we can't be well-rounded."

"I'll keep that in mind when your contract comes up for renewal. Well, I guess I'd better get back home."

"Yeah. If you're going to be of any use to us, you have to keep up your normal life—you know, being obscenely wealthy and arrogant beyond belief," Pete said with a sardonic smile. As Garr turned to go, Pete held his arm. "Alex, *be careful*. Not just for yourself, but for the rest of us. We all gave up our outside lives. That was hard, but at least we don't have to keep up the pretense. If *you* slip, it's not just *your* neck on the line."

"*Semper fi*, Pete. Old Marines don't forget."

"We'll be in touch with you."

Garr saluted and left. A moment later, Lauren came into the office with some burn ointment for Pete's face. "Unbutton your shirt. How far down did it spatter?"

"Oh, give me a break, Lauren. I'm fine."

She scowled at him. "You're well on your way to being a doctor—you're already an awful patient, just like Daddy." She ignored his protest and sat down, reaching for his face with a Q-tip. "Now you know very well you need this on the spots where the venom got you, or you could wind up with God knows what infection. That was like getting hit with acid, Pete."

"Is it gonna hurt?"

"For God's sake, don't be such a chicken! Do you want a bullet to bite on?"

He squirmed again. "*Sit still!*" she snapped.

Pete obeyed, and she dabbed the ointment onto the raw patches on his cheek and forehead, working down onto his neck. "Do you always do what women tell you?" she asked, grinning.

"Only when they're incredibly bright and unspeakably beautiful. Have you ever thought of medical school? We could do our homework together—I'd play doctor with you *any* time."

She laughed in spite of herself and they gazed at each other for a timeless moment. "There—all done," she said, breaking eye contact first.

"Will I ever tap dance again, Doc?"

She rolled her eyes and capped the tube of medication.

"Uh, I, um—" Pete stammered, then ground to a halt.

"Are you always this articulate?"

Now *he* laughed, a little self-consciously. "Only when I'm trying to think of a way to thank someone for saving my life."

"I reacted without thinking," she said slowly. "I really don't deserve much credit. I barely knew what I did till it was all over."

"Hey," Peter said, "the fact is, you *reacted*, whatever you thought while you did it. If you hadn't, I would most likely be dead right now. Ergo, you saved my life. For Chrissakes, will you let me thank you?"

"Well, okay. You're welcome, if that's the proper response for the situation." She smiled, and their eyes held again.

"I can only guess how hard it must have been for you to pull that trigger," Pete said softly, looking up at her.

"A month ago it would've been even harder."

"You mean because you didn't know how to shoot a gun?"

"That and the fact that I *really* disliked you at first." She faced him directly. "You're arrogant and cynical and make obscene amounts of money playing a little boys' game, and—and—" She smiled a little, shrugging. "And I still know all those things about you, but somehow they don't matter anymore, I guess. I was wrong about you, and I'm sorry."

"I'm glad you're sorry," Pete said, a little confused, absently fumbling at the buttons on his open shirt.

"I thought you were glad I saved your life."

"Oh. Well. Yeah, I'm glad about that too." He gave her a sideways glance. "I don't know how you kept your head—I'm still getting the shivers every time I think about that . . . tongue snaking out at me. No pun intended."

"Me too. It was pretty grotesque." She sat down beside him on the old sofa, which creaked alarmingly but held together.

Pete sighed. "Yeah. It may have left me with terrible traumas that will be the ruin of my social life."

"Huh?"

"I may never be able to French kiss again."

Lauren glared at him. "You are so *crude*, Peter."

"Wanna help me get over it?"

"What?"

"My trauma."

Tentatively, he put an arm around her shoulders, then pulled her against him. They sat that way for a long moment. At first Lauren's body was stiff, but finally she relaxed, then after a couple of minutes, she asked, "Getting untraumatized?"

Pete's voice had lost the kidding tone. "Yeah. I haven't felt this good in a long time. I . . . " He swallowed. "Guess I'm still kinda shaky, but it feels awfully good to touch another human being."

"Feels good to me too. Guess we're still sort of shook up, both of us."

"Yeah. That must be it."

Very gently, Pete reached over and put a finger under Lauren's chin, turning her face over to his. After another second's hesitation, she met him halfway, her mouth warm and inviting.

The kiss was nothing but a reassuring comradely gesture— for about the first ten seconds. Then Lauren felt a rising excitement—the same excitement she'd felt under the mistletoe at the Christmas party. It was a feeling she'd convinced herself was due to the eggnog. But now she was cold sober, and her heart began to pound like a trip-hammer anyway. Pete's body felt hard and strong against her own. She slid her hand across his bare chest, felt his heart beating, and put her arms around him, pulling him closer. She felt him pushing her down onto the lumpy couch. His weight felt good.

Finally he pulled away for a moment, his blue eyes betraying the same surprise she'd felt. "Wow," he murmured. "And to think I ever thought you were cold—"

"You talk too much, Forsythe," she said, and pulled him down again. The kiss was even better this time—

—until the ancient couch gave up the ghost and collapsed beneath them with a resounding crash.

Lauren and Pete yelped loudly with indignant surprise.

"Hey, what's wrong?" Joey Vitale flung open the door of the old office, saw the two of them together on the floor, and blushed to the roots of his black Italian hair. "Sorry," he mumbled, backing out and closing the door.

Pete looked over at Lauren hopefully, but the barriers had come back up, at least partway. "Gee, I'm sorry about that," he said.

"Don't worry about it." She stood up and pulled her sweater straight without looking at him. "Just a natural reaction to danger. Happens all the time in the trenches. You okay?"

He nodded. "Fine."

Sitting morosely on the remains of the couch, now only five inches off the floor, he watched her leave.

Chapter 23

Just One of Those Days

Heavy winter storms attacked New York City with blustery force during the remainder of February and early in March, so the White Christmas group used this relatively inactive time to work on their weapons and demolitions skills. One of the bus drivers, Manfred, had worked as a demolitions expert in the Navy, and gave lectures, demonstrations, and practice sessions in the fine art of setting and detonating explosives.

Jennifer, true to her promise to aid the group in their resistance efforts, came through with maps showing the location of the Visitor chemical plants in New York, as well as in nearby Newark and surrounding New Jersey towns.

The armed Visitor forces at these plants, however, precluded the underground's making a direct frontal attack, and due to a new voice-check security system, infiltration was equally out of the question. However, by judicious checking, plus a couple of night reconnaissance trips to New Jersey by scouts rowing across the Hudson River under cover of darkness, Pete Forsythe was able to contact a Newark underground group Jennifer had located. Working with the Newark resistance leader, a woman named Marcia, Forsythe was able to find two Visitor plants close enough to two now-closed factories to give him an idea.

He explained it to the White Christmas people the day after his second reconnaissance visit one sleety and miserable March evening. "There are two factories, gang, both less than a quarter of a mile away from each Visitor operation. If blowing 'em up doesn't take the Visitor plants with 'em, trying to fight the fire is gonna put a crimp in their productivity for a while."

"What kind of factories?" Lauren asked.

"One's an oil refinery." There was an approving murmur, and mutters of "Yeah, that'll keep 'em busy!" and "It'll go sky high!"

"But wait, there's more," Pete said, trying to suppress a grin and nearly wriggling in his seat from excitement.

"What?" they all asked in suspense.

"The *other* one—" Pete let the grin out. "It's a *nitroglycerin* plant."

They all sat in silence for a long moment, then everyone spoke at once.

Lauren said, "But we're apt to blow ourselves to Kingdom Come trying it!"

Manfred said, "We're gonna need more dynamite, Pete. Plastic explosives and blasting caps too. Those things have special safeguards to prevent a mass explosion. We'll have to plant a shitload of charges!"

Joey said, "We'll have to warn all the people who live in the area, but not too long before we do it—"

Denise said, "Maybe we'll be lucky and Roger will be visiting that day!"

Winston Weinberg—whom Denise had recruited—said, "Hey, guys, I got stock in some of those Newark-based companies!"

Alexander Garr added, "So do I!"

Pete held up a restraining hand. "Slow down, one at a time! Then we'll take on the questions of whether to do 'em, and when."

They "did" the chemical factory in late March and the nitro factory in late April—and by dint of Manfred's expertise, managed to demolish both Visitor plants at the same time, with no human loss of life or injury. White Christmas was definitely becoming a threat to be reckoned with, they congratulated themselves, feeling cocky.

Of course, during the lulls between the big projects, their usual harassment of Visitors continued—blowing up squad vehicles with Molotov cocktails, sniping from roofs and windows at shock troopers, bollixing Roger's schemes (thanks to Jennifer's warnings) for gathering up groups of citizenry on assorted pretexts and transporting them to the Mother Ship food-storage chambers.

But even as spring began to softly arrive, and the forsythia yellowed, then ruffled out with bright green leaves, their luck ran out. At first it was just a dearth of targets, as the Visitors grew more and more wary. Then one of their ammunition dumps was discovered and raided. Lauren's cautious foray to attempt a rapprochement with Julio and the Diablos was scornfully rejected.

Things finally culminated in a disastrous raid on the Brooklyn processing plant during which they suffered their first casualty—Winston Weinberg was killed when he was caught in the crossfire from two Visitor shock troopers. Even more disconcerting, the group discovered that the Visitor shaken, troopers were now wearing new and improved head and chest armor that deflected all but their most high-powered slugs.

When they regrouped, shaken after the fiasco, the White Christmas fighters discovered that one of their resistance members was missing. Sal, Manfred's fellow transit worker, had been captured.

Though the group as a whole mourned the loss of their comrades, Peter Forsythe took it the hardest, as he was forced to confront that ultimate horror of leadership—the knowledge that two men would still be alive if it weren't for his decision to stage the raid.

Late that same night, as the group unpacked in its new headquarters in yet another deserted lower Manhattan warehouse—a precautionary move after Sal's capture—Lauren looked around and realized that Pete had disappeared. Leaving Sam, Brenda, Denise, Sari, Manfred, Alex, Joey, and the others to the rest of the unpacking, she wandered off in search of him.

She found him outside, behind the warehouse, sitting on the dilapidated pier. She almost missed him—he sat in the pool of shadows between feeble streetlights, so motionless that if it hadn't been for his blond hair, she would have missed him. His shoulders were hunched beneath his navy-blue Yankees sweat-shirt, and as she walked toward him, silent-footed in rubber-soled shoes, she saw a bottle resting beside him.

Lauren stood there for a long time, debating whether or not she should turn away before he saw her, or speak, or put her hand on his shoulder. She didn't realize he even knew she was there until he spoke. "I haven't opened it."

"What?"

She came a few steps closer as he pointed at the bottle of vodka. "That."

Lauren sat down beside him, dangling her feet out over the chill, oily darkness that was the Hudson River. The night was very quiet, nippy for the middle of May in Manhattan. There was no moon, and a slight overcast obscured all except the brightest stars. After a long silence, she asked, "Are you going to?"

"I don't know," he said. "I bought it to drink, but—" His voice broke. Suddenly he grabbed the bottle, then lobbed it far out into the water. Lauren heard the distant splash only faintly.

"You sure can throw," she said irrelevantly, not sure what else to say. Her throat was very tight—she wanted to tell him she was proud of him for not losing himself in the liquor, she wanted to tell him she was sorry, truly sorry about Winnie and Sal, she wanted to put her arms around him—

"A waste of good money," he said distantly. "If my old man were here, he'd skin me for doing that." He laughed shortly. "He likes his booze too."

"Where are you from, Pete?"

"Virginia. Took me years to get rid of the accent."

"Oh," she said, faintly surprised to find out he was from the South. Several minutes went by, and she simply sat, trying to think of the right thing to say. Finally, when she stirred and looked over at him, he took a deep, shaky breath, letting it out very slowly. "I'm not being very good company, am I?" he said.

From the sound of his voice, she knew he was crying.

"Would you rather be by yourself, Pete?"

"No," he said. "But I don't think I want to talk."

She nodded, and in silence reached over to put her hand on top of his. Their fingers entwined, and held tight.

"So the raid the humans tried on the plant failed?" Roger turned to face Jennifer, who nodded soberly. "Well, after the way they wiped us out in Newark, it's about time."

"The lieutenant assured me it was repulsed with little difficulty, Roger. No casualties and only one injury on our side, and one killed on theirs."

"What about the man we captured? Did you get anything out of him?"

"No, sir. I'm sorry. He apparently had a weak heart, which of course we didn't know when we began questioning him. He died before we could find out the location of their headquarters."

"Typical," said Roger bitterly. "I don't know why *I* had to be assigned to this damned city. Even Ivan on the Moscow ship doesn't have to put up with the kind of bad luck I've had here. And these damned stubborn New Yorkers!" The Commander thumped his fist softly into the conference table.

Jennifer, watching him, was very glad that Roger had no way of knowing that she'd personally slipped Sal the drug that had caused his "heart attack." Since some of Angela's specially trained technicians had been assigned by Roger to do the questioning, it was all she'd been able to do. She felt a great sadness, thinking of the way the gray-haired man had mouthed a silent "Thank you" to her when she'd palmed the only means of escape into his hand under cover of roughing him up a little. She wished bitterly she could've done more.

"Well, sir, at least the raid failed," she said. "The new armor proved to be a success."

"Small consolation," Roger grumbled. "And we're far behind on our food-storage quota! I'll have to think about ways to do some quick harvesting. John is bound to make an inspection sometime soon, and he's going to want a satisfactory explanation."

Jennifer nodded sympathetically, schooling her face to the proper level of concern for a second-in-command toward her superior officer. "By the way," Roger said, "I had a conversation with Diana today. She wants to know how you're coming with President Morrow."

Jennifer tensed. "Well, as Angela discovered, he's an awfully tough subject. Not by any means a good candidate for conversion, Roger. I can't report any more success at this point than Angela had made. Frankly, I think we'd do better to consider drugging him and dubbing in a speech if we ever need him, rather than trusting that our conversion techniques will succeed."

"That's what I was afraid of," Roger said morosely. "Diana wanted to know if I thought we should ship him out there so she could attend to him personally. What's your opinion?"

"Well," said Jennifer slowly, thinking fast, "knowing Diana's . . . temper . . . as we do, I'd resist that suggestion, Roger. I really would. She's just the sort to lose her head over his stubbornness and either kill him or burn his mind out until he's on the level of one of those rodents over there." She gestured at the stacked cages at one end of the conference room.

"Yes, and I suppose it *is* conceivable we might still need him," Roger said thoughtfully. "Keep doing your best, and I'll tell Diana it's just going to take time."

"Yes, sir," said Jennifer, trying not to let her profound relief show. It had taken her the months since Angela's death to return Morrow to even a semblance of the man's former health, and undo the damage inflicted on his mind. If Diana were to insist on seeing the President anytime soon, she'd surely suspect something was going on.

Jennifer watched as Roger went over to one of the cages, taking out a plump greenish frog. "Care for a late-night snack?" he asked.

The second-in-command wasn't really hungry, but she accepted a mouse just to be sociable. As she watched the Commander rapidly consume the occupants of nearly half the wall cages, she found herself thinking that if the pressure on Roger increased much more, he was definitely going to have to go on a diet—or requisition a larger uniform.

Chapter 24

The California Connection

As she stood on the bluffs overlooking Oyster Bay Harbor, Hannah Donnenfeld scanned the evening horizon. In the east, a few early stars twinkled in the blue-black of their cosmic ocean. Toward the west, the last tendrils of orange sunlight tickled the bottoms of clouds already darkened on top, as if charcoal-smudged.

She turned to look back at the outline of the main house against the sky. It was closed and blacked out—the remaining staff both lived and worked in the underground facilities. But it was comforting to know the big old mansion was still there, close by. She kept thinking of Dorothy in *The Wizard of Oz* saying wishfully, "There's no place like home, there's no place like home." This was Donnenfeld's home and there *was* no place like it, no place that could spark her energy the way this lab and its grounds and beach could. That was a simple fact of her existence, and if she'd ever doubted it, the weeks on the run, bunking in Peter Forsythe's apartment and the downtown warehouse headquarters of the resistance, had convinced her.

Her experience away from her home had strengthened the conviction that had grown quietly in the back of her mind: she'd rather die here than run again.

"A penny for your thoughts, Hannah," Sari James said. "You looked like you were coming up with the wisdom of the ages."

The older woman smiled. "I was just thinking that I'm

getting old," she said, turning back to the view off Oyster Bay Cove. The summer day had been hot, and the rapidly cooling breeze coming in over the water was a welcome breath against her face.

"I know what you mean," Sari said, wrapping her arms across her chest. "These last couple of months have been enough to age anybody."

"How is Peter holding up?"

"Mentally, pretty well," Sari said. "He still feels terrible about what happened to Sal and Winnie, of course, but that's kind of fading by now. Lauren's taken over a lot of the administrative and supply details since she gave up faking it at the UN."

"Did she move into the warehouse full time, then?"

"Yes, just about everybody ended up having to go into hiding. Joey held out the longest, but one night when he went back to his place he barely missed being nailed by a squad vehicle parked on his roof."

Hannah made a *tch-tch* noise. "Poor things, all of you. Living in that drafty old warehouse."

"Yeah," agreed Sari. "We froze all winter, had about two comfortable weeks in spring, now we bake all day. I wondered if we could borrow some fans?"

"Of course," Hannah said. "But when I asked about Peter, you said he was well *mentally*. Has he been wounded?"

"No, nothing like that. He fell during that action up in the Bronx last week and threw an old knee injury out, but he seems better now. We really need an M.D. in the unit, Hannah. All of us are afraid to go to the doctor anymore since the Visitors have all their offices under surveillance and their phones bugged."

"Poor Pete," Donnenfeld murmured, "I wonder if this will be the final straw that permanently wrecks those legs of his." She shook herself, suddenly barking a harsh, mirthless laugh. "As if it's likely that any of us will ever see a professional baseball game again, whether or not Peter Forsythe can play in it. I think that's the thing I hate the most about the Visitors— they've deprived this country of its sense of fun, of enjoying life. No baseball, no football, the amusement parks are closed."

Sari nodded sadly. "Yeah. It's been rugged, all right. Not much to keep our spirits up."

Hannah reached over and squeezed the younger woman's hand for a quick moment. "Well, maybe our VIP guests tonight can offer a little hope."

"Hannah!" Both women turned to see Mitchell Loomis struggling up the bluff, panting audibly. In the months since they'd gone underground, Mitchell had gotten even plumper than he'd been before. In fact, none of them had gotten proper exercise, afraid as they were to go out in full daylight.

"They here yet?" he asked, reaching them.

"No," said Donnenfeld.

"Wait," Sari said. They turned to see her pointing up into the ruddy sky. "Look!"

Donnenfeld and Mitchell followed her finger and saw a small aircraft gliding toward them with running lights off. It was a Visitor squad vehicle, and it whispered overhead to settle gently on the mansion lawn. Its gull-wing hatch lifted and a petite young woman with blonde hair pulled back in a single braid ducked out and stepped onto the grass. She was dressed in jeans, a red T-shirt, and a denim jacket. As she started toward them, Hannah saw she walked with a tiny hesitation in her gait, not quite pronounced enough to be called a limp. Under one arm she clutched a large vinyl folder.

Donnenfeld and her assistants approached. As they got closer, Hannah thought in surprise that the young woman couldn't be any older than twenty-five—she could have almost passed for a teenager. The newcomer smiled, holding out her hand. "Doctor Donnenfeld? I'm Juliet Parrish. We spoke on the phone. It's a real honor to finally meet you. I've been one of your admirers since I was a little girl."

The older woman took the outstretched hand. "Heavens, child, you're *still* a little girl! You must be somebody pretty special to be running that group we've been hearing about in Los Angeles! That television broadcast where you people broke in and ripped John's mask off right on camera has brought us more new recruits than we can train!"

Julie shrugged. "I've had to grow up fast since the Visitors came," she said with a self-deprecating smile. "But who hasn't? And I've had a lot of help from the people in our group." She turned as another young woman, much taller than herself, climbed out of the squad vehicle. With honey-blonde hair and high cheekbones, she looked like a model except for the laser gun she wore in a shoulder holster. "This is Maggie Blodgett, our pilot, who performed the miracle of getting us out here without a single challenge from the Visitors. Maggie, Doctor Donnenfeld."

Hannah hastily introduced her own staff members. As pleasantries were exchanged, a voice echoed from within the squad vehicle. "Awright, ladies, let's put a lid on it. You can coffee-klatsch when we've sent the scalies back to Sirius with their butts in a sling."

A slender man of medium height with steel-gray hair and flat, pale-blue eyes ducked out of the hatch. Hannah raised her brows. "Who's your MCP charmer here, Julie?"

Julie Parrish made a face. "I'm happy to say he's *not* mine, Hannah. This is Ham Tyler, our resident professional intelligence agent. He's managed to cobble together a makeshift system of communications between resistance groups around the world, and since it's definitely a case of hang together or hang separately, we put up with his . . . eccentricities."

"Moonlighting as a consultant, eh, Mr. Tyler?" asked Donnenfeld, thinking that Tyler had an ideal face for his undercover kind of life—it had no very distinctive features. He'd fade into any crowd.

"Yeah, and wait'll you amateurs get my bill," he said, unsmiling.

"We're Ham's favorite charity," Julie said sarcastically.

Tyler ignored the dig. "How about taking care of your business so we can get home before daylight?" His voice carried the authority of one used to being obeyed. Scrutinizing him, Hannah decided that behind the macho chauvinist demeanor, there was a keen intellect. As she met his nonreflecting eyes, the scientist shuddered to think what kind of covert mayhem and bloodshed that intellect had been reserved for up till now. Still, she knew they needed professionals in this business, and Tyler was definitely one of them.

"Since the meter's running," Hannah said, beckoning to Julie, "follow me."

"You coming?" Julie said to Ham and Maggie.

"Might as well see the setup." Ham shrugged.

The Brook Cove trio led them toward the shack sheltering the hidden stairway down to the labs.

"I hope 'setup' doesn't turn out to be the operative word,"

said Tyler. "I got real trouble trusting this Visitor Fifth Column Alliance thing."

"Why, Mr. Tyler? As a professional agent, you must be well acquainted with enlightened self-interest as a reason for doing things against the grain," said Donnenfeld. "I've seen a lot of strange bedfellows in my seventy-five years, and the CIA has been paired with a number of them."

"But never lizards from another planet," said Tyler.

"Look, Ham," said Julie, "the Fifth Column knew about us, and they knew about this New York group. They could just as easily have killed us as put us together. But they didn't. This Jennifer from the New York Mother Ship says she wants our scientists to be able to work against the Visitor takeover—what other motivation could she have?"

"Nothing I can *think* of—not yet anyway. But that doesn't mean it ain't there, honey. And if it is, I'll figure it out."

"And if it's not?" said Sari.

"We're here, aren't we? Courtesy of your friend Jennifer?"

They entered the shed and descended the stairs. Down in the lab, it became apparent from the activity that there was no shortage of effort here. Even Ham looked marginally impressed.

Julie was positively wide-eyed. "God, if I'd had all these facilities since the start—"

"Well, as Mr. Tyler might say, 'You've got 'em now, honey,'" said Donnenfeld. "Now tell us more about this crazy pregnancy, and the possible toxin."

Julie sat down at a computer console, Donnenfeld and the others pulling up chairs around her. "Well, it's the damnedest thing I've ever seen," she began. "This girl, Robin Maxwell, about seventeen years old, was taken to the L.A. Mother Ship, held captive for several hours, and during that time had intercourse with a male Visitor—and somehow the Fifth Columnists there set her free and she turned up pregnant."

"That's impossible," said Mitchell flatly. "There's no way plain old sex could have gotten her pregnant."

"What then—something kinky?" suggested Tyler mockingly.

"No, something in a lab," said Donnenfeld.

"All I'm telling you is what Robin told us," said Julie. "I believe her—at least I believe she's told us what she recalls.

I'm sure she *did* have sex with the Visitor male called Brian, but God knows what they might have done to her without her knowing. She *was* subjected to some kind of special examination in one of the labs. My own hypothesis is that Diana masterminded some sort of genetic engineering alterations to *both* Robin and Brian as some sort of horrible experiment. They had to make *some* modifications in her immune system to get her body to accept and retain the growing fetus. I did an exploratory on her to try to abort it, but it was no human pregnancy. The fetus had established a whole network of blood-vessel and neural links with her body—it wasn't neatly contained in a relatively simple amniotic sac like we have. No way could we get it out without killing the girl."

"Get to the meat of it," Tyler urged. "We ain't got all night."

Julie gave him a dirty look. "Who's in charge here, Ham?" she barked, and Tyler subsided.

"Well, in Robin's eighth month, I wound up doing a C-section and delivered twins—the female one looks almost human, but is definitely a hybrid. The other was definitely reptilian, a male, but with some human characteristics."

"Did they both survive?" asked Sari.

"The lizard baby kicked off inside of a day," said Ham.

"Cause?" asked Donnenfeld.

Julie shook her head. "Maybe the computers can make some sense of it. The other infant did survive—in fact, it's thriving. She's grown an incredible amount. I mean *incredible*. She's the size of a five-year-old."

"How long will it take to enter all this stuff?" asked Ham. "I'm getting antsy—and I don't trust your boyfriend, Donovan, out there without me to keep an eye on him."

"About an hour," Julie said, controlling herself visibly.

"Okay, get to it, honey," snapped Tyler.

Tyler checked his watch. The hour was up and Julie was exhausted, but she had finished. Donnenfeld put a motherly hand on her shoulder as she handed her a can of soda.

"We'll get right to work on it, Julie. Between us, I'm sure we'll find something. Thanks to Jennifer, we've got the means to keep in touch and the codes to protect what we're doing. It won't be long now."

Julie managed a weak smile. "I hope you're right." She winced as she stood, bracing herself for a second on the table.

"What happened to you?" asked Donnenfeld.

"Old war injury," said Tyler.

Julie laughed. "He's right. Laser wound from the early days of the fighting—before I learned to duck when being shot at. It only bothers me if I sit too long."

"No time for teary farewells," Tyler snapped. "We've got a long trip back to the Coast—that is, *if* Maggie can manage to fly us past whatever Visitor patrols are out there."

"He should've been a soap opera villain, he's so melodramatic," Julie said to Donnenfeld.

"That he is, but it *isn't* exactly safe—be careful. You're too valuable to the resistance to risk losing, Julie."

"What the hell am I—chopped liver?" asked Ham Tyler peevishly.

"No," Hannah deadpanned. "Definitely chopped *pork*."

"Let's hit the road," said Julie, smothering a grin. Donnenfeld led them toward the stairs.

The pattern of contact between the East and West Coast rebel groups adhered to the plan worked out by Ham Tyler and Jennifer—following a random irregularity that would have been senseless without the complex code. And as far as they could tell, it was working. Jennifer assured them in her own infrequent contacts that their messages and computer exchanges remained undetected by Visitor Security. Jennifer's supplying them with different clearance codes and a mixture of long-line and communications satellite channels helped form the carefully calculated chaos that maintained all-important secrecy.

The breakthrough they'd hoped for took only a few days. It hummed across the paper of the Brook Cove high-speed printer at the appointed hour for Julie's report on the work being done in her own makeshift lab. Mitchell's eyes smoothly skimmed the words laid down by the printer's back-and-forth sweep. When it was done, he tore off the sheet with a theatrical flourish and waddled quickly to Donnenfeld's office.

"I think they've got something," he said.

Indeed they had. Julie's team had isolated a hybrid strain of bacteria in the surviving twin, something harmless in itself but excreting a waste product that appeared to have caused the reptilian baby's death. It was present in the intestinal tract of the humanlike mixed-breed infant, but seemed to be doing her no harm. The questions it raised were fascinating and critical ones—would this hybrid bacterium kill Visitors? And in the process, would it also be fatal to humans? Julie's scientists were trying to come up with the answers, and the computer printout issued a good-natured challenge to the Brook Cove team: "We'll race you!"

The competition turned out to be brief—Brook Cove's computer models predicted that a toxin made from the bacteria *would* kill Visitors and would *not* harm humans. Sari James typed that information into the machine and sent the message to the West Coast headquarters. Two hours later, the printer clacked out a reply:

THANKS FOR THE CONFIRMATION. POWDERED TOXIN INAD-
VERTENTLY TESTED ON VISITOR PRISONER—DEATH NEAR-
LY IMMEDIATE. ARGUMENT ENSUED OVER HOW TO TEST
ON HUMANS. I TOOK BULL BY HORNS AND STEPPED INTO
ISOLATION CHAMBER WITH DEAD VISITOR. BREATHED
DEEPLY FOR A MINUTE—NO EFFECT. DON'T KNOW WHO
SHOULD GET THE TROPHY FOR FIRST CONFIRMATION—
THAT'S SCIENCE FOR YOU! NOW NEEDED: TOXIN IN
QUANTITY AND MEANS OF DELIVERY ON TARGET. ANY
IDEAS? JULIE

A steady stream of data on the toxin came east, and the Brook Cove scientists eagerly dove into the project. Serendipity had handed them a substance that was intensely poisonous as soon as it entered a Visitor's respiratory tract. The eastern team used their superior analysis and data processing systems to advise the best ways to manufacture large amounts of the substance in the shortest possible time. Dr. Donnenfeld's admiration for Julie Parrish grew each day. She was barely more than a kid, a fourth-year medical student, working with comparatively primitive equipment, but Julie seemed to have an inborn knack for looking at problems from just the right angle, breaking them down into simple components, and cutting through the extraneous to find the most direct solution. As often as not, Julie had already thought of what the Brook

Cove computers recommended. *Somehow,* thought Donnenfeld, *I've got to talk this girl into coming to Brook Cove when all this is over—if we're all still alive!*

The West Coast group moved its headquarters to a dairy, according to Julie's progress reports, and within ten days after risking her own life to test the toxin on a human subject, they were culturing the hybrid killer bacteria as per suggestions made by the Brook Cove team.

First, cultures were begun in vials, then transferred to hundreds of petri dishes. When a reddish mold formed, it was stirred into vats filled with plain yogurt—Julie and Donnenfeld agreed it was the best medium at hand. In the next processing step, the pink yogurt was poured into a heated condenser, producing a red liquid collected in buckets. In the final step, the liquid was turned into powdered concentrate—dubbed "cherry Tang" by Brook Cove's resident wag, Mitchell.

Faster than they would have guessed, enough "Tang" was being made to begin shipping it to other resistance groups around the world, with instructions on how to set up their own cottage bacteriological-warfare industries.

A few days after the routine manufacture of the substance was begun, Sari watched the printer tap out a new message from California. "A vaccine?" she mumbled. "Julie Parrish says they need our help to come up with a vaccine against the toxin. Do we have time for this?"

Pete Forsythe, in from Manhattan rebel headquarters for one of his periodic visits, sat on the edge of a desk. "We'll have to *make* time," he said "We never would have gotten this far without Jennifer's help, would we? We can't kill the Fifth Column members who are helping us, can we?"

"I guess not," Sari agreed. "I'll get some people to work on it."

"Good," said Pete.

Even after the antitoxin vaccine was developed, a most prickly problem remained—how to actually deploy the reddish powder as a weapon. Donnenfeld convened a meeting to consider alternatives that her people and the West Coast rebels had drawn up. Pete had driven out from the city to join them.

"Julie and I both agree that we would prefer minimizing the amount of toxin we introduce into our own atmosphere," Donnenfeld said. "We've tested it, and it *appears* to be ecologically harmless, but our testing and computer modeling has been scanty, at best. We have to think about the future of life on Earth—"

"Now, hold on a minute," said Pete. "Do we really have that luxury? There may *be* no life left on Earth—no human life, at least—if we don't use this weapon to its maximum effect on the Visitors. If we undershoot and it kills *some* Visitors and wreaks general havoc, but doesn't get rid of them, what we'll have left are a lot of very angry surviving lizards bent on getting even. If things are bad now, I shudder to think what'll happen then."

"All right, Pete, you make some good points. But I think we can have our toxin cake and eat it too," said Donnenfeld, a sudden light in her eyes. "I think we can come up with a way to have huge quantities of the stuff, but with a safety valve."

"Hannah, I hate it when you sit there like an elf," said Mitchell. "It means you know something the rest of us *don't*, and you're about to get a great deal of satisfaction out of making us feel like idiots for not guessing what it is. So cut the crap and tell us."

The old scientist curled her mouth into her trademark half-smile. "Balloons."

If the members of the group didn't say it, they thought it— the unanimous response was a nonplussed "Huh?"

"Balloons!" Donnenfeld repeated gleefully. "We put the powder into hot-air balloons and float them up into the air, and we fill them with just enough pressure so they pop when they reach the altitude we want. Or we equip them with detonators. As soon as the Visitors realize we've unleashed a biological weapon, they'll know there's nothing they can do but get the hell out of here. Because if they shoot the toxin carriers down themselves, all they'll be doing is releasing more 'Tang' and accelerating its spread and its entry into our air, water, and food chain. The whole planet will become poison to them. So, what do you think, boys and girls?"

Around the conference table, quizzical looks became small grins, then broad smiles, and finally laughs and chuckles and cackles of delight and triumph.

"That's cruel, Hannah," said Mitchell, "very cruel. Diabolical. I *love* it!"

It was simple, elegant, and something that could easily be

done all over the planet without complex equipment. Julie's
L.A. group seconded Brook Cove's enthusiastic acceptance
with alacrity. Ham Tyler and Mike Donovan came up with a
suggestion for a decoy plan to be leaked to the Visitors, to keep
them too busy to discover the actual plan.

Ham Tyler had lived much of his life dealing with people
who barely fit the classification "human." It was in the nature
of covert intelligence activities, and that was his specialty.
Hannah Donnenfeld had been right about enlightened self-
interest making for strange bedfellows. Once, long ago, Tyler
had harbored doubts about using whatever means were needed
to reach a desired goal. When he'd first joined the CIA, he'd
carried a straightforward belief in goodness overcoming evil.
He'd kept it to himself, thinking it didn't fit the macho image
of an intelligence operative. But ideals hadn't prepared him for
the raw realities he'd later faced.

For every romanticized actual liberator struggling to throw
off the shackles of totalitarianism, there were a hundred sleazy
political parasites, bribe-addicted generalissimos, and drug-
dealing murderers. They were all part of Ham Tyler's education, and the lesson hammered into his brain over and over
again was even simpler than his old credo about goodness
overcoming evil: in the modern world, good could triumph
only one way—by using the same means and methods as evil.

Once Tyler had grasped and absorbed that sobering concept,
he no longer blinked when he had to descend from the civilized
world into an underworld hell to find some ruthless creature to
help him accomplish a job. Few forms of life were lower than
drug dealers, who made themselves wealthy by addicting
human beings to substances that would kill them if they used
them, or make them *want* to die if they tried to stop. So it was
somehow fitting that Ham Tyler turned to drug dealers to help
distribute the deadly toxin many places worldwide. He put the
word out lightning quick, and meetings were arranged. Crates
and cans and sacks of red powder were moved out of the
dairies where the poison had been processed. It concerned
Tyler that the limited quantities made were the entire arsenal.
There would be no time for other rebel groups to duplicate the
stuff, not for this attack. Ham just hoped that the Visitors
wouldn't manage to weather the first offensive and stick around

to see if there'd be a second wave. Because there *wouldn't* be, not for weeks, if ever. But if the eggheads were right, if they'd done their jobs and created something as surely fatal to the Visitors as they claimed, if this crazy delivery system cooked up by the old lady at Brook Cove was as foolproof as she asserted, then Tyler's worries about what came next would be for nought.

The toxin was transported by stolen squad vehicle, by jeep and truck, by bicycle and burro. All through the day and into the night—perhaps the most crucial day and night for human civilization—members of the California resistance traveled around the world. In a half-dozen languages, they explained the master plan. And a world sick to death of Visitor arrogance and tyranny roused itself from numb acceptance. Finally given a weapon, people were eager to fight. For the first time in the history of humankind, there was a single enemy. And if spirit alone could carry the day, that enemy didn't stand a chance.

Sam Yeager and a troop of five other rebels in dark dress and blackface camouflage crossed the Hudson River from Manhattan to New Jersey in a small motor launch. They tied up at an abandoned Hoboken slip and found the waiting jeep.

As the driver accelerated slowly away from the river, she shook her head. "I worked with these things for four years, and I'll tell ya we had a ball. Every Thanksgiving we'd be out there on the street for the parade, and when these things went by, seeing the kids' faces made you forget that you'd just gone without a night's sleep gettin' everything shipshape." She pulled up and stopped in front of a mammoth warehouse with a Macy's sign on it. "But y'know," she continued, "I'm happy to trade it all to get rid of those creeps. I just pray for the chance to see one Visitor's face when they see a seventy-foot-tall Kermit the Frog comin' at 'em."

Chapter 25

Grocery List

The trickle had become a torrent. Roger could no longer ignore what field reports were telling him, what he could see with his own eyes when he flew over his command zone of New York City and environs. The strategic situation was deteriorating. There were increasingly frequent and damaging terrorist attacks on Visitor installations and facilities, dwindling cooperation from ordinary citizens, and less leadership than ever from John and the High Command. And now, reports of a growing Fifth Column conspiracy among their own troops!

Roger slammed his fist on his desktop, grimacing in anger. *How could it all have gone so wrong?* How could the Great Leader have chosen such incompetents to carry out this critical mission? Would their failures splatter over onto him too? *I'm not letting my career be flushed away without a fight,* Roger decided.

With the death of Angela several months earlier, Roger had isolated himself, taking daily reports from his new second-in-command, Jennifer, leaving her and other senior officers to run the day-to-day occupation according to his blueprint. But now, faced at last with John's upcoming inspection tour of his ship, he had to think of a bold stroke, something to spotlight himself as a commander to be reckoned with, to draw the Leader's attention, to single himself out for praise while his colleagues drowned in a tidal wave of condemnation for bungling beyond belief.

Finally he knew what he would do, and he called Jennifer to his quarters.

When she entered, he was scanning a computer-screen map of New York City and its suburbs. Without preface, he launched into his idea.

"We've been handcuffed in completing our water and food harvesting by having to keep up appearances, having to maintain the fiction that John introduced," he said briskly. "As a result, we're barely at ten percent of our assigned human storage capacity. Do you agree?"

Jennifer nodded tentatively. "Yes, sir, that's correct."

"But I've discovered that *none* of the Mother Ships have yet achieved a hundred percent of their food harvesting. And as the resistance of the humans stiffens, more and more of our efforts have had to be diverted toward security and actual offensive action against rebel pockets.

Roger leaned back in his chair, a satisfied smile on his face as he looked at his second-in-command. "However, after considerable thought, I've determined a way to rectify the food situation. We're at nearly eighty percent of our water storage capacity, so that's not my main concern. But John has planned an inspection tour in two days. We must bring our food storage supplies up to capacity before then!"

"What do you have in mind, sir?"

Roger looked crafty. "I'm going to keep the precise location details to myself until the last minute. I've received reports from the newly arrived Supreme Commander Pamela in the Los Angeles ship that there is a growing subversive movement among our people, a Fifth Column, that's attempting to undermine our takeover here."

Jennifer expressed credible shock. "Are they certain? Has there been any report of it aboard this ship?"

The Commander shook his head. "No. And keep this quiet, Jennifer, I don't want to put ideas in anyone's head. But they're having a considerable amount of trouble on the West Coast."

Silently, Jennifer congratulated Martin, her counterpart aboard the Los Angeles ship—he really had the top command running scared!

"But at any rate," Roger was continuing, "in case there *is* a potential threat aboard our ship, I'm going to release the precise location for my plan to you only minutes before we make our move."

She looked slightly hurt, stiffening a bit. "Yes, Roger."

"Now, don't get all formal with me, Jennifer," he said, waving a conciliatory hand at her. "It's just a precaution to make sure the thing goes off smoothly."

"What 'thing'?"

Roger activated another map on the screen and leaned forward. "I propose to use a supposed chemical leak at our Brooklyn plant as justification for clearing out one of the nearby neighborhoods."

"Which one?"

"That's what I'll decide only at the last minute. But which one doesn't matter for our purposes. Using this announced danger from the chemical spill, we'll remove the people in the appropriate area, and in one massive sweep, fulfill our food quota—even surpass it. But I can't do it without you, Jennifer. I need your intelligence and efficiency."

"I'm at your service, of course, Commander," she said, trying to keep her voice neutral and control the tremor she felt deep in her gut.

"Just as I expected," Roger said with a satisfied smile. "Here's my proposed plan of action. Feel free to make any suggestions or comments. Now is the time to get any problems out of the way."

"Yes, sir."

He leaned over the map. "Here's the processing plant. We'll make use of the local mass transit rail system in the area to evacuate the humans living there. That will lessen their suspicions, leaving our squad vehicles free to patrol."

"Sir, tens of thousands of people live there. We don't have the security manpower to force them from their homes."

"Ah, we won't *have* to force them. They won't question us—they'll be too frightened of the chemical leak menace. *And* we'll do it in the middle of the night and catch them off guard, asleep, and confused. They'll have just a short time to gather a few belongings and get aboard the trains. Then we'll transport them to a staging area elsewhere where we'll have shuttles waiting. Once we have them isolated and detained on the trains, it will be much easier to herd them aboard our shuttles for transport to the Mother Ship. Do you think you can handle it?"

"Are you sure we can make the chemical accident serious enough to convince them to leave, without actually damaging the processing facility, sir?"

"Yes, I've already consulted our engineers. One opened tankful of the substance we've been manufacturing will give off sufficient fumes to convince the humans something dangerous is leaking into their air. We can arrange to actually poison some of them and when they convulse and die, the rest will be terrified."

Jennifer smiled confidently. "Your plan is a work of *genius*, Roger!"

He waved off the compliment. "No, no, just pragmatism."

He was interrupted by the urgent red flashing of his communications screen. He tapped the switch. "What is it, Lieutenant?"

"A class one override bulletin from the Supreme Commander, sir. Simultaneous broadcast to all Mother Ships. Coming on . . . now!"

The flashing red beacon was replaced by John's face, a worried frown furrowing his usually placid brow. "This message is coming to you directly from my command post on the Los Angeles Mother Ship. Thanks to the foresight of your Supreme Commander and my staff, a spy planted with a human rebel group in California has returned important information to us. The humans claim to have developed a biological weapon for use against us, and they are planning to spray it around their planet by stealing jets from Air Force bases. This plan is to be implemented tomorrow morning. We don't believe this weapon is really a threat, but as a precautionary measure, we are launching a preemptive maneuver to prevent any such actions on the part of underground groups. This will require immediate cooperation from all of you as we concentrate our forces at those air bases targeted by the humans. This action takes precedence over all other tasks to which your troops have been deployed. I instruct each of you to contact my staff within the hour to coordinate our coverage. Out."

Roger watched impassively as John's face faded from the screen.

"That means we can't proceed with your plan, sir," said Jennifer, trying to mask her relief.

"No, it doesn't. While all the other commanders blindly and unimaginatively follow that fool's limited strategy, *we'll* make the extra effort that will set us apart. And we *will* succeed. We'll just move the plan up to tonight." He smiled. "When I'm promoted to the Supreme Command, you'll be in line to take my place as commander of this vessel. You could become the youngest commander in the fleet, Jennifer. That will be your reward for the good work you've done, the support you've given me. I'll see to it."

"Thank you, Roger."

As soon as she was able to get away from Roger, Jennifer frantically set about finding Lisa. They met in an empty conference room on the lab deck.

"Lisa, I have a special assignment to be given to someone I can trust. I think you're that person. I know you're part of the Fifth Column aboard this ship—"

Lisa stiffened in her seat, her young face revealing sudden fear as her eyes darted nervously toward the closed door.

"Relax," Jennifer said, trying to reassure her without wasting time with excess verbiage. "You've done nothing wrong. And you needn't be surprised that I know about the Fifth Column."

"Well, you *are* second-in-command," said Lisa. "I would expect that you'd know what was happening on your own ship."

"Roger doesn't know about it. In fact, I've spent a fair portion of my time making certain he *didn't* find out."

"*You?* Why?" Lisa was genuinely surprised.

"One of the important measures taken was to organize into small groups, with each member knowing the names of only a few others. That way, no one could betray many others. For instance, you don't know the name of the overall leader of the Fifth Column on this ship, do you? Be careful how you answer—this could be a trap."

"I don't know who the leader is."

"You could be lying to me," said Jennifer icily.

Lisa swallowed. "I'm not."

"I know." She paused for just a beat. "You're looking at the leader."

Lisa was speechless. Jennifer allowed herself a brief smile, then continued. "I need you to relay a critical message to the New York resistance group. I've been in touch with them myself, but we'll be going on alert status any moment now. We're mobilizing for a major new offensive to counter a planet-wide rebel attack and it may be impossible for me to leave the ship—but it's imperative that they know what's about to happen. Will you do it? It'll be a dangerous job. You could be stranded on Earth if the rebels succeed. You could be killed if *we* do."

Lisa took a deep breath. "I'll do it."

"Good. Did you get your antitoxin shot?" Lisa nodded. "Don't forget your oxygen mask. They don't want us taking any chances, even if we've been immunized. Now, I'm only going to brief you once, and there'll be a lot for you to remember. But we have no choice. The message has to be verbal. If you're captured before you get to the rebel headquarters, there can't be any hard copy of the information you'll be carrying. Now, listen carefully—"

The klaxon rang in the corridor and the console on the conference table flashed an alert signal—making Lisa's task that much more urgent. Jennifer could only hope she'd succeed.

The shuttle bay was already teeming with crews readying every available squad vehicle when they arrived. Platoons of shock troopers fell into line, heavy laser rifles slung over their shoulders and packs of equipment on their backs. Even technicians were being pressed into service as line soldiers. As she led Lisa through the maelstrom to her personal fighter ship, Jennifer knew the same thing was going on aboard every Mother Ship in the fleet. She struggled against a hollow feeling inside, but couldn't shake the anxiety: how could those humans, poorly armed and equipped, hope to fight against such odds? She'd learned not to underestimate their resourcefulness—and she was thankful the Visitor leadership hadn't yet mastered that lesson.

Lisa boarded the small ship and Jennifer nodded to the pilot, a loyal female of the Fifth Column. As she watched it float out of the bay and dive toward the planet, Jennifer thought of the human deity the Cardinal had told her about—and said a silent prayer for the humans who didn't yet realize it would all be over soon—one way or another.

Chapter 26

Thrown Gauntlet

Jennifer's radio message was terse—danger was imminent, she could no longer contact the White Christmas group
directly, and was sending someone else to the appointed spot.
Joey was designated to make the pickup at the Battery Park
City construction site near Manhattan's south end.

He hid in the skeleton of an unfinished high rise and watched
the Visitor ship descend from the hazy summer sky. It landed
some distance away, let out a passenger, and took off again.
Jennifer's messenger glanced up after it for a moment, then
walked toward the building. Joey could see it was a female, but
she was not in Visitor uniform. As she neared, he realized it
was Lisa. He bit his lip, not sure whether he should say any of
the things that were on his mind. For now, he opted to keep it
all business.

"Hello, Joey," she said neutrally.

He nodded a curt greeting. "Let's go. Pete and Lauren are
waiting."

As they walked the few blocks to the latest warehouse
headquarters without exchanging another word, Joey realized
he'd never seen Lisa in anything but her Visitor uniform before
this. Now she wore tight-fitting blue jeans, sneakers, and a
tank top, and she looked just like any woman he might meet in
a bar or on the street. But she wasn't. Joey couldn't flush from
his mind the nightmare image of the face beneath Angela's
human mask as she lay dying in the dim subway car. Suddenly

he stopped, took Lisa's arm, and turned her toward him. She didn't resist, and he looked directly into her eyes—the day was cloudy enough that she didn't need her dark glasses.

Lisa tried to fathom what he was thinking, tried to decide whether she should say something, or wait for him to speak. She didn't have to wait long.

"I—I saw Angela . . . what she really looked like," Joey stammered. He touched Lisa's cold cheek with his hand. "I know this isn't real. How could you go on not telling me . . . knowing how I was *feeling* about you?" He looked away from her, only the lines around his mouth drawing tight to reveal his anguish.

"How can you ask me that question? We weren't allowed to reveal anything. I was *never* part of the horrible things that were going on. I was always an Alliance supporter, and as soon as I found out, I joined the Fifth Column. I'm sorry, Joey, sorry for all of it . . ."

"*Are* you like Angela?"

She thought of turning away. Instead, she summoned all her dignity and faced him, eye-to-eye. "Physically, yes. And as physical attractiveness is measured among us, I want you to know I'm considered quite attractive. But you knew the answer to that, Joey. I guess I can't blame you for wanting to hear me say it. But we're *not* all the same, any more than all of you are the same inside. I wouldn't be here now if we were, if I were evil like Angela, like Diana. Jennifer warned me I might be stranded here when she asked me to come down with her message." She shrugged. "I don't expect a medal or anything for doing this—I'm a military officer. I'm doing what I have to do."

"Were you doing what you had to do, following orders, when we first spent time together?" he whispered.

For a second, the words caught in her throat and all she could do was shake her head sadly. "Were *you*? Was it your job to distract me, to find out about us by getting to know me?"

"Getting to know you wasn't a job—it was my choice."

She managed a little smile. "Well, it wasn't a job for me either. You know, I've never really liked anyone like this before. We're mated young—I've mated twice—"

Joey looked surprised, even hurt. She touched his hand. "Don't be shocked. It's not like here. We mate when our bodies are at their strongest. It's purely physical, and the male-female matches are made for us, based on genetics, not feelings. Oh, later we might stay with the same mate—but that's for convenience and perpetuation of the species. Not love."

"Can two people from different species love each other?" he wondered.

"I don't know. I don't know if I love you, Joey. But I do know I feel closer to you than I've ever felt toward anyone from my own world. Maybe being stranded wouldn't be so terrible—" She glanced away, "but who knows how long my immunity shots will last?"

"Let's go." He led her around a corner and they entered the warehouse through a basement doorway.

Inside, the remaining members of the White Christmas cadre waited. Lisa told them that the Visitors knew about tomorrow's rebel plot to steal jets from air bases—and she was confused when they started to laugh. "Why is this funny? Jennifer is worried you'll be prevented from getting to the aircraft and you'll never have the chance to spray your biological toxin."

"Not like that we won't," said Lauren gently. "That plan was a deliberately planted decoy—and they're falling for it. Great!"

"But there's something else you need to know about. There is a plan Roger is instituting on his own in this area alone."

They listened seriously as she related the details of the Brooklyn evacuation plan—it would take place tonight, at four A.M.

Joey looked worried. "Brooklyn someplace? We've gotta stop 'em!"

"We will," said Pete. "Or at least we'll make a damn good try."

Lauren was already bringing out road maps of Brooklyn and the rest of Long Island as Pete asked, "Who knows the Long Island Railroad?"

A woman named Michelle raised her hand—she was about thirty with a broad-shouldered, athletic build and frizzy brown hair. "I'm a conductor, and my dad works in the yards. I know the railroad top to bottom."

"Great, Michelle," said Pete. "We've got to intercept the transport train before it gets to the staging area. If we don't, thousands more people are going to end up as frozen dinners aboard that Mother Ship. Anybody who's got an idea, now's the time to suggest it. We've only got a few hours to put this together. Lisa, did your pilot go back to the Mother Ship?"

"No. She's hiding in a hangar near the docks."

"Can you contact her?" asked Lauren.

Lisa held up a cigarette-pack-sized communicator. "I can try."

"Good," said Pete. "We're going to need her."

Roger sat alone in his quarters, hunched over a desk and peering at a succession of maps on his wall-sized computer screen. With a laser stylus, he moved symbols representing troops and squad vehicles from outlying areas to the Brooklyn evacuation site, simulated the loading of approximately five thousand residents onto railroad trains, then had them move to a staging area where the humans were transferred to squad shuttles for conveyance to the Mother Ship.

"Estimated time for mission," he said to the computer.

"Three hours," came the answer.

Roger smiled, then closing his eyes, stabbed the point of his stylus into an area in Brooklyn near the chemical plant. Opening them, he drew a small circle around a number of city blocks.

The coyote nibbled at the last shreds of meat clinging to the bones of the rabbit. The desert glimmered in the moonlight and shivered with the calls and hoots of other animals and birds prowling for a nocturnal meal—or hiding to avoid becoming one. The coyote's senses were diverted suddenly, his pointed ears twitching and pricking to attention.

Across the valley, silence spread around him like a blanket that was being gently lowered until all sounds were smothered beneath it. The coyote listened, as did all the other animals of the night. The more sensitive felt it before they heard it, a whisper from the east that made the coyote's fur bristle. Flying machines were certainly familiar to him, but this was a sound he'd never heard before . . .

The squadron of Visitor ships skimmed across the California desert and landed in the hills surrounding Edwards Air Force Base. Hidden from view, troops deployed and waited, knowing that other Visitor forces were doing the same thing all over the world.

The coyote licked his paws, nosed the rabbit carcass one last time, then trotted off to find a safer place.

There was a light tap on Peter's office door deep in the dim warehouse. With an effort slowed by fatigue, he looked up to see Lauren wearing a Visitors' red coverall uniform. "Definitely your color," he said, managing a small grin.

"Isn't it time you got changed?"

"Yeah. Though I'm not sure why. I don't think we can pull this off."

Lauren moved behind him and looked at the maps spread out on the desktop. Yellow and red highlighters marked the routes to be used both by the Visitors and the rebel rescue forces. Pete's fingers tracked aimlessly over the lines.

"We just don't have the equipment. We've only got the one squad ship that Lisa came in," he said, his voice a hoarse whisper. He slumped forward to rest his head on folded arms. "I feel like we're failures. Other rebel groups captured more ships, more weapons, they're better prepared, while we've got slingshots and peashooters. We're sending our people out, and we're going to get clobbered, Lauren."

"Pete, it's not a competition. We've done things others *didn't* do, but that doesn't matter either. What matters is that every group, no matter where it is, no matter what equipment it has, does what it can."

"Well, that's not gonna do a thing for those people who've already been taken to the Mother Ship, or the ones that get taken now if we can't stop them tonight."

They both looked up as they heard a low clamor from the warehouse entrance, then the scuffing of footsteps coming quickly toward the office. Pete and Lauren exchanged glances of surprise when Jennifer stepped through the doorway.

Pete found his voice first. "What are you doing here?"

"I had to meet with you one more time, and Roger agreed with my suggestion that I handle the Brooklyn evacuation in person. So I took a little detour."

"Is he really going to do it?" asked Lauren.

"He will if you people can't stop it."

"Has he chosen which area will be grabbed yet?" Pete asked.

Jennifer looked grim. "No, damn him. He's going to communicate the information by radio at the very last minute."

Pete looked stricken. "You're asking the impossible, Jennifer! We don't have enough people and we don't have the tools or arms we need to—"

"Would two more squad ships with laser cannon help?" Jennifer asked.

Pete did a double take. "Are you serious?"

The Visitor nodded.

Pete rubbed his eyes. "Wouldn't hurt," he said wearily.

"I'll divert two of my Fifth Column pilots. We have so many ships and troops deployed between this evacuation operation and the one surrounding the air base, no one will even notice that two small ships are missing."

"We could also use more laser rifles," Pete said.

"I'll do what I can," Jennifer replied. "There are also some last-minute things you should know about the schedule. I've arranged for the evacuation train to arrive at the Farmingdale Airport staging area at eight A.M. Eastern time. If it's late, the shock troopers there are going to get suspicious. So whatever you do to that railroad, it's got to be done quickly and you've got to keep to the schedule. Security on the train will be light, so the humans on it won't think anything's wrong beyond the chemical spill at the plant."

"That means we shouldn't have too much trouble stopping the train," Lauren suggested hopefully.

"Piece of cake," Pete said.

Jennifer looked at them questioningly. "I don't understand. Cake? Isn't that a snack food?"

Pete and Lauren both laughed. "I'm sorry," Lauren said, "we didn't mean to laugh. It's just an expression. It means 'easy.' "

"Well," said Jennifer, "I hope the two extra squad ships do help. But it won't be so easy once you get to the staging area at the airport. Roger has ordered a heavy concentration of troops there, and there wasn't anything I could do about that."

"Why do we have to bring them all the way to the airport once we've captured the train?" said Lauren.

"What are we going to do with five thousand people in the

middle of nowhere?'' asked Pete. "And don't forget, it's all part of the overall attack—timing is very important."

"That's right," said Jennifer. "If you capture the transport train too early, a patrol is sure to be sent to check on the train's whereabouts. You'll lose the element of surprise, and you won't have the toxin to back you up yet. The confusion that breaks out when the toxin starts spreading over the area is what's going to save you and those evacuees on the train. You just don't have the firepower for a sustained battle with our troops."

"Will we have enough for the fight at the airport?" asked Lauren, deeply concerned.

"I think you will," said Jennifer. "And if you keep close to the schedule, it should be a short fight."

"Do your people have enough gas masks?" Lauren asked. "Have they all been inoculated?"

Jennifer nodded. "We'll be covered—besides, I've managed to transfer a majority of the Fifth Column members off the planet and back up to my ship. That way, they not only won't be exposed to the toxin, but they'll also be there to help me try to take it over."

"Take it *over*?" said Pete. "Are you crazy?"

"Not that I'm aware of. We have to try. If this plan works and your toxin really does force us to leave Earth, my people in the Alliance still have the problem of trying to take control of our world back from Our Leader and his group of madmen in the military. A few Mother Ships would help us immeasurably."

"Take me aboard with you!" Pete blurted. "You've *got* to!"

"Are *you* crazy?" Lauren demanded.

"No—I want to try to free the humans they've already got in deep freeze."

Jennifer glared at him. *"Absolutely not,"* she said sharply.

Pete and Lauren were stunned by her commanding tone, the first time they'd heard her speak as if she truly were capable of giving orders—and expected them to be obeyed.

"If there's anything I can possibly do to save those people," Jennifer continued, "I will. But you can forget about anything like raiding a Mother Ship. Security has been tightened considerably since Mike Donovan made it onto a Mother Ship in California."

"My father is on your ship," said Lauren quietly.

"I know," said Jennifer. "A lot of good people are. But as important as those individuals are, you have to remember you're fighting to save billions here on Earth. Hundreds or thousands may have to be sacrificed." She touched Lauren's hand and the human and alien gazed evenly at each other. "I'd better go now," Jennifer said.

"Good luck," Pete said.

"Thank you. Good luck to you too."

They guided the Visitor officer out of the office. Lisa was waiting with Joey.

"Do you want to go with me or stay here and help them?" asked Jennifer.

Lisa stood tall. "I think I'll help them, Jennifer."

"This may be your last chance to get back to the Mother Ship—and I could use you."

"I know," Lisa said.

Jennifer smiled at her protégée. "You all should know that even though she's a sociologist, she also scored in the top two percent in gunnery training. Put her in the weapons seat of a squad ship and you'll have a big plus on your side. Well, good-bye, Pete . . . Lauren." She clasped hands with both of them, then followed Lisa and Joey to the headquarters exit.

"What if this doesn't work, Pete?" asked Lauren, watching them go.

Pete shrugged. "Could be the end of our world. We could all end up as a Visitor smorgasbord."

Lauren stared at him. "Thanks for making me feel better. I don't think I'm ready for the end of the world. There's too much I haven't done, too many people I wasn't nice to when I had the chance—"

He looked at her for a long second, then grinned wickedly. "Do you mean me?"

"Among others," Lauren admitted. "Have you parceled out the assignments yet? Where am I going to be?"

"I thought I'd send you on ahead with a couple of others to the staging area so you can take charge of the civilians when we get 'em off the train. Somebody's going to have to keep them under cover and out of it, and you're good at diplomacy."

"*What?*" She hefted her laser gun. "I came here to fight,

and dammit, you're not relegating me to some back-lot action! Who do you think you are, Peter Forsythe?"

He watched her through narrowed eyes, then unexpectedly began to chuckle. "Did you by any chance listen to yourself just then?"

Lauren thought over her words for a moment. "Sounded pretty bloodthirsty, didn't I? Daddy would be shocked."

"Yup." He looked at her appraisingly. "In view of your assignment, you ought to change into civvies; it'd be more reassuring to the captives than having you in a Visitor uniform. How many do you think you'll need to control the crowd?"

"Wait a minute." She stared levelly at him. "I didn't say I was going to do it your way. I didn't slug it out this far to miss out on the showstopper. I'm a dead shot, and you need good fighters. Let somebody old with crumby eyesight play nursemaid. How about Alison Stein? Can you get her to come out and do it? They'll pay attention to the Mayor a lot better than they will to me."

They stared at each other for long moments, the line of challenge drawn so clearly between them it was almost visible. Lauren broke the silence. "Dammit, Pete, I mean it. I want to be with you—and the rest of White Christmas. Why are you trying to schlep me off like this?"

He glared back at her. "Damn, but you're pushy, Ms. Stewart. Did it ever occur to you that maybe I didn't want you to get hurt?"

Her mouth fell into a round O of astonishment, but after a second she rallied. "I've waited too long for this day—worked too hard, just like we all have—to be shut out now."

"Okay," Pete sighed. "Call Alison."

Chapter 27

The Long Island Railroad

Lying on his side, elbow crooked, Antonio Vitale stared at the alarm clock on the nightstand. The green, luminous hands and numbers told him it was almost four in the morning. It was chilly in the air-conditioned bedroom, and his wife, Rosie, had the quilt bunched up under her chin as she snored gently. Antonio got up to turn down the machine, moving clumsily in the dark but not wanting to switch on the light.

He realized unhappily that he was now wide awake. Night had always been the only time he wasn't busy, the only moments he had free to consider his own problems, and the world's, and try to solve them. But he had no hope of solution to the current state of affairs. *Milk and a cookie*, he thought . . . They might convince the worry-demons to let him fall back asleep.

Trying not to wake Rosie, he lifted the bedcovers ever so slightly, stood up, and slid into his slippers.

The night's stillness was split by a whooping siren. Antonio stumbled in shock, rammed his knee into the nightstand, and hissed a curse as his wife sat up in fright.

"Tony, what's happening?" she whispered, awake instantly.

"I don't know, honey, I don't know." He limped to the window and looked out. The siren continued to wail—and a Visitor ship floated overhead.

"Attention, attention," called an alien voice from the ship's loudspeaker. *"There has been an accidental chemical spill at*

the Beach Processing Plant. Toxic fumes have been released into the air, and the imminent explosion of the plant is a danger. You are ordered to evacuate your homes immediately and report to buses that will take you to trains and to a place of safety until the spill can be contained and the danger eliminated. Fifty people living nearest the plant have already been overcome by fumes—twenty-five have died. Our doctors and yours are working to save the rest. To avoid further loss of life, they urge you to leave immediately . . ."

The message repeated. Antonio could see other Visitor ships flying over other blocks. An ominous cloud had risen above the chemical plant like some malevolent genie released from its container. Cracking the window open, he could smell an acrid odor. He coughed and slammed the window shut.

"Tony—"

He shrugged at his wife. "We better go, Rosie."

On the street, helmeted Visitor troopers armed with laser rifles and side arms stood at intervals, brusquely herding frightened residents toward the buses parked every couple of blocks. Most of those fleeing carried little or nothing with them; a few seemed to fear they would never see their homes again and they clutched framed family pictures grabbed quickly off pianos and mantels, or held pillowcases hastily packed with keepsakes.

When the seats and aisle of a bus were filled, the soldiers waved it away and an empty one took its place. The operation was efficient and well planned, and the flow of people and traffic was tightly controlled. No room was left for panic.

The buses rolled smoothly to the Long Island Railroad's main station in Brooklyn, where more Visitor soldiers directed the evacuees onto a waiting train. Again, seats and aisles were filled with people who remained surprisingly calm—or perhaps they were simply numbed by fear and uncertainty.

Jennifer surveyed the train depot from her hovering squad ship. She wondered how those humans below could be so docile, and admitted grudgingly to herself that Roger's plan *was* inspired. Routing sleepy and frightened people from their beds in the middle of the night had the necessary component of surprise. She hoped the rebels' own planned surprise would have the same advantage.

The Visitor officer sat back in her seat, thinking how tired she was. Mentally, she ran through her list of tasks and was conscious suddenly of an uncomfortable certainty that she'd forgotten something. Something *important*. But her memory wouldn't cooperate, so she shelved the notion temporarily. Maybe it would come to her . . .

"Time for pyrotechnics," she said to her pilot, a stocky, dark-skinned Visitor. "Let's go."

Her ship turned and rose into the paling sky, heading back toward the chemical plant. When they were within sight, Jennifer moved to the laser cannon at the ship's rear and punched into the targeting computer the coordinates of a tank truck standing dormant in the plant parking lot. She squeezed the trigger and a red bolt lanced out, hitting the tank. An instant later the truck flared into a fireball, a fist of flame and black smoke churning a hundred feet high, painting the pipes and concrete of the building in a hellish glare.

"There," said Jennifer. "We've done everything Roger ordered."

"He should be very pleased with himself," said the pilot, Phyllis. "I wonder how pleased he'll be when the rebel-controlled evacuation train gets to its destination."

"Hopefully, he'll be in no position to realize his plan failed," Jennifer said. "That is, if the underground succeeds *and* we do too."

"What are you going to try?" asked the pilot.

"I have a supply of the humans' toxin," Jennifer said. "Pete had Doctor Donnenfeld run up a specially potent batch. I've ordered a routine check of the ventilation systems this morning, and our people ought to have an opportunity to introduce the stuff into selected areas of the ship."

"Won't that contaminate it for all of us?" Phyllis asked, worried.

"Not if we flush it out into space later," Jennifer said. "And I've made certain that all our people have been inoculated and have gas masks. Thanks to my so-highly-commended "personnel work," the Fifth Column outnumbers the loyalist crew now. All except for the troopers—we only have a few there."

"But almost all the troopers are Earthside," the pilot pointed out.

Jennifer smiled, nodding happily. "To quote one of the more vulgar human statements of affirmation, 'Fucking-*A*.'"

Phyllis chuckled. Jennifer joined her, then suddenly the memory that had been niggling at her dropped into place, and she sat up abruptly. "Oh, *no*!" she exclaimed. "I forgot all about the President!"

Antonio and Rosie Vitale stood huddled on the platform next to the train. Some of the people with them were neighbors, others had faces they recognized but names they couldn't recall or never knew—people they'd see at the market or the bank, or passed in the street, or shared the sidewalk with at a bus stop. At those times, they might have said a word or two of greeting, a complaint about the rain, a kind comment on a new coat or hairstyle. But no words were exchanged now, only looks from hollow eyes. Looks that gave away inner fears that faces tried not to reveal. The Vitales saw Marianne and her parents in the crowd.

Visitor soldiers used their rifles to prod people into the sleek silver and blue-striped train cars where seats or standing room remained. Finally, Antonio and Rosie were pushed inside, and a moment later the doors slid shut on all fourteen cars in the long train.

The engineer—a human who shared the same hollow-eyed gaze as his passengers—nudged the throttle forward. The electric engines powered up, humming a vibrato up through the floor. The air brakes sighed, released, and the train inched out of the station. The platform was empty of humans. The Visitor troops checked quickly for any belongings left behind which could become incriminating evidence, then they prepared to return to their bases or the Mother Ship. One shock trooper lifted his helmet visor, stooped, and picked up a soft, furry thing that lay shapeless on the cement—a stuffed toy rabbit with floppy ears, left behind by some child. He looked at it blankly for a moment, then dropped it into a trash can, covering it with a newspaper.

The Long Island Railroad is the most complex commuter line in the country, moving something like two hundred thousand people on an average work day.

Mornings, the commuters leave their suburban communities scattered out on the 150-mile-long fish-shaped island that has a larger population than most states in the Union. They park their cars at dozens of stations, some little more than trackside sheds, others concrete-and-steel elevated platforms. Then they ride the rails to their offices, shops, and factories in Manhattan to earn their livings. In the evenings, they reverse the trip. Always, they hope wistfully for the trains to run on schedule; often they're disappointed.

This Visitors' evacuation train ran on time, though, swaying as it clacked over rail joints and headed out of Brooklyn on a northeast track to the railroad's main transfer point, Jamaica Station, in a decaying neighborhood in the adjacent borough of Queens. Almost all LIRR trains coursed through Jamaica, where the half-dozen lines fanning out to serve Long Island's north and south shores, as well as mid-island, funneled down into the two tunnels under the East River that led to and from Manhattan.

On work days, thousands of people had to change trains at Jamaica Station to make connections. The eight tracks here constituted a classic bottleneck of frustration for the rushing commuter. But for the unwilling commuters on the evacuation train, it would be their only hope . . .

The two mice scuttled back and forth in the confines of their cage, standing up on their hind legs and chittering in fear. Roger watched them intently.

"They never stop moving," he muttered. "They have no place to hide and yet they never stop looking."

He opened the cage door and pulled one mouse out by its tail, holding it up in front of his face. "You and humans have a lot in common," he said to the mouse as it hung there, twisting slowly. "All over the world, they think they'll just dance in and steal planes from lightly guarded air bases, spread their poison, and be done with us." He chuckled.

He glanced at the chronometer on his computer panel. "In about an hour, they'll learn the folly of misjudging our power. *You'll* learn now." He popped the mouse into his mouth and gulped it down intact.

* * *

Pete took a large bite of his doughnut, chewed and swallowed it, licking the powdered sugar off his lips and fingers. "Where did you get these?" he said to Sari James.

"We had a cache of them at Brook Cove."

"Down in the undergound labs?" asked Lauren.

Sari nodded. "You sound surprised. Man does not live by health food and staples alone. We've got our share of treats hidden away—scientists can be hedonists, too, y'know."

They sat at the head of the four-car train parked on a trackside spur. Outside, several rebels who had worked in the rail yards before they joined the resistance checked the equipment, making sure it would do the job of intercepting the evacuation train before it was too late.

A slim Scandinavian-looking man named Ozzie hauled himself up from the track bed and in through the open side door. His young face was grimy as he looked at Pete. "We're set," he announced.

Pete checked his watch, and Lauren and Sari looked at theirs. "I hate this radio silence," Pete said grimly.

"We don't have much choice. Jennifer said her people were on top alert," said Lauren. "We can't risk their accidentally finding out what we're up to."

"Time to roll?" said Sari.

Pete nodded. They were all dressed in red Visitor coveralls and all were armed, though Pete wished Jennifer had been able to get more laser rifles for them. Even though they were theoretically supposed to be in combat with the heavily armed Visitors at Farmingdale Airport only briefly, being outgunned gave Pete a queasy feeling.

Assuming they were able to chase down the evacuation train and stop it, then actually take it over, there would be about thirty-five resistance fighters, including several brand-new recruits who had never shot at a can on a fence, to say nothing of shooting at people. They would be backed up by three squad vessels, but this would be little insurance against at least a hundred experienced Visitor shock troopers with a dozen aircraft.

Pete was shaken from his nightmare imaginings by the jolt of the train as it accelerated, with Ozzie at the controls. Lauren had a chart of the tracks that included all signals and cut-offs. It was spread out on one of the vinyl seats and Pete leaned over her shoulder to take a look at their route. Their short chase train was coming down from the northwest and the target train would be intercepted just past the Jamaica transfer station. Pete glanced back at the rest of his "soldiers"—Brenda Ortiz, the bus driver and demolitions expert Manfred, Saul Rosenberg and Lenny Honaka, the two transit workers who had guided them when they had to commandeer that fateful subway, and about twenty others sitting in seats that had been occupied by accountants and lawyers and office workers commuting to and from humdrum jobs a few months ago. Many of these people *were* lawyers and accountants just months ago. About a third of the group wore Visitor uniforms, some stolen or stripped from alien bodies, alive and dead, others supplied by Jennifer and the Fifth Column. The rest wore street clothes. *My God,* Pete thought with a terrible sense of unreality, *how the hell did we get here?*

Chapter 28

If the Train Should Jump the Track . . .

"Son of a gun, this is better than a Learjet any day!" Alexander Garr exulted as he examined the control panel of the Visitor squad ship while keeping a firm hand on the joystick that flew the ship manually. He, too, wore Visitor red.

Cardinal Palazzo, in civilian clothes, sat in the navigator's seat next to Garr. He'd insisted on joining the dangerous mission, saying, "Every army needs a battlefield chaplain." He'd served in that capacity in Vietnam, giving last rites to boys who'd been blown to pieces by booby traps and land mines. He'd held dying soldiers in his arms while medics frantically tried to staunch the rivers of blood. He'd hoped, never to have to pray again for eternal life in the shadow of violent death. But he'd felt compelled to go today, to give whatever support he could in order to salve his guilt at not having had the courage to do more and speak out sooner against the Visitors.

"You look like a little boy discovering the bike under the Christmas tree," he said to Garr.

"You're a good pilot," said Lisa from the gunner's nest in the aft compartment as she and the ballistics computer scanned the surrounding airspace for intruders.

"I've been flying for more than thirty years, since our Korean War. These babies are a snap compared to our planes."

"You never flew a more important mission, Alex," said the Cardinal softly. "I just pray there's not too much killing."

"We'll do what we have to do," Garr said. There was a sadness in his voice—but determination too.

Michelle looked up from her railroad-track charts, identical to the ones Lauren had down in the chase train. She peered through the squad ship's side window as Garr banked to give her a better look. He was flying slowly, pacing the four-car train. "Damn," Michelle whispered. "I wish we could radio them."

"So do I," said Garr. "But we can't, not unless it's an emergency. It's a good thing your people are spread so thin, Lisa, or we could never get away with this casual flying."

"Every plan has a flaw," said the Visitor in her throaty vibrating voice. "This is one of Roger's."

"Let's hope his flaws are worse than ours," said Palazzo. He lifted his eyes skyward and Garr noticed.

"A few final words to the Man Upstairs?"

The Cardinal smiled. "Can't hurt."

"Let's head south, higher altitude, and see where the evac train is," said Michelle.

Garr nodded. "Hold on." He executed a graceful half-roll and turned south.

Been driving trains for twenty years now and my hands never shook, the engineer of the evac train thought. *But they sure are now.*

His strong, meaty fingers were clenched around the throttle handle—the only way he could keep the tremor from showing. Sweat stood out on his ruddy face. It was chilly in his air-conditioned cab, and the perspiration soaking his light flannel shirt made him shiver. He was a big man, well over six feet, with a face that bore the scars of more than one barroom brawl. He'd been the master of locomotives driven by thousands of horsepower, hauling fifty-car freight trains behind him, but now he felt as powerless as a small child.

The shock trooper captain, Carl, who stood just outside the open cab door, had made one thing very clear—one wrong move, and Lamarr B. Verdeaux would be one very dead train engineer. Lamarr kept his hand on the throttle, his eyes forward, watching the clear track out ahead. As the rail curved gently up a slight grade, he knew they'd be approaching Jamaica Station soon.

He heard one of those reverberating Visitor voices talking to Carl, who leaned to look out the side window and took out a hand communicator.

"This is Carl, commanding the evacuation train. Please identify yourself and state your orders."

As the message from the train came through the squad vehicle's speaker, Garr and Cardinal Palazzo looked at each other. "I thought we'd be high enough that they wouldn't see us," said Garr.

"Repeat—identify and state mission," came Carl's harsh voice again.

Garr turned in his seat. "Lisa, you've got to answer. He'll recognize a human voice."

Lisa clambered out of the gunner's chamber. "But I don't know what to tell him." Her hand poised at the comm switch.

Garr bit his lip as he thought quickly. "Ummm . . . just tell him reconnaissance."

Lisa hit the button. "Reconnaissance ordered by Roger, Carl. Just a precaution," she said smoothly. "All is well?"

"So far. Out."

The static faded as the channel shut off and the squad ship crew sighed its relief.

"I don't know if my nerves can take another close call," said Michelle. She glanced out the window, then at the chart. "Oh, shit!"

"What's wrong?" asked Garr.

"The evac train is *ahead* of schedule. At this rate, the chase train won't catch them. We've *gotta* break radio silence."

All eyes turned to Garr—he was clearly the one in command as far as they were concerned. "I'd say this qualifies as an emergency. Do you have the frequency Jennifer gave us, Your Eminence?"

Palazzo nodded. "She said this was a channel they *probably* wouldn't be monitoring. I pray she's right." He punched the frequency numbers into the digital tuner, then motioned to Lisa. "If your people are monitoring, maybe they'll pay no attention to an unauthorized communication if it's in a Visitor voice."

She nodded and pressed the activation switch again.

"Chase, this is Skyview. Do you read? Our friends are ahead of schedule—increase speed immediately."

There was a long pause—then a one-word reply. "Copy." It was Pete's voice. Lisa shut down the comm system again.

Julio, Benny Hernandez and three other Diablos huddled in the abandoned building across the street from the structure that had been the Madonna del Sol. A Visitor shuttle was parked in front of the fire-scarred church, the pilot visible in the cockpit window. Two other aliens stood guard at the door. Julio knew that the one he really wanted, the one who had pushed Father Roberto down, was inside.

The Visitors had fixed the damage and moved back in after the first firebombing. But *this* time—

"Julio," Benny said, "let's do it *now*. Why we gotta wait?"

"We gotta, that's all. It won't be long . . ."

Pete stood at the open door to the engineer's cubicle, bracing himself with a firm grip on the handrail at the top of a seat back. "Is this as fast as you can go?"

"The train can go faster," shouted Ozzie, "but the tracks can't take it. It's always been one of the railroad's biggest problems—not having enough money to replace all these old rails and track beds."

"How far to Jamaica?" Pete asked, tension in his voice.

"About five miles—less than five minutes at this speed."

"Okay. Lauren, break radio silence. It's now or never."

She nodded and turned to the portable communications set up in the seat facing her. "Signal control, this is Chase. We're five minutes from X. Ready?"

"Ready," came the answer.

"Skyview," said Lauren, "what's happening?"

"This is Skyview," said Lisa's voice from the speaker. "They're still ahead of you—you *must* increase speed."

Pete and Ozzie looked at each other.

"Pete, we can't. We'll jump the track—"

"Dammit, Ozzie. We've gotta catch them!"

The engineer wiped his upper lip as he edged the throttle open a little more.

* * *

Lamarr Verdeaux saw the signpost that told him he was nearing the crisscross network of tracks that was Jamaica Station, by far the most complicated section of the entire railroad. Reflexively, he backed off the throttle. Almost imperceptibly the evacuation train's speed dropped. Carl took no notice.

Pete leaned into the cab. The speed indicator was a round dial to the left of the rectangular windshield. Small red lights marked every ten miles per hour, with a needle covering the increments between. The lights were lit to seventy—the needle edged higher. The train shook and vibrated, every rail weld amplified by the train's excess velocity.

Ozzie wiped a sweaty palm on his pants. "Pete, there's a curve up ahead—we may not make it. There was a derailment there months ago—they were supposed to do repairs but never finished them. If I don't slow down—"

"We need every second. Maintain speed."

Lisa narrowed her eyes at the tracking computer screen. "Hey, the evac train's slowed down," she called up to the cockpit.

"Call Pete—tell them," said Garr.

Cardinal Palazzo nodded and punched the comm switch. "This is Skyview," he said crisply. "They've cut speed."

"Computer estimates you're still behind," said Lisa. "But this may improve matters."

"Hold your speed, Ozzie," said Pete as they heard the message from overhead.

Ozzie held his breath too as the train swept into the sharpest part of the curve. The wheels shouldered the rails, trying to skip over the steel strips holding them in place. The train shuddered like an airliner hitting turbulence. Ozzie's face was ashen. The train rocked and bucked, metal wheels on metal rails singing a discordant chorus of protest.

"Pete—"

"Maintain speed!"

And then they were through the curve. The tracks gently straightened and the train settled quietly into place.

"Faster," Pete said flatly.

*   *   *

Lamarr peered ahead as they passed the signal-control towers nearest to Jamaica—normally, there would be other trains rolling in from both directions, workmen busy with track and car maintenance, bustling activity. But now the familiar sights and equipment were eerie, mute reminders of how different this trip was from any run he'd ever made. He wondered if it would be his last ride on the railway he'd come to love. He was going fast, too fast, and he cut his speed a bit more.

In a second, Carl's laser rifle was jabbing him in the ribs. "Who told you to slow down?"

"Safety regulations—"

The Visitor bared his teeth in a hideous imitation of a laugh. "New regulations have just been issued—speed up if you don't want to die *here and now*."

Lamarr obeyed.

"Captain, look out the side!" shouted another shock trooper.

Carl leaned quickly from the cab and saw the small four-car train speeding along a parallel track, sweeping into the station from the north side. He hissed an oath in his native language, causing the false skin around his mouth to crack open, and turned savagely on Lamarr. The Visitor's long grotesque tongue lashed out of his mouth in anger. "Do you know what that is?" he demanded.

Lamarr shivered at the sight of the Visitor's alienness exposed but couldn't avoid a truthful answer. "It's—it's a train, Captain."

The tongue flicked out at him again and Carl growled deep in his throat.

"Don't get funny with me, engineer. Can they catch us? Do the tracks intersect?"

"No," Lamarr lied, hoping the Visitor wouldn't notice him shaking with fear. "Their track branches off up ahead."

"Speed up—full throttle."

The terrified engineer followed the order and the heavily loaded train groaned as the motors strained to meet the demand.

Jamaica Station was a massive structure, with elevated intersecting tracks looming over city streets. The eight tracks converged to thread through concrete platforms with roofs to protect waiting passengers from the elements. Ozzie knew there was enough space to fit through, no matter what his speed, but his senses told him he was hurtling toward a narrowing space that would crush his train if he sped through too rapidly. He could see the fourteen-car evacuation train out his side window now, and he dared not slow down.

Pete stood alongside him, watching out the front. His own stomach argued with his brain, telling him they were sure to crash into the platform. Both trains raced toward the station at nearly eighty miles an hour, the evacuation train two tracks over. They were parallel now, like two straining racehorses.

"Lauren—switch, *now!*" Ozzie shouted.

"Switch—now!" she said into the radio mike.

In the control tower, a rebel reached for a relay

—and a hundred feet in front of the evacuation train, a track switch twitched, slid, and clicked into place

—and the long train lurched from its original rails onto the next track to its left. Passengers screamed as they pitched over, Carl cursed, and Lamarr blanched dead white. He was the only one aboard who knew they'd come within a heartbeat of rolling over at eighty miles an hour.

The two trains were side by side now, the distance between them as narrow as five feet in some spots. Neither had slowed down, but Pete could see that the chase train's head was only up to the middle of the other train. They had to overtake the rest of the evacuation train and pass it within the next three miles, maybe less.

Pete knew from Ozzie's description that each car had a pair of electric motors, each pumping out over five hundred horsepower. That meant the much longer evacuation train had that much more power driving it—but it also carried tons of extra weight. A physicist might be able to figure out which train had the advantage, but Pete had no idea.

"Chase, this is Switch—Skyview says you're still behind," said the crackling voice.

Lauren looked at Pete. He was grim, expressionless. "That's right," she said. "Hold next switch until Skyview gives a signal."

"Copy."

Pete glanced out the right side window just behind the

engineer's cab—the evacuation train filled the view. The trains swayed and Pete swore they were going to scrape.

"Faster," he whispered tightly.

As the chase train edged up, Garr circled so he could see both trains out his front windows. The short one was only two cars behind now and definitely gaining. But the switching point was coming up fast. If the *whole* train wasn't in front, the plan wouldn't work. The chase train nosed forward—

"They're ahead," said Palazzo through clenched teeth.

One car, two cars, two and a half. The trains looked like segmented, undulating snakes from this altitude as they thundered along, nearly touching.

"Come on, baby!" Michelle muttered. Then she looked quickly down the rails. "Damn—they're running out of room!"

"Chase, this is Skyview," said Michelle's voice from the speaker.

Lauren reached for the mike. "Come in, Skyview."

"Bad news—you're not going to make it. You've still got a full car overlapping the target."

"Understood."

"Listen closely—there's an old freight siding eight miles ahead. It's straight rail all the way. They can switch you there—but you've got to get in front *by the length of your train* or they'll smash into you as you're switching."

Pete reached over and grabbed the mike from Lauren. *"We'll* switch over to *their* track?"

"Affirmative," said Michelle.

"No way to have them switch to ours?"

"Negative. You switch to theirs and you'll be close enough to kick in the speed governor on their train—they'll automatically slow down. Then both trains will be shunted onto the siding. It'll be tricky, but it may be our last chance."

Ozzie signaled "thumbs up."

"We'll go for it," said Pete. "Alex, are you ready to be our air force?"

"Affirmative. Lisa's ready at the laser. If you can stop 'em, we'll make sure they think twice before they fight."

Chapter 29

The Last Battle

Jennifer and her pilot flew east over Long Island, the huge Mother Ship still looming large even though it was ten miles behind them.

The communications channel beeped, indicating an incoming message. "Jennifer, this is Roger."

"Yes, Commander. Are there any changes in our evacuation plans?"

"No. I just wanted to let you know that the suspected rebel attacks on air bases have yet to take place, though they should have occurred at dawn. Go to full alert—and I want you to *personally* take charge of the loading of humans onto our shuttles once the train arrives. If John and Diana are wrong about the rebel offensive, our little plan will make us look even better in the eyes of Our Great Leader."

"Very good, sir," she responded. "I'll stop at the loading area to make sure all is in readiness before I come back to the Mother Ship to verify that the storage pods are prepared and the food processing technicians are ready."

"I didn't know you were doing that on-board check yourself . . ." Roger said doubtfully. "Do you think that's really necessary?"

"Yes, sir, I do," the second-in-command said earnestly. "Don't worry, my pilot will have me back at the staging area in plenty of time to oversee the loading operation."

"Well, all right, if you feel it's warranted. I just want to make certain *nothing* will go wrong."

Jennifer looked at her pilot, a thin smile on her lips. "Don't worry, Commander. Everything will go according to plan. I'll see to it."

"Very good," said Roger's voice. "I know I can count on you. Keep me posted."

"Jennifer out." She turned to the pilot. "You heard our courageous Commander. Let's do a quick flyby at the airport, then head back to the Mother Ship."

They made a quick turn and headed toward the staging area some twenty miles to the east. After a few minutes, Jennifer spotted the fourteen-car train headed the same way.

"I wonder if Pete's group was successful," she murmured.

"We could contact the train," said Phyllis.

Jennifer shook her head. "Not under full alert—too risky. We'll just have to wait and see."

Farmingdale sprawled at the border of two suburban counties, Nassau and Suffolk, about thirty miles outside of Manhattan. Farmingdale Airport was built to accommodate the needs of the several aerospace corporations that had plants in the vicinity.

It was small as airports go, with just a couple of runways and several hangars scattered around the perimeter. It housed a fair number of private and corporate planes, and railroad tracks passed directly by the northern side. The Visitors had used it to store some of their equipment and vehicles in preparation for today's coup. A dozen of the largest Visitor shuttles sat on the runway, waiting to take loads of humans up to the Mother Ship. Eight smaller fighter and squad ships were parked nearby, along with a handful of wheeled ground-support vehicles bearing the Visitor symbol.

Paul, the young officer who had helped Jennifer raid the Brook Cove Lab, was in command of the ground forces. His blond curls peeked out from under the visor of his black cap. The hand-held communicator clipped to his belt beeped for his attention and he raised it to his mouth.

"This is Paul."

"This is Jennifer."

He unconsciously straightened his posture at the sound of her voice. "All is quiet here."

"Good," said Jennifer. "Maintain full alert." Her ship swept by overhead. "I have to make a quick run to check the preparations in the Mother Ship. I will join you in a few minutes."

"Yes, Jennifer," he said.

"You begin the operation when the trains arrive—and Paul?"

"Yes?"

"I want you to keep most of your troops *away* from the rail depot—do *not* panic the humans. They've been told they're being flown to a place of safety, so they expect to be escorted to the shuttles. They do *not* expect to be treated as prisoners. I would like that illusion maintained."

"Yes, Jennifer. We'll have minimal troops and visible weapons to greet the passengers as they disembark."

"Good—I'll see you shortly."

Paul returned the communicator to his belt, then looked up to see Jennifer's squad ship streaking away as the train pulled into the station. He signaled ten shock troopers to advance. One of them stopped and pointed skyward.

"Paul, look. A second ship—"

Paul looked up as the doors of the train cars slid open. Soldiers dressed in Visitor uniforms crouched in the doorways —and fired at the surprised shock troopers on the runway. Half of them were hit and fell dead before the others could even aim their weapons to return fire. Laser blasts ripped the quiet morning.

The second squad ship screamed out of the eastern sky, the rising sun directly behind it, its laser cannon blazing as it strafed the Visitor ships caught on the airfield.

"*Yeee-haaah!*" Garr crowed from the cockpit as he looked back at Lisa's handiwork. She continued to lay down a stream of fire, hitting both Visitor craft and the troopers trying to get closer to—or away from—their vessels. At least three of the alien ships took direct hits and burst into flames.

Garr pulled the stick back sharply; Michelle and Cardinal Palazzo were thrown back in their seats as their ship nosed toward the heavens. Lisa kept shooting to cover their tail.

On the side of the train facing away from the battle-littered airfield, plainclothes resistance fighters were helping confused passengers jump down to the gravel track bed, then hurrying them across the road into a warehouse for protection. For the moment, the Visitors on the runway were too busy to notice or care that Roger's precious prisoners were escaping.

"Let's hurry now, ladies and gentlemen," Alison Stein said. "For your own protection you must move as quickly as possible. We want you grouped together in the middle of the area, behind the protective sandbag barriers we've set up. Hurry now, please. Parents, please try to keep hold of your children. That's it, hurry, but don't run . . ."

On the other side of the crowd, Joey Vitale shouted similar instructions when suddenly his voice faltered. "Marianne!" He darted into the crowd and emerged, holding the dazed young woman by the arm. She was still wearing a nightgown and robe, battered sneakers on her feet. "Are you all right?"

"Joey!" She looked puzzled at his commando-style dress and laser sidearm and rifle. "What are you doing here?"

"Helping get you folks safe before we join the rest over there," he jerked his chin at the airfield. "Hurry up now, folks!" he shouted. "Right through those doors and behind the sandbag barriers. Hang on to your kids!"

"You mean you're gonna *fight*? You're one of the resistance members?" Marianne looked terrified as the implications of Joey's garb and weapon sank in. "Joey, be careful!"

"Were my parents on the train?" he asked urgently.

"Yes, I saw them in the crowd," she replied, "but, Joey—"

"Damn!" He took her by the shoulders. "Find 'em for me, Mare, if you can. Make sure they're all right. Promise?"

"I promise, Joey," she said, her mind whirling, realizing this might be the last time she'd ever see him. "Take care of yourself, please? Oh, Joey—" She threw her arms around him and gave him a hurried but quite passionate kiss.

Joey left her and moved back toward the train, surprised at the intensity of emotion she'd displayed and his own response to her embrace. As he returned to his crowd-direction duties again, none of the harried evacuees noticed he was smiling.

Paul watched his troops return laser fire from behind vehicles and retaining walls, whatever protection they could find. Some soldiers tended to the wounded, while dozens already lay dead out on the field. The Captain paced in the open doorway of a hangar, shouting angrily into his communicator.

"Where the hell is Jennifer's ship? Hasn't anybody seen it? She was arriving with the train." He paused to listen. "How could they have shot her down? No, I don't believe that! *Impossible!* Get someone in the ground-rover—lay down fire and give the pilots a chance to get to the fighters and get them in the air. It's our only chance."

Two shock troopers leaped into the tanklike vehicle that had been stored in the hangar. It was low and squat, with a laser-cannon turret behind the driver's compartment. Armored skirts covered its drive tracks. Moments later its engine roared to life and it rumbled out onto the tarmac, laser blazing away. The gunnery officer hunched over in the open turret, the hatch propped behind his shoulder. He spun the cannon quickly, spraying energy bolts like a lawn sprinkler. He wasn't trying to hit anything in particular, just to pin the resistance fighters down, disrupting their offense.

The strategy worked—the underground fighters had to duck and pause, and Visitor air crews ran serpentine patterns to those craft that weren't too badly damaged.

Garr rolled his squad ship and saw what was happening below. "Damned lizards," he growled. Then over his shoulder, "Sorry, Lisa."

"Don't apologize—just give me a clear shot at that ground-rover."

"It doesn't fly?" asked Palazzo.

"No," said Lisa. "But it sure can shoot."

"Here we go," said Garr. "Look sharp."

He dove at a frightening angle—and felt a blast that shook the ship. He wrestled the stick, trying to pull out of the dive. The instrument panel spat sparks as the electrical system shorted out. Smoke filled the fore and aft compartments.

"We've been hit!" Lisa shouted over the whine of the damaged engines. "Michelle's been hurt—cabin wall breached."

"Oh, dear God," said the Cardinal as he clambered back to Michelle, who had pitched forward, still strapped in.

A gash had been ripped in the vessel's metal skin right behind her and a laser bolt had burned into her back before she'd even had time to scream. She was obviously dead.

Palazzo made the sign of the cross, saying a quick and silent prayer.

The small ship shuddered and bucked as it spiraled toward the ground. Garr tried to aim it away from the main fighting, hoping to find a safe spot on the far side of the tracks and praying he'd still have enough control to keep from crashing. Out of the corner of his eye, he spotted a fighter zooming away—somehow they'd blindsided him.

Garr knew he hadn't had a chance.

Lauren looked up at the sky as she heard the muffled pulse of a laser cannon, then saw a small squad vehicle falter after being struck by a blast from a larger one. Obviously crippled, it made a bumpy, labored landing behind a nearby hangar. She saw the hatch open, and Cardinal Palazzo's gray head appeared.

Turning, she shoved Peter Forsythe in the side as they lay behind a hastily assembled barricade of metal benches, doors, and assorted junk. "Alex and the Cardinal just landed over there! I've got to cover them!"

"Take Denise with you," Pete said, aiming carefully and squeezing off a shot with his laser rifle. As she turned to crawl away, he yelled, "And *be careful*, for God's sake!"

Beckoning to Denise, she ducked low and the two women ran to the end of the barricade. Cupping her hands around her mouth, Lauren screamed, "We'll cover you! Get ready to run!"

At her wave, three figures sprinted toward them at top speed. Lauren and Denise fired steadily, laying down a barrage of laser fire that made the shock troopers duck. The turret on the tanklike ground vehicle began to swing in their direction— "Hurry!" shrieked Denise.

Lisa, Garr, and the Cardinal dived behind the barricade just as the first blast exploded.

"Are you all right?" Lauren asked them. "Where's Michelle?"

"She's dead," Palazzo said. "Can you use some help here?"

"We're doing okay so far, but that damned tank thing's got me worried. We don't have anything that can stand it off."

They all crawled back to Pete, Joey, Manfred, and the rest

of the White Christmas group, as they hastily dragged junk from the sides of the barricade to strengthen the middle. Blasts from the laser cannon were eating away at their protection.

As Garr reached Pete, he asked, "Where's Jennifer?"

"Damned if I know," Pete said. He looked at his watch. "And where the hell are those balloons? If they don't get here soon, we've had it."

Garr peered over the top of the barricade. "What the hell is that thing? Is it armored?"

"Very," Lisa said. "You can't destroy it from the outside using anything less than an explosion that would wipe out this entire airport. A fighter ship might be able to do it, but—" She shrugged.

They all flattened themselves as a burst of laser fire rocked their barrier, raining dust and shards of metal and flaming wood down on them. "Whew!" Pete said. "We can't take many more like that!" He felt desperate.

A small squad ship zoomed in toward the armored vehicle, frontal, pilot-operated laser cannons spewing fire. "Jennifer!" they chorused.

"Give her cover!" Pete yelled. Two Visitor fighter ships turned to intercept the rogue craft before it could attack the ground-rover. The resistance members turned their rifles on the other craft. Manfred launched a hand-held surface-to-air missile, and the heat-seeking shell bore in on the enemy ship. It hit and penetrated. A second later it detonated, and the ship burst into a fireball showering the runway with burning debris. White Christmas cheered.

A moment later the rogue fighter swooped in again, letting loose a blast at the ground-rover. Its front erupted in flames. The vehicle's forward motion stopped, but its turret kept spouting gouts of blue laser fire. Pete turned to Lisa, gesturing at the firing cannon. "What the hell?"

"The rear compartment housing the gunners is protected by internal armor," she shouted. "But at least it can't move anymore!"

The rogue fighter swerved violently away from the other, larger ship, swooping toward the hangar in back of the resistance fighters. Manfred loosed another shell at the larger pursuing craft, and it bobbed suddenly, dipped, then nose-dived into the hangar behind them. The blast shook the ground violently.

"Did Jennifer get away?" Lisa yelled anxiously.

Pete turned to crane his neck at the small rogue ship just as it came to a decidedly ungraceful landing, throwing up clouds of dust in back of the destroyed hangar. A single uniformed figure leaped out of the craft and raced toward them, ducking low. As the Visitor approached, Pete realized it *wasn't* Jennifer—it was a man, heavy-shouldered, with thick gray hair.

Ducking low, he scuttled toward them. "Jennifer sent me," he gasped, flinging himself down between Pete and Denise behind the barricade. Pete realized with part of his mind that the voice was a human one, not the Visitor reverberation.

"We need all the help we can get," Pete mumbled. "Glad to have you." Most of his attention was focused on the ground-rover, which still continued to fire, whittling away at their barricade. *Dammit, where are those balloons?*

"Can I get something to shoot with?" the newcomer asked.

"Yeah," muttered Pete, glancing at the man. "Denise," he called, "give our hero here a weapon and some ammo."

Denise pulled out an M-16 loaded with the new Teflon ammunition Ham Tyler had supplied them with, handing it to the man. "We're all out of laser rifles," she yelled as another shot made them all cower, "but these bullets do pretty well if you don't aim for an armored spot. You ever shoot before?"

"Been a long time," the man shouted back, "but I think I remember."

Denise watched him efficiently load the weapon and nodded in satisfaction. "You'll do," she yelled. "I'm Denise."

"Bill," the man shouted back. They exchanged a brief handshake before diving for cover against another barrage.

"We've gotta knock out that fucking cannon!" Pete yelled. "Where the hell is Jennifer?"

Another squad vehicle rocketed by overhead, strafing the barricade with laser fire. Screams of agony from several fighters marked where its run had succeeded.

Suddenly, a new squad ship soared into the battle zone, but it was at high altitude and its side hatch was open.

Two large balloons emerged from the hatchway, and they hung in the sky as the squad ship moved back and away from them. "Lisa!" shouted Joey. "Get your mask on, *now*!"

The newly arrived ship fired two short bursts and the balloons ripped open, releasing a red powder that twisted into clouds and spread on the air currents. Then the ship paused in the sky, dipped its nose, and swept low over the Visitor gun emplacements, spewing a fine red mist from a spray gun aimed out the hatch opening.

The immobilized ground-rover continued flashing shot after shot at the fast-moving aircraft.

"Gotta stop that cannon!" Alexander Garr mumbled. He grabbed two grenades from a munitions carton and scrambled past Pete and the others before they could stop him. In a second he was out in the open.

"*Alex!*" Pete screamed. "*No!*" Then he swung his laser rifle up to provide the best cover he could for the running man. Too damn many Visitors were still shooting across the tarmac. The rest of White Christmas followed suit, laying down a near-constant stream of blue energy bolts, forcing the shock troopers to take cover behind their emplacement. As he fired, Pete saw that some of the red powder was finally filtering down—in a few moments it would reach the enemy.

"I'm out of shells!" the newcomer shouted to Denise Daltrey as the resistance members continued to blaze away. They saw Alex Garr crouching on their side of the ground-rover, heart-stoppingly close to it. But he was safe for the moment since its cannons could not point directly downward.

"Here," Denise said, passing the man another couple of clips. He took off the Visitor cap, wiping a dusty arm across his forehead, and suddenly, for the first time, Denise really *looked* at him—

"Oh my God!" she yelped. "Mr. President! You can't—"

"Shh," said William Brent Morrow, laying his finger over his lips in a cautioning gesture. "Don't yell like that. These people have too much on their minds to worry about who the hell I am. You want to get us all killed?"

"But—"

"Besides," he said as he finished loading the rifle, "after all those bastards—Jennifer excepted, of course—put me through, I deserve a chance to get back at them." Coolly, he squeezed the trigger, firing at a shock trooper who was leaning out trying to get a clear shot at Alex. The Visitor dropped. "Got 'em," the President said, grinning.

The powder continued to rain down on the aliens in gentle, nearly microscopic, flakes . . .

Paul saw the red stuff rain down on his troops. They stopped firing and looked at the substance questioningly as it dusted them. The soldiers out in the open were covered first, and it took just a few seconds for their breath to catch in their throats. Paul watched, horrified, as their chests began heaving. They gasped for air, clutched their throats, and fell to the ground in wracking convulsions.

Only a few Visitors had masks. They kept shooting. Of the others, those not immediately affected recoiled, trying to get away from the deadly mist. But it was already drifting back into the hangar where Paul stood. He watched his shock troopers claw their own faces, ripping their outer skins off in a vain struggle to breathe. He searched frantically for a gas mask.

Then Paul felt the tickle in his nostrils—his lungs twitched and his gullet constricted. His body was strangling itself as the red dust seeped into his air passages. He took a step, stumbled and fell onto his face. Like his soldiers, he tore at his face and throat, rolled on the floor of the hangar, spasmed in a brief flare of agony and realization—and died. With their commander gone, some of the surviving aliens ran for the shuttles to escape.

But the rover cannon kept blazing. The spreading panic and death among the shock troopers gave Alexander Garr the unimpeded moments he needed to reach the vehicle.

Still firing his machine gun with one hand, he leaped up onto the fender of the ground-rover, hidden from the gunner in the turret who'd closed the hatch to protect himself from the toxic powder. Garr clambered on top of the rover, pulled the grenade pins, wrenched the hatch open, and tossed them inside.

Watching from across the runway, Pete gritted his teeth. He saw Garr start to climb down—then his friend lost his footing on the metal and tumbled to the ground. He hit his head and lay there for a long second.

"Shit," Pete spat, leaping over the barricade wall and running toward the fallen Garr, who shook himself and got to his feet. He weaved unsteadily—

"Alex, move your ass!" Pete yelled.

The grenades inside the rover detonated. Pete heard two muffled rumbles, saw smoke puff out of the vehicle's hatch. Then the whole thing blasted itself apart. The shock wave threw Pete onto his back and he skidded five yards on the oil-slicked tarmac. What was left of the rover was engulfed in fire, thick black smoke roiling up into the blue sky. Pete saw Garr lying face down, still.

On hands and knees, trying to keep below the intense heat of the flickering flames, Pete grabbed Garr and half carried, half dragged him back to the rebel area. Joey moved to provide covering laser fire and Palazzo ran out, crouching low, to help Pete carry the injured man. Garr's Visitor uniform was shredded and blackened, and dark red stains covered him. By the time they reached a nearby shed and gently stretched Garr on the ground, it was all over. The ground beneath him began to turn muddy as blood mixed with the dust.

Pete tried to catch his breath as he wiped blood and dirt from Garr's face with his fingers. He felt tears on his own cheeks.

Gentle hands lifted him from his crouch beside the body. "You jackass, Alex," Pete whispered, allowing Joey and Lauren to move him away after a moment of resistance.

The Cardinal knelt next to Garr's body and crossed himself. He spoke softly in Latin: *"De profundis clamo ad te . . . Domine . . ."*

Pete turned to Lauren, who wiped tears from her own eyes.

"Jennifer radioed," she said. "She said resistance forces have attacked all over the world. The Mother Ships have ordered all Visitor ground forces to leave immediately. She had to go. They're running, Pete. We've won—"

But neither could do any more than cling to each other tightly. As they hugged, Pete became aware that the firing had stopped. The airport was quiet. The battle had lasted all of twenty minutes . . .

Julio stood in the doorway of the vacant building across from the church. In the brilliant morning sky, filled with June sunshine, Visitor shuttles and squad ships were flying up from all sides. Balloons floated overhead—he almost laughed when he saw Kermit the Frog and Snoopy drifting above the city. He whispered a silent cheer when the seventy-five-foot blue and red form of Superman headed directly for the Mother Ship.

Some balloons burst and the fine red dust of death wafted out of the sky. But Julio had only one task. He knew he'd have his chance within minutes. They would *have* to leave the church —*now!* The pilot in the squad ship in the street started his engines. The guards at the door glanced into the church, and then hurried down to their ship. Finally, the one Visitor Julio wanted the most ran out.

Julio stepped into the open and tossed the homemade canister grenade. It landed two steps below the Security Commander and exploded with a *pop!* no louder than a small firecracker. But the red poison enveloped the alien as he tried to cover his mouth and nose. The guards nearest to the ship leaped in as the hatch closed and the vessel lifted off without their fallen leader and their dying comrades who were simply too slow.

With arrogant strides, Julio walked across the street and stood over the commander, who had fallen headfirst down the church steps. His skin was gouged from his face, and his body shook as if a charge of electricity coursed through it. Then he was still. Julio spat on the body.

After a few moments of silent triumph, he turned to find Benny Hernandez beside him. "Well, we did it," the bearded Diablo said. "What now?"

Julio thought for a moment. "You and the others go look for Father Roberto. Tell him the moneychangers are gone. He'll understand."

"What are you gonna do?"

Julio moved to drag the first of the fallen Visitors away from La Madonna del Sol's steps. "I'm gonna start cleanin' up this mess," he said. "We've got a lotta work ahead of us, and not much time. Tomorrow's Sunday, Benny."

Chapter 30

When the Battle's Lost . . . and Won

"Look!" Joey Vitale said, pointing up. The New York Mother Ship lumbered toward higher altitudes. A comet's tail of smaller Visitor ships trailed, trying not to be left behind.

The whisper of an approaching squad ship caught the resistance fighters' attention as they huddled around the train and the equipment shed that had been turned into a makeshift first-aid station and morgue. Brenda Ortiz had lost a leg, and Saul Rosenberg was dead.

The exhausted fighters tensed and their hands reached for their weapons. The vehicle landed and the hatch swung open; Sam Yeager, Hannah Donnenfeld, and Mitchell Loomis climbed out and trotted over. Lisa's pilot was with them, wearing her mask.

"They're scramming like bats out of hell!" Yeager crowed. Then he saw the casualties laid out in rows and his grin disappeared. "Oh, my God . . ."

"Did you dump all your toxin?" asked Pete in a leaden voice.

Donnenfeld nodded. "It was a pretty sight, all those balloons. The Visitors didn't have any idea what they were for—until they shot one down and saw what was inside. They're no dummies—they figured out pretty quickly that the toxin was not only deadly on contact, it was also going to make this planet one giant poison pill to them."

But there was no cheering. Donnenfeld surveyed the group.

Lisa, wearing her mask, sat with Joey in a corner. His parents were with them. Donnenfeld spoke up: "We monitored their communications before. They're not just fleeing from here. This is happening all over the world. We've done the impossible—we got our planet back."

"But we don't know what happened to Jennifer," said Pete. "She was our only hope for saving all those people on the Mother Ship, and now she's gone."

"There's nothing we can do about that, buddy," said Yeager. "If there's any way she can save those people, I'm sure she'll do it. Meanwhile, we've got our people *here* to worry about."

With deceptive grace, the balloons decorated the skies around Earth. Brightly patterned hot-air balloons, advertising balloons, small party balloons, massive balloons spray-painted with the red "V" for victory, red-white-and-blue balloons that had been destined for the next American presidential conventions . . .

They lifted up on breezes from lawns and balconies . . . from the Pacific Palisades in California and the cliffs of Dover towering above the English Channel . . . from the Acropolis in Greece.

And as the invaders scrambled to escape the certain death carried by those lovely floating balloons, bells began to sing, heralding the return of freedom.

In London, Big Ben chimed, though it was nowhere near the hour. The bells of Notre Dame pealed their deep harmony over Paris.

In small towns across America, church steeples rang out a jubilant chorus through the countryside. Even at the Kremlin, bells etched the air with their sounds.

The chill of reaction had begun to seep into Lauren's bones as the sun sank low. The injured had been stabilized and could be moved now. Six hours had passed since the battle began here at this suburban airport, and around the world. The United States once again had a President. Under a special guard quickly organized by Sam Yeager and Denise Daltrey, William Morrow was flown back to Washington in one of the undamaged squad ships. He was to be spirited up to Camp David in the Maryland mountains for maximum security while a search began for other national leaders—those whose minds were untouched by Visitor conversion techniques.

Lauren and Pete had roused themselves to give commands that would preserve order in their tiny corner of the world—until better contact with the outside world could be reestablished. Lauren had kept up the attempts to use their radio to signal or receive someone else's messages, to no avail.

She'd had to face the apparent reality that she would never see her father again. She kept that thought to herself—she didn't want to deflate the spirits that were beginning to rise in others. For them, every moment following the Visitors' departure was another moment to savor regained liberty. For Lauren, every moment without word from Jennifer or the return of that Mother Ship was another lock on her father's fate and the fate of all the captives taken away over the past months.

Whispers had given way to more relaxed chatting during the day, then to an occasional smile, and finally to boisterous voices and laughter.

But the sudden hum that shook the ground cut off all conversation within seconds. Nightmare memories crushed out the new happiness abruptly. It was the soul-shaking, chilling throb they'd all felt only once before, months before . . . when all this had begun.

One by one, faces turned up, not wanting to see what they knew would be there.

Lisa gazed up through her mask, her heart churning with mixed desires. Would this be her chance to go home, or was a vengeful Roger or Diana returning to rain destruction on the humans who had triumphed against all odds?

Peter's hand involuntarily tightened on his laser rifle as they saw a Mother Ship glimmering in the fading sunlight out on the eastern horizon.

The radio crackled to life. "This is Jennifer. Mother Ship secured. All your people on this vessel are being revived—we'll bring them home by shuttle. Oh, and Lauren, I'll be down on the first ship. I have someone who's very anxious to see you. I figured you'd rather have the news than wait for the surprise."

But Lauren didn't hear the last few words—she was crying into Peter's shoulder as they held each other tightly.

All around them, the air splintered with cheers that made the stadium crowd at the last Yankees World Series victory sound sedate by comparison.

Overflowing happiness and relief was tempered by more sad news for Pete. When she landed, Jennifer took him aside. Even through her filter mask, he sensed something was wrong.

"Peter, not everyone survived the pod revival process . . ."

"Who—?"

"Bobby Neal. He died without pain, if that's any consolation," she said softly.

Pete bowed his head, and took a breath to steady himself. "Lost two of my best friends today. Alex Garr was killed."

"I know. I'm sorry." She gestured toward Lauren joyfully hugging her father while Joey and Lisa stood by. "I'm glad we were able to save some friends at least."

Pete managed a smile. "Me, too. Hey, Doc," he called, "I can't get over how great you look."

"Why shouldn't I?" Stewart said with a shrug. "From what Jennifer told me, I've essentially been asleep for the last few months. Talk about vacations . . ."

"We didn't think you were going to make it back," Pete said to Jennifer. "What happened?"

"I didn't think so myself for a while. We introduced your toxin into the ship's air supply. My people kept the engineers in Auxiliary Control from shutting down the vent system, but some loyalists managed to barricade themselves into key sections and grab masks. I had to kill Roger myself. Then there were pockets of resistance to clean up."

"What happens next?" asked Lauren.

"Well," said Jennifer, "we'll get out of your atmosphere and purge the ship of toxins. At this point, I have no idea how the other Fifth Column groups are doing on the other ships. But I have a feeling at least some will win—and then we'll go home to continue the fight. With a little luck, the Alliance can either convince Our Great Leader of the error of his ways—or we'll overthrow him. Whatever happens, we'll try damned hard to prevent any other worlds from being destroyed the way Earth almost was."

"Will the people who've been converted, like the Pope and Farley Mason, be all right?" asked Cardinal Palazzo.

Jennifer shrugged. "I wish I knew. The process was new and untested before Diana introduced it here. I should tell you that your President, William Morrow, resisted the conversion process, and that his mind is untainted, in case suspicions arise after we leave. He's a stubborn man."

"Guess that's what saved him," Pete said. "You could've knocked me over with a twig when I found out I'd been hollering orders at the Commander-in-Chief!"

"Morrow was able to fly the vehicle I put him in?" Jennifer asked.

"Fly it?" Lauren said. "The guy saved our *butts* at one point. I *may* even vote for him next time around, just on the strength of that!"

The group laughed wearily, then sobered as Jennifer continued, "But a lot of leaders from all over the world were killed, or taken away on the Mother Ships that weren't secured by the Fifth Columnists. I'm sorry . . ."

"Well, you certainly did all you could do, Jennifer," Pete said. "And we owe you a lot of thanks."

"I only wish my people and yours had met under more peaceful circumstances," the Visitor said wistfully. Then she gave them a soft, thoughtful smile. "Your world will recover, and when you do, you'll go out into space sooner or later. It may not be in your lifetimes, but all this is something you have to pass on to your children. Make sure they never forget what happened—make sure they understand that not *all* civilizations they may encounter will be evil. And make sure that *your* people never go to another world to try to do what we did here."

Joey took Lisa off to the side. "You were one of the things that got me through all this," he said simply.

"That goes for me too, Joey. Thanks for teaching me about baseball."

He gently kissed the faceplate of her mask. "Hey," he said, "you're the only alien girl I've ever brought home to meet my parents."

"I'm honored," she said, smiling up at him.

"Lisa," Jennifer called, "let's go."

The younger officer joined the older one and they waved to their human friends, then climbed into their squad ship with Lisa's pilot. The antigrav drive whispered softly as the ship lifted off and left Earth behind for the last time.

Epilogue

The Visitor on the Roof

The halls of the United Nations were blessedly quiet. Lauren had honestly thought she'd never return here—she didn't think there'd be anyone left to argue at this institution whose sole reason for existence was to save the planet's bickering nations from snuffing out life on Earth.

The tattered remains of most governments around the globe had yet to find ambassadors to send back to the UN. But Lauren found herself looking forward to returning to work.

By their nature, diplomats had to possess stubborn streaks of optimism. How else could they go on believing in the ability of persuasive words to keep countries from going to war over every crisis, real or imagined?

After what the world had just been through, Lauren had to hope that maybe—just maybe—the petty squabbles over borders and resources, the now meaningless feuds that had dragged on for centuries, might now give way to a different perspective.

Perhaps humans had finally gained a new respect for an old philosophy—coexistence. *After all*, she thought, *we've all seen the alternative close up*.

She smiled as she thought of Olav Lindstrom agreeing to take two weeks off and go skiing in Austria. Lindstrom had wanted to wade right into things at the office, but Lauren wouldn't hear of it. She'd given him his marching orders, and he'd sheepishly obeyed. The pace was so deliberate and tentative here now, his presence wasn't really required. He'd been through hell too, and Lauren wanted him to be refreshed as the heartbeat of world affairs picked up again. For him, skiing was the right prescription.

For herself, solitary reflection on the long ordeal was the way to get back up to speed. Being more or less alone in the offices gave her that time. She had to come to terms with the person she was now—no one could be unchanged by what the world had experienced, and it was one of Lauren's passions to be fully self-aware.

For one thing, she cherished her father now more than she'd ever imagined was possible. Getting someone back you'd thought was gone will do that, and she smiled as she glanced at the framed photo of him on her desk.

Her mind sifted through all the faces that were in her memory, all those who'd become a part of the resistance—and a part of her life. Denise Daltrey, now back at CBS News . . . Cardinal Palazzo, off to Rome to clean up Church matters and try to determine if the Pope was still the man they'd elected to lead the world's Roman Catholics . . . Joey Vitale, who'd helped to save his own parents and truly become a star-crossed lover, and who would never again be the simple Brooklyn kid he'd been before . . . poor Alex Garr— "Alexander the Great," as Pete had facetiously dubbed him— who turned out to be pretty great after all, giving his life in the best tradition of the Marines . . . Alison Stein, who'd truly emerged from this crisis a leader to be reckoned with . . .

And Peter Forsythe. She hadn't heard a word from Pete in the week since V-day. She sighed as she tried to picture his face—she'd spent most of the last ten months with him, and suddenly she couldn't summon a clear image of him. That made her frown. *Damn him*, she thought. *Why did he have to turn out to be so goddamned complicated? When he was just a cynical, alcoholic ballplayer, I didn't have to pay any attention to him at all . . .*

Perhaps he'd gone off to spring—no, make that *summer*— training with Joey. Even though the season would be so late, President Morrow had specifically requested the baseball commissioner to get the major leagues going as quickly as possible. Something normal like baseball would be a soothing reminder that the world still circled the sun—and that the human race was again in control of it.

Lauren was interrupted by her phone. "Hello?" She listened. "To the *roof*? What for? Oh, all right . . ."

Lauren emerged from the elevator on the top floor and was dismayed to find that walking along the corridor to the roof gave her the chills. She hadn't been here since the October night when Lindstrom had first greeted the Visitors.

She quickened her pace, and a guard opened the exit door for her when she reached the top step. The hot air smacked her in the face and she cursed for having worn her navy suit. Her breath caught in her throat and the pit of her stomach turned over in queasy déjà vu when she saw the Visitor squad ship parked in *exactly* the same spot as the Supreme Commander's vessel on that long-ago night. She edged uneasily toward the dormant ship, telling herself the bad guys were gone—

"Hi, Lauren," Peter Forsythe said cheerfully as he ducked out of the open hatch.

She stopped, hands going to her hips in an angry stance. "You dumb shit, Forsythe! I'm going to have nightmares for a week because of this! I thought—I don't know what I thought! If you *knew* what kind of dreams I still have . . ."

"You want to have some of them in Hawaii?" he asked innocently.

"Wha—?"

"Hawaii—you know, those paradise islands in the middle of the Pacific—palm trees, semi-naked hula dancers?"

"You're asking me to go to Hawaii? With you? Are you nuts? I've got tons of work to do. And what the hell are you *doing* with this thing? How did you get it up here?"

"I carried it in my hip pocket. How do you think? I flew it. Alex taught me how the week before V-day. I've been practicing all week. Today I borrowed it from the authorities, cleared my flight plan with the FAA, and called my kids to tell 'em I was coming. I've got a week before I've gotta report for training. Now, are you coming with me, or not?"

Lauren looked at him closely. "You haven't been drinking, have you?"

He smiled gently. "You know better than that, Lauren—or you should. I'm cold sober, scout's honor."

She narrowed her eyes suspiciously, but Forsythe picked up a dancing gleam beginning to shine in their dark depths. "Were you ever a scout, Mr. Forsythe?"

"No. But I want you to know that my intentions are equally honorable. You set the terms, and I'll abide by 'em. I even started out by asking your father's permission to take you away from all this."

"And he agreed?"

"Actually, he was overjoyed. His exact words were, 'If you can drag her away to someplace where she'll enjoy herself, you have my blessing, Peter.' So how about it? I guarantee you'll enjoy yourself."

"But I need to pack—"

"Bullshit. We'll buy what we need when we get there," he said lightly. "Don't forget you're traveling with a guy who makes obscene amounts of money." He stepped away from the hatch and came over to her, taking her hand. "Now, if the two people who practically saved humanity singlehandedly—"

"Oh, come on!"

"Well, at least the entire population of New York City. Anyway, if *we* don't deserve a vacation, then who does?"

She began to laugh. "Pete, you're certifiable!"

"Certainly," he deadpanned. "I stopped by and picked up my weekend pass from Bellevue on the way over." He touched her cheek. "Please come."

Lauren rolled her eyes. "Oh, what the hell." She turned back to the guard by the roof door. "Tell them I went fishing."

"That's the spirit!" Pete said. He took her hand and helped her into the squad ship, then hopped into his own seat.

"Are you *sure* you know how to fly this thing?" she asked nervously.

"Does a bear shit in the woods?"

He switched on the engine and moved a lever, and the ship lifted a few inches, swaying precariously. "Air current," he mumbled. "It gets better."

She smiled. "We'll see. Does this thing have all the niceties?"

"Anything you could want, m'dear."

"How about an autopilot?" she asked, too innocently.

His blue eyes widened as he scanned the control board. "If it doesn't, I'll invent one."

Lauren's laughter reached the guard as he watched the squad vehicle lift off the roof and turn gently. It circled the UN Building once, then steadied and picked up speed, heading west.

THE BATTLE IS NOT OVER . . .

Watch for

THE PURSUIT OF DIANA

first of the brand-new "V" books—based on
the upcoming fall NBC-TV series—from Pinnacle.

Coming in December!

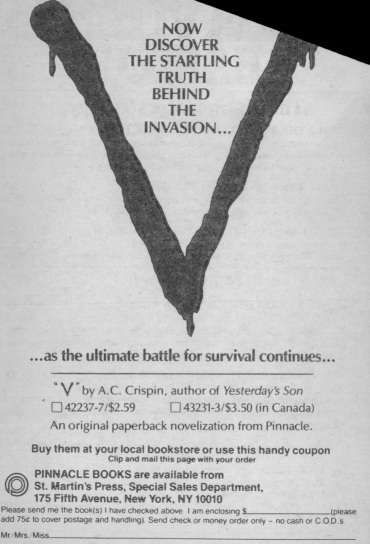